The B

Jane Reid

© Jane Reid 2015

All rights reserved

No part of this publication may be reproduced, stored in a retrieval system, or transmitted in any form or by any means, without the prior permission in writing of the publisher, nor be otherwise circulated in any form of binding or cover other than that in which it is published and without a similar condition including this condition being imposed on the subsequent purchaser.

All paper used in the printing of this book has been made from wood grown in managed, sustainable forests.

ISBN: 978-1-78003-837-7

Printed and bound in the UK
Author Essentials
4 The Courtyard
Falmer, East Sussex BN1 9PQ
www.authoressentials.com

A catalogue record of this book is available from the British Library

Cover design by Jacqueline Abromeit

1/24
fr

Dedicated to my father, William Reid

About the Author

Jane Reid was born in Hurstpierpoint, and has lived in Sussex all her life. She always wanted to write, but also had art training, specializing in flowers and plants, and Architecture. Among other things she used to do paintings of people's houses. In 1979 she did black and white illustrations for a book of herbs.

At the request of someone running a bookshop in Lindfield. West Sussex, she wrote and illustrated a little handbook about that village, which has been on sale since 1983, the most recent edition was published in 2007.

PART 1

Richard Randall's house in Sussex

Late Spring, 1794

On his return from his customary saunter round the estate, Mr Randall had only one aim in view – to go straight to his study and continue the almost gloating examination of the newly-bound volume, which had only arrived the day before, and all the time he had been out, while he interviewed his steward and spoke to his tenants, his thoughts had been of his book, his very own *History of the Family of Randall, in the County of Sussex down to the present day*. Turning author in his fifties had almost turned his head, Mrs Randall had remarked crossly coming upon him lovingly turning the pages. She was a good wife, but how few women could appreciate an achievement of this kind!

However, upon entering the hall, Mr Randall received a check to his enthusiasm. A letter lay on the large round centre table, and as he picked it up with a slight frown, he became aware of his wife, hovering rather anxiously in the doorway to the dining-room. To her he addressed himself as he broke the wafer; "Can't think why Sturgis should be writing to me, when he'll be dining here this evening."

"Perhaps he is writing to say something is wrong," said Mrs Randall, ominously calm. "The servant awaits an answer. I sent him to the kitchen to quench his thirst."

"Oh, dear," said Mr Randall as he read. His wife sighed.

"I knew it," she said. "He cannot come. Is he ill?"

"No, no – it is John – his nephew, you know."

"Of course I know John. Dear me, without him we shall be an odd number at table. Why is he not coming? Has he been delayed on his journey from Norfolk?"

"He has indeed. He has broken his leg."

1

"How very unfortunate, poor young man. But why should that prevent Mr Sturgis from coming? Because his nephew is laid up, must he shun company? It is most annoying, I have just heard that Mr and Mrs Fellows cannot come, and it looks so pointed to have the Carters and nobody else."

"Ah!" said Mr Randall, enlightened. "I presume that Sir Charles Carter is paying his uncle another visit?" His tone was lightly bantering and his wife stiffened.

"It is not a matter for jesting," she said. On reflection he was inclined to agree. To his mind, her matchmaking efforts were slightly ludicrous, but with four unmarried daughters, two of them in their twenties, her concern was understandable. And Sir Charles was such a matrimonial prize. A trifle dull, perhaps, but good-natured, undeniably handsome, and a baronet in possession of a considerable estate in Hertfordshire.

"He does seem to admire Lucy a great deal," Mrs Randall continued.

"So he should," said Lucy's father. "After all, she is the beauty of this neighbourhood, and if there are prettier girls in Hertfordshire, I should be surprised." Mrs Randall made a half-hearted protest, but her husband stopped her. "Come, Anne," he said. "We all know that Lucy is one of the loveliest creatures one could wish to see.

"But it does not *do* for us to say so," said Mrs Randall gloomily. "If our only guests are Mr and Miss Carter and their nephew, we will seem to be pushing her forward." She sighed. "If only one of the elder girls were married, it would not look so pointed."

Mr Randall was anxious to escape from this topic, and picked up his friend's letter, effectively silencing his wife until he laid it down, when she said impatiently, "Well, does he explain why John's accident should prevent him from dining here?"

"It does not do so, exactly. But he did not receive the news by post; it appears that when John Sturgis broke his leg he had been planning to travel to Sussex and knew a friend was going to Lewes next week. This young man offered to bring a letter, it seems. Sturgis writes that he had asked him to stay for a few days before he recalled the dinner engagement, and very properly asks if he may bring this – Thomas Martin – in John's place."

At any other time Mrs Randall would have appreciated such thoughtfulness, but her anxiety not to entertain the Carters alone appeared to outweigh all other considerations, and scorning their friend's scruples, she said of course he could bring his young visitor to dine. "You have no objections, have you, Richard?"

"None at all, my love. I must confess I myself would be sorry not to see Sturgis this evening."

"Oh, you are thinking of your book. I do hope you will not bore Sir Charles with that."

"I am sure he will be very interested," said Mr Randall reprovingly. "He also comes of an old family, though not as old as mine." He sighed. "Though his is likely to continue."

"Yes, well, that cannot be helped," said his wife abruptly. "I am sure I tried hard enough to give you an heir."

Mr Randall was dismayed. "Yes, my love, of course you did," he said hastily, "And in fact, I was thinking as much of the loss of my brother than of our little Dick. No, there are other males in the Carter family and Sir Charles himself is a young man, that is what I meant."

"True, true," Mrs Randall changed the subject. "I suppose this Mr Martin is not unsuitable?"

Feeling that this was a bit belated, her husband asked in what way the youth might not be suitable to dine with them. "I assume him to be a gentleman. But if you prefer not to take the chance, Sturgis will understand, only he can hardly come without him."

This seemed to settle the matter. "No, no, they must both come. And here is the servant come for your reply. You do not need to write, he can tell his master."

"It would be safer to write, my dear. Poor Sturgis does hear so badly these days. If you will wait a minute or two more, Jarvis, I will have a note for you to take back." Thus provided with an excuse to retreat to his study while his wife returned to the dining room, Mr Randall dispatched his note and was free to relish his own words in print until it was time to dress for dinner.

He came downstairs to find his wife and three older daughters already assembled in the drawing room awaiting the arrival of the visitors. How long was it since anyone unfamiliar had dined there? He found himself wondering what Mr Martin would make of this household. For a moment his perception was intensified to a point where he perceived the familiar scene as if for the first time, noticing as never before the way his own colouring and that of his wife was reflected in their children. She was going grey now, but as a young woman she had had light brown hair and a pale creamy skin. This was echoed less attractively in the eldest daughter. His own hair was still aggressively red, and the second girl's abundant curls were the same startling colour as her father's. But in eighteen-year-old Lucy, the two elements had blended to produce pink-and-white cheeks, with sapphire blue eyes and hair so bright it could only be called golden.

She looked so attractive, seated demurely on a sofa between her older sisters, that when Sir Charles Carter entered the room with his uncle and maiden aunt, it was not surprising to see a dazed expression spread over his face. Mr Randall felt that if the young man's manners had been less exquisite, he would barely have stopped to greet the parents before moving on to the daughters.

Mrs Randall was beginning to tell the Vicar and his sister about the substitute for John Sturgis that was about to arrive, and her husband was visited by a sudden uneasiness as he watched Sir Charles greeting, in order of age, Anna, Caroline, and Lucy. John Sturgis, who had known the family for years, was safely engaged to a girl in Norwich. He would not have grudged the young baronet the opportunity to converse with Lucy, but his unknown friend might not be so obliging. Would he be so willing to entertain her older sisters?

Until he actually saw Mr Martin, his host had imagined him to be of the same large, uncomplicated type as John Sturgis, and fill a similar place in the company. John was amiable, but he was not clever; he was hearty but not talkative; and in spite of his physical proportions, he would have provided a usefully negative element against which Sir Charles could shine.

Thomas Martin was not handsome; the first impression he gave was of a negligible youth of medium height and insignificant features, with hair that was neither dark nor fair. This in itself drew attention to him, since his was the only male head that had not been powdered. It was perhaps no longer a universal practice, but even Sir Charles, under thirty and not unfashionable, had not cropped his hair and would not have appeared in company without having dusted it. To do either thing was still almost the sign of a Revolutionary, especially in the country. True, the young visitor had not had very much notice that he was to dine out, but it had been sufficient. Clearly he never did powder his rather short hair and the fact that he didn't seem at all conscious of the difference surely confirmed this.

By the time the introductions were over Richard Randall was beginning to wonder how he could ever have thought of the visitor as unimpressive. He was the youngest man in the room, and also the shortest, but he showed no signs of unease. He greeted the ladies with calm assurance, bowed almost condescendingly to his host and the vicar, and seemed singularly unimpressed to learn that the only other young man present was a baronet. It was irritating that he appeared almost more at ease than Sir Charles.

At least he was not trying to single out the youngest daughter, which clearly relieved Mrs Randall. Having greeted all three girls, he showed more interest in Anna and Caroline, and took a seat beside them. The eldest girl looked modestly down and seemed dismayed, but Caroline's smiling response and willingness to enter into conversation, perhaps not so maidenly, seemed to attract him more. Though it was pleasant to see his second daughter so animated, Mr Randall began to feel a little disturbed.

Even Lucy's loveliness could not entirely eclipse Caroline at any time, but whereas the younger girl's perfect little face looked equally enchanting in repose, much of her sister's charm came from the glow that interest and enthusiasm gave to her features. Knowing the sort of thing likely to produce this effect, her father was not entirely surprised, when they went in to dinner, to hear their visitor speak with earnest admiration of William Godwin, the social reformer.

If he had not been concerned about how it would affect his own peace, Mr Randall would have derived some amusement from watching the expression on his wife's face change as she became aware of the sort of man they had let into their house. He was acutely aware of her feelings, after thirty years of marriage and he could see that though she was irritated that the humiliation was seen by the vicar and his sister, the final exasperation came from the knowledge that owing to his increasing deafness, Mr Sturgis was the only person unaware of the trend his guest's conversation was taking.

The first hint of this came when the subject of the terrors happening in France was brought up by the vicar, deploring the execution of the King and Queen in Paris.

"Dreadful!" said Miss Carter, shaking her head, "Quite appalling." In spite of her words she sounded comfortably detached, but her brother seemed honestly dismayed, and shocked when he spoke of the state of things in that unfortunate country.

He addressed Thomas Martin, "You come from London, I believe? Are there any fresh news?"

"I merely passed through the capital on my way from Norfolk, and I only heard what I had learnt before. As a humane man, I am sorry to hear of these many executions, but one can hardly blame the people of France, so long suppressed, for taking their revenge upon the Aristocrats!"

One could almost listen to the silence that followed. Glancing round the table, Mr Randall watched the reaction ripple from the vicar to his sister and nephew. That anyone could voice such sentiments was not something likely to have come the way of these comfortable country gentlefolk and to the young baronet it was clearly a complete novelty. Richard Randall's late brother had frequently discoursed on the subject

6

of inequality and the need for general reform, but that had been in the days before the French Revolution had given so sinister a meaning to the sentiments. Events since his death in 1791 would surely have caused him to modify his opinions? But Caroline had lived in her uncle's house most of the time between her nineteenth and her twenty-second years, and she was probably the only other person at the table who had ever had the rebels in France presented as other than fiends incarnate. Mr Martin's words had certainly left her unmoved, her grey eyes held a familiar glint as she watched the company.

Sir Charles was the first to find his voice. "You cannot mean that seriously!" he exclaimed, possibly unwisely. His host felt he could have predicted the visitor's response, Mr Martin seemed somewhat amused as he said firmly that indeed he did.

"If we in this country would avoid a similar Revolution, we should immediately abandon these foolish preoccupations with rank and wealth. Perhaps you have not read what Mr Godwin and Mr Holcroft have to say on the subject? They both make it plain that future civilisations will not have rich and poor, servants and masters, but that all men – and women – will be equal!"

"No servants!" Sir Charles was incredulous.

"Certainly not. Why should people in full possession of their health and faculties require others to do for them what they could well do for themselves? Only the very young, the old, and the incapacitated should require people to assist them, and they should not be subordinates."

Mr Randall could see that his wife was anxious to change the subject, but the young baronet had clearly never encountered a revolutionary theorist before and he seemed gripped by a fascinated curiosity. "Would you equate a gentlewoman with her maid?" he demanded.

"With her maid, and with her husband. Women should be considered the equals of the men in their family, as well as of each other. Have you heard of Mary Wolstoncroft?"

"The name is not unfamiliar," said Miss Carter, pursing her lips. Thomas Martin did not seem to notice her disapproval.

With unabashed enthusiasm he continued by asking if anyone had read that lady's *A Justification of the Rights of Women*.

"Yes," said Caroline, causing her mother to fidget. Miss Carter gave a little shudder. Since the known immorality of Miss Wolstoncroft overshadowed all her brilliance of mind for respectable ladies, Richard Randall was relieved that his old friend now innocently created a diversion.

Cupping his hand to his ear to catch the reply, he questioned his hostess about her other daughter. "I don't see my little Harriet, where is she?"

"She's not well," said Mrs Randall, slowly and with some volume. Those who knew the youngest daughter exclaimed with concern, Mr Sturgis looking dismayed, Sir Charles murmuring questions to Lucy, Miss Carter sighing fatalistically, and her brother exclaiming how very sorry he was to hear it; hadn't they had a better report from the doctor the week before?

"Why yes, so we did, but she has bad days and this is one of them. She was not well enough to come down tonight."

"Is your doctor good? I could ask my mother to recommend a London man, if you like," said Sir Charles. From some this might have seemed officious, but his genuine sympathy was patent. His hostess smiled at him cordially.

"You are very kind and I thank you for the suggestion, but we have every confidence in Dr Bowen," she said. The introduction of such a personal topic appeared to have temporarily silenced the stranger in their midst, and Mr Randall admired the assiduity with which his wife and Miss Carter managed to keep the conversation on subjects like health in general and that of Lady Carter in particular, pursuing that and other non-controversial ideas until it was time for the ladies to withdraw.

Mr Randall watched them leave the room with less enthusiasm than he would have felt earlier. He had been looking forward to producing his family history for the edification of the vicar and Sir Charles as well as his oldest friend, but he found himself wondering if he could avoid doing so in the company of young Mr Martin. Unfortunately, he had not only mentioned it to the Carters, he had written of it to Mr Sturgis, promising to give him a copy. This had been received with interest, and now, rendered insensitive by his deafness, he cut through any attempt to introduce a different topic.

"I say, Randall, what about that book of yours, eh? Thought you were going to show us that." He turned to the vicar, "Clever fellow, isn't he, Carter? Writing a book like that. Puts us all in the shade, don't you think?"

Mr Carter, who had published a volume of sermons only the year before, seemed uncertain what to reply to this, but his nephew seemed to share this enthusiasm.

"You have really written a book, sir? And is it to be published?"

"I have had it printed privately, Sir Charles." This caused Mr Martin to look sardonic, and his host said a little defensively that he made no claim to be a great scholar, but felt such a volume would be of interest to his family and friends.

"Yes, indeed," murmured the vicar, and Sir Charles echoed his uncle. Mr Martin still said nothing. Mr Sturgis had been straining to catch what was being said, and apparently gathering that the subject he had introduced had not been abandoned, now broke in with a comment on the Randall family.

"One of the oldest in Sussex," he told the others. "Doesn't it go back to before the Conquest?"

"I have heard that this is possible," said his host cautiously. "But I have not said much about us before the time of Elizabeth."

"Ah, that is further than we can go," said Mr Carter frankly. "The first record we have is of the time that the baronetcy was conferred upon the first Sir Edward, after the Restoration of Charles the Second, in recognition of what his father did during the Civil war."

"How interesting," said Mr Randall uncomfortably. What he had found out about his family at that time had not been very inspiring, there had not seemed to be any record of

9

heroic support of either side in the Civil War. Yet the Randalls appeared not to have suffered financially during the conflict and some of the new building of the manor dated from the Restoration of Charles the second. He began to speak of the way his more recent forebears had improved the property, especially his grandfather who had completed the new façade that made the building look so much more elegant, and his father who had been responsible for landscaping the grounds.

Thomas Martin seemed to find it all hugely amusing, his smile was almost a grin, but at least he was content to listen, until Sir Charles, who did not seem to have learnt from the earlier encounter, asked if he did not find it admirable, that their host had written this book?

"Splendid!" agreed Mr Martin cheerfully, but sounding slightly patronising.

"And to trace one's family back so many generations," continued the young baronet. "That is some thing to be proud of."

"Why so? We all of us go back to Adam, I suppose."

Even Sir Charles could not mistake the scorn in the other's voice. His reply was the sharpest his host had ever heard from him. "Oh, really. No doubt you can trace your ancestors back to the Flood at least?"

This attempt at sarcasm simply glanced off his opponent. "Yes, if my father is to be believed, that is just about where we do originate," he retorted. "When I lived at home, he was for ever boasting about how we came over in 1066. I used to tell him that it was of no significance, that half the yeomen on his estate could probably claim as much, and that in any case they were most of them far better specimens of humanity than those who prided themselves on their gentle birth. He was greatly annoyed."

"I am not surprised," said Mr Randall, slightly disconcerted to find that the visitor possessed anything as conventional as a father. He found he was being regarded thoughtfully.

"Yes, I should imagine that you and my father would have a great deal in common. He used to talk of writing a book

10

about the Martins. Not that he will ever do so, it would be too much of an effort."

His coolness, and the contempt he showed towards his father, jarred upon everyone except Mr Sturgis, who had given up trying to follow the conversation and was consoling himself with a second glass of port. The disapproval of the rest of the company was clearly a reaction that Thomas Martin encountered frequently. Not in the least disconcerted, he returned their gaze with another unpleasant smile, "Ah, does it pain you to hear me abuse my father?"

"Since you put it like that, yes," said Richard Randall.

"My father died when I was five," said Sir Charles mournfully, "It has always made me feel so very sorry that I never really knew him."

"Of course it has," said his uncle, looking sternly at the other visitor, "I must say that as a clergyman I am greatly pained to hear a young man so lacking in respect for his progenitor."

"Well, if my father had died before I grew up, I might have continued to respect him. Unfortunately he did not, and as an adult, I can see nothing about him to be respected. I do not doubt that I was begotten by him, but I find that rather depressing than otherwise. To be truthful, I think him an old fool, and I told him so."

"I wonder that he endures it," said Sir Charles.

Thomas Martin laughed. "Oh, he does not! We have parted company."

"On what do you live, then? Surely he does not make you an allowance?"

"Naturally not. With your inherited wealth, it would not occur to you that a man might earn his own living.

"So you have a profession," Mr Randall was intrigued in spite of his disgust. For the first time the visitor seemed uneasy. He frowned, and from the disjointed remarks he made about "Help others, and others will help you," he conveyed the impression that just for now he was dependent upon the generosity of a friend on whose behalf he was on the way to Lewes, where they were both destined to spend the summer.

11

"However, he will not lose out in the end, I shall be able to repay him when I inherit my father's estate."

"You are likely to do that, are you?" said Mr Randall ironically.

"I must. I am the only son, and the property is entailed. My father cannot leave it away from me even if he wishes to. No doubt he does so wish!"

"But then," said Sir Charles brightly, "You will be living on inherited wealth, will you not?"

Mr Martin was not to be caught like that. "I suppose it might seem like that," he said kindly. "But then you see, I shall not consider it as mine. I shall endeavour to cut off the entail, and regard wealth as a trust, to share with my fellow men for the good of all."

Sir Charles was speechless, but his host was interested to see that his hands had clenched

"Hey!" said Mr Sturgis, draining his port and preparing to resume his struggle with the conversation. "What about that book, Randall? I'm sure this young man has an interesting family, but we want to hear about yours."

"I will fetch it from my study, if you will excuse me a minute." Richard Randall still regretted having mentioned it, but was glad of the excuse to leave the company and fetch the volume, so sumptuously bound in red leather and embossed in gold, that was sitting on his desk.

Having picked it up, he paused before returning, looking from his study window at the view over the Weald of Sussex, across fields and farms to the great hump of the South Downs that reared so protectively between the fertile lands and the sea. The sight brought to mind his early childhood and how his nurse had told him that the downs were specially provided by Providence to keep the sea from lapping at his father's land. Those Downs were a potent part of his affection for the county of his birth, speaking to the deepest layers of his soul. No doubt young Mr Martin would sneer at such emotions.

"Why should I care what that young puppy thinks? He may be intelligent, but he has no manners!" But however much he told himself not to let it affect him, he was very conscious of the hasty temper that had so often caused him to lash out with fists and tongue in his youth. Even now he found it difficult to control, yet he owed it to his own dignity not to let this impertinent youth know how much he had provoked him. He took a deep breath as he returned to the dining room, to find only his old friend, and the vicar awaiting him.

"Silly young men," grumbled Mr Sturgis. "Couldn't wait to get back to the ladies, it seems. What's the matter with the youth of today? Where's the stamina we used to have, eh?"

Mr Carter elucidated, "They asked us to apologise to you, Mr Randall. I know my nephew would like to see your book some time, but perhaps they felt it was of greater interest to us." His look conveyed the impression of certainty that his host would not mind the absence of Mr Martin, but he said no more, and though Mr Sturgis continued to murmur about the milkiness of modern youth, he was soon absorbed in studying the book.

Mr Randall enjoyed the luxury of a perceptive audience very much, but was uneasy about what sort of atmosphere he would encounter on returning to the drawing room, and looked round with some concern when the three of them finally rejoined the rest of the company. Things seemed peaceful enough, though the vicar's sister, wore a slightly pained expression, and did not look as calmly complacent as usual. Anna was not present, and the six occupants of the room were grouped in pairs. Mrs Randall and Miss Carter on a small sofa, Lucy and Sir Charles over by a window examining a portfolio of prints, and Caroline in her elder sister's absence dispensing tea and coffee. She was engaged in discussion with Thomas Martin, who leant attentively over the back of her chair.

He became aware that his wife's attention was focussed more on this pair than on the progress of the young baronet's courtship, and continued his conversation with Mr Sturgis to avoid her eye.

At least while the visitor was concentrating on Caroline, he was neither shocking Miss Carter nor enraging her nephew,

13

how ever little good this was doing for her reputation with the vicar and his sister. Richard Randall felt troubled about his second daughter; he had always been fond of her, not only for her own sake but because she had been dear to his much loved younger brother, yet he was always conscious of discomfort in her presence. Expecting a female to be less intelligent than he was, he was prepared to be indulgent to such weakness, but since her early teens, Caroline had shown herself to be almost his equal intellectually. Sometimes he suspected that it was only her tact that prevented her seeming his superior.

Mr Sturgis was moving slowly in search of a cup of coffee, and suddenly noticed Anna's absence. Was she ill, too? he enquired anxiously. No, she was sitting with Harriet, his hostess informed him.

"Oh. Kind of her. But, my dear, I really must congratulate you on your husband's book. Magnificent, isn't it?" For half an hour poor Mrs Randall had to sit and listen to the praises of the "History of the Randall family," while her husband talked to the Carters and the young people entertained each other.

None of the guests stayed to supper, and Anna did not rejoin the company, she sent word that she would take the meal in Harriet's room in the hope that the poor child might follow her example. There was little conversation at the table, it seemed unwise to discuss the visitors and Mr Randall prudently refrained from mentioning his book, but when the silence became a little oppressive, he decided to ask his daughters how they had spent their day. Lucy seemed dreamily abstracted, and Caroline warily amused by the questions. Had they gone riding, early?

"Yes, Papa," said Caroline, "We went in the direction of Bolney. Sir Charles joined us. He has a splendid new mare. Good points, hasn't she, Lucy?"

"A pretty horse," Lucy agreed. Her father felt that she had been more interested in the rider to notice much about the mount.

"And, later?" he persisted. "Did you draw? How is your work coming on, Lucy?"

Lucy looked up with a start, "Oh, quite well. We walked to the Dell and I drew while Caroline read. The new green coming out makes everything look delightful."

"I should like to see the picture." His daughter promised to show it to him when she had finished the painting, but it was hard to find much more to say on the subject and his wife seemed too absorbed in her own thoughts to contribute anything to the conversation. As soon as he could decently do so he escaped to his study, where he had deposited his book on his way to the drawing room. Picking it up to bring it into the circle of light, he caressed the embossing on the cover, wishing that Mr Martin's scorn did not obtrude itself into his thoughts. He turned the pages, resenting the implication that he had been classed with the senior Mr Martin as a senile fool preoccupied with petty concerns. He felt some sympathy for the father, mixed with a certain degree of envy. However unworthy, this man did at least have an heir.

Suppose his little son had grown up to despise him and laugh at all he valued? He had been spared that, but it could not have been worse than watching the child fade and die before his sixth birthday. Sixteen years had done nothing to ease the bitter feelings about that time. A faint noise attracted his attention, he must have failed to latch the door properly as he entered the room, and it was swinging open, giving him a clear view of the painting that hung in the hall. It had been done in 1775 showing his wife and their three children, and spoke of happier days. Not merely because little Dick had been alive then. There was Anna, smiling as she nursed her doll, with Caroline, a chubby three-year-old, romping with a large benevolent dog. How well the painter had captured the glint of red hair on the two younger children, especially the baby who sat chortling on his mother's lap, reaching out to the dog, looking the image of health.

The child's death, just before Harriet's birth, seemed almost more of a tragedy in retrospect. At the time, it was the loss of a loved individual, but it had not put an end to all

15

hopes of an heir to the Randall name. The new baby might have been a boy, there might have been other children to come, and even though Harriet remained the youngest, there was always the possibility that Charles Randall might have married. If only their older sister had not made his busy life as a barrister in London so very comfortable! Perhaps if she had died sooner, he might have looked for a wife! But Miss Lucy's death had occurred only three years before that of her youngest brother, and by then his favourite niece and god-daughter was old enough to come and keep house for him.

And here he was back on the subject of Caroline. He looked up and found his wife was crossing the hall in the direction of his study. He realised that it was too late to get up and shut the door properly, and lifted the bound volume a little higher in the faint hope that she would think him absorbed and leave him alone.

Ostentatiously she knocked on the open door, but stepped into the room at once, saying quietly, "Can we have a word in private?"

"Why, yes, my love," said Richard Randall resignedly.

She closed the door behind her and seated herself in a high-backed chair that was just outside the circle of light from the lamp, making it impossible for him to study her face when she unburdened herself of her reaction to the guest Mr Sturgis had brought to dinner. She did not speak at once, and in the silence the mournful cry of an owl came distinctly through the still night. He felt it was almost an embodiment of his thoughts, and he drew a deep breath, letting the family history fall from his hands. It hit the desk with a gentle thud, and the slight sound seemed to break the spell. Mrs Randall stirred.

"Richard, if I had known that Mr Martin was an admirer of immoral, freethinking men like Mr Godwin and his friends, he would never have set foot in this house," she said. "And do not tell me that it was partly my fault, I am only too well aware of the fact!"

"No," said her husband.

"What do you mean, No?"

16

"Why, that I would not have welcomed him, had I known."

"And we should have known! How could Mr Sturgis... yes, yes, you need not say it, I am aware that he has become so deaf, he can have had no notion of what sort of visitor he was entertaining. I blame John Sturgis, myself."

"For breaking his leg?" asked Mr Randall mildly. His wife was clearly in no mood for pleasantries.

"No, of course not. Do not pretend to be foolish! I mean, for giving his letter to that man to deliver. It was obvious, with a room prepared, and being hospitable, that his uncle would be certain to ask his friend to stay."

"Knowing that Mr Martin was bound for Lewes, in a few days," Mr Randall agreed. "But though you or I might have anticipated that, I doubt if John would. He is not a thinking man, you know, and it probably never occurred to him."

"I understand that the young man does not have much money, he must be thankful not to have the expense of putting up somewhere while awaiting the friend he is to meet. But I cannot understand how John Sturgis came to know him in the first place. Those theories would not interest him. All he cares about is sport."

"I understand that Mr Martin is an excellent horseman. That may explain their friendship. If they were at school together this interest in Reform may have developed since they last met."

"That may well be, but it is a great pity he did not discover it before using him as his messenger. How long is he likely to remain, do you know?"

"Sturgis said a few days, no more."

"Well, he must not come here again, however long he stays," said Mrs Randall firmly. "Richard! Surely you agree with me on that point."

"Um. Well, I am certainly not anxious to meet him again, but nor do I wish to offend one of my oldest friends. How could I explain it to him?"

"Oh, you mean his deafness, but surely you could write?"

"I suppose that I might do that, but it would make us seem to be making a great deal of it, just because we do not care for the youth."

"It is a great deal more than that. I do not consider him a fit person to associate with young unmarried women. Surely Mr Sturgis would understand that?"

"Only if it were explained to him in great detail. My dear Anne, I do think you are over anxious. Mr Martin, however displeasing, and however immoral his theories, is at least a gentleman, by birth and education, and I do not think him a libertine."

"I am not so sure about that. Immoral theories may lead to immoral practice. Did you not hear him speak warmly of that shameless Miss Wolstoncroft, who is well known for living with an American to whom she is not married. A fine example to set before your daughters! Before you came in to the drawing room, he was spouting some nonsense about marriage not being considered necessary, in the future."

Mr Randall tried to be soothing. "These reformers all talk like that. I do not think it need be taken very seriously. It is simply a theory."

"Perhaps it is; but it provides a wonderful excuse for immorality at the present time. Poor Miss Carter was shocked and upset."

"She can never have encountered anybody like that before."

"I could wish she had not had to do so in our house, Richard. And the worst of it was the encouragement he received from Caroline. What must Miss Carter have thought, to see a daughter of ours take so much interest in all his theories?"

"But she must be aware that Caroline was educated quite differently from her sisters. Surely it might have been expected, once he spoke of some of the ideas that my brother held?"

"*I* did not expect it, Richard. I knew that she had her head full of a great many foolish notions that her uncle and his friends had put in it, when she returned from London, but more than two years at home should have shown her how impractical they were."

Mrs Randall's words dismayed her husband. He had been thinking how little he really knew his second daughter, yet her response to Thomas Martin had come as no surprise to him. If his wife had not foreseen it too, she must be possessed of a greater capacity for self-deception than he had realised. Her belated discovery did not look good for future harmony in the home.

"Oh, if only we had not permitted her to keep house for your brother when your sister died," she said dolefully. "We really ought to have known better."

Thinking back, Mr Randall wondered. They had indeed had their doubts about the invitation to a daughter not quite nineteen to take charge of a house in London, but it had been a relief in some ways, removing a disturbing element from their quiet life in the country. "It would have been hard to refuse, my love," he said. "After all, she was already as much at home there as she was here, she knew his ways so well, and she was his god-daughter. Naturally he thought of her."

"It is not natural at all, a bachelor in his forties having a young girl in charge of his household."

"But much younger girls have to do so, if they marry," he argued. "And he did leave her his money and his property."

"I do not wish to sound ungrateful, Richard, but I cannot help but think it would have been a great deal simpler if he had not made her his heiress. Of course I am pleased that the money should stay in the family, but why could he not have given you control?"

"I daresay, when Charles made his will, he expected to outlive me, and that Caroline would be in her thirties or forties by the time she inherited his fortune. But he also believed that a young woman had as much right to independence as a young man."

"Oh, Richard! Your brother had so many foolish notions, I wonder he made enough money to have a fortune to leave at all."

"Charles was an extremely able lawyer," said Mr Randall defensively.

"I am sure he was, I did not mean to belittle him. But he was also what one might call quixotic, would you not agree? He might easily have wasted his money on schemes to persuade people to treat their inferiors as equals."

"If he had done so, it would have been money that was in every way his own. Except for what my father paid for his education, which I hope nobody would grudge him, none of the Randall money came his way at all."

His wife became conciliatory. "No, I am quite aware of that, and of course he was very generous to Caroline. Only, consider how much easier things would have been for us if she had not inherited that house and money at the age of twenty-two."

He thought about that, and said cautiously, "I have sometimes wondered if it might have been better for her to remain in London rather than return here. Anna could have kept her company – no, perhaps that would not have done – but if we could have found an older woman to act as her companion?"

"I trust that is not your idea of a joke," said Mrs Randall, "Caroline herself did not seriously consider such a thing for very long. It would have been most unsuitable. Of course she had to come home to Sussex."

"However, Anne, you must admit that she has behaved well since her return. It can not have been at all easy for her, after being practically her own mistress for over three years, to come back here and take up her old place as one of our daughters."

"But had she married, she would not have had to do that, would she? And it is not as if she lacked the opportunity. You know how many offers she turned down saying she would prefer to remain single. I thought – I still think – that these ideas may be the result of what she heard while living with her uncle. Surely Charles did not advocate such very revolutionary theories as those that young man spoke of?"

"No, I think not. His interest in reform was general, and stemmed more from dissatisfaction with customs that he felt had become meaningless than from a desire to change everything. Do remember that the French had not gone to such extremes, in his lifetime."

Mrs Randall made no reply, she seemed wrapped in thought, and her husband was beginning to hope he could turn his attention to his book again, when her voice came sharply out of the gloom, saying ruefully that she really ought to have known.

"What do you mean, Anne?"

"I should have been prepared for Caroline to do something outrageous. Think of Selina Coleman."

He was somewhat mystified, failing to see any logical connection between the recent departure from their neighbourhood of Caroline's earliest friend, and the expression of unmaidenly interest in theories about social reform and the emancipation of women. He said as much, "Selina has married, the very thing that Caroline appears to hold in abhorrence."

"I am certain that her elopement was entirely Caroline's idea! Selina is far to timid to undertake such an enterprise on her own. You spoke of Caroline behaving well, but encouraging her friend to defy her parents is hardly good behaviour."

"Surely the young man in question must have played some part in the matter?"

"Richard, you have been acquainted with that girl since she was a child. You must be aware of how much support and reassurance she would have needed if she was not to falter in her resolve. Since *our* daughter affects to despise matrimony, it must seem to the Colemans that she simply took pleasure in disrupting the arrangement they had made for theirs. She knew they had chosen a husband for Selina, yet she promoted her marriage with an obscure Welshman she had merely met on a visit to her aunt."

Mr Randall had tried not to take much notice at the time, but he had seen enough to be aware that there was more to the story than that.

"Whatever the Colemans thought of Mr Penry, at the time the young woman met him there was no question of her being engaged elsewhere. He cannot be said to have behaved dishonourably. The idea that she should marry Mr Jobson was not suggested until after her return from her visit, and Mr Penry only learned of it when he came to Sussex to ask for her hand."

"Nevertheless, upon hearing that she was to marry another, he should have taken himself off at once, not hung about waiting to see her."

"Would you not expect him to want to see her once more if only to say goodbye? It may have been all he intended to do, till he saw how much she disliked the man her parents had chosen for her? That must have been obvious to him. I saw how miserable she was, and he was in love with her."

"Because she chose to imagine a preference for him," Mrs Randall began, but her husband stopped her.

"No, I cannot agree that it was her imagination," he said, "Selina is not a simpering miss in her teens, she is nearly as old as Caroline and not unintelligent. Setting aside her prior attachment, how could she help but dislike Mr Jobson?"

"She could have refused to marry at all," said his wife rather bitterly. "It was most undutiful to set up her choice against that of her parents."

Richard Randall demurred. "She and her parents did not disagree about that unfortunate young man who died a month before they were to marry. And in this instance, it really cannot be said that her parents had chosen better for her than she had for herself. I encountered both men, and Mr Penry was far superior. The proposal to marry a well-bred young woman to a booby like Jobson does no credit to either her father or her mother. I am surprised at Coleman, he at least is a gentleman, if his wife lacks breeding, and with the son virtually adopted by his Irish uncle, it really should not be necessary to consider wealth above all else in marrying their daughters. My dear Anne, what would you think of me were I to propose such a match for one of our girls? Would you not imagine I had taken leave of my senses?"

She seemed to think about this, finally saying reluctantly that, yes, she would not have found Mr Jobson at all appealing. "But nevertheless, it was wrong for Caroline to assist her friend to deceive her parents like that."

"Do you not think that she was honour-bound to respect Selina's secret?"

"No, I do not. In the first place, I am sure that she did more than keep quiet about what was planned, she actively helped them, and in the second, what has honour to do with young women? Honour is for men to concern themselves with. And it made things extremely difficult for me. I am sure Mrs Coleman blames me – she hardly speaks to me now."

"I would have thought that was something to be grateful for," said Mr Randall dryly, knowing how trying his wife had always found their neighbour. From the curious sound she made he suspected that she was suppressing a laugh, though her next words were grave.

"I suspect that she writes to her, Richard."

"Who writes to whom?"

She sounded impatient, "Why, Caroline, to Selina."

"Did you forbid her to do so?"

"I should not need to. But, no, I did not. I merely hoped that it would not happen. But I fear I was too sanguine."

"Why not ask her, Anne?"

"I am afraid she would admit it, and say that she would continue to do so. Caroline never tells a lie."

"No," he said thoughtfully, "Truthful as well as honourable. A strange combination for a female."

"I do not object to veracity! That is a virtue that all young women should possess."

"I wonder if they do, in general?"

"Is there any reason why you should doubt it?"

"Ladies are popularly supposed to be practised in bending the truth to suit their own convenience, are they not? If you

23

do not care to raise the subject with Caroline, would you like me to ask her if she writes to her friend?"

"Would you prohibit the correspondence?"

"I do not think so. Whatever the circumstances of her marriage, I cannot believe that contact with Selina Coleman could harm any young woman, let alone Caroline. In any case, I agree with you."

"In what way, Richard?"

"Why, if she were to defy us, we would be powerless to make her obey. Perhaps we ought to be grateful that so far, since her return, she has treated us with respect and not flaunted her independence. Think of the way – oh, of course, you were not present then. But the way that youth spoke of his father, it was not merely disrespectful, it was contemptuous! I was quite sickened."

"And you wonder why I do not wish for further contact with Mr Martin."

"Did I say that? But I thought it was his principles that you were concerned about."

"So it is, but I am also afraid of the influence of his theories. Caroline is just beginning to settle down at home after her sojourn in London, in time she would surely have forgotten all that nonsense about Equality, and the Rights of Women. But now she has received fresh incentive to pursue such ideas, and Heaven only knows when she will come to her senses. That is why I do not wish her to meet Mr Thomas Martin again."

"And how are we to achieve that end, Anne? Even were we to make my old friend understand that he must not bring him here, he might meet her out walking, or riding with Lucy. We could hardly keep both girls at home until he has left for Lewes. Unless you were to ask Caroline not to converse with him should they meet him? As a favour."

These words seemed to lash Mrs Randall, she made an impatient noise and said sharply, "I should not have to beg favours from my daughter! This is what happens when a young woman is given inflated ideas of her own importance. Also, if I were to do that, it might only make her think about him more. I would like to prevent him from crossing her path, so that there is some chance that this evening may be forgotten. I suppose if he is not invited here, he may take the hint and not approach our daughter."

"Hint! My dear Anne, I might as well expect a hint to be taken by one of my pigs, I doubt if they have any thicker skins. That man is armoured at all points, I can assure you."

"That I can believe. I am most concerned about his meeting the two girls when they are out riding."

"It is not as if they go unattended, my love. Batehup is always there."

"Batehup is a groom. He could not prevent that man from joining their ride, unless we made an issue of it, and that would mean everyone knew we were anxious to discourage Mr Martin. After all, Sir Charles has frequently accompanied them, as he did this morning."

Mr Randall could not resist the temptation to tease her: "It would never do for Sir Charles to be discouraged," he agreed slyly. His wife's response made him regret this imprudence.

"It would be bad manners, apart from anything else," she said with stiff dignity. "It seem to me that the solution would be for you to ride with the girls for a while, you could at least engage him in conversation."

The mere thought appalled him, and he was chiding himself for not seeing the way her remarks were tending. Marshalling his thoughts for objecting to her suggestion he said hastily, "But that would seem very peculiar of me. Everybody knows that I do not care to ride these days. I am not so young as I was, and I have got too heavy to do so with any comfort. I much prefer to walk round my estate than ride further afield. Caroline would certainly be aware if I were to take it up again while that man remains in our vicinity."

"Of course she would. You must continue to do so when he has gone, so that nobody connects the two things. It will do you no harm, Richard."

Mr Randall was indignant. How would she like to find herself bumping about in the company of younger riders who were more accustomed to the exercise. The image of her on horseback was not incongruous. "Why do you not accompany Caroline and Lucy yourself, my love?" he asked solemnly, "You used to have as good a seat on a horse as either of them."

"Really, my dear! Your idea of humour. What a figure I should cut! It must be twenty years since I was last in the saddle," but her tone was not quite so sharp, and recalling their courting days and the gratification with which she had received compliments on her skill, he wondered if a little judicious flattery might help, and pointed out that she was some years his junior, but she cut him short.

"Please do not continue this farce, Richard. Even were that possible, what could I say to that man? And if you fear that your taking up riding again might seem strange, that would be nothing to the sensation that I would cause."

With a sigh he had to admit that she was right. He tried to think of other reasons against her suggestion, but he did see her point. Better to capitulate now than to argue about it, disturb the harmonious terms on which they lived and have an atmosphere of ill feeling for days.

"Very well," he said with a sigh, "I will speak to Batehup in the morning. I only hope that Jupiter will still be up to my weight!"

PART 2

The Old Schoolroom in Mr Randall's house

August 1794

Those encountering the Randall's handsome building with its brick façade often expressed surprise that it was called "Old Manor," but the present owner was wont to explain that some sort of building had occupied the site for at least six hundred years, and this was merely the latest of many. And even that was older than it appeared for concealed within the shell of symmetrical brickwork was a timber-framed house that the taste of the 1730s had considered utterly barbaric. The original ground floor rooms had been enlarged, plastered and generally brought into line with the façade. A grand staircase now led up from the hall, but above that the modernisation was external only. Most of the bedrooms were small, and even before the recent departure of the governess, the schoolroom had increasingly been used as a sitting room for the daughters of the house rather than a place for lessons.

Here Caroline kept most of her books, and wrote at her little portable desk, and here Anna, Lucy, and till recently Harriet, practised on the old spinet since the new pianoforte in the drawing room was reserved for more formal performances. Being situated over Mr Randall's study, it commanded an even more extensive view of the Weald and the South Downs.

In the mornings Caroline was generally out riding, but her mare had picked up a flint and was temporarily lame, forcing her to withdraw from a party consisting of the groom, her father and her sister Lucy, and by arrangement, Sir Charles Carter who had just returned to Sussex from his home in Hertfordshire. She was not accustomed to write letters at this time, but Anna having done her practising and departed, it seemed a good opportunity for her to finish off the letter to her friend Selina that was long overdue.

Seated near the window, she read through what she had already written, drinking in the warm air that came in, impregnated with the scent of summer flowers and alive with the buzz of insects and the distant sound of cattle. The downs were partly hidden in a heat haze, a promising sight, and the whole thing made such an impression on her that it was the first thing she mentioned when she picked up her pen and wrote the date and time.

"It really is a perfect summer morning, not unbearably hot but warm enough to make one feel alive all over. You might wonder why I am not out riding, but Lady Molly has gone lame. A pity; it is just the day for a ride, and after a fine July we have had such wretched weather this month. I shall hope to walk to Cuckfield later, as I have been doing frequently, wet or dry. As you know I prefer to take my letters in myself and collect any that have come for me, and at the moment I am trying to do so more often than usual, because Dame Anscombe is very near her end, and it gives her pleasure to see her youngest daughter. Becky, you will remember, is one of our maids, and my mother insists that she accompany me when I go to Cuckfield on my own. It seems strange to me that she would not give her permission to leave her work to visit her sick parent, but will spare her from it to attend a perfectly healthy young woman on a walk! And Mama is generally considered an easy mistress, almost indulgent. This is the sort of thing that makes me understand why some servants might rebel, especially when I consider that some of them are treated by their employers as if they had no right to ordinary human feelings.

"I see I have yet to answer your query about Harriet. I am afraid the poor child shows little sign of improvement, and this is high summer. Dr Bowen would have us continue sanguine, but I am sure he privately regards her case as hopeless. Words cannot express my emotion. I am probably thought cold, because I do not weep easily, but that does not mean I do not feel! If only there were something I could do.

"Apart from that, we all keep healthy. Sir Charles Carter is at present paying his third visit to his uncle and aunt in the last few months. My mother pretends not to know what brings him so often to the neighbourhood and to this house, which I find amusing. I feel that Lucy is perfectly sincere in her surprise, she is not at all coquettish, in spite of her beauty. She is prettier than ever, and looked delightful when she set off for her ride this morning, dressed in a dark blue habit with her hair braided up under a little hat. She has such lovely hair that it seems a shame to hide it, but the effect was very elegant."

Footsteps were approaching the room, and Caroline began to put her sheets of paper tidy. She looked up to see the person she had been writing about enter from the passage. "Why, Lucy, I had not realised how the time was going. Did you have a pleasant ride?"

"Very, but we missed you."

Caroline was tempted to reply sardonically that she doubted this, with Sir Charles there, but her sister's blue eyes were fixed on her so innocently that she hadn't the heart to say it, and merely thanked Lucy for the concern she had expressed.

"It does seem a shame, when you enjoy riding even more than I do. Oh! But you could have ridden Seraphine, Caroline – I did not think of that!"

"Thank goodness," Caroline responded, thinking of how the young baronet would have felt about such a suggestion. "My dear creature, you really are too good. As if I would have permitted that. It is a pity that Lady Molly should be lame during the first fine spell since July, but it is not serious. Which way did you take?"

"Some distance towards Cowfold. Caroline, I must take this hat off, it feels a little heavy on my head. She went out to her bedroom, returning quickly without the hat but with her bright hair still pinned up in the graceful classic style that made her look older than when it was flowing loose, though it really enhanced her lovely little face. Lucy became aware of her sister's scrutiny, looked momentarily anxious, but seemed reassured by a smile, and seated herself at the table. She glanced at Caroline's papers with some interest, but said nothing.

Caroline replied to the unanswered question, "I am writing to Selina, Lucy."

Her sister looked alarmed. "Oh, Caroline," she began, but was cut short.

"Well, she is my oldest friend." Caroline was annoyed with herself to find she was on the defensive.

"But she eloped!"

"And you feel that that ought to end our friendship?"

"Well, Miss Yare said..." Lucy faltered. "I mean – it is so – so shocking – to elope, is it no?"

"It is an elopement to Scotland that is considered so very disgraceful," said Caroline thoughtfully, "Selina did not do that, Lucy, she was married in Horsham, by special licence, on the day she left home."

"And that was not such a bad thing to do?" asked Lucy innocently.

"Indeed it was not. Only consider, a couple going to Scotland would be together, unmarried, for several days, before the ceremony could be performed."

"Oh. Oh, I see." To Caroline's amusement her sister blushed prettily as she gave this some thought, "I can see that this would make a difference, but even so..."

"You still feel that I should drop the acquaintance, since her family disapprove of the match, do you?"

"Oh, no! I mean, it is not for me to say – but did not Mama forbid you to write to her?"

Caroline looked at her in silence for a minute, very conscious of the difference between the ways they had been brought up. She was fond enough of her mother, but from an early age had been aware of the critical view her uncle had had of both her parents, causing her to question their authority as absolute. It had plainly never occurred to Lucy that one could go against any edicts from Mrs Randall, and she wondered how easy it would be to bridge the gulf thus revealed. To show too clearly how very much she differed in her opinions – if it did not shock her sister – would certainly distress and

30

bewilder her. When she came to reflect on it she realised that they neither of them knew as much about as each other as they might have done. Lucy had been a pretty, sweet-natured child when Caroline left home to live with her uncle, still very much in the schoolroom, too young to hold a conversation with, and only just emerging from that stage when she returned. They had never discussed anything like this before and it seemed wise to be cautious in her explanation. "No," she said finally. "Mama did not tell me not to write to my friend."

Lucy still looked puzzled, and her sister, wondering exactly how Selina's marriage had been presented to her, asked if she had been surprised by it?

"Oh, yes – when Georgina Coleman told me that her sister had eloped with a strange Welshman, I could hardly believe it."

"Ah, you heard it that way, did you. Not from Mama, or Miss Yare?"

"No indeed. Mama did not mention it, and Miss Yare would not let me discuss it with Harriet."

"Really?" Caroline was slightly surprised. "Did you not discuss it with her when you were alone? I know you said nothing to me."

"But I had been told not to," said Lucy, her eyes widening. By Miss Yare, thought Caroline, who had exhausted that lady's meagre knowledge before she was eleven and regarded her with scorn which had later turned to pity. It seemed strange to think of her sisters treating those feeble utterances with such respect.

"You must surely have thought about it?" she said gently.

Lucy put her hand to her mouth and looked guilty. "I am afraid I could not help doing that. It seemed incredible that Selina, of all people, should have done such a thing. She seemed so quiet – almost timid, perhaps. I used to like her, more than I like Georgina."

Selina's sister, about a year older than Lucy, had always struck Caroline as a rather spiteful creature, no doubt people

31

expected the younger ones to have a similar friendship, but this didn't sound as if it were true on Lucy's side.

"Did you talk more about it to Georgina?" she asked.

"I tried not to, but she mentions it when we do meet." Lucy seemed a little embarrassed, not meeting her sister's eyes. Caroline laughed.

"I can guess what she says, she probably suggests that I am to blame for Selina leaving."

"Er – yes, I am afraid she does. I do not understand what she means. She seems to think that you helped Selina to elope, how could she think such a thing?"

"It is true that I enabled her to get away without the family knowing where she was going, no doubt they credit me with far more involvement than that. But you do not know why the wedding had to be so secret? You did not meet a Mr Jobson?"

"Oh, I did once, at the Coleman's house. He had rather bright clothes and a silly laugh."

"What did you think of him?"

"I know I should not say so, but he did not seem to me to be a real gentleman. Caroline, I remember now, Georgina said something about him wanting to marry Selina. Could that be true?"

"It was, and her parents were insisting on it. They refused to consider Mr Penry's offer, though she had met and become fond of him before she had ever heard of Mr Jobson, her parents would not listen because that uncouth creature was richer."

"That seems terrible." Lucy was distressed. "No wonder she seemed so unhappy. But her parents have the right to say who she should marry, do they not?"

"Not legally," said Caroline firmly. "She is over twenty-one. Parents may have a claim to a child's affections over that age, but they cannot forbid marriage. What right had Mr and Mrs Coleman to Selina's affection if they were prepared to force Mr Jobson upon her? What would you think of our parents, if they proposed a man like that for one of us, Lucy."

"They would never do such a thing!" Lucy exclaimed. "You cannot think it!"

32

Her sister laughed. "No, of course I do not. But that was what the Colemans intended for their daughter, imagine how she felt, quite apart from the fact that she loved someone else."

"Oh, Caroline!" Lucy was obviously torn between her natural sympathy and the strict code of behaviour in which she had been reared.

"So you can see, the situation is not as simple as it might seem. It was not even a question of their merely forbidding her to marry the man she cared for, was it? You might say that they had forfeited her affections."

"Oh, dear, I can see how difficult it was for her. And you suggested that she should marry him in spite of them?"

"She asked for my advice, about a situation that already existed, I did not put the idea into her head, and I told her that given the choice of marrying the man she loves or displeasing her parents, she might be better off with Mr Penry than doing what they wanted and have the misery of being tied for life with a man she could neither love nor respect."

"And is she happy with her Welshman?"

"I think so," said Caroline, "She was distressed to have to go against her parents' wishes, but Mr Penry is a good and honourable man. He would never have agreed to the secret wedding if he had not felt it was the only thing to do."

"Then, I am glad for Selina," said Lucy, rising and half turning to look out of the window. "I still feel it must be wrong, but in this case..."

"Exactly," said Caroline, "General rules cannot always be applied to particular circumstances."

Lucy nodded absently; her attention seemed to be held by something in the garden below. If she had looked happier, her sister might have wondered if Sir Charles had returned, but she had stiffened as she went to the window. Concerned, Caroline joined her and together they watched their sisters walk down the path. Harriet was clinging to Anna's arm and before they were out of sight they paused to rest on a bench.

"Oh, Caroline," said Lucy brokenly, "I cannot bear to see Harriet like this. Just think how she was a year ago, she would have been skipping ahead, teasing Anna. Or riding with us!"

"Yes, I know," said Caroline sadly, wishing that tears would relieve her as they did her sister, who sank into a chair and buried her face in her hands. She moved to pat her shoulder and Lucy raised drenched blue eyes to her and asked piteously how bad she thought Harriet's illness was. "Is she really as bad as little Dick was?"

"What gave you that idea?" Caroline's thoughts were carried painfully back to her early childhood.

"Oh, it was old Harden. I heard him saying to Batehup this morning that it put him in mind of the young master, and then they both saw me and stopped talking. It isn't really so, is it?"

"I fear it may be," said Caroline reluctantly. "It pains me very much to say so, but when I think about it, she does seem to be ill in a very similar way. I am sorry to upset you," – Lucy had begun to weep desolately – "I would deny it if I could, but it would not be honest to do so."

"No, I would not like you to hide the truth from me, that would be worse. You really think it is so? Is there no hope?"

"There is always hope," said Caroline soberly. "But I fear she is very ill, and it is like Dick. His sickness was brought on by just such a fever as she had last January."

"I had not realised that. I do not remember him, you know. I think of him as the baby in Mama's arms, in that picture in the hall. But he was older than that when he died, was he not?"

"Indeed he was. I was eight, and he was over five. You were still in the nursery."

"And Harriet?"

"She had not then been born. When Dick died, Anna and I were with Uncle Charles and Aunt Lucy in London. We returned to find there was a new baby and were told that Dick had gone to Heaven."

"Oh, Caroline! Did you have any idea that that was going to happen?"

"I think so, Anna possibly understood it more than I did at the time, but I can now see the significance of some things that happened then, like the way the servants whispered to each other, and the look on our parents' faces, but I am not sure I really the gravity of the situation, all I knew was that Dick was very ill. I think what made the greatest impression on me at the time was the unkindness of the vicar."

"Mr Carter was unkind!" cried Lucy, stricken, "Oh, Caroline, surely not. He is a most tender-hearted man."

Caroline was amused at the defence of Sir Charles' uncle, and said gently, "Dear Lucy, I am sure he is, and I do not think he would be unkind. This was before he came, our vicar then was a Mr Boxall, whom I thought most unpleasant."

"I think I have heard Anna speak of another clergyman. Can that be the one? Only she described him as a good man."

"How like Anna," said Caroline bitterly. A puzzled look came into her sister's face as if she were trying to work out what her sister meant.

"Are you saying that she thought him better than he was? Do you not think that a good thing, to look for the best in people?"

"It is certainly kinder than seeking out their faults," Caroline agreed. "As long as one is not perceiving virtue where it does not exist, where one's trust might be betrayed. But that was not exactly what I meant about Anna." She checked herself on the point of saying that this particular folly was not one that their eldest sister was likely to commit. Whatever her private feelings about Anna, it seemed an ugly thing to speak of them to Lucy. "I do not suppose she found him so unpleasant as I did. She was a good, quiet child, the sort he approved of. Dick and I were too noisy and mischievous for his liking."

"But I thought Dick was a good little boy."

"Yes, that is how he is spoken of, as a little angel. He was not a bad child, but had he lived, I am sure his mischief would have been remembered as well as his good behaviour. He was a normal five-year-old boy, it would have seemed unnatural if he had had no faults."

"I can see that," said Lucy thoughtfully.

"And he had red hair just like mine, and the temper to go with it. No doubt it needed to be curbed, but Mr Boxall thought it ought somehow to be erased, I think he saw it as a sign of the devil. Also, he spoke of it being the colour of Judas. He was always rebuking us even before Dick got ill. Then he threatened him with Hell-fire, all because a footman we had at the time had taught us to play cards to cheer up the sick room. The poor little fellow was in tears, I found it hateful and did not understand that the man thought it was for the good of his soul..." Caroline broke off abruptly, finding the memory too painful to speak of with a steady voice. Lucy looked aghast, obviously moved by her words, and put up a hand.

"Oh, Caroline, I cannot feel that was necessary. And I am sure that Mr Carter would not have done that."

"No, he is a much kinder man. I believe that some people do not consider him as zealous in his teaching, but to my mind he is a far better clergyman than Mr Boxall. He has certainly put me more in charity with his profession."

This remark seemed to have startled Lucy. She gazed at her sister wide–eyed for a moment, and then said unexpectedly, "Was it true that Uncle Charles had lost his faith? That he had become an atheist, by the time he died, as Anna said once?"

Caroline tried to hide her disgust at this evidence of her elder sister's attitude. "No, it is not true. He never lost his faith, but he came to lose confidence in the way it is presented by the Church."

"Is that not the same thing?" Lucy seemed perplexed.

"Only if you regard the Church of England, as it has become, as the only way to believe in God," said Caroline, "There are many sincere believers who do not go to church. Some of them set up a new Christian religious group, such as the Quakers or the Methodists, but my uncle came to feel that was only starting the whole circle of authority all over again. He considered that what he disliked about it was the fact that such a body needs organisation, he used to say that this process put barriers between Man and God, so that over the years more and more interpretation is needed for the ordinary mortal. Since he himself was more intelligent than most of the clergymen he met, he became impatient when they tried to assert their authority over him."

Lucy was looking very troubled and her hands moved nervously among the papers in front of Caroline, stilling as she caught her sister's eye. She was plainly far from being reassured about her uncle – if he had really been the person she was worried about. "Why did you mention Uncle Charles, and ask about his faith, at this moment, Lucy?"

Her sister looked at her reproachfully and her eyes filled with tears. Deciding she was afraid to ask outright, Caroline wondered aloud if she had thought that hearing what views Charles Randall held would explain their effect on his niece.

Lucy nodded, "I knew how much time you had spent with him, and I wondered…." Her words faltered to a halt and she continued to move her hands restlessly.

"If I shared his views? I might have gone further, though."

"Oh, Caroline, No!"

"Or, never have agreed with him at all. I did not share all his views, you know. I think my position is somewhere between those two extremes. I can understand what he found to criticise about the Church and admire how he coped without it. But he was a very exceptional man, not everyone can manage without some kind of direction…." She paused. If she spoke of her own feeling that she might prefer some other form of worship, her sister might imagine that she was actually about to seek one out. Possibly not, from the worried frown on Lucy's face, she felt that the notion of a faith existing without all the ceremonies of the Church of England was beyond her comprehension. The next remark showed this fairly clearly.

"But you do believe in God, Caroline? Please understand, I do not want to seem impertinent, but I should be so distressed if I thought that you – doubted…"

How could she say much on the subject without terrifying her sister? Lucy would probably sense if she were prevaricating, and it was against her nature to do so. Finally she said cautiously that she was unable to except the idea of God that some people seemed to hold.

"If it seems cruel in a human being to terrify a small child the way Mr Boxall did, how could one believe that an omnipotent Deity would do so? Many imperfect men and women would be more loving that that."

Lucy continued to look frightened but though Caroline could see that it upset her to hear even a bad clergyman criticised, she felt the need to make some effort to explain her meaning.

"Even when I was small, I felt that Mr Boxall had his own idea of God – someone much sterner and more cruel than when Mr Carter speaks of Him. Clergymen are only human, after all." She doubted if her sister would be able to understand how her uncle had accused some of them of creating their maker in their own image.

Lucy suddenly started to behave rather oddly, her fidgeting with the papers had caused some to become dislodged, and she had gone very pink, trying to hide a particular sheet under others, studiously avoiding her sister's eyes as she did so.

Caroline put out her hand and grasped the paper just before it disappeared from sight. She had a suspicion which one it might be, and this was confirmed when she glanced at the signature on the bottom. In a flowing hand it said, "*I am, my dear Miss Randall, your obedient servant, Thomas Martin.*" Lucy looked at her miserably and coloured even more. "Caroline, I am so sorry, I did not intend to pry, but that is no excuse. I do not know why I was playing with your papers, it is not something that I do as a rule."

"No, my dear, you were disturbed, I could see that."

"You do believe that I would not pry? I only saw who it was from, I did not read it! I will forget even that, I promise."

"That is easier said than done, Lucy, memory is not dependent on will, we will leave the subject if you prefer, but I would not like you to worry over it in silence. There is no dark secret, you know."

"No?" said Lucy faintly. "But you have never spoken of it."

"I have not wished to advertise the fact that I am corresponding with Mr Martin, because people will misunderstand, think this is a matter of sentiment. He is simply the most intelligent and rational being that I have encountered since I lived in London."

Lucy seemed to be making calculations and after a moment she said tentatively, "Is that the reason why you go to collect your letters so frequently, now?"

"It is one of them," said Caroline carefully. "Once I knew he was going to write, it seemed as well to do so."

"Did he tell you that when he came to dine?"

"No, he was still in the neighbourhood then. He asked if he might do so, that day when we met him and Mr Sturgis out riding – do you remember?"

"Oh yes. That was about the time when Papa started to ride out with us, surely?"

"Of course," said Caroline, feeling a surge of impatience when her sister looked at her with an apparent lack of comprehension.

"Do you mean there is a connection between Papa's decision to ride again, and Mr Martin?"

"Oh, yes, Lucy, it seems quite clear to me. He had declined to ride so often, saying he had become too heavy. It cannot be a coincidence that he should suddenly change his mind about it the very day after that dinner party."

Lucy looked distressed for a moment, but then her face brightened and she pointed out that their father had continued to do so ever since. "It is over three months since Mr Martin went to Lewes!"

Caroline decided that she must disillusion her. "Lucy dear, he could not stop as suddenly as he started, that would have made his real motive all too apparent. There is a line in Shakespeare's Hamlet –'Tis sport to see the engineer hoist with his own petard' – That is Papa. Until he can find an excuse to do so, he cannot give up riding! Though I think it has been good for him, and perhaps he enjoys it more than he expected to."

"You sound cross about it," said Lucy wonderingly.

"I am a little angry, I must confess. Not so much with Papa, poor man, I doubt it was his idea. I am sure that Mama thought he could stop me talking to Mr Martin. I do not care to have schemes made against me behind my back."

"But you did talk to him," said Lucy innocently. "You ride so well, and so does he. Papa and Mr Sturgis could not keep up."

"And Papa had to talk to his friend at the top of his voice," Caroline was amused at the recollection, and her sister gave a reluctant smile before asking if she really thought that their mother had been responsible for their father's decision to resume riding.

"I do not like being treated like a child. She might have spoken to me," said Caroline, hoping her sister would not ask how she would have responded if Mrs Randall had requested her not to converse with the man. It did rankle that her mother had tried this roundabout method of circumventing her. "All I wanted was the chance of an intelligent conversation, it had been so long since I spoke with a rational human being."

"Are we not rational, then?" asked Lucy, in a small, hurt voice.

"Oh, I am sorry. I did not mean it quite like that. But there are many things that would not interest you, and I doubt if you would understand them. Some might be thought unsuitable for a young girl. No, it is I that out of place, not you or the rest of the family that fail."

"Was it leaving home to keep house for Uncle Charles that made you so different? I think that is a shame."

"You pity me for being different?" asked Caroline with irritation, and saw her sister wince.

"I did not say that, but I have always been sorry that you had to go away like that. Miss Yare was most concerned…"

"Miss Yare! What did she tell you about it?

Lucy blushed again. "She did not speak of it to me, I happened to hear her talking to Anna when I came in here one night to collect something. She was saying how sorry she was for you to be forced to go away to London."

Caroline tried to picture the scene. "What did Anna say to that?" Her sister looked horrified.

"But I did not listen!" she cried, "I knew their conversation was not intended for my ears. I only heard those few words before I called good night and went off to bed."

Caroline wondered what their older sister's reaction to the remarks of their governess had been, and on an impulse said abruptly, "What was your opinion, Lucy? Did you feel upset that I might have been forced to go to London?"

Lucy wrinkled up her forehead in a way that made her look like a serious baby, and was so long in replying that her sister repeated her question.

"Oh, Caroline. I am afraid you will think it dreadful of me, but the truth is, it did not seem to matter too much to me at the time. I mean – you had so often stayed with Uncle Charles and Aunt Lucy for months, so I did not really miss you as much as I ought to have done." She was near to tears again, and Caroline patted her hand.

"Bravo!" she said, and Lucy looked up in surprise.

"What do you mean? I thought you would be hurt to hear me sound so callous."

"Nonsense, I thought nothing of the kind. Why should you care a great deal about me at that time? As you said, I was so often away from home, you and Harriet could not have known me very well. I was applauding your courage in admitting the fact."

"It is kind of you to take it like that," said Lucy. "I should miss you much more now."

Caroline laughed.

"I mean it. I feel as if I hadn't known you properly since you returned."

"Exactly. You cannot be expected to care a great deal for a person you do not really know, even if they are relations. And of course you were very much enclosed in the world of the schoolroom."

"That is how it felt. These last two years, it has seemed as if I have been released into a different life. Now I understand what you were giving up, in having to leave home."

Caroline was decidedly taken aback. "My dear Lucy!" she exclaimed, but before she could comment further her sister continued rapidly and rather anxiously to say that she had cared much more later.

"I was leaving the schoolroom by the time you returned, and Miss Yare did speak about that to me. She was so glad for you."

"Glad!" said Caroline blankly, remembering the misery she had felt at having to leave London and resume her place in the family after her uncle's unexpected death.

"Yes, glad that you should be released from that obligation."

"I begin to see. Poor dear Miss Yare, she always did try to find the best in all of us. I suppose she thought I had sacrificed myself for Uncle Charles."

"That must have been what she meant. But you were pleased to go and look after him?"

"Certainly I was. I was very fond of him, he had been like a second father to me since I was a child. I was happy to be able to be of assistance to him, but I also liked having the chance to live in London and I actually enjoyed keeping house for him."

"In spite of what you were giving up to do so? Surely that meant you had no chance of marrying while he lived?"

"Not necessarily. Had there been any question of that, I do not think he would have prevented me," said Caroline. She wondered if she could make it clear to her sister that in many ways she had counted it a gain to be freed from the status of dependant daughter without being forced into the bonds of matrimony. So few people seemed to believe this. "Why, Lucy, you know I have always said I have no desire to marry."

"Yes, but... No, I should not say any more."

"Why not? What should you not speak of?"

Lucy looked nervously down at her hands, now folded in her lap, and seemed to be keeping them still with some effort. "It is simply that when some women say that, I am afraid I wonder if they are anxious not to be pitied."

"You think that they conceal a genuine desire for it under a pretended indifference? Did someone tell you that, or is it your own observation?"

"I could not help noticing," said Lucy after a moment's hesitation. "People like – well, Aunt Lucy, or Anna. I do not blame them for it, I think it is very sad."

"So do I," said Caroline quietly. "And most unfair. It is bad enough that a woman should be despised for not marrying, it is almost tragic that she should have to hide her feelings with a lie to protect herself from ridicule. I think that may have been so with Aunt Lucy, a little, though I believe she was once engaged to a man who died. But Anna has certainly had the chance to change her status."

"Anna has?" cried Lucy, and immediately looked guilty, "I am sorry to seem so surprised, but it is something I was not aware of."

"This was something that happened when I was about fifteen," said Caroline. "Mr Carter had a young curate and he proposed for her. Though I was still in the schoolroom, and about to go on one of my visits to London at the time, I saw enough to be sure it was mainly her decision to dismiss him. I am not sure if our parents were very eager for the match, but there was nothing to object to about him. Only Anna did not care to marry him."

"I did not know Mr Carter ever had a curate," said Lucy.

"I believe he was ill for a time, about nine years ago, and needed assistance with the services and work in the parish. He was not here for long, but you must have seen him sometimes. Rather a little man, with a big nose."

"I think I do recall something, but not very much. I do not think I ever saw him at this house."

"Once Anna had refused him, he probably did not come unless he had to."

"Poor man! Was he very unhappy?"

43

"That I cannot say. I went to London at that time, as I mentioned."

"What did you think about him, Caroline? Were you sorry that she turned him down?"

Lucy might be surprised at how little her sister had thought about the matter at the time, and looking back, she was conscious that she had found the young curate slightly repulsive, especially the rather arch way he had treated her when meeting her out with her mother and older sister.

"He would not have suited me, even if I had been old enough," she said thoughtfully. "But he might have appealed to Anna, I suppose. She did not tell me why she did not wish to marry him."

"And she has never had another offer? Do you think she is sorry now?"

"I never heard of another, but as you know, I was away for some years. Perhaps she had others, but like me does not desire to marry." Probably not for the same reasons, she said to herself, thinking how difficult she had always found Anna to converse with.

"I have just remembered, surely there were two men who wished to marry you after our uncle died? Or have I got it wrong?"

"In fact there were three of them," said Caroline. "Much too soon, even if I had cared for them. It was far too obvious."

"Do you mean that this was due to your having his money? That could not have been the only reason?"

"Possibly not, though one of them was quite candid about the fact. I suppose were prepared to take me along with the money. But I doubt if they would have been so eager if I had not had it."

"But you are not plain!" cried Lucy.

"It is kind of you to say so, but I have other defects in their eyes. Not one of them would have cared to have a wife who was cleverer than they are, which was one of the many reasons why I would never have considered them as husbands! But I can conceive of a man who might want me in spite of that. While I was with my uncle there who was one who asked for my hand, and he certainly seemed to admire my brain."

"But you did not care for him."

"I liked him well enough, but certainly not enough to exchange the life I had with my uncle for life with him."

"But it would not be true to say that you had no chance of marriage."

"No indeed, though in years to come, I might not be believed if I spoke of it. I daresay some women do lay claim to proposals that they had never had." She thought of poor little Miss Carter's reference to a faded romance that had ended sadly. But perhaps it was true, after all.

"It is strange that neither you nor Anna seem to mind not being married," remarked Lucy, sounding puzzled. Caroline thought again of their very different motives, but hesitated to try to explain to the younger girl her suspicion that in her older sister's case, that it might be the physical aspect that repelled her, whereas she herself had little objection to the idea of intimacy.

"I cannot speak for Anna, but I feel that matrimony can be rated too highly. I resent the idea that even married to a fool I should be considered to have improved my position. I prefer to control my own life." She checked any further comment, they were nearing an area that unmarried young ladies were not supposed to discuss. Yet by the way Lucy had blushed at the explanation of why a trip to Gretna Green would have been worse for Selina, she was clearly not as ignorant as she was supposed to be.

"You speak of marriage as though it was a mere contract between people. Surely it must be more than that?"

"It can sometimes be a contract arranged by the parents, with the couple barely acquainted, to merge two fortunes, perhaps. In such cases, they may come to care for each other, but in some instances, such as the match proposed for my poor friend, it could be disastrous."

"But people do marry for love, surely, Caroline?"

45

"It is a convention that they do so, even if they had hardly met before the ceremony, but I am inclined to doubt if it is real romantic love, something I have rarely encountered. That appears to me, as an observer, to be a sort of bewitchment. I have not experienced it myself. How do you feel about it?"

"I?" said Lucy, turning pink, "Why do you ask me that?" Caroline felt a surge of irritation at this maidenly modesty.

"Oh, Lucy, you do not have to be coy with me! Surely between us you can admit your feelings towards Sir Charles Carter?" To her surprise her sister looked indignant, and her voice was full of reproach when she replied.

"Oh, Caroline, I did not expect you to tease me like that!"

Caroline felt as if she had picked up a wrong thread. "My dear girl, I merely thought that you were being less than candid with me. Why should you imagine that I was trying to tease you?"

"Because that is what people like Georgina Coleman do. 'Don't you like him, Lucy?' or 'You surely find him very handsome!' I wish they would leave me alone, I have done them no harm! Can they not see how it hurts me?" Lucy finished her little outburst with a storm of tears, and Caroline in dismay set about trying to soothe her.

"My dear creature, pray forgive me," she began, "I did not realise that." Lucy was now sobbing more gently, and turned a piteously appealing face to her sister.

"Oh, Caroline, I do love him so very much but I know I must not speak of it, unless he offers for me. I feel I should not admit it even to myself – but I do!" More tears rolled down her cheeks and she fumbled blindly for a handkerchief. Caroline silently produced a clean one, and patted her gently while she mopped her face and blew her nose.

"I am sorry, Lucy, I misunderstood about that. But I cannot see anything wrong in your admitting to me how much you care. It is not as if he were indifferent to you, he plainly admires you very much."

"Do you think so? I am not imagining it?" said Lucy wistfully.

"Certainly not. I should say it was apparent to anyone at all observant. Depend upon it, that is why the other girls were teasing you, some of them may envy you for his preference, and they possibly think that you will enjoy being teased about it."

"Enjoy it!" cried Lucy, "How could they think that?"

"I believe some girls do take pleasure in being teased about their admirers. I suppose it feeds their vanity, makes them feel important."

"Goodness, how strange. But, Caroline, you would not deceive me? What is your opinion about Sir Charles – am I foolish to think that he might come to love me?"

"No, Lucy, I do not think so. I would have said that he shows every sign of caring as much as you do. But he may be somewhat in awe of you."

"Of me? How could that be? I cannot believe it!"

"Yes, I know, he is a great tall man, and a baronet into the bargain, but he could still be shy and diffident."

"But I am shy, sometimes, with him."

"He may be aware of that, and is being careful not to go too fast. But he might mistake your diffidence for disdain. You have a delightful smile, perhaps you have been afraid it might seem too forward to show much of it. I do not think it would be flirting, for you to give him a little more encouragement. Not that I think there is any doubt of his intentions."

"Oh, thank you, Caroline!" cried Lucy, rather to her sister's embarrassment embracing her as if she had done her a great service. "I feel so much happier now. I must go and change my gown." She moved to the door, turning back to add earnestly, "If – if he does propose for me, I do not think Papa or Mama would raise any objection, do you?"

She was perfectly serious, and her sister decided that there was no point in suggesting that their mother had been working hard to bring about that very conclusion.

PART 3

The grounds of Mr Randall's house

Early September, 1794

Caroline and Lucy were on the point of taking an afternoon stroll when Anna called to them. They turned to see her hurrying out of the front door gesturing frantically.

"Wait, wait, Mama and I are bringing Harriet out, since it is so warm!" The day was not merely warm, it was almost stiflingly hot and Caroline was surprised that her mother should consider it suitable for the sick child, even if this had been one of her better days. Possibly after the recent wet spell, Mrs Randall feared the cold more than anything else.

They checked their progress and waited in the sun, till the others joined them and the party got under way. Anna bustled out again carrying a rug and cushions and hovering round as her mother tenderly supported her youngest daughter down the steps, she indicated that Caroline and Lucy should bring up the rear.

Forced to go much more slowly, they accompanied the little party round the house and across the smaller lawn, Lucy cheerfully willing, if abstracted, her sister trying hard not to feel rebellious. She would have been happy to do anything to help Harriet, but Anna seemed to be providing all the assistance that was needed, and this progression was dreary in the extreme. Ever since an understanding with Sir Charles Carter had been reached ten days before, Lucy had been moving in a state of bemused happiness, insulated against any trivial irritations, and it had not been easy to get rational conversation with her. Caroline would have been happy enough with her own thoughts had they continued their walk at a normal pace, but it was difficult to ignore the dull platitudes that passed for conversation as they all made their way over the lawn to the rose garden at the top of the avenue that led to the East gate.

A small bench had been placed looking down among the shady trees, and by the time they reached it Harriet was panting painfully, clearly in need of a rest. Anna placed the cushions on the bench and spread the rug in front of it, as her mother set about making the girl comfortable. Lucy sank down on the rug and dreamily began to pick daisies, but Caroline stood by, feeling helpless and excluded, and aware that the temper she tried so hard to control was in danger of escaping.

Anna's self-important manner in tending the child irritated her, and the wistful smile on Harriet's wasted little face pierced her to the heart. Now that the doctor had almost given up hope, little effort was being made to conceal from her how very sick she was, and sadness had been added to the languor of ill health. Possibly little would have been gained by letting her think she had a chance of recovery, but did Anna have to make so much fuss about her spiritual welfare?

No doubt the oldest daughter believed she was doing the right thing, but the effect on Harriet was almost agonising to watch, and Caroline sometimes wondered if her parents shared her feelings about it however much they ought to approve, Hoping she had got her expression under control, she turned to look at the bench and found that her mother was leaving to speak to the gardener who had just approached. This left an empty space and the sick girl looked at her hopefully. Caroline would have been willing to join her, but Anna solicitously adjusted her position so that there was not really enough room for third person, putting a sisterly arm round Harriet and squeezing her hand gently. Her calmly self-righteous look was almost too much to bear. She then smiled indulgently at Lucy, now starting to weave the flowers she had gathered into a daisy-chain, it seemed the last straw when she appeared to expect their other sister to join in this harmless employment. Caroline looked down the long avenue and moved towards it.

"I think I will walk down to the old East gate and back," she said over her shoulder, and strode off without waiting for a reply.

Her thoughts as she walked ebbed and flowed as the shadows cast by the foliage of the trees came and went upon the mossy ground. Had Harriet felt snubbed, poor little thing, or would she realise that Anna had deliberately prevented her sister from joining them on the bench? Would she be hurt? Oh, but how could anyone think that Caroline would be prepared to sit and make daisy-chains at this juncture? This seemed like a deliberate insult, of course one could never tell with Anna. Everything she did appeared to be motivated by pure selflessness, but it was hard not to suspect that somehow there was an undercurrent malicious enjoyment.

A flash of light where the trees thinned out brought a mental image of Harriet's sweet, sad little face and in the patch of shade cast by the next lot of leaves, Caroline lived again the bitterness of her first encounter with death. Her unspoken cry at the time repeated itself in her mind "If God had to take one of them, why could it not have been Anna?" At the age of eight, she had shocked herself by the thought, at twenty-four it no longer seemed a sign of the irredeemable wickedness that the vicar had warned about, but it still disturbed her. She quickened her pace and emerged into the sunlight.

The avenue of trees ended just before the East gate, and in the clearing she felt almost assaulted by the heat. In spite of the large shady hat she wore, her eye were dazzled by the glare that met them, and she almost clung to the metal bars as she adjusted herself to it. "Pouff! What heat!" she exclaimed aloud, gazing at the lane outside. She turned and put her back against the gate, feeling the relief at looking at the green trees rather than the white dust. She had been heated as much by her anger as by the strength of the sun, she found she was trembling a little and at first was quite grateful for the warmth behind her. It gradually became almost too much, but before she could move away her ears caught the sound of footsteps in the lane.

There was not a great deal of traffic on this road, especially in the afternoon, and the only people likely to walk along it would be the villagers. But no farm labourer's boots would produce that crisp, light sound – it must be Sir Charles Carter, claiming a fiancé's privilege by walking in the back way. Caroline's heart sank. She hoped Lucy would never know just how boring she found the man. He was good looking, he was amiable, and he was devoted to her sister, but she dreaded the prospect of going back to the others in his company. Still, he must have seen her, difficult to avoid him without appearing either rude, or shy, and she turned, forcing a welcoming smile as the visitor addressed her by name.

Not Sir Charles, Thomas Martin stood there, looking very pleased to see her. "Ah, I was beginning to fear I had taken the wrong direction," he said. "It seems further from Mr Sturgis's place than on horseback, but he assured me it would be quicker if I came to this gate. I did not expect to meet you here, but I am very glad to see you. It does not look as if I can enter it easily. Is it locked?"

"I don't think so," said Caroline, smiling. "It looks very much more formidable than it really is. If I recall correctly, the lock was broken some time ago and it is merely tied up with string!" She struggled to undo a knot and unwind the string, eventually pulling open the heavy iron gate so that he could come inside. He assisted her to close and refasten it, displaying some interest in the strange arrangement. She agreed that a proper lock would be preferable but explained that this entrance was so seldom used that the gate had been low on the list of things repair. "You see, this used to be the main entrance at one time, that lane was the only road that ran anywhere near us. Then the new road was made, to the East, and my grandfather had a driveway made from that. This was when he was altering the house. Later, the grounds were rearranged, and this merely leads to the Rose Garden and the lawns. Well, it is a pleasant surprise to see you. I thought you were not to leave Lewes until October."

"That was my original intention," he agreed, sounding dispirited. "And my friend is still fixed there until then.

Unfortunately, the people with whom I have been staying have had to leave for Somerset where their son is ill. Since I must perforce return to London, I decided to call in upon Mr Sturgis and bid you all farewell. I was merely intending to pause to rest my horse at his house till it is cooler, but he has kindly invited me to stay overnight."

"You must have had a hot and dusty ride, if you have come all the way from Lewes since this morning," said Caroline sympathetically.

"Yes, it was tiring. These white chalk roads made my eyes ache."

As they made their way back up the avenue, Thomas Martin asked after the rest of her family, especially the little sick girl she had mentioned in her letters.

"Today she is well enough to be out in the garden," said Caroline. "But I fear that the prospect of her recovery has grown very faint."

"I am so sorry to hear that." He sounded genuinely distressed about a child he had never met and Caroline was a little surprised. She had thought his enquiry merely formal, but his concern was almost tender, and was disconcerting. It did not fit the picture she had built up of him as a cool, intellectual, rather unemotional man.

"It is kind of you to take such interest in my sister," she observed.

"I could not help but do so. I lost one of my sisters some years ago, and had she lived, she would have been about the same age as Miss Harriet. She was only ten years old when she died, poor little creature."

"Oh dear," said Caroline, adding with fierce misery. "No doubt everyone said it was a blessing that she was taken from this wicked world so early."

"But of course," Thomas Martin picked up the note of irony. "A merciful relief was the phrase they used. Though," he added reflectively, "Perhaps in her case it was. She developed water on the brain, you see."

"That must have been very distressing."

"It was indeed. She was a sweet little thing, but she would have got worse as she grew older. However, I do detest the pious way people accept the idea that it is all for the best – 'God's will be done,' when they would give anything to prevent an early death if they could only find a cure. I do not believe they really resign themselves."

"I suppose that comforts them," said Caroline. "What I find so distressing about my sister's illness is the fact that she is not being permitted to be happy in the last few months of her life. She used to be so joyful, but now seems almost afraid to laugh. I cannot see what harm it could do for her to forget how ill she is as much as possible."

He sounded moved. "Oh, surely it could not."

Caroline felt that however much he might have shared her sentiments, she ought not to indulge herself in complaints about her older sister to him, and changed the subject. They were passing a massive, somewhat damaged statue, and it caught the visitor's eye.

"Did that come from Italy?" he asked, as she walked round it to sit on the small stone bench placed pleasantly in the shade.

"I believe so. I think my grandfather acquired it when he went on the grand tour. I cannot say I care for his taste, and possibly my father did not either, since it is not displayed to advantage!"

"We had worse objects from my grandfather," said Thomas Martin gloomily, joining her on the bench. "Is it not amazing the way they wasted their money on such frivolities?"

"Quite," said Caroline, glad to divert him to the subject of how people had too much money and the majority so little. Earnestly he said he still felt there was grave danger that this inequality might lead to the sort of violent revolution that had recently occurred in France.

"We must seem an idle lot, to our servants," she remarked. "Did I tell you one of our maids has an elderly mother very sick?" She told him about it, ending, "It is thought a great concession that she should be allowed a little time in the evenings to visit her, yet she can be spared from her work to accompany me when I go for my letters. But I seem to be the only person who finds that strange. Even Becky herself accepts it as perfectly reasonable. Perhaps our poorer people are more placid than the French, and their peasants were a great deal worse off than ours. Many of them were no better than slaves."

Mr Martin was attentively surprised. "You do not consider a revolution in this country as inevitable, then?"

"I think and hope that the change will be more gradual," said Caroline, remembering things that her uncle had said. "But of course they must improve, or the poorer classes will grow desperate."

"Exactly! That is what those who are blind to social unrest fail to see in their comfortable lives. I think a revolution would teach them a lesson."

"I wonder if it would," said Caroline. "I have met some French Émigrés, and most of them do not seem to have learnt anything from the experience, simply feel that Fate has been very unkind to them. And if the Revolutionaries had not proceeded to extremes, it might not be so difficult to arouse sympathy and understanding for their cause."

"That is the best argument for gradual reform that I have ever heard," cried Mr Martin a little over-enthusiastically. Had he not had this put to him before? She had hardly gone very deeply into the matter. A little breeze refreshed them and she rose to her feet to start walking again, becoming aware that her companion was gazing searchingly at her. She smiled, and he seemed to kindle.

"Miss Caroline, how charming you look this afternoon!" he exclaimed, adding with concern, "I trust you do not mind my saying so?"

"No indeed," said Caroline, amused, as they continued up the avenue. "You must think me a strange kind of female if you imagine me averse to a compliment."

"I do not think you strange, but I find it amazing, with your brains and the ability to use them, that you do remain truly feminine. I wish my friends in London could meet you, most of them maintain that beauty and brains do not go together. And some of the women actually discourage compliments, I assure you. I think they feel that praise of their looks, means that they are considered mere playthings."

"Dear me, I can see why you were so cautious."

He regarded her seriously. "I would not have you think that I admired your features more than your mind. I hope I can appreciate both."

Caroline was touched, recalling the number of men who had been repelled to find that her looks did not mean that she lacked the intelligence that they regarded as a male prerogative. "Unfortunately, though beauty and brains do not always go together, plain women are not necessarily intelligent," she commented, reflecting sadly that compliments might be welcomed by the plainer women.

"How very true," said Mr Martin.

"Perhaps it ought to be a law of nature, but it is not," said Caroline, and fell silent as the Rose Garden came into view.

As they approached, Lucy had just finished a second daisy chain, Harriet had one round her neck and was leaning forward to look at this one, the shawl in which she had been wrapped slipping off her shoulders. There was no sign of their eldest sister, and the sick girl looked much more relaxed without her. They both looked round at the sound of people coming, and Caroline wondered if Lucy had also thought the visitor might be Sir Charles. If so, she hid her disappointment well and her good breeding meant that she greeted him politely.

Caroline took firm charge. "Mr Martin is on his way back to London," she remarked, and Harriet looked up with something like her old animation.

"Oh, Caroline, is this the gentleman who came to tell us about poor John Sturgis having an accident?"

"Yes, this is he. Mr Thomas Martin. Mr Martin, my youngest sister, Harriet."

Caroline was pleased to see him bow over the little limp hand with as much ceremony as if she had been an elegant lady, especially as it clearly gratified the sick child.

Timidly, Harriet asked after his horse when he mentioned visiting Mr Sturgis, had it suffered in the hot ride from Lewes? He reassured her that it was safely in the stables, and asked if she were fond of animals, which produced an eager response. Harriet had been a keen rider till her illness, still took apples to the horses when she was fit enough, and liked smaller pets. She had once had a canary. The visitor seemed to sympathise, and began to speak of his own sisters, with a certain amount of affection in his voice, as he remarked upon their childhood interest in unusual pets. He had written quite harshly of their stupid behaviour, and interfering ways as adults, but this talk of the past showed hat he had not completely lost his affection for them.

Lucy looked almost hypnotised by his sudden appearance, and started when Caroline moved up to her and asked in a whisper where Anna was.

"Oh, she has gone to fetch another rug, she feared Harriet might be cold when the sun leaves this part of the garden, Caroline," she lowered her voice so that her sister could hardly catch her words, "Mr Martin is being very kind to Harriet!" She sounded so incredulous that Caroline chuckled.

"Well, my dear, he is human! And he was telling me about how one of his sisters died at the age of ten."

"Oh dear," said Lucy. Leaving her to digest this information, Caroline went to sit beside Harriet, who seemed delighted, leaning gratefully against her sister's shoulder while she listened to the visitor. Lucy, after a moment's hesitation, resumed her seat on the rug, and Mr Martin included her in the conversation, remarking that when they had last met she had been on horseback.

"You are also fond of riding?"

"I am, but I am not as good at it as my sister."

He bowed to Caroline. "Indeed, I have seldom seen a better horsewoman. Tell me, have you ever ridden upon the downs?"

"Only once, when we stayed at Brighton for a week or so. They are a little far for the rides we go on. We have occasionally been there for picnics, in the carriage. I believe it is fine turf for riding."

"Very fine, I was fortunately able to ride most days while I was in Lewes, which is right in the heart of the downs. I was able to get down to the sea once or twice and I found the views magnificent. I wonder that those who write of the Picturesque do not mention the South Downs."

"Perhaps they do not consider them rugged enough," Caroline suggested.

"No, I suppose you could not call them that, but the clear sweep to the skyline is superb. I am no artist, but I have wished I had the power to portray them."

"Lucy can paint," said Harriet shyly.

Thomas Martin turned eagerly to Lucy, "And have you ever considered doing a picture of the South Downs?"

"I have placed them in the background of some studies, but as my sister said, we are never really close enough to see them properly."

A crunching on the path made them all turn. Mrs Randall was coming round the bushes. She must have heard a male voice, and like Lucy assumed it was Sir Charles, the smile of welcome she kept for her future son-in-law was just fading from her face as she recognised the visitor, to be replaced by a reserved expression. The eloquent look she gave Caroline was more than reproachful.

"Mama, Mr Martin has called in to see how we do. He is on his way to London. Caroline got to her feet and Lucy took her place beside Harriet.

Mrs Randall inclined her head towards her daughter and accepted Mr Martin's greetings without any thawing of her attitude. Into the slightly strained silence came the sound of Anna's returning footsteps, which increased in speed as she caught sight of the visitor causing her to reach them at the nearest thing to a run she had ever displayed since she grew up.

Caroline had expected her eldest sister to disapprove of Thomas Martin, but her almost frenzied reaction was worse than she could have imagined. Anna dropped her burden of wraps as she shrank past him with a shudder, rushing to Harriet's side. Practically pushing Lucy out of the way, she clasped the child in her arms, and ignoring anybody else, addressed her mother.

"Mama, I must take Harriet indoors, it is growing cooler." She indicated the pile of wraps on the ground. "Ah, Lucy, will you please bring these."

Harriet was looking bewildered and a little frightened, "Oh, Anna, I am not cold, I assure you. It is so pleasant here, may I not remain a little longer?"

"No, dear, it is for your own good. Come along now, come, Lucy."

Caroline was too angry to trust her voice, and was interested to see that even her mother had been taken aback by this vehemence, and was clearly worried by Harriet's distress. Possibly she felt that a cool manner to the visitor was one thing, outright rudeness another. "Wait, Anna," she said firmly, holding up a hand to prevent the little group being swept off. "I appreciate your concern, but I think it would be sufficient for Harriet to move to the seat on the West lawn, where the sun is still warm."

"Very well, Mama," said Anna meekly, her dutiful words not corresponding with her resentful glance. She began to lead Harriet away, again urging that Lucy to follow with the things she had already gathered up.

Lucy looked questioningly at her mother and Caroline and Mrs Randall's expression softened. "Would you mind assisting Anna, my dear," she said gently. Harriet waved rather forlornly, and Lucy made the visitor a little curtsey before following.

Caroline was glad to see that Thomas Martin did not appear aware of her sister's animosity, and his reluctant hostess seemed to feel that some explanation was called for and she remarked stiffly that her eldest daughter was very worried about her sister.

"Of course, you must all be," he agreed sympathetically and Caroline felt indignant that her mother continued to treat him coldly, speaking of John Sturgis and his recovery in a manner designed to express her opinion that a slight acquaintance with the nephew had been presumed upon to obtain the hospitality of the uncle. If she had expected him to be disconcerted, she was to be disappointed.

"I am very glad to hear that he is better," he responded. "But I think you possibly imagine that he and I are greater friends than is actually the case. It is true we were at school together, but had largely lost touch. It was quite by chance that I happened to meet him in Norfolk when I was on my way to Sussex, and he remembered me when he broke his leg and asked me to convey the information to his relation."

Mrs Randall was the one to look uncomfortable. While she struggled for a reply, Mr Martin turned to her daughter, "Miss Caroline, you understood how little I knew John Sturgis, did you not?"

"Why, certainly," said Caroline, watching her mother with rueful amusement.

That lady had recovered herself. "Oh, I beg your pardon," she said with heavy irony. "I thought it was as a friend of his nephew that you stayed with Mr Sturgis."

As they began to walk towards the house, the visitor looked perplexed. "I hope that was not why anyone thought I was a greater friend of John than I am. I do not think that his uncle did, I had the impression that he extended his hospitality to me because he is fond of company."

Mrs Randall was well aware how true this was, and Caroline felt that she was vexed that her attempt to shame this forward young man had had this result. She frowned repressively at her daughter and coldly assured him that he was correct in his assessment of Mr Sturgis, who was a man fond of any company. Did she hope to convey her opinion that their old neighbour was incapable of being selective? Thomas Martin did not see it as a reproof, and he began to compliment her on the beauty of the gardens, which silenced her again until they were within sight of the front door, and about to encounter her husband just returning from a stroll round his estate.

Caroline could not help feeling that her father's displeasure at the sight of the visitor was caused more by his apprehensions about his wife's feelings than from any hostility. The hunted look he gave them all made this painfully apparent to her.

"Here is Mr Martin, Richard, come to say goodbye on his way back from Lewes," said Mrs Randall stiffly, and having set the two men talking, did her best to detach her daughter. Caroline obstinately refused to be detached, remaining in their company, to the visitor's evident gratification and somewhat to her father's relief.

She was very conscious that this came closer to open defiance than anything she had done since her return from London, but she was still gripped with indignation at the poor reception her family were according Mr Martin. The way Mr Randall was edging them away from the door and heading down the drive made it plain that there was no intention of offering the guest a drink. Of course, dinner would be awaiting him with Mr Sturgis, but Sir Charles Carter would certainly have been given wine.

Fuelled by her resentment of this to the point of recklessness, when her father eventually said goodbye, Caroline smiled sweetly and said, "Papa, I will just see Mr Martin a little way down the drive," and did so firmly. She noticed that her companion was a little despondent, probably not at the shabby way he had been treated but because he did not relish the prospect of having to return to London a month before his wealthy friend and possibly having to scrape a living copying legal documents.

"Do write and tell me how you are managing," she urged, and his face lit up.

"I will indeed, you can have no idea how much your interest means to me," he said, and shook hands very warmly. She watched him till he reached the gate before returning to face the reaction of her parents.

Richard Randall did not seem at all anxious to speak to her. As Caroline entered the front door she could see him hovering just outside his study, looking so miserable that she felt it was only his wife's stern eye that had prevented him from slipping away from domestic worries and taking refuge in a book. Mrs Randall was so busy watching him that she had not noticed her daughter's arrival until his expression made her turn round. Neither of them said anything for a moment, and he seemed almost incapable of speech. Eventually she frowned and exclaimed, "Well, Caroline?"

She may have been pausing for effect, but anything else she had been going to say was checked by the arrival of Anna, who rushed in from the side door looking distraught. Had she been watching out to make sure the visitor had left? "Harriet is very upset!" she announced dramatically. Her usual response to what she considered disagreeable would have been a dignified distaste. It seemed ominous that she had departed from it, and Caroline decided to try to control her unruly temper as long as she could. She bit back her irritation and endeavoured to meet her sister's accusing eyes with reasonable calmness. This seemed to have the effect of fanning a flame, and Anna almost spat out her next words, "Of course, I would not expect you to care!"

"On the contrary, I care very much."

"Oh! How can you say such a thing? *You* care? You, who would not even stay with Lucy and poor little Harriet! But of course, I understand that now. No wonder you chose to leave when you knew that man would be waiting."

"I beg your pardon, I knew nothing of the sort." Caroline hoped that she was maintaining an even tone in the face of provocation, but something in the way she spoke seemed to have alerted their mother to possible storms ahead.

"Anna, Caroline, you forget yourselves," she said sharply, indicating with a gesture that the hall was far too public for an argument.

"But Mama, it is Caroline that is to blame," Anna began defensively and rather loudly, and her mother's frown was turned in her direction.

"Hush, Anna, I would have thought that you at least would have refrained from unladylike abuse." She looked round, but none of the servants seemed to be in earshot.

Anna dissolved moistly into noisy sobs, and her father gave his wife a haunted look. Caroline decided she had taken pity on him. Or did she realise how useless he would be at this juncture? It was chillingly amusing to see her give him the dismissive nod that permitted him to take refuge in his study.

Mrs Randall approached her tearful daughter, and with an almost fastidious air, urged her towards the drawing room. On the threshold she turned to Caroline, who was so consciously holding herself in that she felt breathless and said almost curtly, "Please will you accompany us."

Caroline obeyed with slow deliberation, really worried about Harriet hearing any of this As she shut the door behind her she heard her mother ask if the child was calling for her. "No, Lucy is with her, and I have procured them some lemonade," came the reply, and as she caught sight of her sister, Anna huddled with increased sobs on her mother's shoulder. With a grim nod, Mrs Randall indicated the open window, which Caroline obediently closed before leaning back on the sill to watch the soothing process.

Gradually, under the influence of pats on the back, Anna's sobs died away to the occasional sniff, and her mother looked dispassionately from one daughter to the other and said in a quiet and conversational tone, "Well, Caroline, what have you to say?"

Caroline considered the words carefully, "Do you mean about this afternoon, Mama?"

"Of course she does!" Anna raised a tear-stained face. "You made an assignation to see that Mr Martin! You – you..." she subsided on to her mother's shoulder again, and was again patted, though rather less gently.

"Let me speak, my dear. Caroline, were you aware that Mr Thomas Martin was going to come to the East gate this afternoon?"

"No, Mama, I was not."

Anna sat up indignantly. "Oh, how can you tell such a lie? Mama, I am sure she did know. She has been corresponding in secret with him for months, and today she had arranged to meet him. I wanted her to stay with us, but she would go, she would, she would, she would!" More sobs swallowed up her voice, and her mother resumed her patting, the expression on her face now suggesting that she was starting to lose patience.

"Anna, my dear," she said, "Now, listen to me if you please. I know you mean well, but you are making things more difficult for me. Please leave me to deal with the matter. Caroline, if it is true that you have been writing letters to this man, I think you owe me an explanation. And I should like to be told exactly what did happen this afternoon, after I had left you all settled in the Rose garden."

Caroline was still feeling indignant about the way Anna had taken charge and treated herself and Lucy as if they were younger than Harriet, but there seemed no point in trying to explain. She simply remarked that she had felt in need of more exercise, and decided to walk down to the gate and back. "I reached it and was about to start back, when Mr Martin chanced to come along."

"Chanced!"scoffed Anna.

"That was what I said. If I had not met him, he would probably come round to the front and asked for us. And, Mama, if I have concealed my correspondence with him, it has simply been to avoid being misunderstood. I am not in love with Thomas Martin, he happens to be the first person I have met with recently who shares some of the interests discussed at my uncle's, and to whom I could speak of them."

"I see," said Mrs Randall. "Well, Caroline, I am disappointed. I had hoped once you came home you would have settled down and forgotten all that nonsense. But you must have been aware what people would say about a correspondence with a man who is not a relation and to whom you are not engaged."

"I was. That was why I did not advertise the fact. But I was prepared to speak of it, if asked, as I have done now."

Her mother sighed heavily and looked away. Caroline was sure she had at least suspected the correspondence and preferred to avoid confrontation. Perhaps she now annoyed at having her hand forced.

During this exchange, Anna had been regarding both her mother and her sister with hot, angry eyes, and now moved convulsively crying out, "Mama! I tell you she was deliberately concealing the correspondence!" She clutched at her mother's arm, which made Mrs Randall throw her other daughter an irritated glance, gently remove the hand and shake her head.

"Now, Anna," she said, "Without excusing Caroline, I must be fair. She always tells the truth, and I am certain she would not have made a secret assignation with Mr Martin in that way. The mere fact that she brought him into the grounds is proof of that." Her tone was only mildly reproving, but it had an effect upon her eldest daughter.

Anna, for all her meekness, could never bear to be rebuked. A noisier burst of tears followed, but though her mother automatically soothed her again, she showed less sympathy. Without encouragement Anna stopped crying more quickly, raising her head and looking pathetically round as if to seek justification for her actions. "Perhaps it would have been better if it had been a secret assignation," she said sharply. "That way, Harriet would not have been disturbed. I could not believe my eyes when I saw that man there, and I learned from Harriet's own lips that he had been permitted to speak to her. How could you let that happen, Mama?"

She sounded almost accusing, and Mrs Randall frowned. She did not say she had only encountered the visitor a minute before Anna did, but gave them both a searching look. Before her mother could reply, Anna turned her attack upon her sister, saying with distaste that she supposed it was only to be expected.

"If that is how you feel, why mention it?" This flashed out before Caroline could stop herself.

"I have to speak of it! The dreadful thing is that I cannot make the child understand."

"What cannot you make her understand? What do you mean, Anna? Oh, please do not start crying again. Anna." It was the scene in the hall all over again, but this time their mother did not check them. Caroline wondered if it was only because they were more private or whether Mrs Randall was getting tired of intervening between her two eldest daughters.

Gulping, Anna gave her sister an indignant glare. "What have you done?" she wailed. "Even Lucy does not seem to agree with me, and as for Harriet, she has no idea what is wrong! When I told her that man should never have addressed her, she grew quite distraught. Oh, what can he have said to her?"

"Really, Anna, I think you must have taken leave of your senses," said Caroline scathingly. "It seems the only charitable explanation. What do you think he said to her? Do you imagine that he told her indecent stories, or asked her to be his mistress? Try to be rational, do. Thomas Martin may hold views that you disapprove of, but was there anything improper in his manner to you? If he could behave like a gentleman to you, a grown woman, how could you think for an instant that he would say anything to pollute the ears of a sick child? You are a fool, Anna."

Gasping and sobbing, Anna seemed incapable of speech, but was it misery or rage? Caroline turned to Mrs Randall sitting erect as if in judgement and said, "I am sorry Mama, I don't suppose you like to hear me say that. But he was so sincere in his distress about Harriet, and so particularly kind to her, talking about horses and pet animals and the ones his sisters had. Mama, whatever you think about me, I hope you will believe me when I say I would never have let him near Harriet if I thought he could do her any harm, either in this world or the next."

Her mother looked as if she had bitten into something unpleasant, but she plainly saw the justice of these words. "Yes, Caroline, I do believe you," she said quietly. "I am also prepared to concede that his concern was not feigned. Hush, Anna – now listen to me, please. I have not changed my opinion of this man's principles, but you own father has pronounced him a gentleman, and that being so, he could certainly be trusted to respect Harriet's innocence. I do not think you need worry about that, it will be quite sufficient to talk of other things. Calm yourself my dear, wash your face, and go to her when you have. It will be time for her to come in soon, and I have a few words to say to your sister alone."

For just a moment, Caroline wondered if Anna was going to protest. Her excessive emotion threatened to overcome her habitual deference to the commands of her elders, but after one shuddering sob, she hearkened to the call of duty, rose from her seat, smoothed her gown and went off to repair the damage to her blotched face, dishevelled hair and reddened eyes. As she reached the door, she turned and bestowed on her sister such a look of conscious virtue blended with reproach that Caroline feared for the future.

Along silence followed her departure. At last Mrs Randall stirred, moved to the sofa, looked at Caroline still leaning back on the window-sill, and motioned her to take a seat, which she did, taking a slightly bitter pleasure in being a little more dutiful than usual. Prepared to defend but trying not to take the defensive, she folded her hands demurely in her lap and waited to hear what her mother had to say. The next pause was even longer, Mrs Randall sat wrapped in thought, and her daughter, feeling that the course of action to which she was now committed was not one she would have desired, was not without sympathy for her.

How was she feeling about Anna having practically forced her hand? Probably, not as grateful as that young woman might have expected. Caroline found herself speculating about what her sister really imagined herself to have achieved. Had she any idea that her recent disclosures might have embarrassed their mother? Though so sensitive to personal slights, she did not seem to have much perception of how other people might feel, and the idea that Mrs Randall's authority would have less effect on Caroline would probably never occur to her. "No, I am expected to tremble at the prospect of being rebuked!" she thought wryly.

"Oh, Caroline!" her mother's voice sounded quietly despairing. "If only you had married Mr Fosse, or Mr Sharpe, or Mr Smith."

This indication of the line Mrs Randall's thoughts had taken was disconcerting enough in itself, but the inclusion of the last name seemed excessive. "Oh, Mama, you know you found Mr Smith quite unbearable!"

This produced a tiny, reluctant smile. "That is true. But he was not a radical. And in spite of what you thought about Mr Sharpe being anxious to restore the estates that his father had gambled away, he was not a gamester himself. Also, I am sure Mr Fosse did not only want your inheritance to advance him in his military career. Both men were interested in you for yourself, and either would have made you an excellent husband."

"Possibly, if that had been what I desired," said Caroline. "But as you are aware, I had and have no desire to marry at all. Mama, we talked enough about it at the time, why are you now expressing regret about those gentlemen?"

Her mother gave her a sharp look. "You must know that I mean, had you done so, you would not have been in the house when Mr Sturgis introduced that young man into it."

Caroline was tempted to point out that she might have been on a visit to her parents on that spring day, but decided not to take the hypothetical argument too literally. And on reflection, she conceded that had she been fool enough to marry either of those men, she would have abandoned all interests that would have drawn her to Thomas Martin. "And my self-respect," she thought. But did Mrs Randall suspect her of an emotional attachment to the man? "Mama," she said aloud, "I think you may misunderstand the nature of my friendship with Mr Martin. We are not in love, I merely take intellectual satisfaction in discussing the subjects that are of interest to us both."

"Oh, do you indeed?" Her mother sounded completely unconvinced. "Even so, I could wish that he had not come along to unsettle you by reawakening your interest in these unsuitable subjects like politics and social reform."

"Unsettle me," said Caroline with a sinking heart. "How do you mean, Mama?" Had her mother never noticed the books and papers that she occasionally received from an old friends of Charles Randall?

"I think you are perfectly aware of what I mean," said Mrs Randall firmly.

"No, Mama. That suggests that you expected me to lose all interest in all that had meant so much to me, once I left London. Did you?"

There was no immediate reply. Glancing across, Caroline had the impression of embarrassed irritation. Yes, she probably had expected just that. She had been forbearing, but not because she'd accepted that her daughter had agreed to give up her independent life in return for retaining her independence of mind. Both her parents had tacitly refrained from insisting on more than the appearance of conforming what people expected of an unmarried daughter, but she had not thought that they knew her so little. Trying not to sound bitter, she put the question slightly differently, asking in what way she had been expected to forget all about the years she had spent with her uncle. "He was part of my life," she pointed out.

"Caroline, of course I knew how fond you were of him. Your memories of him would be pleasant and grateful. But that was just an episode that was behind you, naturally you would be drawn into the family circle once more. I knew you had had some notions put into your head at the time, but it was quite time you put them away and became practical. All this nonsense about not marrying!"

Even now, it seemed, Mrs Randall had not abandoned the hope that her daughter could be persuaded to alter her views about matrimony. Not, of course, to Thomas Martin, but to one of the unmarried men she occasionally invited to dine. Someone like John Sturgis, for instance. Perhaps she had not even completely given up all thoughts of Anna finding a husband! Caroline ceased to listen to the oft-repeated lecture on how much better off she would be would be with a man to order her life.

She continued to look at her mother, but her mind was working busily, wondering how she could have been so foolish as to imagine that by being unobtrusive about her activities she had gained acceptance of her different views,

68

instead of simply increasing the hopes that she was "settling down".

...''If it were to be known that you openly correspond with a man like Mr Martin, what do you think people will say?" she heard her mother say. Was she still clinging to the idea that this would damage her reputation in the eyes of possible suitors?

"They can say what they like, Mama, it is a matter of indifference to me," she said abruptly. Mrs Randall sighed. It must be dawning on her that confronted by this sort of rebellion, she was almost powerless. Caroline had full control of her own money and was not really dependant. They had never before reached the point where this might have to be admitted, and the way she now regarded her was almost appealing.

Before either could speak again there came the sound of approaching footsteps and then a light tap on the door. Mrs Randall looked round, frowning. "Yes? Who is there?" she called impatiently.

The door opened a few inches and Anna put her head round it. Avoiding Caroline's eye, she addressed her mother in a sober, deprecatory voice which still had overtones of the previous emotions. "Mama, I am sorry to disturb you, but is it convenient for you to come to Harriet? I feel concerned, she looks very flushed and seems over-excited, though I have done my best to calm her."

Mrs Randall rose, possibly almost relieved, and said that she would come at once, adding as she left the room, "Please consider what I have said very carefully, Caroline."

As the door closed, Caroline caught a glimpse of her sister's expression. She thought she noticed a glint of satisfaction beneath the meekness. Was Anna convinced that her mother's admonition was the culmination of a severe reprimand? "Oh, dear Heaven! What am I to do?" With her elbows on her knees and her chin on her hands, she stared blankly at the elegant drawing room, seeing only past mistakes and future anxieties.

It was far too easy to feel that the present situation was the direct result of her earlier concessions, should she not have foreseen it two years before? When upon her uncle's death her parents had pointed out the impropriety of her remaining in the house left to her, her mother being especially eager, she had perceived some validity in their arguments. Charles Randall, with the assistance of a friend who was an expert on financial matters, had tied up his legacy in such a way that she would not forfeit her money should she wish to marry, he regarded his niece as a rational being who could be trusted.

He would probably have done the same even if he had foreseen that she would inherit so young, but at the time he made his will he must have envisaged her coming into the money and the house when she was in her thirties, surely able to remain there without scandal, even if she had to employ a nominal older woman as a chaperone. She had thought of doing so at twenty-two, but the outcry this produced had been difficult to bear, grieving as she was for one who was as dear to her as her father, and the reasons for giving in had seemed not without merits.

She reviewed the arguments she had used to herself ruefully. Though still reluctant to sell the property, she had let herself be persuaded. She still had some affection for her childhood home, and for her parents and the younger sisters she barely knew. If memories of disagreements with Anna did surface, the years of absence had softened them, and she had hoped to achieve a state of neutrality. As an adult she would surely be accepted very differently from the girl who had left Sussex four years earlier. Then there was her great friend, who although not permitted the same freedoms had intelligence and appreciated some of her ideas about equality, she had looked forward to having contact in person instead of merely by letter.

"And Papa, too," she thought. "I had hopes that I could exchange a few ideas with him, now that I was grown up." It had not seemed impossible; he might not have quite the intellect or the range of interests of his brother, but he was a scholar, read the classics for amusement, and when she returned had just begun to pen his family history. Her uncle Charles had been somewhat cynical about the importance of the Randalls, especially those of earlier centuries, but Caroline had been willing to show interest and even give her father some assistance, only to find him reluctant to let her look at any of the archives he had turned out, and the routine of the household made it difficult for her to spend much time in his company.

Had her mother actually warned him against indulging her in any kind of debate, she wondered, remembering his lack of response to her views. Since he had taken up riding again he had spoken more about the estate and the tenants, and she gave him credit for caring for those who looked to him for support. Considerably better than many of the local landowners, perhaps his brother's strictures had not fallen entirely on stony ground and when she had mentioned housing conditions that seemed to have been overlooked by the steward, he had listened to her and made sure something was done. All the same, he continued to seem uneasy in her presence.

If, in hindsight, she blamed herself for not fighting harder for her independent life in London, what would have been the alternative had she held out? Her uncle's friends would probably not have cast her off, but it would have been difficult to remain on good terms with her family. It might have proved very lonely!

Still, she should have acknowledged sooner that there was really no chance of her ever being accepted on her own terms within the family circle where she was regarded as merely an unmarried daughter. If her mother had been remarkably patient with her, not trying to impose too many restrictions, it was probably partly because she felt that to do so would slow down the recovery she had been so certain of. She and Mrs Randall had each been fooling themselves that things were settling down and it had created a semblance of normality that had now been shattered.

"Mama blames Thomas Martin for unsettling me, but I was already becoming less content before he reminded me of

71

what I had missed," she thought, painfully aware of the way Harriet's illness and the effect it had on Anna had indeed dismayed and disturbed her. The way that the eldest girl was acting as if the responsibility of caring for the invalid was hers alone might appear admirable, but it was a source of increasing irritation to Caroline, and she suspected that her mother was not happy about it either.

When she looked back to their childhood, she realised that she and Anna had always brought out the worst in each other. The first time this had come to her notice, had been at the time of their little brother's death, when they had been sent to stay with their uncle and aunt. In spite of the distressing circumstances, she had enjoyed this first of many visits to that house, particularly because she had been treated so differently by these relations. She had never been preferred to her sister before; but her uncle had singled her out for his interest and intelligent conversation and even Aunt Lucy had seemed to enjoy her company most. They had been perfectly kind to Anna, but perhaps without treating her as though her good behaviour made her the automatic favourite. Jealousy was not a fault that the older girl would ever admit to, but perhaps she had envied Caroline the close relationship with her uncle that developed from that time onwards. "I did not see that," she thought, "Everything about Anna that was praised at home, must have bored him, and he seemed to like my having a mind of my own."

Looking at the clock, she realised that it was almost time to dress for dinner, however little she desired to do so or to eat, to be late would only make trouble. She made her way upstairs. In order to reach her own room she had to pass Harriet's, but Anna pushed it shut with unnecessary firmness, sending her on her way fuming and in no mood to be gentle with Lucy who was waiting for her anxiously at her bedroom door.

"There you are, I wanted to see you!" she cried thankfully.

"Well, here I am," said Caroline brusquely, and saw tears forming in the blue eyes. "Oh, Lucy, don't cry, I did not mean to be sharp with you. I am sorry. What is it?"

"I heard Anna say that she knew about your writing to Mr Martin and I was afraid you would think I had told her. I have not even told Charles."

Caroline was touched by this admission. "I never thought you had, my dear. As I told you, I simply did not advertise it in case the wrong construction was put upon it."

"I am sure I did not let it out by accident," said Lucy timidly.

"Dear Lucy, please stop worrying. I know very well what has happened. Anna has been going through my papers again. Do not look so shocked, she often does it if I have been unwise enough not to lock them away."

"But that is prying!" cried Lucy indignantly. "I would not have expected that of Anna. How can she do such a thing?"

"I suppose she feels it to be her duty," said Caroline. "And of course if one has nothing to hide, it does not matter."

Lucy still looked troubled at the idea of her older sister reading other people's private papers, apart from finding it distasteful, she was obviously thinking of her own correspondence with Sir Charles Carter.

"I do not think she would read your letters," Caroline was reassuring. "It is because she suspects me, you see. You are entitled to correspond with your fiancé." In spite of her conviction that Anna was capable of malice, she did not like the idea of saying so to Lucy. Having tried not to recognise the fact even to herself, she felt it would be unkind to expose it to the younger girl who clearly regarded Anna as a very good person. She wondered if Lucy would ever come to see it for herself.

She sent the younger girl away comforted, and in the sanctuary of her own room began mechanically to prepare for dinner, her heart filled with apprehension for the coming months. Unless she was prepared to sacrifice half her personality, she could see no alternative to the domestic conflict she had hoped to avoid. "However hard I tried, will it be enough for Anna? I really think she delights in provoking my temper!"

73

She was filled with dread as she finished dressing and prepared to join the rest of the family in the dining room.

PART 4

Randalls Manor

Late October, 1794

Coming in from the hall, Lucy found the drawing room fire blazing cheerfully away to chairs grouped round it but in an apparently empty room. It had been unusually cold out, and she hurried to seat herself and hold out chilled hands to the flames. The walk she had just had with Sir Charles Carter filled her with a deep contentment, even if it was occasionally pierced by twinges of unpleasant recollection, one of which nagged at her at the moment. What had caused it? Poor little Harriet's worsening condition was always at the base of her thoughts, and so was the upheaval Caroline had brought about so recently, but something with echoes of both these had occurred after she entered the house. Oh, yes. Becky Anscombe, the maid who had taken her pelisse and bonnet at the door, had smile her eyes reddened with much weeping. Caroline's absence might have upset her, she had been particularly her maid. No, of course, the girl had just lost her mother.

Lucy's was a practical nature, and both her mother and her governess had discouraged idle brooding, so she looked for the sewing she had put down before she went out and tried to shake off the momentary depression by working on it, pausing now and then to look into the fire and think of her fiancé. Dear man, how lovingly he had urged her to hurry in out of the cold! All the same, she had stayed and watched him out of sight, warm enough in her fur-trimmed pelisse.

"Well, Lucy, where is Sir Charles? I thought he was coming in to see my father?" It was startling to discover that she was not alone, Anna had been sitting out of sight, on the window sill, all the time.

Disconcerted, she apologised. "I am afraid I had not seen you there, I was not ignoring you."

"I realised that you had not noticed me," said her sister stiffly. "It does not matter. But what of Sir Charles?"

"He will be coming in, he has gone with Papa to inspect the new plantation to the West. The lane would have been too muddy for my shoes, so I had to come in. They will both be back in time for dinner."

"Ah." Anna fell silent. After a minute Lucy turned from her own work and noticed that her sister was not sewing on one of the useful garments for the poor that usually engaged her attention but working much finer material with more delicate trimming. Part of Lucy's trousseau, in fact. On her face as she concentrated on it was a rather sour expression.

Lucy exclaimed, and Anna looked up and in a neutral tone of voice said, "You seem surprised that I should be doing this."

"Yes, I am, but very grateful, I assure you. Thank you…" her words were cut short.

"It was a request, from my mother," said Anna coldly. "I agreed, since there is so much still to be done and she has so many other calls upon her time."

Her feelings hurt, Lucy struggled to finish expressing her gratitude. "I thank you for it," she said with dignity, hoping she did not sound tearful. Her sister gave a little frown and seemed to shrug away the thanks as if they were unwelcome Rather repressively she commented that she endeavoured to do her duty.

At these words, Lucy was surprised to discover a sudden impulse to leap up, cry that her trousseau was not to be regarded as anyone's "duty" and take the work into her own hand. But she was restrained by her upbringing, and since what she was doing was also part of her trousseau there would be no excuse even for removing it politely. She continued to embroider an edging, but her usual placidity had been deeply stirred and in the silence that followed she began for the first time to think back over the events of the last few weeks.

Neither by training nor by nature was she accustomed to think constructively and she had difficulty in assembling her impressions to let her examine them. Before her engagement she would not have dared to draw comparisons between her two older sisters, this was something she was now starting to do but had to look back at what her youthful, innocent eyes had perceived in the past and pursue it through a host of distractions, notably her present preoccupation with Sir Charles Carter and her future life in his company. As long as she could remember she had thought of Anna as good, meek, and long-suffering, Caroline she saw so little of in the early days that it was only in retrospect she was aware that of the arguments she knew others blamed on the red-haired temper. Until recently, if asked, she would have assumed that it must be Caroline's fault, that she must have provoked her elder sister beyond bearing. But had she? Lucy reflected upon the time she had spent in the company of her elder sisters with the status of an adult. There had been less of the quarrelling between them that she vaguely recalled from her childhood, at least until the last few weeks, but she suddenly thought of the old saying "It takes two to make a quarrel." Had it always been Caroline who provoked those arguments? "When did she ever quarrel with me – I know I am not as clever as she is, and she did get a little impatient, but she said she was sorry, she was never angry with me, or try to make me angry." So had Anna in fact been blameless?

Memories of how kind Caroline had been in the days before Sir Charles had proposed flooded back to her. No one else had seemed aware how worried she had been. "Dear Charles," she thought, "I wonder when he and Papa will be home... how lovely to think that in a very few weeks we will be married and I shall be away from this house. Oh, what am I saying! Away from my home? But it is all so different now, with Caroline gone, and in such a way... And Anna is so cold and unfriendly. Did she have to be so unpleasant about working on my trousseau?" She glanced at the pinched lips and narrowed eyes as her sister made tiny stitches on a ruffle. The frothiness of Lucy's new underwear was as sharp a contrast with Anna's plain dark gown as the knot of hair scraped so severely back was with Lucy's flowing curls.

"Poor thing, how plain she is," thought Lucy uneasily, looking away quickly in case their eyes should meet. But Anna's cold manner still rankled, there was some reason just now, perhaps, but she had never been very enthusiastic about the engagement even though she had given her congratulations when she was told of it. She had seldom shown much interest in the plans for the wedding, and once mid-November had been chosen for the ceremony she had seemed to disapprove, almost reproaching everyone with reminders of Harriet's state of health whenever it was mentioned. That was distressing, but Lucy trusted her elders to know what was best. If only there had been a chance for her little sister to attend her as bridesmaid! Still, Harriet was looking forward to seeing her in all her finery. She thought of the wasted appearance she had seen only that morning, and silent tears rolled down her cheeks. Hastily she turned round so that Anna could not see her face before dabbing at her eyes with an inadequate handkerchief.

And how solemn the poor little thing was these days, when healthy she had had such a pretty smile! "Caroline could make her smile, it must distress her not to know why she has gone away. But I do not think Anna thinks she ought to smile, Harriet seems almost as if she is afraid of Anna." This thought made Lucy wonder if she also feared her eldest sister. Once, perhaps, but not any longer. Unbidden, the idea that she was not very fond of her either, came into her mind and horrified her. What a dreadful thing to think, especially with her sister in the same room with her! But even as she chided herself, she caught a glimpse of Anna's head bent over her sewing and it did not increase her feeling of guilt. It struck her that for all she knew, her sister might be thinking worse of her. Caroline had once said something about mere relationship not guaranteeing affection, this direct contradiction of what she had always assumed had upset her at the time, but now it almost seemed a sort of comfort. "Oh, Caroline!" she thought sadly, and let her work fall on to her lap as she gazed into the fire.

"Dreaming, Lucy?" at the cold reproof she picked up her embroidery again and started sewing again with quick, nervous movements. "I was thinking, Anna," she said over her shoulder.

"Indeed. And does that prevent you from working?"

Lucy had an unaccustomed temptation to snap at her sister, which she suppressed as she concentrated on her embroidery, still resenting the words. She could not remember when she had last been alone in a room with Anna, and wished she were not so now as she turned back to look at her again, finding the impression of plainness distressingly obvious. Without being conceited, she valued the effects of her own beauty too much not to pity the lack of it in another. She thought of Caroline, and Harriet before her illness, even of her parents, and felt what bad fortune it was that this sister should not have inherited some of the handsomeness.

But when one looked closer, Anna's features were better than the initial impression, and her hair, if a dull shade of brown, would have waved if she had not pulled it back so severely. "If her hair was better dressed, and she wore a prettier gown, she could be quite attractive," Lucy thought in surprise. She tried to picture her sister in a fashionable gown, with her hair perhaps rippling down her back, but found it almost impossible. Could it really be that Anna deliberately made herself look plainer than she needed to? Surely not, yet the thought remained, and she took a further glance. Yes, the features were certainly more regular than Caroline's, if they were more animated, perhaps she would not seem plain at all.

Anna raised her head as if aware that she was being scrutinised, and said sternly, "Thinking again, Lucy?"

"Why, yes," said Lucy, ostentatiously continuing her work and conscious that she no longer felt guilty about the things she had been thinking.

"Take care not to become too abstracted, it does not do to get into the habit of ignoring others, Lucy, simply because Sir Charles Carter occupies so much of your thoughts."

"Well, he does," said Lucy, rather crossly.

"Quite. No doubt that is natural and I would not reprove you for it in general. However, you should have a care that you do not give offence by doing so."

"I am sorry if I have offended you, Anna, but I did not think you wished for conversation."

Her sister frowned. "I do not care for idle chatter," she said repressively. "But it is very uncomfortable to sense that the thoughts of one's companion are so far away. You are to leave us soon enough. Could you not spare some attention from Sir Charles while you remain with us?"

This remark jarred so badly that Lucy was stung into responding more frankly than she had intended. "It is not only Charles who occupies my mind, I have been thinking of Caroline as well," she said, meeting a horrified gaze unflinchingly, and deriving a certain amount of satisfaction in noticing that her words had actually caused Anna to lay down her work for a moment.

"What did you say, Lucy?"

Lucy obligingly repeated it.

"How can you do that? You know very well that she is not to be spoken about."

Though vaguely aware that Caroline's name was not mentioned, Lucy did not remember an absolute embargo, but she contented herself by saying, "I cannot refrain from thinking about her."

"But you know that she has disgraced herself!"

"Has she?" said Lucy slowly. Anna's frown increased.

"You must be as well aware of the fact as I am," she said abruptly.

Lucy considered this for a moment and then spoke with care. "All I really know is that Caroline went to London, taking the footman with her, and that James returned without her, bringing a note which only Mama and Papa read. They told us that she would not be coming back." She did not add that she suspected that this had something to do with Thomas Martin, but her sister was not so reticent.

"It is quite obvious she went to that man, that Mr Martin. Even if she did pretend that he needed her help."

"Do you know this for a fact?" Lucy felt a little hurt that her parents should confide in Anna and not in herself. "Have you have seen her letter?" There was no direct reply to this beyond a comment that their sister had taken an irrevocable step.

"If you are thinking that he might marry her, Lucy, you are fooling yourself. And our father would never permit it." Under the circumstances this seemed a ridiculous thing to say, and Lucy had the impression that her sister was trying to avoid explaining her familiarity with the contents of a letter only Mr and Mrs Randall were supposed to have seen. If they had shown it to her, why had she not said so? The time that Anna had made it obvious that she had read their sister's correspondence came back to her and she was suddenly convinced that she had pried into their parents' papers. Caroline had said that she would probably not read Lucy's letters, but she found herself trying to remember if she had been indiscreet in any way. It altered her conception of her oldest sister and she found it distasteful, especially when Anna made a reference to how their neighbours must be speculating on the whole subject.

"It makes me want to hang my head in shame," she said, bending low over her sewing

"To think that our affairs have become a matter for common gossip."

Lucy had heard her say how much she disliked gossip, but only recently she had been censorious about the split between a local couple. Was it not gossip, if one took a moral stance? She had a feeling that Anna had taken some pleasure in the discussion. She would have liked to point out that however much their neighbours might speculate on Caroline's reasons for leaving home, if all her parents admitted was that she had gone, they could not be certain. She did not feel inclined to discuss the subject further, and picked up her work, but it seemed that Anna had something more to say.

"Please understand, Lucy, that you should not mention Caroline again. Indeed, you should endeavour not to think about her either, that would be being disobedient in spirit if not in fact."

Again Lucy had to suppress an impulse to snap at her sister. "Keeping silence is one thing," she said quietly. "It is not so easy to control one's thoughts. I am very fond of Caroline, Anna."

"Ah, so was I, until she did this dreadful thing."

Lucy was too incredulous to hide her reaction. "*You* were fond of her!" she exclaimed, and Anna flushed unbecomingly before going on the defensive.

"You are no doubt thinking of the many times we had disagreements, and it is true that I frequently had to find fault with her. That does not mean I did not care for her. I have always been anxious for out sister's welfare, and though she often pained me by her attitude to serious subjects, I believed her to have been misdirected for years by my uncle and his friends. Once she returned, I was in hopes that I would be able to help her to a right way of thinking. But it was not to be, she continued to follow her misguided inclinations and look where it has led her!"

Lucy could think of no suitable response to this, and simply reiterated that she did not find that she could stop loving Caroline, whatever she might have done.

Anna was unsympathetic. "A charming sentiment, my dear, but one that does no credit to your reason. I think you had better try to conquer such notions, lest people suspect your own principles. You would not wish it to be said that you condoned a sinner, would you?"

"Certainly not," said Lucy, rejecting the idea of asking where was the proof in this case. She found that her sister's condemnation was having the reverse effect from what was intended, and though the idea that Caroline had consented to live with Mr Martin on terms other than marriage distressed her, it did not alter her affection. Had Anna really had any love for Caroline? Could she speak so glibly of overcoming such feelings, in that case? She found that she was being addressed again.

"Lucy! Have I your attention? I was saying, that you should consider how Caroline's action will affect other people's opinion of us all. You in particular – though the Carters have been magnanimous."

"What are you talking about?" demanded Lucy indignantly. Anna shifted uneasily and would not meet her eyes.

"Have you felt no concern that their disapproval might affect your engagement?"

"Who has been suggesting such a thing? Is that something else that has been discussed behind my back, with Mama and Papa?"

"Not exactly," said Anna evasively, "It is something that must have been thought about, I felt I should give you a hint."

Had her parents actually mentioned this? Lucy wondered, noting the same avoidance of direct reply. "How can you think so poorly of Charles?" she exclaimed, shaken by anger such as she had never before experienced.

The fierceness of her response seemed to have shaken her sister as well, and she was immediately on the defensive, "Lucy, how you twist my words. I have the greatest respect for Sir Charles Carter, who appears to be all that a gentleman ought to be, both in manners and in morals. You are very fortunate, my dear."

"Well, I should hope I know that," said Lucy, her eyes filling with tears. She blew her nose almost aggressively and continued, "But if that is how he seems to you, how can you think that he would behave so. In such a – a knavish way?"

"I thought nothing of the sort!" exclaimed Anna. "It was simply that Caroline's disgrace might have made the Carters feel an alliance with our family less desirable. Since nothing has been said, you have been spared unnecessary pain. I think you should be grateful."

Lucy was far from feeling gratitude. "I should think poorly of Charles if I consider him capable of letting his family persuade him to act dishonourably."

"It would hardly be dishonourable for him to do as his family wished."

"Oh, Anna – Charles is nearly thirty, he has been the head of his family for years and I am sure they regard him as such. He is not a child, to be directed by his elders. And once he had pledged his word to me, the only thing that ought to influence him is my behaviour."

"Lucy, be careful. You sound like Caroline when you speak like that."

Somehow this remark annoyed Lucy more, and she persevered with the subject firmly. "If Charles had been so unmanly, I think I would have been ashamed of him, and I think, a little ashamed of myself, for loving him."

"Lucy! Even if Sir Charles had so far forgotten his duty to his family, you could not have accepted him if they had set their faces against the match, and our parents would never have permitted it."

Lucy found that she was doubting this. But if this idea about the Carters had any real foundation, could her parents have kept all signs of anxiety from her? "But there is no question of that." she said, firmly. "All the Carters have welcomed me into the family."

Anna broke in, "Lucy, one moment," she said tensely, "If I understand you correctly, I am amazed. Can it be that you would entertain the idea of marrying a man whose family did not wish it?"

"But I love him," said Lucy simply.

"Where is your delicacy?" exclaimed Anna.

"Surely it cannot be indelicate to say that you love the man you are about to marry? Or to say that you would be unhappy if you were asked to give him up once you had said you would do so?"

Anna gave a little moan. "Oh, again you sound dangerously like Caroline. I beg you, have a care what you say."

"I sound like Caroline?" Lucy was suddenly impatient. "She is my sister, after all. However, I can assure you that she has never tried to influence me in any way. I think she took pains not to do so."

"Ah, yes, we know that, but the Carters might not."

"Mr Carter and his sister are very well aware how differently Caroline was educated, and Lady Carter…"

"Yes," said Anna, "She was not at all anxious for the match at one time, I believe."

She sounded almost triumphant, and Lucy felt hurt. It was almost as if her sister wanted to make her unhappy, she thought, and felt pleased to put her sister right on this point. "Lady Carter had hoped that he might marry the daughter of a friend, but once she was aware of his wishes, she was prepared to accept his choice, and now that she has met me, I think she likes me for my own sake. Even if she had not done so, I think she would have endeavoured to be friendly to his wife-to-be."

Anna gave her a strange look and said after a slight pause, "Lucy, I trust you will be a good wife to Sir Charles, but I must confess that I am not quite sure what you mean by that."

Lucy had to think for a moment exactly what had brought her to say this. "I – I suppose what I meant was that I was glad to find that she will not be jealous of me," she said thoughtfully.

"Lady Carter may be a trifle frivolous for a woman of her age and situation, but I believe her to be a Christian woman," said Anna stiffly. "As such, she would certainly not permit herself to indulge in such a sentiment. I doubt if she would have approved of you had she known that that was your opinion of her."

Lucy looked at her sister helplessly. Anna had put an interpretation on her words that had nothing to do with what she had been trying to say. How could she explain? The word jealousy did not really fit the complicated emotions that she had sensed a mother might feel about the girl her son was to marry. Picking her words carefully, she said, "Surely one might feel an impulse of jealousy and overcome it? I only meant that as a mother, she might fear that her son's affection would have to be shared. It cannot be easy for her to give him up to a younger woman."

"And that is how you see it, Lucy? As Lady Carter surrendering her son to you?" Anna's tone was stern, and Lucy felt impelled to defend herself.

"Of course I would not like Charles to cease to care for his mother, but I should not like to think that he loved her more than me. I can sympathise with Lady Carter, indeed I cannot help wondering how I would feel were I in her place, to have her son's affections divided. Why, the thoughts I am having now, she might have had about Charles's grandmother when she married Sir James."

Pleased with this thought, she turned to see what effect it had had upon Anna. To her surprise her sister had coloured up and was averting her eyes. "What have I said to embarrass her?" she thought. Could it be because she had revealed that she had been looking ahead to the possibility of becoming a mother? Questioned, Anna admitted regarding this as indelicate, and Lucy became a little impatient. Sounding even to her own ears a little like Caroline, she pointed out that there could surely be nothing wrong with hoping to provide an heir to the baronetcy. "The Carters must surely wish that? It is not something I would generally speak about, but it cannot be shameful to think it."

Anna seemed still more embarrassed, and made no reply. They continued to work in silence for a few minutes, till the butler entered and addressed Lucy saying that her mother wished her to go to the sewing room, where she was closeted with Miss Dart, the dressmaker.

She laid down her work and gave him a smile, knowing that the summons must concern her wedding gown. "Oh, thank you, Sayers," she said, putting her sewing aside. She found that Anna had got to her feet and was gazing anxiously at the man. In a strained, hard voice, she asked if her mother was with that woman at the moment.

"Indeed, Miss Randall," he said formally.

Anna turned sharply to her sister as if she held her to blame, "That will mean that Harriet is all alone! Mama was sitting with her."

"I am sure she would have asked one of the maids to take her place," said Lucy soothingly. "Is that not so, Sayers?"

"Certainly, Miss Lucy. Joan has been there ever since Mrs Randall went to speak to Miss Dart."

Anna was gathering up her work in a determined manner. "Ah, Sayers, I shall go to Miss Harriet at once," she said distantly.

"Very good, Miss Randall. Shall I inform my mistress?"

"Do not trouble yourself. Miss Lucy will do so." Anna stalked out of the room leaving her sister to follow, trying to choke back her tears so that she could smile apologetically at the butler, who remained impassive but must surely have been hurt by the abrupt way he had been addressed.

Lucy's wedding gown was shaping well, and normally she would have enjoyed standing while it was fitted on her, but the interview with Anna had left her feeling very disturbed. Patiently she let her mother and the excellent little London mantua-maker (recommended by Lady Carter) crawl round her arranging folds and deciding where tucks might be needed. They surveyed her from a distance and then advanced to take pins from a china dish held by one of the maids. Lucy felt as if she herself was on secondary interest to them, only spoken to when they wished her to move. She would have liked to think over what had taken place downstairs, but found it difficult to shut out the sounds of their voices. She found that trying to concentrate on her thoughts seemed to sharpen her ears, and when she finally left the room she had got no further in sorting out her impressions of the talk with Anna, only a confused memory of the words that had eddied round her.

"Stand there, Lucy... Bodice a trifle full, perhaps, Miss Dart?"

"I would say so, Mrs Randall. Pins, please, Molly. There, is that better?"... "Oh yes, but the shoulders..." "Ah – excuse me, Miss Lucy, could you please move a little this way. Now, how about this?"

"Oh, very good, Miss Dart, a great improvement. Yes, excellent... I like it. But now, about the waist? Is that not a trifle high?"... "Why, the raised waistline is quite the latest fashion, Mrs Randall..." "Do you say so? Well, well... That seems strange to me... How do you like it, Lucy, my love?"

Rather dazed, Lucy was confronted by her reflection in a long mirror. With pins everywhere and only one sleeve finished, the dress looked odd, but she could see how becoming it was going to be, and said so while Molly helped her out of it.

Miss Dart's round rosy face beamed with pleasure at the praise, and she set about her work with renewed energy while Mrs Randall smiled approvingly at her daughter. Lucy had not been able to mention Anna's message but delivered it while the dress she had been wearing was replaced. Her mother made no comment, but pursed her lips and turned away almost as if it was unwelcome.

On her way back to the drawing room Lucy caught a glimpse of Joan, pink in the face and gesticulating as she talked to Becky. They fell silent as she passed by, dropping curtseys and looking abashed. She was sure that they had been talking about the way Anna had ejected Joan from Harriet's room, and wished she could apologise for her sister. She recalled Caroline's remarks about the servants and was momentarily sad that her presence should seem to repress these girls.

While she had been upstairs, Sayers had had the fire made up in the drawing room, and Lucy resumed her seat beside it, but did not start sewing again at first. The room was really quite warm, but she felt chilled. The earlier talk had left her shaken, as though a door had opened on aspects of her eldest sister that she had had no idea about. In spite of what Caroline had said, the possibility of Anna prying into other's papers had been hard to believe, but now she began to feel that this might be regular practice in one generally held up as a model of rectitude! "Miss Yare would surely be horrified," she thought, and what about her parents – would they believe her if she told them? Not that she would do such a thing, it would feel like a betrayal. But that dreadful sultry day when Thomas Martin had called to say goodbye came to mind and she found she was now critical of the way Anna had blurted out the knowledge of his correspondence with Caroline. She could not escape the feeling that this was intended to provoke trouble.

Lucy shivered and held out her hands to the blaze. She had been trying to forget the last few weeks, the stormy atmosphere that had threatened to mar the days before her wedding. She had an impression that attempts had been made to spare her the worst of it, but it had been impossible not to notice the tension between her two older sisters. It was certainly more peaceful without Caroline, and much as she missed her, it was some relief not to have her cause discord by mentioning her ideas for reform and other subjects considered unsuitable for a young lady.

But until that visit of Mr Martin, she had not said so very much, had she? And how dreadful was it really? "Surely much of it was deploring things like rich people throwing their money about, not caring for others, that is quite Christian if you look at it. Why did Anna keep saying it was unladylike, or shocking?" Lucy tried to think of all the good work her eldest sister did in the parish, her piety, her selfless caring for Harriet, but the conversation that morning seemed to come between her and an appreciation of these virtues. Especially the attitude to Harriet, it was almost as if she was trying to keep anyone else away from her. Even Lucy found difficulty in being alone with the girl, and as for Caroline, Anna had recently found every reason to exclude her from the sickroom.

"I am sure Harriet misses Caroline, and she does not understand what has happened. She would like to ask me, but Anna will not allow it." With her new comprehension, she was beginning to realise how often the arguments had arisen not because Caroline had provoked them, but out of some subject that Anna had introduced, generally when one or other of her parents were present. Lucy was even-tempered by nature, and from childhood had been taught to control any fits of pique, and had always found it hard to understand the difficulty Caroline had at keeping her anger within bounds. For the first time, she was realising something of the provocation that she had received from the older sister.

Lucy discovered herself hoping that Anna would not return to the room soon, it felt uncomfortable to be aware that she was not quite what she had always seemed. "She is good, but she is also not as kind as I imagined," she thought. Caroline had been so cautious in her comments, she had not complained to Lucy of the way Anna behaved, but she must always have known the side that had shown that morning, and tried to shield a younger sister from that knowledge. This was a sobering reflection, Lucy was finding that she must adjust how she perceived things now. The pity she had felt for Anna's plainness had changed along with the respect for her virtues, but she would clearly have to make other adjustments to her view of her sister.

Gazing into the depths of the fire, she again thought with pleasure that she would soon be leaving, no longer quite so dismayed. But the loss of Caroline hovered behind the anticipation, and she applied herself to her work in the effort to keep back her tears, starting when she heard the door open.

Sir Charles Carter came into the room, looking round him cautiously and Lucy had a sudden conviction that he was relieved not to see Anna. With her new insight, she realised that he might often have been ill at ease with her. He come to sit near her, speaking warmly of the new work her father had been showing him.

"This plantation will enhance the grounds greatly," he observed. "I have some idea of doing something similar in part of our estate. I long for you to see our home."

Lucy beamed, and they discussed the property in Hertfordshire. She found that her fiancé was enchanted to find what an interest she took in the grounds as well as the house, saying that for his dear mother this had no great appeal. He praised her painting, saying that he looked forward to seeing how she would portray her new home.

"And that picture of this house you have just finished, will you allow me to have it framed? I think your parents will be very pleased to have it."

"Do you really think so? I make no claim to be a great artist, but I did feel I had captured it well on this occasion."

"My house is more modern than this, it was only completed in 1734, but it is quite handsome, with a delightful dower house built at the same time, where I think my dear Mama will be very happy."

Lucy felt a pang. "I do hope so, I should be so distressed to feel that she missed the great house and felt that I had supplanted her."

"Oh, my love, you must never feel that. For a long time I think she has desired to move from such a large building. She knows that we will always make her welcome."

"But, of course," said Lucy. "It has been her home for so long, has it not." She smiled lovingly at him, and saw that he was looking round the room.

"When I came into the house I was told that you and your sister were both here," he observed, and once more she had an impression that he did not mind Anna's absence. She explained what had happened, feeling a little shy of speaking about her wedding gown, and he was concerned to hear that this had been one of Harriet's bad days when she was unable to leave her bed. His sympathy brought the tears to her eyes again and she was grateful for his comforting arm, and soothing picture their life together. Her grief, though she did not mention it, was not only for that sister. It was devastating to think that however long she or Caroline lived, they would never see each other again.

PART 5

Lodgings in Islington

June, 1795

"Oh, Mrs Randall, is that you?"cried Mrs Basset, bouncing out of her room as her lodger shut the front door and moved to the stairs. "I am so glad to see you back again, it grows very hot at midday now. Far too hot for anyone to be out, let alone a person in your condition. You look tired, my dear. You must be careful, for your own sake as well as the child you are carrying."

"I thank you for your concern," said Caroline, forcing a smile. "But I assure you I am not over-tired. I have often walked much further, on hotter days, and come to no harm."

Mrs Basset shook her head. To her, it was plain, walking was a necessary evil, to be avoided whenever possible, and it was difficult to convince her that some people did it for pleasure. On the other hand, whatever Caroline knew herself to have been capable of in the past, her new landlady had had experience of the later stages of pregnancy. She respected the advice she was given, though the motherly solicitude could be cloying, but only listened with half an ear to her reproaches, occasionally wondering how Mrs Basset would react if she knew that the black clothes were worn in mourning for the death of a beloved younger sister and she was not really a widow. But Mrs Basset had a poor opinion of men in general, and knowing the full truth might simply cause her to see her lodger as an innocent seduced, the victim of a man's heartlessness. It seemed best to maintain the deception suggested by the clothes and the wedding ring.

Mrs Basset had come to the end of her advice. "Now, my dear, you must go and rest. I will send you up some dinner in a little while. You must keep your strength up, these last few weeks are very important."

Caroline thanked her meekly and was permitted to escape upstairs with her precious letter, hoping as she took it out of her pocket that it would compensate for what had really been a rather tiring walk of over two miles, at least this time she had not returned empty-handed.

Having gained the sanctuary of her sitting room, she sank into a chair and was surprised to find that her hands were trembling so much that she could not open her friend's letter until she had steadied them. It was probably largely physical weariness, but she was in a state of nervous tension very unusual for her. This was the first letter she had received from Selina since she had left Sussex, and she was not quite sure of her friend's sympathy and understanding. She no longer had the old faith in her own judgement, and the girl she had known from infancy might have changed in a year or so of matrimony. At least she had replied, and not with a mere note.

Leaving the letter lying on her lap, she closed her eyes, leant back, and tried to envisage the friend who had once been more familiar to her than her own sisters. A little figure, by the time they were twelve Selina came barely above Caroline's shoulder, with pale features and hair and a sweet, shy, smile. To outsiders they must have made an incongruous pair, and she was sure that the Coleman family were not the only people who thought the pliable girl completely under Caroline's influence.

To some extent this was so, Selina was timid and glad of her friend's guidance, but she had a basic integrity that would have prevented her being led astray. Without help she might not have found the courage to leave home and marry the man she loved but nothing would have made her yield to her parent's persuasion where she felt a principle was at stake, however miserable they made her. She also possessed a quiet wit, and Caroline valued her perception. No, the friendship had not been as unequal as it might have seemed. "If she were to turn away, I should be lonely indeed," she thought, picking up the two sheets of paper and bracing herself to read their contents. Would she find that she had not known Selina as well as she thought she had?

"But of course, she may feel that she has never known me. Perhaps she did not think I would really go as far as I have. In fact, she might have been more surprised than those who considered me capable of wrong, since she knew what the theories I learnt from my uncle and his friends really consisted of, unlike those who assume the worst if you do not agree with them." Caroline turned to the first page of the letter, and finding it opened "My dearest Caroline," was encouraged to read on.

Selina was too honest to pretend not to be shocked to hear of a young woman consenting to live with a man she had not married, even though this was her greatest friend; but disapproval could not alienate her affection, and she said so. Whatever her friend had done, she was still Caroline. Did Selina not owe her present happiness to her? "Why do you not know that you can trust me," she wrote reproachfully. "You are not really living at that Inn under the name of Mrs Smith, are you? I would not give anybody your true address, I assure you. Caroline. After the way you kept my secret, can you imagine that I would betray yours? Oh, and I was so thankful to hear from you at last. Since I had your note in October I have been waiting so anxiously for a letter.

"Though I sensed that things were going badly for you, I hardly expected to hear that you had left Sussex, I am so glad that you warned me not to write to you there, but I had certainly hoped to hear from you before now. I had begun to fear that you had met with an accident. It was distressing that I had no way of discovering what had become of you. I was delighted to see your writing the other day, even if you have still not given me very much detail. I must confess that I felt sure that you had gone to London because of Mr Martin and I hoped that perhaps you were changing your ideas about matrimony. From what you wrote, he sounded most congenial, and if you are expecting a child, is it not possible to forget your aversion to matrimony? Has he treated you badly?

94

Please tell me more about what has happened since the Autumn, and also if you are keeping well.

"Of course I shall want to hear all about the baby when it comes. I wish I could tell you that we are to have one, but alas! There is no sign of it. Strange, that it is you who are pregnant, when I have always been the one to love children. If that Mr Jobson had been a shade less obnoxious and I had never met Ifor, the only thing that would have reconciled me to the man would have been the thought of consolation in my children, and oh, Caroline, if I am not to have any, how thankful I am to be married to one who means so much to me in himself! We both owe you so much! I have told Ifor that you have moved to London, but nothing more. I do not think he would censure you even if he knew more, but unless you would like to come here, it might be as well to keep it like that for now. I think he would sympathise with you, but he might want to fight Mr Martin, which I should hate, and I do not think you would approve of even if you did part on bad terms.

"Am I to address you as Mrs Smith, now? Do write soon and give me your direction." Selina concluded her letter with information about her house, garden and the dairy she had begun to take an interest in, and the letter ended "Ever your most affectionate friend Selina Penry."

Caroline found to her annoyance that tears were starting to her eyes as she laid the pages down. It was disturbing to find how much meant that there was one friend left for whom she would not have to act a part. "I must reply at once," she heard herself say out loud, and struggled out of her chair to see how much paper she had in her little portable desk, which lay on the table beside the dining chair. She had barely opened it when she heard footsteps outside and a tap on the door.

"Come in," she called, shutting her friend's letter up in the desk. There was a pause during which the doorknob turned first one way and then the other, as of its own volition, but eventually it yielded and Mrs Basset's little maid-of-all-work staggered in with a loaded tray.

"There you are, Mrs Randall," she said, putting it down on the table. "A nice piece of lamb for you."

"Thank you, Nancy," said Caroline, smiling.

The girl's pinched little face was thoughtful as she arranged the plate and cutlery on the table. "Hope you fancy it, Mrs Randall. Mrs Basset said to tell you to try and eat it all." She sighed, "My Ma, she fancied a bit of young meat when she was expecting – not that she got it, as a rule. Pa, he didn't care who went hungry as long as he didn't. Might have been more of us left, if Ma had been able to eat better before they came. Six, she buried."

"There are still three of you, did you say?"

"Yes, and it was hard enough for her to find food for us all as it was. P'raps it was just as well in the end, what with him being knocked down and killed by a Brewer's van. Seemed like a judgement, that did! Not that Ma saw it like that, she was so fond of him, in spite of everything, I really think it killed her, she just faded away after he'd gone. Men!" said Nancy scornfully. "I've not much use for them. Look at my brother. He's been more trouble than us two girls put together."

"But he is doing well in that shop, now, isn't he?"

"Not too bad," Nancy was off-hand. "Better than most men, at that." Caroline smiled, aware that the girl was speaking of one she had helped to bring up, and was reminded of something.

"Oh, by the way, how is your sister? Is she better now?"

"Yes, she does pure now, thank you for asking, Ma'am. I must say, Mrs Basset's sister has been kind as kind to her, had the apothecary round and Sal only a kitchen maid. Well now, is there any more I can get you? A pillow?"

"To sit at the table?" Caroline protested, laughing. "Oh, no thank you. But I wonder if Mrs Basset has any writing paper, and perhaps ink? I seem to have used most of mine, and I want to write a letter. Would you be so kind as to ask her for me?"

"I'll see what I can do," promised Nancy. "But don't you go wearing yourself out, now. Remember what Mrs Basset said."

This was clearly so well-intentioned that Caroline suppressed her irritation, and assured her that she would take care, wondering how it was that some people seemed actually to enjoy being the object of solicitude. Possibly the girl sensed her reaction, regarding her with shrewd little eyes, she said unexpectedly, "Kill a cat with kindness, they say. I guess you know better than Mrs Basset or me, what you can do."

"In general, probably," said Caroline. "But this being my first child, I think she may know more about my present condition. But writing is not something that tires me."

"Oh, it does me! I can write a bit, but dreadful hard work I find it. Still, I expect it comes easier to you than what it does to me."

"Well, I have had more chance to practise it," said Caroline. "Please do not think I am not grateful for the concern that you and Mrs Basset both show me, it is simply…" she hesitated, but Nancy appeared to understand.

"I know, Ma'am," she said. "You wants to be let alone, sometimes. I does myself, not but what Mrs Basset has been ever so good to me. There is many that would take advantage of a person being poor. Well, I'll see about that paper, then." She picked up the empty tray and left the room. As she watched her go, Caroline felt relieved that she was not the only one to find her landlady's overflowing sympathy a little cloying, however preferable it was to animosity. Even a virtue could be overdone, she thought as she sat down to her meal.

But Nancy's sturdy independence was interesting, in the course of conversation with her the facts gleaned had made Caroline aware of her pitiable history. She and her younger brother and sister had been born in a back street and reared on the borderline of poverty, though their parents had been tradespeople, the children seemed to have been left almost destitute by their mother's death, Nancy, the eldest barely twelve. Mrs Basset had discovered this and come to the rescue, taking them into her own home, and employing the girl at once, then finding places for the others as soon as they were old enough. And she kept an eye on them to make sure they were well treated. Yet Nancy, though clearly grateful, did not entirely welcome too much maternal solicitude.

Often, in the few months that she had known her, Caroline had mentally contrasted Nancy with the young woman who had tended her in Sussex. How miserably stunted the girl would have seemed beside the well-grown, country-bred Becky Anscombe, who was much the same age. Nevertheless, it was much more interesting to be in her company.

Becky had no doubt been glad of the opportunity of visiting her sick mother that Caroline had afforded her by frequent visits to the village, but had seemed almost embarrassed by being treated in a friendly manner, almost as if she was happier with the ordered world in which servants were expected to know their place. "Becky would be a great disappointment to those who are convinced that the poor yearn for equality," she thought. "Not that she would consider herself poor, of course! That man who tried to fix his interest with her a while ago, she was pretty scornful about him, even if his father had known hers." The disgust with which Becky had spoken of a mere ploughman aspiring to a respectable upper servant like herself had made it clear that she hoped to marry some gentleman's valet, or at least a farmer. And farm workers in regular employment probably felt superior to the day labourers.

"So many idealists imagine such distinctions to be the prerogative of the upper classes. Is it perhaps only when those right at the bottom outnumber the rest of the population that revolution becomes likely, as with the French peasants?" The structure of Nancy's background puzzled Caroline. The rigid hierarchy she had been accustomed to did not appear to apply to people like Mrs Basset, whose servants in the eyes of an outsider, appeared to belong to the same social class as themselves. Nancy undoubtedly regarded the landlady as a benefactor and accorded her respect as her employer and an older woman, but did not treat her with the sort of deference that Mrs Randall demanded from her servants.

Caroline chuckled inwardly at this thought. "Mama would hardly be flattered at being compared with a woman who keeps lodgings! No doubt she would also regard Nancy as very ill-bred for a servant, one who does not know her place. But Nancy at least is neither pert nor underhand, unlike some I have seen in well-to-do households."

When Nancy returned with the tray, she brought some reasonable quality paper and a bottle of ink, and showed both concern and interest. Caroline had not written many letters since her arrival at Mrs Basset's house and Nancy was clearly fascinated by this one. She seemed genuinely glad to hear that contact had been made with a friend not seen for some years.

"Oh, that is nice, Ma'am. I was so sorry that you don't have anyone like I do with Sal and Billy," she said as she departed with the tray, leaving Caroline touched and amused as she began to think about her reply to Selina. What exactly had her friend said? She had been so anxious to get the gist of it, she had not taken in the derails, and decided to read it more carefully. There was a postscript, too – Selina luckily did not cross her letters, but she had a habit of wrapping any afterthoughts round the main body of the page, forming a border often three lines deep and not easy to read. But in this one a familiar name caught her eye and she turned the page round and round till she had taken in the message; "I was about to close this letter, dearest Caroline, but having read it through, and realised that I had said nothing of poor little Harriet. It was with distress that I saw the announcement of her death a few months ago. What can I say, except that I am so very sad for you. It must have been a bitter thing to see that in the paper."

Was there a hint of reproach in this final statement, Caroline wondered, or was she feeling slightly guilty herself? She decided to open her own letter with this subject, and once she had thanked Selina for writing, she continued, "It may perhaps seem heartless of me to leave home when Harriet was so ill, I would not blame you for thinking so. I was very unhappy about it myself. But I was not permitted to nurse her, and I even wondered if my presence at home was making things worse. That was one reason for leaving, but life was becoming impossible, and I was less and less suited to occupy the position allotted to me. I recall when I returned to Sussex that you expressed some doubt as to whether I would be able to continue to pursue the interests I shared with my uncle and his friends. I thought then that you were not aware of how different my parents were from yours, but now I think it was I who was blind to facts. I hoped that giving way over remaining in London would be enough, but I should have known that to my mother in particular, this was only the beginning of what she expected of me. She imagined that I would 'settle down' and forget all I had done before. To her, my education, the rational approach that my uncle had always encouraged meant very little. Unless I married, she felt that I should be prepared to be merely a daughter, subservient to my elders. She did not insist too much, so it took some time for us both to realise how differently we envisaged our future life together.

"For quite some time I did my best to appear not to disagree with my parents. This may have been a mistake, since it enabled her to feel that I was coming round to her of way of thinking, till she had to recognise that this was not so. I am not sure that my father was ever convinced on that point. What neither of them wished to admit was that they no longer had any real authority over me. I am in full control of the money my uncle left, and at any time I could have defied them over what I did. I chose to try to fit in and not to scandalise the neighbours, because I felt I had not seen enough of the younger girls. And I had you to visit, of course. But by the time Mr Martin came into my life, I was finding life at home tedious and the prospects bleak. You had left the area, Lucy was about to be married, and Harriet deathly ill, I would be left with my parents, and my sister Anna.

"When we Randalls are healthy we are often long-lived, my grandfather was eighty when he died, and *his* father, nearly ninety. My parents may live another twenty or thirty years, and Anna and I possibly as much as fifty! Selina, for the first time I came near to regretting that I had not married, if only to escape! With most of those who asked me it would simply have been exchanging one form of bondage for another, but there was a pleasant soul who proposed when I lived with my uncle with whom I might have rubbed along well enough, if I had not expected my life there to continue longer than it had. Do you know, I have often thought that some unsuitable marriages may have been brought about because a woman is desperate to leave home at all costs!

"You are familiar with my older sister, Selina, and I think you will understand what I mean when I say that had it merely meant my living with my parents, I might have faced the prospect without dread, but Anna and I have never been close, and in the last few months that I was at home, the situation had grown a great deal worse. Of course she would never have admitted how much she disliked me, but I have had to try, all my life, to feel the affection that was expected of me."

Caroline paused as she wrote those words, and recalled how often the way her older sister ordered her about when they were in the nursery had caused her to lose her temper and be reproved for bad behaviour while Anna sat looking as good as gold. Yet she had formed a bond with her little brother almost at once, though the age gap between them was about the same. Had Anna resented this? A few months ago she had thought that those weeks with her aunt and uncle when little Dick died had been the first time she had not been made to feel inferior to her sister, but hadn't their governess praised her for learning to read fluently while Anna was still struggling. That was probably one of the reasons why Charles Randall had preferred her to her sister.

Caroline sighed, and dipped her pen in the ink. "You are aware how pious Anna is, how earnest in doing things for the poor, but it does not seem to give her any pleasure. In fact, I have sometimes suspected that she secretly enjoys making others miserable. From the time Harriet became seriously ill, she tried to take on all the responsibility to herself, as if nobody else was capable of nursing her. Once she discovered that I was in communication with Thomas Martin, she apparently decided that I was unfit to be alone with Harriet, and did her best to exclude me from her company altogether. I did insist once or twice, but Anna grew hysterical, which was so distressing for Harriet, I had to give in. How she could say she cared for Harriet, and not see that she was upsetting her needlessly, I cannot think. That was the situation I was faced with, and it was increasingly difficult for me to control my wicked temper. I had never regretted leaving my house in London more, and if I could have simply gone back there and resumed the life I led there with my uncle and his friends, I think I would have done.

"I was also beginning to be concerned for Thomas Martin, he had been hoping that the friend who helped by employing him would to return to London when expected; but he had had to go to Devon to assist a relation, and Thomas was becoming distressed for money. I had offered to lend him some, I felt at the least that would mean I was of use to someone. His response was to write and ask if I would consider coming to London to share his life and meet all his like-minded friends. The one who was away was almost the only one with much money. He wrote that though neither of us approved of matrimony, we were good friends, and perhaps we might change our minds if we discovered that we were suited. You will feel that this is not the sort of proposition that I ought to have considered for a moment, but I had seen that idea succeed for some friends of my uncle's who married after being together for a year or two.

"His letter came on a day when I had had an appalling time containing my anger over Anna trying to keep me from visiting Harriet, even though the poor little thing was asking for me, I began to feel that if this went on much longer my temper might have got the better of me, creating an unbearable situation. To go right away seemed the only thing to do, and if I did something irreversible, it would be difficult for my parents to try to force me to come home I felt that this would relieve the whole household from the worsening tension. I went to London very correctly, taking the footman with me, and sent him back with a letter next day."

Caroline looked thoughtfully out of the window and remembered how she had gone to join Thomas Martin at the rooms he had taken when he knew she was coming. The whole episode seemed more remote than the days preceding her departure from Sussex. Every room in the house where she had been born remained as clear to her as if she had just left it, but she could hardly recall what those rooms near the Haymarket consisted of.

"And Selina wants to hear about it all!" she thought, dismayed. Where should she begin, and how many details could she go into? Thinking of her feelings, going to meet her lover and how he had seemed to her then, she thought how illusory her preconceptions of unemotional involvement been. Though later events had overlaid that first impression she could still see his face light up with pleasure as he saw her, coming forward to take her hands in his exclaiming, "My dear friend, you have come!" She had been startled by her own response, since until that point she had remained convinced that there was no passion involved in their relationship, simply the attraction of sympathetic minds. "Mama was sure it was not only his mind that I cared about," she thought. "And I was equally certain that I knew better!"

The consciousness of his child quickening within her meant that her memories of those first weeks with Thomas Martin were of their times in bed as well as the more mundane aspects of living in London and meeting new friends, but it was not something she wished to communicate to Selina. She had never been prudish, and she had been married for some time, but how would she react to the idea of Caroline having these experiences outside marriage? How much did married women discuss such matters with each other, she wondered. Probably simply assumed that others felt as they did, however differently they regarded the experience in fact. She decided to tell Selina about the feeling of freedom the move had brought, not having to watch her words the whole time, "What a relief not to have to act as a dependant daughter," she wrote, "And to be in charge of household again, however small. And to meet like-minded people who were considering how life might be improved for those so often regarded as inferior."

Again she paused, thinking of how for a month or so she had really felt that this was the man, and these the people, with whom she would be happy to spend the rest of her life. It was embarrassing to have to admit her mistake, but she would have to do so if she was to explain why she was not going to marry the father of her child. "It must have seemed unlike me to take this step, Selina, and I have to admit that I did not approach it as calmly as I would normally have done. If the situation at home had been more comfortable, I might not have been quite so eager to throw my lot in with a man I did not know as well as I thought I did, and I am afraid that I was not quite honest with myself about what attracted me to him.

"I thought it was his brains and his interests more than his person, I liked him well enough, but if he had not appealed to me as someone I was happy to live with, I might have tried a little harder to discover what he was really like. I found him intelligent, and thought he admired me more for my mind than my looks. He had several sisters whose brains he despised, and I imagine it was refreshing to find a female who was capable of taking a reasonable interest in radical ideas. But I doubt if he had ever considered the possibility that a woman might have a better brain than he has. He had a remarkably high opinion of his own ability, but after a while it became apparent that I am not only better read than him, thanks to my uncle, but that I am probably more intelligent. He did not care for that at all!

"Of course, I had never pretended to find him unattractive, but if I had not liked his looks as well as what he said, I wonder if I would have been so slow to realise that much of his intelligent conversation consisted of ideas he had adopted from his friends. Sometimes I fear, without really understanding them properly. I began to suspect that one reason why he had become interested in revolution and reform was that his father had refused to make him an adequate allowance unless he returned home after leaving

Cambridge. His refusal to bow to tyranny brought him a great deal of sympathy from his friends, and undoubtedly his having been influenced by radical ideas was anathema to Mr Martin senior, but I think that even before that he wanted to keep his son in Lincolnshire under his eye. He certainly sounds a narrow minded man, and even more fanatical about his family than my poor father.

"The mere idea of reform, of all men being equal would have been the final straw, and cutting off the allowance made Thomas take still more interest than he might have done otherwise. His friends certainly regarded him as a martyr to the cause, and helped him as much as they could. Particularly Mr Forster, the wealthy and brilliant idealist with whom he had visited Lewes last Summer, who has the kindest heart in the world. I came to know most of the little group of friends that he had gathered round him, and I do not think it ever occurred to any of them to doubt Thomas Martin's sincerity. After living with him for a while, I began to feel that his enthusiasm was waning, but I said nothing; after all his friends had known him much longer than I had.

"It was towards the end of January that I began to suspect that I might be with child, but I hesitated to mention it to Thomas. By that time we had found that we were not as well suited as we had hoped but of course this could not be postponed indefinitely. Then in February, Mr Forster came to say that he had had a letter from Mrs Martin, who knew of him, begging him to find Thomas and tell him that his father was dying. The poor woman was in great distress, and Forster was moved to urge Thomas to go home and make up the quarrel (I said he had a kind heart).

"I am not sure that Thomas needed a great deal of persuasion, after hearing the news he left the next day. But, as was clear from the notice in the newspaper shortly, he was too late to see his father alive. Of course he had to see to the funeral arrangements, and it was over two weeks before he returned to London. I found that I was not sorry for the delay, it gave me time to consider my own position very carefully." Caroline was conscious of a cynical smile on her face as she wrote those words. How unnecessary all that painful consideration had proved to be!

She thought ruefully of how even the most idealistic of Thomas Martin's friends had begun to notice a change in him, when they started to realise that this was not the anticipated return in triumph to place his fortune at the disposal of the causes they espoused, but a visit to wind up all his affairs in London before going back to Lincolnshire for good. Though worried on her own behalf, she had still felt concern for their disappointment, and was still haunted by the hurt expression on Peter Forster's face when he came to see her later. "He not only paid me back every penny I'd ever let him have, when I'd have been happy to give it to him," he had lamented, "He insisted on paying me interest. I feel as if I had been regarded as a mere moneylender!" He had sounded bitterly disillusioned, and Caroline, who had experienced the same thing, had felt apologetic. How much she had been accepted in their circle? She had been a little afraid that they were thinking she had in some way influenced him. Possibly Mr Forster guessed this, for he assured her earnestly that he in no way held her to blame. And of course they must all have realised that Thomas Martin had changed most of all in his attitude to her, though exactly how much, only she knew.

When he finally returned to London, he'd seemed embarrassed, and his general behaviour toward her took on a sort of arrogant truculence that she found quite exasperating. Asked about his time in Lincolnshire, he had replied in monosyllables, and when after an uncomfortable supper they retired, he insisted in sleeping in the tiny dressing room. Even after a quarrel he had never before shown any aversion to her bed. She had wondered if seeing his mother and sisters in their sorrow had revived his affection for them, influencing the way he regarded Caroline. Had the perception of how she would appear in their eyes, added to his growing distaste that she had a greater intelligence? With a little shock of surprise, it occurred to her, that to them she would simply be his mistress, someone he would not present to his female relations, someone to be provided with money, if he were a gentleman, but discarded.

It was of course awkward from his point of view that Caroline belonged to his own class and had in fact paid for practically everything in their association, he had been scrupulous in his insistence that she accept money for that, but she was certain that he felt consenting to live with him outside marriage unfitted her for the company of his mother and sisters. She thought of the plans for redistributing his wealth which he had discussed with her and his friends, how had the rest of his family featured in those? Was this something he had ever considered?

"Perhaps he had persuaded himself that he did not care for them, and have enjoyed the idea of shocking them," she thought. His father's death had made a remarkable difference – apart from anything else, he was now the head of a household where he had formerly been a mere dependant. The women in his family probably looked up to him as never before.

Caroline moved to the more comfortable chair while she considered how to continue her explanation to her friend. She was growing drowsy as she thought of the last time she had seen Thomas Martin, aware that her problem had been solved for her. He was clearly unlikely to repeat his suggestion of marriage and she was thankful that she had postponed telling him that he was to become a father. Though she was sure that he no longer wished to marry her, might he have felt it his duty to offer, "He could have thought I was trying to force him! What a dreadful foundation for matrimony that would have been. He would have blamed me for separating him from his mother and sisters."

Yes, if he had brought her to his house under those circumstances, they might have felt driven out. Or, worse, would they have considered it their duty to accept and reform this fallen woman? That would have been worse still. Almost asleep, she thought yet again what a narrow escape she had had. Supposing the senior Mr Martin had lived a while longer, and she had reluctantly decided that she ought to marry for the sake of the child. "I might had been a mother before he became possessed of his estate!" She was sure that he would still have reverted to the attitudes he had affected to despise. "A lifetime of misery, as bad as if I had remained in Sussex," she thought sleepily. Her present situation was better than that.

Caroline was roused from a rather uncomfortable slumber by a faint tapping at her door, and realised that it must be time for supper, calling for Nancy to come in, she returned to the table and put her half-finished letter in the little desk.

"Did you notice the new buildings, Ma'am?" asked Nancy as she took the light meal off the tray. Still slightly dazed with sleep, Caroline looked at her without understanding what she was referring to. "In Islington, I mean. While you was out?"

"No, I did not go in that direction. But I know the ones you are speaking of, I saw them a few days ago."

"Well, I hadn't seen them for about a month," said Nancy, folding her arms over the empty tray. "The walls were hardly above the ground."

"They were up to the first floor when I was there," said Caroline, suppressing a yawn. "Have you seen them more recently?"

"I had to go that way for Mrs Basset this afternoon, and some of them's got their roofs on!" Nancy sounded almost triumphant.

"Good gracious, not tiled, surely."

"Ah, no, just the rafters, but they do grow quick, don't they. Pity really, all those terraces, make it less like a village."

"Still, people have to live somewhere," said Caroline, yawning. Nancy was immediately concerned, wanting to know if she had been over exerting herself.

"No, no, it is this heat." The atmosphere seemed to have grown more oppressive while she slept.

"Storm coming up, I shouldn't wonder," said Nancy darkly, "I hope it won't bring your baby on before its time!"

"Well, so do I!" said Caroline, only half-laughing at the suggestion as the little maid-of-all-work left the room.

"But it will have to come some time," she told herself ruefully as she picked at her supper. She was prepared to do her best for the child, but she found it hard to regard the prospect with any great enthusiasm. She had had very little experience of babies, and had never sought the company of children, as so many women seemed to. Unless they were old enough to talk, they bored her.

The storm broke in the middle of the night, but the only effect it had on Caroline was that she woke refreshed and somewhat cheered, in spite of the rain still streaming down the window. Once she had reassured Mrs Basset, who seemed to share Nancy's apprehensions about thunderstorms and pregnant women, she returned to the half-finished letter to Selina. She hoped her description of how greatly Thomas Martin had changed on his return from his father's funeral would be enough to convince her friend that marriage was now impossible. "Thank goodness he did not know about the baby," she wrote. "We did not part on good terms, but nor did we really quarrel, and I have spared him from having to break it to his family. I do not think any of his friends have heard from him since, but a little while ago I saw an announcement in the paper of his engagement to a Lincolnshire lady of great fortune. This is probably the girl he spoke of with scorn as a match his father had hoped to arrange for him. She was rather young at that point in any case, but no doubt she appeals to him now. Perhaps it might be thought my duty to tell her about our living together, but I do not think him a libertine, I was not seduced, and I am certain she will be perfectly safe with him. She will probably think him quite a scholar, which he is in comparison with many country squires."

Caroline then explained the precautions she had taken to establish herself in a new life and her reasons for doing so, describing how she had moved several times and settled right away from the group of people she had met through Thomas Martin.

"His friends were very kind to me, after he left, and I feel sure they would have been welcoming towards the child, not seeing it as a disgrace. But had I remained among them, all would have known my story, I would have had to stay for the rest of my life as part of their community, and much as I sympathised with a lot of their ideals, I was not so attracted that I wished for that. For one thing, what ever the future may have in store, there is a stigma attached to illegitimacy, and would it be right to declare one's independence from conventions at the expense of a child? I saw the effect of this in some couples, and the daughter of one pair, a girl of twelve, seemed miserable, she knew there was no reason why they should not have married, indeed they were very happy together. There was some talk of founding a colony somewhere remote, where nobody married, making it the norm, but even if this could be managed, it would be unlikely to attract many followers. My uncle was eager for reform, but I think he would have admitted that the time is not yet.

"I have therefore decided that if I am thought a widow, my child may have a better start in life, so I am calling myself Mrs Randall, I am entitled to use the name after all, and as I have put on black because of Harriet, I seldom have to say I am a widow. I shall not pretend to grieve too much for my 'husband' I prefer to be as honest as possible and not prevaricate unless it is necessary. I shall hope to remain at this address for some time, it is quite a pleasant area and my landlady is a friendly, motherly soul.

"I hope that by the time I write again, my child will have come, but this brings me to something I feel I must say before I close this letter. I might never be able to write again, women do die in childbirth, and though I am told that I am exceptionally healthy, I ought to face the possibility that I might not survive. If the child does, I would like to think that it would be brought up by somebody that I know. I am therefore going to leave instructions that you should have the care of it. I know that you would be kind to it for my sake, and I have already made a will leaving money in trust for it. I realise that then your husband would have to be told the whole story, but everyone else could simply be informed that it was the child of a friend. Selina, do not let this letter worry you, I think if ever you see my child it will be in my company, but it seems sensible to take precautions. Will you burn this letter as soon as you hear from me again? I did want you to know the whole story, and I know I can trust you, but from now on we can correspond without reference to the full facts."

Caroline closed the letter with regards to Selina and her husband, and sealed it using the signet ring she had inherited from her uncle. As she put down the taper she had used to melt the sealing-wax, it occurred to her that it would be as well to destroy Selina's letter, or at least part of it, and found herself surprisingly reluctant. It had been so heart-warming to feel she was not quite cut off from all that was familiar. Never before had she been so long without some contact with this friend, as little girls they had played together, they had shared drawing, music and language teachers and when apart, had corresponded frequently.

She had always imagined herself to be less dependant upon emotional attachments than most women, but now, deprived of intellectual stimulus and in the company of comparative strangers like Mrs Basset and Nancy, she had been feeling very desolate. Hearing from Selina had helped, but as she rang the bell, she was conscious of still being depressed. Perhaps this was partly due to her pregnancy.

Nancy arrived in response to her ring, and having asked her to take the letter to the post office, Caroline roused herself to go to the window, where she stood looking out at the rain trickling down on to the damp earth of the little square of garden. "Really good for the soil, that is!" she thought, recalling the words of the Randalls old gardener, and in spite of her reasons for leaving Sussex, she was momentarily visited by homesickness. As Nancy had remarked, Islington had grown more town-like even in the few months she had known it, and even though there was still plenty of green to be found, there was no sign that the rate of house building was abating. It seemed unreasonable to object, but the prospect did add to her depression. Could it be that her roots were more firmly planted in the countryside than she had realised? Her uncle's house had been in an almost rural area of Chelsea, and they had also paid visits to Richmond and other nearby villages. Still, Islington was an improvement on living in the heart of London among all the traffic.

A faint gleam of sunshine penetrated the clouds and it seemed to stab at her heart.

She turned and walked back to her chair, finding as she settled down again that the rain was coming down as heavily as ever. She found she was very near to tears and told herself fiercely that this would not do. "I have to look forward, not back." The future did not look very encouraging, but she would be able to be more active once her baby had arrived. "One may not need brains to bring up a child, but having intelligence can do no harm, surely, once it is old enough to communicate with."

PART 6

A house near Hampstead

March, 1798

"Mr Carpenter will arrive about half past six," said Mrs Dewsbury at dinner. She addressed herself principally to Lady Lassiter, but a murmur of interest ran round the table, although all the boarders present waited for her Ladyship to comment, which seemed to gratify her.

Inclining her head with gentle condescension, she said, "Ah, that will be the gentleman you have spoken of, who is to occupy the two rooms at the back of the hall. I did observe that they were being made ready."

"Oh, so they were!" exclaimed Miss Watt, sounding surprised, though little escaped her eyes and she must have been well aware the fact. "Is this gentleman to live entirely upon the ground floor, Mrs Dewsbury?"

"Mr Carpenter is recovering from a bad accident, and when he wrote he asked if it would be possible for him to avoid stairs as much as possible till his leg is stronger."

"Poor man," said Lady Lassiter gravely, and was echoed by a spontaneous chorus from several of the other people. The low-pitched rumble of Dr Field and the melting coo of Mrs Price particularly distinguishable. Caroline still found it surprising that these people could glean so much excitement from small events. The prospect of a new addition to their small circle seemed to be absorbing Mrs Dewsbury's boarders; once the subject had been raised it was clear how much quiet speculation had been taking place. Mr Price turned directly to the owner of the house and asked if she were acquainted with the newcomer.

Mrs Dewsbury smiled. "Nay, we have only corresponded," she said, "Though I have known of his existence all his life, I knew his mother as a girl."

"Good gracious, he must be very young, then!" Mrs Dewsbury looked amused. She certainly had the timeless serenity that Caroline thought of as a special quality of Quakers, but she was certainly over sixty and the hair peeping out from under her cap was snow-white.

"Thee flatters me, Doctor," she said dryly. "John Carpenter must be over thirty years of age by now. May I offer you some more pork, Mrs Randall?"

"Yes please, Mrs Dewsbury," responded Caroline, passing her plate. She had been at Little Park for nearly six months now, but was still cautious about joining in any conversation uninvited. Not only were the other residents a great deal older than she was, they had all lived under the same roof for so long that they had grown almost like one family. Though they retained strict formality in the way they addressed each other, they seemed to have developed the sort of familiar mannerisms usually to be found in blood relations. She was sure that there was no deliberate intention to exclude her from their discussion, but as they conversed about Mr Carpenter she felt they had almost forgotten that she was there. However, she derived quiet amusement from being a spectator, and was grateful for the genuine friendship that had been extended to her.

As she finished her meal and listened to the other residents, she wondered what had been said about her and her little boy six months before. How would they have taken to the idea of a small child being introduced into this secluded community? The first new faces for nearly a decade, she gathered. Lady Lassiter, for many years a widow, had a married daughter and grandchildren, but the Prices were childless and so was Mrs Dewsbury. And apparently none of the others had ever been married. Surely they must have greeted the idea with some apprehension, yet they had shown no signs of it in her presence.

114

Lady Lassiter turned to Caroline as the dessert was brought in, and almost as if echoing her thoughts, addressed her with some anxiety, "Oh, Mrs Randall, I meant to ask you sooner, how is little Dickon tonight? Is his cold better?"

Before she could reply, Miss Watt chimed in, "Ah, yes, poor little fellow. We have all missed the sight of him playing in the garden."

"Thank you for your enquires," said Caroline, smiling. "If there had not been such a chilly wind, I would have been inclined to let him go out today, but it did not seem wise to risk it."

"You were perfectly right, my dear," said her ladyship earnestly. "I recall the time when my Julia was about six or seven, she contacted the whooping-cough, and for a long time after that any sharp wind would bring on a dreadful spasm."

"Does he mind having to stay upstairs in your sitting-room?" asked Mrs Dewsbury anxiously. "Thee may always let him play down in the hall, Mrs Randall."

"That is so very kind," said Caroline, "And I am truly grateful, if this bad weather continues I might to do so. But until today he has been happy to play with his bricks or if he tired of that, to make marks on pieces of paper, which he was convinced were beautiful drawings! They all looked much the same to me, but I was assured that some were trees, some dogs, and many were horses. He loves horses, you see. I must admit he was a trifle restless this afternoon, but Nancy took him up to the attics to romp about for a while. She said the other servants did not object – I hope you do not mind, Mrs Dewsbury?"

"Mind? My dear Mrs Randall, of course not."

"But would it not be better for him to run about the hall?" asked Lady Lassiter. "Surely you do not think that anybody would be disturbed by a dear little boy like that?"

Caroline addressed her respectfully. "That is so kind of you," she said, privately wondering how popular this suggestion might be with the other residents. She felt Miss Watt was really fond of the little boy, and Mr Price seemed almost wistful in the company of any children, but his wife was subject to nervous headaches and both Dr Field and the sixth boarder, Mr Peters, were elderly and not too steady on their feet. Once in a while might be all very well, but a lively child dashing about in that part of the house must make most of them nervous, however hard she tried to make him walk sedately.

However, everyone, with the exception of Mr Peters who was dining out with friends in the neighbourhood, actually followed up Lady Lassiter's suggestion, and as she left the room to see her child into bed, Caroline was a little puzzled by this. Climbing the stairs, she called to mind the doting expression on Mrs Dewsbury's face as she spoke of Dickon. She had been aware almost from the start that the gentle, elderly Quakeress was held in great affection by all the household and they were obviously prepared to put up with the little boy underfoot if it gave her pleasure.

But she still felt concerned about it, apart from anything else, she was reluctant to let her child spend too much time with the other boarders. They were inclined to indulge him with toys and sweetmeats, and she remembered all too clearly a child she had once encountered that had had the misfortune to be brought up elderly grandparents and several aunts, he was hopelessly spoilt and most visitors avoided the house whenever they could. She had often felt that it was hardly fair to the child, either.

Dickon, recovering his spirits with his health, was remarkably boisterous that evening, so that Caroline was only vaguely conscious of the sounds of arrival from below. It was well after seven before she felt he was settled enough to be left, and made her way down to the drawing room, which she did very quietly. There was screen round the door to protect against drafts from the hall, and she was able to enter without the occupants being aware. Part of the room was hidden from her, but she could see that the doctor was engaged upon his customary game of chess with Mr Peters who had clearly cut short his visit so as to continue the tradition. He was hunched over the board as usual, his wrinkled face pink with

116

concentration. He was perhaps the more enthusiastic player but Dr Field had the most skill.

Caroline moved round the screen, and Mrs Price came in sight, absorbed in a serial story in the Ladies Magazine. A step more and she could see the whole room without being noticed. Lady Lassiter was inclined to deplore Mrs Price's taste, and was diligently perusing the writings of Dr Johnson, while Mr Price was engaged in conversation with the new arrival, a tall young man who sat with one leg out stiffly, a stout stick by his side emphasising his lameness, though he bore no other signs of ill-health, seeming fitter than the other men in the room, most of whom must be over thirty years his senior. While still unobserved herself, Caroline regarded the latest resident with interest, wanting to gain an initial impression that she could measure against later experience.

John Carpenter was fair, light brown hair rather than yellow, thrown into sharp contrast by really dark lashes and brows that had a touch of ginger. His face was pleasant rather than handsome, and his expression was strained, she felt that he was almost certainly in pain after his journey. And conversation with Mr Price was disconcerting to those unfamiliar with that gentleman's staccato way of talking and sharp "Hey? Yes?" after stating an opinion, however, the newcomer seemed amused rather than bothered.

Beyond them, near the fire, sat Mrs Dewsbury, placidly sewing some linen while giving an ear to Miss Watt, who managed to work at her netting, talk, and glance round the room at frequent intervals. Inevitably it was she who caught sight of Caroline first and exclaimed, "Ah, here is Mrs Randall now!"

Mrs Dewsbury laid down her work and smiled welcomingly. It was accepted that the chess players were not to be disturbed if a female came in once they had settled down, but Mr Price rose at once and to Caroline's dismay, Mr Carpenter struggled out of his chair and stood leaning on his stick while introductions were made by their hostess.

"Mrs Randall, this is Mr Carpenter. Mr Carpenter, Mrs Randall."

As the new arrival took Caroline's hand and bowed over it, she had a feeling that he was slightly embarrassed. She wondered uneasily if they had been telling him about her. No doubt kindly, but if she had been described as a perfect mother, devoted to her child, she would not blame him for feeling awkward as he greeted her. Once they were seated she noticed that whenever he thought she was not looking, Mr Carpenter seemed to be regarding her with a sort of anxious commiseration, and she was dismayed at the idea that he was pitying her as a young widow. Never feeling that she felt she deserved sympathy, she had from the start made it clear that she had not had a happy time with Dickon's father, but this only seemed to cause her companions to pity her more.

"Tea will be here shortly and I must go and see about supper," said Mrs Dewsbury, folding up her needlework and rising to her feet. "Did thee find Dickon well, Mrs Randall?"

"You were absent so long, we were beginning to worry," said Miss Watt amid a general murmur. Mr Carpenter said nothing but seemed concerned.

Caroline laughed. "Oh no, nothing wrong, on the contrary, he was so lively he did not want to go to bed!"

"I am so glad to hear it," said Mrs Dewsbury warmly. "And you have left Nancy with him, of course."

"Yes, she is sitting in the next room in case he stirs, but once he falls asleep, it takes a great deal to wake him! Still, I am glad to think of her there, just now."

"Thee is fortunate to have a girl like that for his nurse," Mrs Dewsbury was moving to the door. "One hears such dreadful tales of some nursemaids, I am sad to say."

Miss Watt chimed in with an account she had read of children drugged to spare the nursemaid's trouble, and though Caroline had heard this before, she nodded gravely and agreed that such women probably had no affection for their charges. "However, Nancy has been devoted to Dickon from the day that he was born."

When Mrs Dewsbury had gone, the boarders settled down to their various occupations, while Mr Price, clearly relishing a male companion who was not addicted to chess, drew the newcomer back into conversation. Caroline threaded a needle and took up her own work, politely listening to Miss Watt rambling while privately wishing the garrulous old creature would concentrate more on her netting so that a little of the gentleman's talk could filter through to her. Although she had schooled herself not to repine, she had not lost her interest in wider topics. Mr Price had a great deal to say about the current situation in France and the war at sea, and was regaling Mr Carpenter with his opinion of the Government. Caroline was curious to discover what the newcomer thought, and some of his responses seemed less hidebound than she might have expected, sensible and moderate.

Unfortunately Miss Watt found these issues as dull as ditch-water, and politics a matter of concern only to the opposite sex. She was innocent of any suspicion that she was trying Caroline's patience, and chattered on. When the weather, Dickon's cold, and her own state of health had been exhausted she produced a new pattern for netting that she had just come across, which she handed over for inspection. This was for a purse and would involve threading beads into the rows as they were worked.

Caroline looked at it almost apprehensively. She had no great love for netting in spite of associating it with her dear Aunt Lucy, who had always had some in hand. She had found it fiddly and meticulous then, and Miss Randall had been good at it, which Miss Watt was not. She was too impatient to work it properly and the result of her labours was often a tangled mass of yarn, looking as if a rather untidy spider had been playing at Cat's Cradle. "Heaven knows what she will make of this," Caroline thought, affecting interest in the pattern and discussing where the beads might be purchased. She had an idea that what her companion was longing discuss John Carpenter and his lameness, and was glad she was too timid to do so. He was far too close and like other slightly deaf people, Miss Watt had no idea how far her voice carried to those not so afflicted.

Just as Mr Peters succeeded in beating the doctor for the first time in days, tea was brought in and placed on a table near the fire. The whole company gathered round to drink it, and to Caroline's relief, Mrs Price had found an embroidery pattern in her magazine that distracted Miss Watt's attention. Dr Field sat down next to Lady Lassiter, and on noticing what she was reading, launched himself on the tale of his one and only meeting with Samuel Johnson, when he himself was a younger and rather nervous man. With a general comment on Hampstead, Mr Price brought Caroline and Mrs Dewsbury into his conversation with Mr Carpenter, and Mr Peters, pleased at his success, ambled over to join them. He was an inquisitive old man, and it was plain that he had come in after the newcomer had arrived and had not been told of the accident mentioned at dinner.

"I knew a Carpenter," he observed. "Years ago. Met him when I was staying with friends in Wiltshire, who were not as keen on hunting as I was – Carpenter was a bruising rider to hounds, and this made a bond between us. You are not unlike him."

The new arrival had inclined his head to listen, but had gone rather pale, and gripped his stick very hard. Caroline wondered if anybody else had noticed this. Mr Peters certainly did not, he was gazing past them at the fire. "Why, it must be over fifty years ago," he said plaintively. "Dear me. You would not think, to look at me now, that I was once a sportsman, would you? Though I was not up to the standard of my friend Carpenter. You *are* like him, can he be any relation? He owned a place called Coombe Park, in Wiltshire."

"My grandfather," said John Carpenter in quietly restrained tone. "He died about eighteen months ago."

"Dear me, I am sorry to hear that," Mr Peters sounded dismayed. "Mind you, he was some years my senior. Is it your father that now owns Coombe Park?"

"My father was the eldest son, but he died when I was a child," said Mr Carpenter, meeting Caroline's eye and swiftly looking away again. "I am the present owner of Coombe Park."

Mr Peters seemed surprised. "Indeed? But you are staying here."

120

Mr Carpenter flushed and Caroline noticed his jaw set as if facing an opponent. "No doubt that seems strange to you, sir," he said stiffly. "But at the moment the property is let."

Embarrassed, Mr Peters sought to change the subject. "Uh – do you hunt – like your grandfather?" His voice trailed off as he noticed the younger man's stick, and the other conversations ceased as most of his fellow boarders turned looks of reproach in his direction.

"I was not as eager as my grandfather, but I have done," Mr Carpenter gave a rueful smile. "But last summer I had a bad accident when schooling a restless horse, and it smashed up my leg. I hope to ride again, but it has taken some time to heal."

His questioner stammered out an apology, and there was a collision of words as the others tried to condole with the newcomer. Caroline sympathised with the hunted expression this produced, and remarked gently that she too had been used to ride, at one time. Everyone else looked anxious, Mr Price tried to change the subject, but Mr Carpenter turned to her eagerly, saying that she did not sound as if she had wanted to give it up. Had she enjoyed it?

"Indeed I did. I never hunted, but I believe I was considered a good rider. I must confess that I do miss it." She did not give any details but her tone must have carried conviction for he looked sympathetic and said how unpleasant it was to have to abandon an activity one enjoyed.

Tea being over, Caroline took up her work again, and listened to the conversation between the new boarder, Mr Price and Mr Peters. Lady Lassiter and Dr Field discussed Dr Johnson, while Mrs Price and Miss Watts went into a huddle about embroidery. It would never have occurred to the two older men to ask Caroline's opinion, but as they talked she noticed Mr Carpenter glancing in her direction as if he would have liked to know what she thought. She wondered what was passing through his mind, and found herself admiring the adroitness with which he steered the talk to other topics whenever Mr Peters showed signs of reverting to the subject of Coombe Park and its late owner.

Had anyone else noticed that it was the reference to his grandfather that had upset the young man more than mention of his lameness? Or that there was something unusual about his response? Caroline had a feeling that he resented the suggestion that he resembled the old man and he had not seemed unduly distressed in speaking of his death. Nor did he appear very willing to discuss the property with anyone, especially the man who had visited it. He had sounded almost bitter when he spoke of Coombe Park being let, as if he resented the fact. Perhaps he was heavily in debt? But in that case, surely his creditors would have forced a sale, rather than letting him raise money in this manner.

"Supper will be in about ten minutes," said Mrs Dewsbury, returning to the drawing room, and Mr Carpenter rose to his feet and saying he must speak to his man, hobbled out. Once he was safely out of earshot, Lady Lassiter and Miss Watt turned reproachfully upon Mr Peters, chiding him for his tactlessness in mentioning hunting to a lame man, which he took quite calmly. Knowing that he really had a kind heart, Caroline decided that he was comfortably sure that he had not really upset the newcomer.

"I had not noticed his stick," he told them, when he was permitted to speak. "When I did realise its significance, it would have looked far worse to break off than to continue."

"But surely you heard Mrs Dewsbury allude to the accident? – Oh, no, you were not present at dinner," said Dr Field.

"And we were all so careful not to speak about it!" said Miss Watt.

"I wonder," said Mr Price thoughtfully, and having gained the attention of the room he addressed his next remarks to the whole company, "Was that really what he wanted? It seemed to me that he was almost relieved when Mrs Randall spoke of having ridden. Perhaps he has grown tired of people avoiding the subject. No, it seemed to me that he was far more distressed when you spoke of his late grandfather, Mr Peters."

"Really, Mr Price," said Lady Lassiter disbelievingly, but he persisted. "I thought he was anxious to avoid that subject, did not you, Mrs Randall?"

Caroline reluctantly agreed, wishing he had not been so acute as she saw the complacent expression fade as Mr Peters took in the meaning of the words.

"Oh, dear!" he exclaimed. "Oh, dear, dear me. Oh, Mr Price, do you really think so? I see now. How dreadful, it never occurred to me – I was so interested to discover that he was related to my old acquaintance I did not think of how much he must have been distressed about him dying." The poor man looked so forlorn and deflated that Mr Price, in turn, became disconcerted at the effects of his comments, possibly aimed more at Lady Lassiter, Miss Watt, and the doctor, and began to try, rather awkwardly to console Mr Peters. Caroline had a sudden thought and asked Mrs Dewsbury about Mr Carpenter's mother.

"You spoke as if she had died, was that a long time ago?" she asked.

Mrs Dewsbury had also been regarding with concern the dismay of Mr Peters, and she nodded, "Yes, indeed, I ought perhaps to have mentioned that she died only a month or so after her father-in-law." Her voice shook slightly, "I was so fond of her myself, I find it hard to speak of her," she said apologetically. "It is a long time since we met, but we corresponded frequently, and it was a great shock to me to hear from her son of her sudden death."

"Oh, it must have been," said Caroline with sympathy. "If that was so close to his grandfather dying, what Mr Peters said may also have been reminded him of her."

Mr Peters revived a little. "I could not have known that," he observed.

"Of course not," said Lady Lassiter kindly. "The loss of his mother must have been a great sorrow to him."

She looked enquiringly at Mrs Dewsbury, who nodded, and said sadly, "Yes, he was devoted to her, Though I had not seen her for a long time, it was with much sadness that I heard of her passing. He is very like his mother. Thee saw a likeness

123

to the grandfather, Mr Peters, I only met him once, but surely he was darker, and not so tall? Penelope — Mrs Carpenter — was tall for a woman." And almost to herself she murmured, "A tall laughing girl with light hair." She sounded so sad that everyone fell silent until supper was announced.

When Caroline came up to bed, and entered her sitting room, Nancy rose from her seat by the fire and glanced at the bedroom door which was not quite shut. "Oh, he's fast asleep now," she said, smiling.

"Poor Nancy, did you have a great deal of trouble with him?"

"Oh, no, Ma'am," Nancy sounded almost aggrieved. She would never admit that Dickon had behaved badly if she could possibly put it down to high spirits, or fatigue, or lay the blame at someone else's door. "He was still excited, but he went off like a lamb in the end."

Raising her eyebrows, Caroline went to look at her son while Nancy coaxed the fire into a blaze. "He is breathing much more easily," she observed as she returned. "That shows his cold is better."

"Oh, yes, Ma'am, it is — thank goodness!" Caroline was a little surprised at the fervour of the reply.

"I don't think he was in any danger, Nancy," she said, "His lungs are very sound, the doctor says, and after all this is only the second cold of his entire life."

"Ah — well — no, I wasn't thinking that, no what I meant was that now he will be able to go out and play in the garden again."

"Oh, I see. Did you get a lot of complaints about the noise he made up in the attics, from Mrs Dewsbury's servants?"

"No, not at all!" said Nancy sharply. "They was all pleased to see him, bless him — no, it's him I'm thinking of. The passages up there are very narrow, not much room for him to run about. If only he was let to play down in that big hall when he can't go out, it wouldn't be so bad. Surely those old people could put up with it for a little while?"

"They have all assured me that they could," said Caroline, "But I feel that it would put a great strain on them, and I

124

should feel shockingly responsible if he were to knock into some one and cause them to fall."

Nancy shook her head despondently. "All these old people," she reiterated. "There's so many of them in this house!"

"Are you regretting Islington, Nancy?" asked Caroline.

"Huh! The old women there was worse than here," said Nancy. "They weren't all that old anyway, but fussy! Oh, they said, couldn't stand a child in the place – Ugh! The people here do seem fond of him at least. Oh no, I'm glad enough to be away Islington."

"Surely you were sorry to leave Mrs Basset? You had been with her for quite a long time, after all."

"So I had, but what of it? Why did she have to get those two lodgers for, anyway? Taking over the garden saying only their little dog could use it, it was downright cruel."

"They paid well," Caroline reminded her. "And Mrs Basset was in need of the extra money, was she not?"

"Those sons of hers, and her daughter, always coming to her for help," said Nancy disapprovingly. "I s'pose she had to find new people for the downstairs rooms, but no one else wanted the garden all to themselves. Those two, any one would think Dickon was a monster, the way they carried on. And their maid! Haughty wasn't the word for it. 'Mai Ladies are not accustomed to children,' she said to me. 'Well, I told her, our Dickon's very quiet for a boy, but I wish he was noisy as noisy.' That would have given them something to moan about all right!"

Caroline had heard all this before, but Nancy's indignation still amused her, and she was moved at the extent of the affection the girl had developed for the little boy. Islington had become increasingly built up by the time Dickon was two and a half, and his mother had already begun to contemplate leaving even before the arrival of troublesome ground floor lodgers hostile towards children. She had not thought of Nancy wanting to accompany them until her spirited defence of the child showed dismay at the idea of parting from him.

"As for Mrs Basset, I'll always be grateful for her kindness to me and my family, but I didn't expect to stay with her for ever, you know."

"Ah," said Caroline. "I certainly hesitated to suggest that you might like to accompany us when I felt I must leave Islington."

"Because of Mrs B? Oh, no. She could get another maid easy, but where would I get another Dickon? And, Mrs Randall, about Dickon, don't you think he's more important than the old people here? Don't you think we ought to worry more about him?"

While Nancy was completing this outburst, Caroline was conscious of several conflicting reactions; that there was some sense in what she said; that she ought not to permit her maid to speak so freely; that she must make it clear once and for all just why she had chosen to live in lodgings like this – and finally, unexpectedly, an almost jealous resentment that the girl had any interest in Dickon at all, any claim to his affections, any say in how his life was managed. Yet on the whole she was fond of Nancy, and often felt glad that the little boy did not depend entirely upon his mother. Perhaps tonight Nancy's attitude had been a little too possessive, criticising when it was not really her place. The result was that when Caroline replied, she heard herself say coldly, "And what do you propose I should do about that? Move yet again?"

Nancy looked as if she had been struck in the face. "No need to take me up so sharp, Ma'am." she said reproachfully. "I was only thinking of his good." This made Caroline pause, reflecting that Nancy too might feel jealousy, and as his mother, she not only had the greater claim, she had the power to separate them completely.

"I am sorry, Nancy," she said more gently. "I know how much you care about his welfare. But I am afraid it would be much the same wherever we went. Those who board at a house like this are likely to be elderly, or widowed, if I could afford to take a house it might be different, but there is Dickon's future to think of, and a house and servants to run it would take a great deal of my income."

126

Nancy seemed somewhat mollified at being taken into her mistress's confidence. "I'm sorry, Ma'am," she said. "I didn't know it was like that. I s'pose it was the new boarder that set me off. When I heard the poor man was so bad, he couldn't climb stairs, I thought – Oh yes, and he'll be so afraid Dickon will knock into him, we'll have to be even more careful when he's around."

"I think not," said Caroline. "I am sure Mr Carpenter will be able to stand Dickon, possibly more than the other men, it is just his leg that is bad, and it may well improve."

Nancy was sceptical. "Old Dr Field, and Mr Peters, they get worse," she pointed out.

"True, but Mr Carpenter is recovering from an accident," said Caroline. "He is not suffering from the infirmity of age."

"Isn't he old, then? I was sure he must be, the way he was spoken of."

"No, he is about my age, or a little older, I would say."

"That is a change," said Nancy as she moved to the door. "But whatever will he do here, in that case?"

Left to herself, Caroline thought "What, indeed." Again wondering why the young man should have chosen this place to recuperate in. Certainly it was not far from London, known to be healthy, and of course more like open country but was that enough? She sensed a great affection for the place he had let to others.

"But it is none of your business, Caroline Randall," she told herself severely, "Remember, you used to despise gossip." She took a candle into her bedroom and began to undress.

Dickon slept in a little bed in one corner of the room, behind a screen which shielded him from the light. He seldom stirred once he had gone to sleep, but his recent cold had made him restless, and she was in her dressing-gown and had just taken out the pins that kept her hair neatly coiled under a cap when she heard the child stir. She put down the hairbrush she had just picked up, and went round the screen to look at him. But he had merely turned over, champing his teeth a little and did not wake when Caroline leant over to tuck him in more closely. She stood looking down at him, still surprised at the strength of her affection for him, particularly considering how little she had welcomed his arrival, and had felt little enthusiasm when he was put into her arms. Newborn babies had never struck her as beautiful, and the complete dependence, which other women seemed to delight in, did not appeal at all.

Considering him now, she remembered the tiny red frog-like object that Mrs Basset had shown her. How long had it been before he ceased to fill her with a mixture of apprehension and pity and begun to exhibit his own very definite personality? Remarkably soon, surely. Of course she had never had much to do with so young a baby before, but both Mrs Basset and Nancy, who had, appeared to find Dickon advanced for his age. Perhaps his character really had developed earlier than usual.

The child moved again, turning his face upwards and throwing off some of his coverings. Caroline leaned forward to replace them, and as she did so, her long plait fell over her shoulder and touched the curly red head on the pillow. The colour matched it exactly, and as she straightened up she was struck with the similarity of his features as well. "Very like his mother!" she thought, wondering why the phrase seemed vaguely familiar. Had someone commented on the likeness in her hearing? Probably they did, but not recently...

Returning to the dressing table where a lamp stood, she undid, brushed, and re-plaited her hair, and suddenly remembered the conversation before supper. "Of course, Mrs Dewsbury said something about Mr Carpenter reminding her of his mother." Thinking about the evening, she had a feeling that the elderly Quakeress knew a little more about the Carpenters and their family home than she had said, even if she did not know exactly what had brought him to Hampstead. For some reason Caroline felt genuine concern about the unhappiness she perceived in John Carpenter.

PART 7

Mrs Dewsbury's Garden

August 1798

The garden at Little Manor was thought to have been one of the first cultivated areas of Hampstead, it was certainly older than the house, which had been built in the time of Charles the Second on the site of an earlier structure. Tradition had it that the fruit trees in the cool orchard had been planted in the reign of Queen Elizabeth, though the high walls that surrounded them and enclosed the whole garden had the date 1669 scraped on them in several places. On a cold winter's day when the trees were bare, the effect of so much enclosed ground could be forbidding, but when the afternoon summer sun blazed down, the cool shade of the trees and the great walls was a blessed relief.

Returning from a walk with her son and John Carpenter, Caroline was interested to note that the extremely fine weather had actually tempted Lady Lassiter and Miss Watt to sit outside, a very rare occurrence. She lifted the hand in which she carried a letter and waved to them both. Dickon, holding her other hand, called out a greeting, and Mr Carpenter looked round, rested on his stick, and raised his hat. The ladies waved back, and Caroline noticed that other chairs had been laid out in the shade near the house. She hesitated, but her companions had already left the drive by the wicket gate to the orchard, and as the last thing she wanted was to open Selina's letter in public, she decided to assume that the chairs were for the Prices, Dr Field, or Mr Peters, so she waved again and followed the others into the orchard.

"Oh look, Mr Tope!" cried Dickon, pointing to the gardener who was scything the long grass at the far end of the orchard. "Can I go and talk to him, Mama?"

"If he does not mind, and you do not bother him," said Caroline.

"Oh, no, he likes me!" said Dickon cheerfully, and ran off. His mother and John Carpenter made their way to one of the green-painted benches situated under the apple trees and sat down, the gentleman letting out something between a gasp and a sigh as he stretched out his stiff leg to ease it.

"I never cease to be surprised, at how peaceful it is here, and yet we are so close to London that a drive of an hour would have us in the centre of the city," he remarked. "Here, we might be in the country."

Caroline murmured her agreement, feeling that beneath the simple words lay a longing for his country home. She was interested to discover that she not only understood his reaction, she shared it. Yet only few years ago Old Manor and the country around it had seemed purgatory, London a distant paradise. Pondering upon this, she laid her letter unopened on her lap and folded her hands on top. Though she had been anxious to hear from Selina, who had not written for over two months, she found herself a little reluctant to read it.

She might not have been as responsible for her friend's marriage as some people suspected, but she felt that it was partly her doing, and was concerned that things might not have worked out as well as it had promised. Selina had continued to be childless, and though she did not complain, some of her letters had seemed a little plaintive, referring to activities like sport and farming in which she could only participate to a limited extent.

"Are you not going to read your letter?" asked her companion almost wistfully. Caroline realised that he was too polite to open his own until she did.

"In a little while," she promised, smiling at him, "Please do read yours, though."

"If it does not offend you? I must confess that I am anxious to discover what my attorney has to say to me."

"I quite understand," said Caroline, and sat dreamily watching the birds in the trees just as she had done in the orchard of Old Manor more than twenty years before. Her eyes wandered to her little son, who seemed to be having a splendid time with the gardener, whom he appeared to be helping sweep up the grass. He was clearly quite happily occupied, and she looked up at the ripening fruit just as a bird trilled on a nearby branch. "A blackbird," she thought, turning to see if John Carpenter had also recognised this. But, looking strangely excited, he was absorbed in what he was reading and suddenly gave a cry of delight.

"Good news?" she asked.

"Oh yes. Oh, indeed!" he was beaming at her. "This is about Coombe Park, the Salfords who have been renting it, have decided to quit by the end of October!" his tone was triumphant, as at the retreat of an enemy.

"Really? I thought you said that their lease had still two years to run."

"That is so. It appears that they are disappointed that they have not been given the option to purchase the property, and desire to look elsewhere. I certainly have no desire to hold them to the contract."

Caroline could understand this, considering the affectionate way he had always spoken of Coombe Park, though it still seemed strange that it should have been leased at all. "But you had no intention to sell, had you?"

"No, never! In fact I did not really want to let the property. If I had not been a sick man, the question would not have arisen. No, it was the suggestion of my uncles. I have mentioned them, Edward Carpenter and the Canon, have I not?"

Caroline agreed that he had indeed spoken of two gentlemen for whom he seemed to have little affection. He sighed and said bitterly that no doubt he seemed feeble to have listened to the idea.

"Not at all, you said that you were very ill at the time."

"I really do think that is the explanation, if not an excuse. So much had happened in less than a year, my grandfather dying, and then my dear mother, and my unwise agreement to help a neighbour school a troublesome horse, which was really untrainable, hence my accident. I was barely conscious

131

when the uncles began to speak about letting Coombe Park since I would need to be in London for the doctors." John Carpenter paused and hit the ground with his stick rather forcefully. "I am inclined to think that any man in the condition I was in then, should be regarded as temporarily insane, or as if under the influence of drink! He certainly ought not to be considered fit to make decisions of such importance."

"Your relations seemed very anxious for you to let your property," commented Caroline.

He looked thoughtful. "They were, were they not? They *said* it would be more convenient for me to be in London, which may have been true. But I suspect that there was more to it than that. I have an idea that my life was despaired of for a time, or they thought it was. I had not then made a will, which would have complicated matters for them both."

He seemed to be sunk in reflection and Caroline wondered if he had remedied this omission since. She did not like to disturb his train of thought, but after a moment he looked up and smiled a little grimly. "I am almost certain that one of them gave those tenants the impression that there would be the option to purchase eventually. Strange, my Uncle Edward has children. You would not think he would want the property to go out of the family. But he made a fortune in the East Indies as a youth and purchased an estate in Shropshire and the Canon is very well situated in the Cathedral Close, besides owning a house in London. They would no doubt have preferred the extra money. Only I did not oblige them by dying. My poor uncles, how they must have suffered!"

Caroline thought that the Carpenter brothers sounded an unpleasant pair, and he had seldom had anything good to say of them, but she hesitated to agree. So often people abused their relations but sprang to their defence if one took up the criticism.

"Have I shocked you, imputing such a motive?" he asked. "Perhaps my uncles would not have desired my death, had I not been so ill, but they neither of them liked my mother and

I daresay they regard me as an interloper. They were never amiable men."

"It does not sound as if they are," said Caroline cautiously. "From what you have told me about them."

He studied her face, puzzled for a moment, and then appeared enlightened. "Ah, possibly you think I do not really mean it, that I am liable to resent other people abusing my relations? I am aware that some might respond like that, but I can assure you that I am not of their number. You may really say what you think."

"I dislike what I have heard, but not having met them I hesitate to say much."

"I understand, you think I am biased. My uncles, even more than my grandfather did their best to make my mother's life a misery, and for that I can never forgive them. But perhaps you might see virtues in them that I cannot."

"Not necessarily," said Caroline. "I simply meant that I would be judging them on hearsay. I might find even less excuse for them than you do, were I to meet them, but any opinions I give at the moment can only echo yours. You would not want that?"

"Oh no, I see what you mean. I am biased, as I remarked, but I do think my uncles are a precious pair. Even my grandfather did not care for them, and he was their father! He was a selfish old man, but I think he really loved Coombe Park, and knew that I shared his feelings. It was almost the only thing we agreed upon."

"And now you will be able to return to it?" said Caroline.

"Within a month or so, is it not splendid! No doubt my uncles will dislike it immensely," John Carpenter sounded pleased at the idea. "But I am no longer in poor health, and thank goodness I never gave them power over what was done. I have an idea that they tried, but my attorney was firm, I am grateful for that." His tone became more subdued as he added, "It will not be the same, without my mother at Coombe Park. Dear me, nothing turns out as one might wish. For years I had longed to be the owner and see her at ease there. My grandfather never really permitted her to feel at home."

Caroline murmured sympathetically, as he sighed, and then examined the last page of the letter. "Oh, I ought to reply to this at once. Will you excuse me? You have your own letter to read, have you not? I hope to return to the garden before it is time for Dickon to go in to his supper."

Caroline watched him limp away, thinking how much more easily he moved now, and looked for her son. The child seemed to be behaving himself and happy with the gardener, and she picked up her letter. As she broke the seal she discovered that her apprehensions had lessened during her conversation. After all, if life with Mr Penry was imperfect, it *must* be better than what her friend would have led with the man proposed for her. But Selina sounded cheerful, though she remained childless, the slightly plaintive note had disappeared.

"Ifor was persuaded to stand for the local By-election," she wrote. "It was very interesting, I had never seen such a thing before. And – perhaps you will understand this better than I do, Caroline – Ifor is very popular even though he was defeated. People tell me that he would have been elected if his opponent, Mr Lewis, had been more honourable. This man is our largest local landowner, and he used his position to force his tenants to vote for him, besides bribing others, but I understand that Ifor had more people willing to vote for him. I am not very sorry he was not elected, even though it would have meant that he would have been able to frank my letters. I do not think I would have enjoyed being the wife of a politician, and I doubt if he would have liked it much. He made some wonderful speeches, but he is rather shy, the quiet life in the country suits him very well, to have to take a house in town would have been a strain on us both. Have you ever seen an election, Caroline? I suppose you must have done, when you lived with your uncle – but it was probably not exactly like what happened here in Wales. Everyone was so enthusiastic! It was almost overwhelming at times. There was music and song, and both candidates had their own harpist.

Ours came to our house at the dinner we gave afterwards, and played such beautiful sad songs, I found the tears pouring down my face. The Welsh harpists all seem to be men, and they perform with such splendid power that I am quite out of charity with the insipid females I have encountered."

The next part of the letter was dated later and the ink was a different colour. Selina was most apologetic about the delay. "My dear, I had left this overnight, but I had every intention of finishing it in the morning. Only the very moment we were finishing our breakfast next day, there came a dramatic interruption to our usual routine. A coach overturned almost at our gates, the crash could be heard from the house and when we rushed out, I fully expected to find the occupants dead or dying. However, the coach was the worst casualty, the people were dreadfully shaken but escaped with only cuts and bruises, no bones broken. Ifor took one look and sent for the blacksmith, and while he and the husband waited with the coachman, I assisted the wife and daughter into the house. We sent for the doctor just in case, and they were all so grateful.

"Their name was Taylor, and they were returning from a tour of Wales. It was some days before the coach was ready, and while it was repairing they stayed with us as our guests. They were very nice people, and the strange thing was that we found they are distant connections of my father! I did remember the name, but my family had not known them very well in my day, it seems that recently there had been more contact. They had been told about me, as an undutiful daughter, but I do not think they believed half of it. Certainly once they had met Ifor, they saw what a splendid person he is. It appears that they were so pleased with our hospitality that they wrote to my parents on their return home, praising us and what we had done for them. This resulted in a letter from my father in which he forgave us! I must say, I found it hard to have patience with that, Ifor is not a whit changed from when he was not thought good enough to marry me, but Mr Taylor, who is very rich, approved of him and *that* makes all the difference. Ifor agreed with me, but thought however ignoble the reason for it being offered, the hand of friendship ought to be accepted.

"I understood what he meant, and wrote at his suggestion to invite my family to stay, though I did not expect them to accept. But they did! At least, my parents and Georgina came. My brother is now settled in Ireland and has recently married an Irish girl, (why should that be better than a Welsh man in their eyes?). But I must not continue in this vein. My parents have forgiven us both, I wish I knew why that seems to make me feel uncomfortable. I felt that they were making an effort to be charitable all the time they were here, it made *me* cross, and poor Ifor suffered on my behalf, he has a hot temper, you know, especially where those he cares about are concerned.

"I think that they have changed, Caroline. They both seem so much older than I remember them, and somehow smaller – I am sure I have not grown! Even Georgina is not quite as sharp-tongued as she used to be. She is engaged to a suitable gentleman from Buckinghamshire and appears to be happy about it. I did not care for what I heard of him, but as you know, Georgina does not possess a great deal of sensibility.

"Your name was not mentioned by my parents, but Georgina did say she had heard you had left home, when we were alone, but she is much more interested in Lucy. She had a great deal to say about what a splendid wedding it was in our little church, and had more recent news of Sir Charles and his bride. She told me how they were on a visit to your parents when their first child was born, a week or so early but a healthy little girl, called Lucy. A year later they had a son, and she had another child this year – imagine little Lucy with three children! I can only think of her as she was when I last saw her, barely out of the schoolroom.

"Oh, but Caroline, what surprised me most and I fear may distress you, was to learn that your family have left Sussex, let the Old Manor and taken a house in Hertfordshire. To be near Lucy, Georgina says. I asked if she did not think that that was very strange, but she said not considering Mr Randall's health. It seems that he had a stroke about eighteen months ago, he has recovered to some extent, but was at first partly paralysed on one side. I suppose that means he cannot travel far, so it is sensible to be nearer Lucy, but it does seem strange to think of Old Manor without your family."

"Strange!" thought Caroline, letting the last page of her friend's letter fall unread on to her lap." "Is that all it seems to her?" To her disgust, the hated tears were pricking at the back of her eyes and for a moment she felt almost angry with Selina for dropping the piece of news so casually. "Still, she did think it might distress me, even though I have seemed to scorn my father's preoccupation with the property." Yes, she had always declared that human beings were more important than places, how could her friend be expected to know the bitter resentment that this information would evoke? She would not know that Caroline's opinion on this subject had modified. Though rationally it should make no difference to her who lived at Old Manor, since she could never return to it, she found herself resenting the idea of the property being occupied by any but members of the Randall family.

"How could Papa bear to do this?" she wondered, "He was so devoted to the property and the family history. To let it must have distressed him greatly. I suppose he agreed when he was ill and *because* he was ill. Oh, how like John Carpenter!" She thought about the story that she had just heard, feeling the poignancy of how it had affected this young man. The tears pricked again when she realised that her father might also be regretting having consented to lease Old Manor. His preoccupation with his home and family had alternately amused and irritated his daughter, but she had never undervalued how important it was to him. She also had a genuine affection for him and was concerned on his behalf.

Possibly she was wrong, and his illness had altered his feelings. Who had advised the move? His doctor, the lawyer, friends, or was it mainly his wife and eldest daughter? "No doubt Mama really did desire to be near Lucy and the grandchildren, and Anna must have enjoyed nursing him." She felt that she ought to suppress her irritation over it but found herself hoping that Richard Randall was not suffering as Mr Carpenter had.

"Mama! Look at me!" Caroline pulled thoughts back to her present concerns, and found that her son was prancing about on an improvised hobby-horse consisting of a small birch broom with his handkerchief tied round it for reins.

"Goodness me, Dickon, where did you get that?" she exclaimed, detaining him as he bounced past. The little boy chuckled proudly.

"Mr Tope made it for me, he says now I can ride my own broom, 'stead of using his when he wants to sweep," he said. "And it's a *proper* one, Mama, I can sweep with it. Did you see me sweeping?"

"I did," Caroline assured him. "I could not imagine where you had got a broom your size. Did you say thank you to Mr Tope?"

"Oh, yes," said Dickon. "Isn't it lovely?"

He leant on her knee while she admired how carefully the gardener had fashioned a small-scale replica of a full-sized birch broom, and suddenly sighed gustily. "I wish I could ride a real horse like Mr Carpenter has," he said plaintively. "By myself."

He had enjoyed being taken up in front of the newest boarder now that he was able to mount a horse again, but Caroline frowned and said he was not big enough for that.

"For a horse – but a pony, Mama? I would like a pony."

"I am sure you would, love, but you are too small even for a pony at the moment."

"I grow," said Dickon in aggrieved tones, "Mr Carpenter had a pony when he was little, not much bigger than me. He said so!"

"Possibly, but his mama had more money than I have. And he must have been more than three. Why, I was nearly five before…." Caroline stopped herself, but her child's ears were sharp and his brain quick.

"Oh, Mama, did *you* have a pony?"

"I used to ride one, once, but it was not really mine. (It had been a piebald pony, Anna had been nervous of it, Caroline had loved it and the younger girls had also learned to ride on

138

it. And these reminiscences could never be communicated to her son.)

"Where it gone now?"

"I do not know," said Caroline truthfully. "It was a long time ago, Dickon. When I was a little girl."

"But people have ponies here," Dickon pointed out, "Couldn't I have a very little one?"

"There would not be room in the stables," said Caroline. "And no one to look after it."

Dickon pouted, swinging his broom to and fro while still clasping her knee, and she wondered what her response ought to be. It was not as if the child was really being unreasonable, she felt it was quite natural that he should wish for what both she and John Carpenter had had when children. But her son was being brought up near London, she was suddenly aware that though she had lived there off and on from the age of eight or nine, all her early years had been spent in Sussex.

"Where Mr Carpenter gone, Mama?"said Dickon suddenly.

Caroline stood up and turned so that she could see beyond the orchard to the house. "He went in to write a letter," she said. "Look, here he comes now. He is talking to the ladies."

"Oh yes. Mama, can I go and show them my broom. Can I? Please!"

"Very well, but remember not to jump about too much. Lady Lassiter and Miss Watt are old ladies."

"Yes Mama," said Dickon and trotted soberly to the wicket gate. His mother watched him go, suddenly a little shaken to realise that her past, her home in Sussex, her sisters, would all have to be hidden from him, or at least kept very vague.

"I shall have to tell him *something*," she thought. "Especially since I have already admitted to having ridden a pony." When she looked back at the times she had been at Old Manor, she found a series of impressions, moods rather than memories of events, it was the times he had been at her uncle's house than seemed clearer, and not just because they had come later. Possibly being the only child in the house had sharpened her perception. She had ridden in London as well as in Sussex, perhaps she could mention visits to relations in the country?

Mr Carpenter and Dickon had left the ladies and were now approaching the orchard together. She sat down to wait for them and returned to her friend's letter. There was no time to read the final page carefully, but she glanced through it, noting the end of the Coleman's visit to the Penry household, and that Selina asked after John Carpenter as well as Dickon. How odd, had she said more about him than she realised. As the other two approached her, she watched the child raising his face admiringly and the man beaming down at him delightedly. "Oh dear, Dickon is going to miss him when he leaves," she thought.

PART 8

Mrs Dewsbury's House

Early Autumn, 1798

Caroline entered the drawing room so quietly that Lady Lassiter and Miss Watt did not notice her. They were standing at the far window looking out at the garden, talking in low voices. She thought she knew what was absorbing their attention, but moved to the other window to make sure.

Mr and Mrs Price were returning from a stroll, and Dr Field had just passed them going in the opposite direction, but it was upon a little group within the orchard that the ladies were concentrating. The tall lame man with the light hair had walked there often enough, but his companions were strangers and seemed to clash with the peaceful influence, almost as if they were consciously keeping aloof from their surroundings. She watched them with fierce interest, wondering if they had been introduced as Mr and Edward Carpenter on arrival. This must be them, the long pale man and his stocky wife standing so stiffly and clearly haranguin poor John, were the embodiment of his description.

She had not realised that she had let out her breath sharply till the two inhabitants of the room showed that they were aware of her presence. They started almost guiltily away from their window and joined her.

"My dear Mrs Randall," said Lady Lassiter majestically. "I did not see you come in. How is Dickon?"

"With Nancy," said Caroline, still watching the group in the orchard and feeling worried about John Carpenter's angry gestures. Miss Watt cleared her throat and moved towards the seats by the fire, while her ladyship gave a little frown and shook her head.

"I was not asking where he is," she remarked, gently urging the younger woman to join Miss Watt. Caroline looked away from the garden and bestowed a blindingly pleasant smile upon the two of them to hide her irritation, and assured them that her son was fine. She knew that Lady Lassiter must be torn between curiosity and shame at being caught observing the visitors. Come to think of it, as the probable cause of this angry discussion, she herself had better not be seen to watch them either. She joined the two ladies and hoped that she did not look too anxious.

They looked at her sympathetically but were clearly avoiding the topic they had been discussing when she came in, beginning one of their characteristic conversations which consisted of her ladyship discoursing on some subject while Miss Watt echoed the last word of each sentence. Caroline was used to letting this sort of thing flow over her, and they either indulged her absence of mind or were deceived into thinking she was listening since she put in the occasional appropriate word.

With the visitors at the back of her consciousness, she found by natural progression that she was recalling the conversation she had had with Nancy a few days earlier after she had broken the news of her engagement to John Carpenter. As she had rather feared, the little maid had not been pleased.

"Oh, Mrs Randall," she had said dolefully, "Why? I seen it coming, of course, but I thought you would be different."

"In what way, Nancy?"

"Why, from other ladies. It seems that once you start marrying you can't stop. It's like drink, my mother'd have done the same, if she had lived."

To Nancy's indignation, Caroline had burst out laughing, and resentfully she had persisted, "It's true, though, Ma'am. Marrying gets to be a habit. Oh, Mrs Randall, have you considered? Dickon doesn't need anyone else, now does he?"

"I beg your pardon, what makes you say that, Nancy?"

"I'm sure they have been telling you that Dickon ought to have a father, Mrs Randall."

"They? To whom are you referring?"

"Oh – people," said Nancy vaguely, and when pressed further, produced the names of Lady Lassiter, Dr Field as well as the other boarders and even Mrs Dewsbury. "They have been on at you, haven't they?"

"Not that I am aware of."

"Not to your face, maybe, but it's been heard."

"It certainly has not been said to me, and if it *had*, it would not have influenced me against my better judgement. I would not take advice that I did not agree with."

"Then you really want to marry Mr Carpenter, Ma'am?" Nancy had almost wailed. "Oh, why? You don't love him, do you?"

Caroline was accustomed to the girl's frankness, but this was going too far. "That will do, Nancy. I really cannot have you talking like that."

Having her speak so sharply silenced Nancy, but she had not looked convinced, and Caroline, had thought for a moment emphasising the liking and respect she felt for John Carpenter, but decided against it, putting forward the aspect that was most likely to make sense to the girl.

"After all, this will mean that you will be able to remain with us." Nancy, looking up from mending some of Dickon's clothes, had exclaimed in horror, "Mrs Randall, was you thinking of dismissing me? Oh, whatever *have* I done?"

"Nothing wrong, I assure you. I am generally very satisfied with you." Caroline had felt that it would not hurt to remind her again that she had overstepped the mark, but continued to explain that when Dickon grew too old to need a nurse, she could not have afforded to keep her on.

"Oh," said Nancy soberly, and had made no further protest, if her mistress marrying was the only way she could remain with Dickon, she clearly had to accept it. However, since this conversation Caroline had noticed a certain amount of possessive jealousy towards Mr Carpenter, this reminded her of her own feelings about sharing the child's affections with Nancy. His devotion to his prospective stepfather did not bother his mother at all.

"Yes," she said aloud, in answer to some query from Lady Lassiter. "Oh, yes!" she had no idea what was under discussion but her response seemed to satisfy, for her ladyship plunged into a long description of a ball she had attended, some fifty years before. This momentarily distracted Caroline from her own thoughts, and she listened to the two of them with some amusement.

"I was in palest blue satin, with silver lace and my family diamonds – I was a Damerel, you know – very full skirts, of course, hoops were always worn."

"...ways worn," echoed Miss Watt.

"What my mother would have said could she have seen the clothes of today, so much less full, I cannot imagine."

"Cannot imagine!"

"And the way that the gentlemen bowed to us, they knew how to do it in those days."

"Oh they did!" Miss Watt appeared to have been moved by some private recollection to essay a remark of her own. Lady Lassiter looked a little surprised and continued her discourse. "Manners of that time were elegance itself," she said, "In general, people are so careless these days."

This was an old grievance, and Caroline's attention wandered. She looked instead of listened, and watching their faces was reminded of the moment when she and John Carpenter had announced their engagement. Perhaps the congratulations of the other residents had been merely courteous, but they had surely not been hiding disapproval. Had they really been as anxious for the match as Nancy appeared to think? "Possibly they all thought it suitable from the time he arrived," she thought, and wryly considered that in this case, it must be the first time she had done what others expected of her.

But it was probably not for the reasons they would have imagined – or was it? Why had she said yes to John Carpenter? Partly for Dickon's sake, certainly, but not even for that would she have contemplated marriage with a man she did not care for, and she thought of how she had rejected the idea of telling his real father of her pregnancy, once she realised how much he had changed.

When she came to examine her motives for accepting the proposal, she still felt ambiguous. Nancy's comment that she was not in love might be impertinent, but she probably did not convey the appearance of passionate affection. But she found her feelings for the man had warmed over the months she had known him, and she was fairly certain that his for her were similar.

The conversation had ceased. Lady Lassiter and Miss Watt were gazing out of the window, their mouths open as if caught in mid-speech. Caroline turned sharply, to see what had attracted their attention. The situation in the orchard seemed to be deteriorating.

The gestures of the plump lady were growing even wilder, and though she was at some distance her face appeared to be verging on purple, while her pale husband had flushed an unbecoming pink. John looked calmer, but Caroline had come to know his reactions very well, and suspected that his manner concealed deep anger. Suddenly he hit his stick fiercely on the ground, and turned his back upon his uncle and aunt. They looked at each other and then at him, finally walking indignantly to the gate and out of sight. John stumped off into the orchard to work off his anger in pacing up and down.

Lady Lassiter caught Caroline's eye and began to speak rapidly and randomly to Miss Watt, who looked anxious and responded, neither of them seemed to expect her to participate, and she was grateful, but though preoccupied with her own thoughts, she noticed that their disjointed speech indicated that they were almost as interested in John Carpenter's visitors as she was. Of course, she had known about these relations for some time, whereas to the rest of the boarders they were a novelty. Only in private conversation had John spoken much about his uncles, and the others had barely known of their existence. Certainly none of them had had any idea how much he disliked and distrusted them, this uncle and aunt in particular.

Caroline had hardly recognised it herself until he declared his intention of keeping them in ignorance of his approaching marriage. "It may seem discourteous," he had said, "But after the way I have been treated by them all, I see no reason to consider their feelings."

She had made no attempt to dissuade him, if he had no desire to be on friendly terms with his relations it was surely his business. Her own experience of family discord had been quite painful enough, she had no wish to encounter it at second hand, especially since he voiced his opinion that though his uncles frequently quarrelled with each other, they would be united in their desire to keep John a bachelor.

Caroline wondered again, how had they come to hear of the prospective wedding. It had been impossible to keep it entirely secret, but his attorney was a man he trusted and most of the people at Little Manor were unaware that he had relations. No doubt it had been impossible to so prevent the Carpenters from hearing that the lease of Coombe Park had been surrendered, and the scale of preparation for the house being occupied again had probably aroused suspicion. Someone had been careless or indiscreet, causing the family to make the enquires that had led to the note dispatched from a nearby inn, which had been brought to John Carpenter as he breakfasted.

Its arrival had taken him completely unawares, and forgetting that none of his other companions would understand, he had exclaimed angrily and passed it to Caroline, saying, "Look at that! My Uncle Edward and his wife are here. I wonder how they came to know about our plans."

"Oh dear," Caroline had said as she read the epistle. Behind the elaborate courtesy and measured phrases she could see resentment and dismay, which only confirmed the impression she had gleaned from John. As she handed it back, she indicated the rest of the company and he nodded, not saying more about the threatened visit until they were alone. Everyone politely ignored the event, but John's reaction had made it very clear that he was not on good terms with these

146

relations and there had obviously been much speculation about what might be happening.

John was very silent for the rest of the evening, and Dickon who had resented being deprived of a promised walk, was fretful and difficult to settle, Caroline had to go up and try to calm him after dinner, returning to find that Mr Peters was out and Dr Field persuading his young friend to join him in a game of chess. The other ladies and Mrs Dewsbury were particularly kind, but both they and Mr Price were exchanging pitying glances when they thought she was not looking. Did they imagine that the other Carpenters had been trying to make John change his mind? She thought she knew better, that it had been anger that made him so taciturn at the meal – but suppose she did not know him as well as she imagined. From what he had said, his relations were perfectly capable of slandering her, sight unseen. She hoped this would have no effect, but having something to hide in her life made her uneasy.

Breakfast the following day was unmarred by further communications from the Carpenters, but the previous note had cast a shadow over the company, and Caroline felt deeply conscious of further scrutiny. John's confiding smile cheered her, and she thought he had recovered his spirits to some extent even before he invited her to walk out with him when the meal was over. Dickon was a little sleepy after his disturbed night, and she felt relieved that Nancy had decided to keep him in bed late, for once his company would have been too much of a distraction.

"Bah!" said John as they went down the drive. "If you want an example of a thoroughly malevolent couple, there you have them!"

"Mr and Mrs Edward Carpenter?" Caroline was delighted at his tone, and the friendly way he put his arm through hers.

"Of course. I would still like to know how they discovered that we are to be married!"

"Does it matter *how*?" asked Caroline. "It is the fact that it has happened at all that we have to reckon with now."

"You are perfectly correct," agreed John with a sigh. "But it was to avoid this sort of impertinence that I wished to keep them in ignorance till after we are married. It was not because I am afraid of them!"

"I did not think so," she said quietly, squeezing his arm.

John relaxed, and his face cleared. "I am so glad to hear you say that," he said fervently. "I suppose some people might think I was, but it is simply because I did not wish my relations to have a chance to make themselves unpleasant, in just the way they have. Of course it is against all their interests to have me marry, but they will not admit it, instead they talk sickeningly of having my welfare at heart! Ugh!"

"You cannot really expect them to admit it," said Caroline thoughtfully, and he gave a sudden laugh.

"No! That would be far too honest. Only I wish they would not pretend to be fond of me, that is almost an insult. Was I sure I was quite recovered – as if it had been my head and not my leg that was injured. Did you see them leave?"

She nodded.

"Good," said John vindictively. "I hope I finally convinced them that the dislike they feel for me is nothing to what I feel for them. They were so infuriated, I trust they will never forgive me! I can never forgive them for what they said about my mother."

"I was afraid of that," said Caroline, reflecting that the couple must be lacking in sense as well as affection if they had not seen that this tactic was the worst approach they could have taken.

"So was I, but by that time what I feared even more was that I might have been provoked to do something I might regret and give them cause to regard me as unstable – threatening them with my stick, for instance. How I managed to confine myself to words, I do not know! My mother was one of the best women that ever lived, it made me so mad to see her treated as an inferior by those unfit to tie her shoelaces! She, and you, are the only women I have ever known who possess brains – brains that they are capable of using rationally, at any rate."

Caroline thought he was exaggerating, recalling how wise Mrs Dewsbury had shown herself, but took the remark as a compliment. She wondered if she had been likened to his mother in the condemnation. Probably they considered his recent behaviour the result of maternal influence, but she did not feel inclined to question him further. But she took some comfort that any accusations they made would only alienate their nephew more.

They had just turned a corner, and John gave a sharp exclamation at the sight of the young couple coming towards them. Caroline looked at him inquiringly, his mouth had set into the line it had worn when he first came to Little Manor, when his leg had been so very much worse. "That is my cousin Edward and his sister Augusta," he said distastefully. "How very unfortunate."

Caroline had been unaware that the Carpenters had brought two of their offspring to Hampstead, and regarded them with some interest as they approached, seeing the parents in each of them. The girl was nineteen or twenty, rather pretty but too tall for her build and with something of her father's pallor, her older brother was pink-faced and stouter and had a discontented expression. They affected surprise, but were plainly on their way to Little Manor.

For a moment John seemed about to ignore them, but the girl forestalled him by exclaiming, "Why, look, Ned, it is Cousin John!" and he and Caroline were forced to pause.

"Ah – Augusta, I did not expect to see you here. Caroline, this is my cousin, Miss Carpenter. Augusta, this is Mrs Randall, who is shortly to become my wife."

While they bowed to each other, the young man almost quacked as he was introduced, in his turn and they both looked dismayed to find that John and his companion had no intention of interrupting their walk. Caroline wondered if they would be quick enough to protest before it was too late. Young Edward seemed unable to speak, and his sister had possibly to overcome some maidenly hesitation before she said plaintively, "But, Cousin John, we were on our way to call upon you."

He paused and looked round, but made no attempt to return to Little Manor, merely murmuring, "How kind of you, but we are on our way out."

Disconcerted, Augusta said, "Oh! Cousin!" and looked to her brother for assistance. Pulling himself together with a visible effort, he stammered out that they wanted to speak to him, "Will you be going very far?"

"A mile or so, it is our usual walk. You may accompany us, if you wish." A look of dismay passed between them, clearly they were under orders to get their cousin on his own, but the youth nodded, and the girl took his arm as they prepared to join the walk.

Caroline thought it was as well that she was not easily embarrassed, John's behaviour was outrageous, cheerfully making it plain that he did not feel any need to entertain the unwelcome relations, and continued to address himself mainly to her, ignoring any remarks coming from behind. It did not seem likely that the young Carpenters would endure this for long, and as soon as the road widened a little, Edward tried to bring his sister up level with the other couple. Though his leg no longer incapacitated him from going at a reasonable speed, John chose to assume that they wanted to pass, pausing and waving them to go ahead. Caroline's hand was resting lightly on his arm, and he squeezed it gently as he succeeded in this manoeuvre. She responded with a quick pressure of her fingers but avoided looking into his face.

Walking ahead, Edward Carpenter was able to turn and address those behind, but his remarks were brief and disjointed, and he seemed more exasperated every time they glimpsed his face. Presently they came to a stile, and the girl, who had been flagging, clearly not accustomed to walking at the speed her brother had to set, begged for a chance to rest for a minute. While she sat there panting gently, John drew Caroline a little way off and grinned at her almost triumphantly. She smiled back, but looking at the pair with some sympathy, she murmured, "Poor things!"

"They are, are they not?" he said. "Such poor things, it scarcely seems worth the trouble!"

"Cousin John." Edward was approaching them, his rather heavy jaw jutting a bit, and a light almost of desperation in his eyes. "Cousin, I must speak to you alone, on a personal matter." He cast an ingratiating smile in Caroline's direction, but it did not quite reach her. John gave an exasperated sigh.

"Oh, very well," he said wearily, and muttered in her ear, "Again!" as if this was a common occurrence. When they moved on, Edward had contrived to walk next to John, and with Augusta still holding his arm for a moment Caroline was left on her own at the rear, reflecting that again, this was not the wisest move the youth could have made. As she could have told him, it enraged his cousin, who brought the whole party to a halt and returned to her side.

"Oh, Cousin John!" cried Edward.

"Well? I understood that you wanted to speak to me alone, I take it this does not concern your sister?"

The young man's expression rather amused Caroline, who felt that the request might have been genuine, but that he was probably following parental orders to snub her. She smiled at the girl, who looked at her brother in dismay, but finally fell back and let the two men take the lead.

For a while the females walked in silence, while Edward muttered into John's ear. Caroline was willing to open a conversation, but Augusta contrived to avoid her eye, even though her mounting colour suggested that she was aware of scrutiny. Irritation mounted at such deliberate rudeness, which must also be the result of instructions from the senior Carpenters. Nothing they knew of her warranted this, and she sensed that the girl's natural manners were telling her so.

Would she be able to ignore a direct remark? As they emerged from a patch of shadow to bright sunlight, Caroline commented on the mildness of the morning. "The sun is really quite hot for the time of year!"

Augusta presented a little more than her profile for a moment, and said, "Yes," very quietly.

"Of course it is often warm about Michaelmas, but this is outstanding. Why, the trees have barely begun to turn colour."

"No," agreed Augusta.

"But perhaps they have begun to do so in Shropshire?"

The girl very nearly looked at Caroline this time, and stammered out that she did not think so.

With the subject of the weather exhausted, Caroline turned to a more feminine topic. "I like your hat," she observed truthfully, though feeling that the colour was not entirely suited to Augusta's complexion. "Surely it came from London?"

"Oh, yes, I bought it when we arrived in Town," said the girl eagerly. "It was delightful to..." she stopped abruptly, looking away again.

Caroline persevered, saying sympathetically that living at such a distance must make it difficult to shop in London. "But perhaps you come for the season?"

"No, no, we do not." Augusta sounded wistful. Perhaps she would like to live nearer the capital? Caroline did not ask that but remarked that for her part she was glad to be a little further out though she had enjoyed living in the centre of town when she was younger. She felt that Miss Carpenter was still trying to steel herself against friendly conversation, but she did not return to her previous monosyllables.

The gentlemen had got so far ahead that they had paused under a tree, young Edward still gesticulating at his taller cousin. Just before Caroline and Augusta came within earshot, the girl stopped and faced her companion squarely for the first time, saying awkwardly, "Mrs Randall!"

"Yes?"

"I – er – that is – well, I was supposed to say, if I saw you – with regard to my cousin – Oh, no! – why should you not marry him?"

"I intend to, my dear," said Caroline dryly.

"Yes, of course, it really is not our affair, is it? My mother and father said... Mrs Randall, I do not know how to put it."

"Perhaps your parents are concerned about their nephew's happiness?" suggested Caroline gravely. Augusta looked searchingly at her, her whole expression eloquent with her disbelief of that statement, though as a dutiful daughter she made no verbal criticism of Edward Carpenter and his wife.

They walked on in silence for a minute, and then the girl said unexpectedly, "I hope you will be happy with Cousin John."

"Thank you. I hope so too."

"He is difficult," said Augusta confidingly. "But perhaps you will not mind that?" There was no time to reply, because they had reached the two men, and John came forward to take Caroline's arm, his expression determined. Edward did not look pleased, but he and his sister turned back and they walked four abreast, not exchanging many words until they reached the road leading to the Inn when John looked in the direction of Little Manor and asked if his young relatives would care to come in for some refreshment.

"No, thank you," said Edward coldly, though his sister appeared willing to accept. "We must return now. Come, Augusta!"

John watched their retreating backs, in better humour than his cousin, and chuckled. "Poor Edward!" he said.

"He would appear to be somewhat annoyed," Caroline commented.

"So he was, not only had I no intention of listening to anything his parents had told him to say, I refused to lend him any more money."

"Ah, so that was why he wanted to speak to you privately."

"Indeed. I have helped him in the past, my uncle is rather close with his money, and young Ned did gamble when he was at university, but now he has a Civil Service post in addition to his prospects from his father, I see no reason why I should pay his debts. Especially as he combined his request with remonstrations about our marriage, hardly likely to make me look favourably on demands!"

"And did he hold me responsible for your refusal?" asked Caroline.

"How quick you are," said John admiringly. "That was the final straw, I would not have mentioned it to you, such impudence! However, I told him that even if I had not met you, I would not have been willing to lend it. I wonder if my uncle has any idea that I have helped his son? Perhaps I should have asked Edward about that."

153

"He may be apprehensive that you might tell Mr Carpenter now."

"That is possible, it may be one reason why he desisted. Do you know, I believe that his parents had some idea that I might be brought to marry Augusta. That child! I suppose she is not quite so young now, but I remember her as an infant. Did she speak of me to you?"

Augusta's comment now seemed clearer to Caroline, "I think she is a little afraid of you, and if they *have* suggested such a thing I do not think she cared for the idea."

"I should think not! So that was why she was dragged along. Poor Augusta! She is the best of that family and I trust she will find good husband."

Dickon was deeply wounded that his mother and Mr Carpenter should have gone out without him, and they had derived so little pleasure from their walk that they decided to have a stroll after dinner in the pleasant late afternoon. The little boy ran ahead to the end of the drive and looked in the direction they had travelled that morning. By mutual consent, they took him towards the heath instead, and by the time they returned it was almost dark.

"Bedtime, Dickon," said Caroline as they entered the hall, and he pouted.

"Oh, Mama, I want to say good-night to everybody!"

She sighed, knowing that he was hoping that one or two of the boarders might have some sweets for him, but the old people liked to see him and if she permitted it, he would be easier to settle on Nancy's night off.

"Very well, Dickon, if you come up at once when I tell you to. But if you make a fuss, I shall never let you do that again."

"Yes, Mama," he said soberly, and took John Carpenter's hand in preference to his mother's as they entered the drawing room.

As expected, all Mrs Dewsbury's boarders were gathered there, but not employed in their usual way. The three ladies and Mr Price were sitting on one side of the fire and regarding Dr Field and Mr Peters, who were not playing their usual game of chess but seated beside a visitor.

"Uncle James!" exclaimed John, still holding Dickon's hand. The clergyman looked up and beamed at him.

"Nephew John," he responded. "How well you look. I had scarcely dared hope for such an improvement."

Caroline noticed a muscle in John's jaw quiver, but he maintained his composure and simply said how kind it was of his uncle to say so. "Caroline, this is Canon Carpenter – Uncle, may I present Mrs Randall and Master Dickon Randall."

"Oh, delighted," rumbled the canon, rising to his feet and bowing gallantly over Caroline's hand. He then turned and Dickon's little paw was swallowed up in his huge chubby one. The little boy looked up at the great expanse of black waistcoat with an awed expression, and when his hand was released he moved to his mother and caught hold of her dress.

"I hope you have been introduced to everybody," John said politely, glancing round. They all nodded, and Mr Peters said brightly that he had been telling Canon Carpenter about knowing his father in years gone by. "Really?" John looked at his uncle. "I am sure you were interested, sir?"

Caroline felt the genial smile with which the gentleman greeted this remark to be as insincere as the words that he addressed to his nephew and Mr Peters. "Most certainly. It always pleases me to hear of my dear father, and this gentleman speaks so warmly of him."

Not only the canon but all the other gentlemen were on their feet, Caroline realised and she urged them to sit down, saying that she would not seat herself since she would shortly take her son off to bed.

"And is our young friend to leave us so soon?" asked the canon, smiling benignly. "What a shame!"

"It is past his bedtime and he is tired – say goodnight to everyone, Dickon."

The child submitted to another handshake from the fearsome stranger and then went round the other inhabitants of the room accepting sweets with gratitude but none of his usual enthusiasm, and his mother had little trouble persuading him out of the room and upstairs. He did not say anything until he was in bed, and then he looked up at Caroline and asked in a small voice, "Who's that man?"

"That is Mr Carpenter's uncle, Dickon."

"Don't want to see him again, Mama."

"I do not think you will, love," she said, tucking him in.

"Good." Dickon half sat up, "But I'm not afraid of him!"

Caroline was touched, and said as she pushed him gently back, "He is a very big man, is he not?"

"So up there!" said the child mournfully as he lay down and let her cover him up again. She went quietly into her sitting room, knowing that though he liked her to stay until he was asleep, if she sat beside his bed he was tempted to bounce up, talking or romping, whereas he could see and hear her through the open door he was satisfied and would settle down tranquilly. He seemed quieter than usual, but one could not be sure and the meeting with Canon Carpenter had clearly disturbed him a little.

Caroline had a letter to write to Selina, but could not collect her thoughts enough to start it at that moment and took up some sewing. Dickon's reaction had been surprising, he was a bold little boy and had never shown any apprehension of much taller or larger men. True, he had not encountered one so stout before, but perhaps with a child's instinct he had distrusted his manner. In view of what she had heard from John, she felt sure the Canon's over-enthusiasm masked animosity, "He may be trying to appear, friendly," she thought, "But he must have come to disapprove."

She wondered what was going on downstairs and whether, like Edward, this relation also hoped to get John alone. It was a relief to realise that her son was now so deeply asleep that he would not stir, and she would be able to join the company for tea or coffee. The light had almost gone as she went downstairs, and she found that candles, but not the lamps had been lit in the drawing room. Nor had the doctor and Mr Peters yet embarked upon their game of chess. Such a thing had never happened in the time Caroline had been at Little Manor, and she had the sensation that a way of life had been shaken to its foundations. Apart from John and his uncle, the company was exactly as she had left it, but all gathered together looking angry and animated.

The very room seemed thick with their indignation, and in the brief time before she was drawn into it she gathered a series of swift impressions. Mrs Price in tears, Mr Peters red in the face, Miss Watt talking so fast and so unintelligibly that it was like an angry insect, and Lady Lassiter, flushed and abandoning her dignified manner, was exclaiming *"Oh!"* The effect of that single word was more eloquent than an impassioned speech, expressing what was clearly the consensus of opinion of them all. As Caroline came up to them she turned to her and exclaimed, "That Man!"

"Canon Carpenter?" What had John's uncle done to produce this reaction? They all tried to tell her together, even Mrs Price gulping out some indistinct phrase, and in the hubbub all she could distinguish was the name Mrs Dewsbury. Light began to dawn, and she looked to Mr Price, who though angry seemed most in control of himself, for an explanation.

"Why, shortly after you went upstairs, she came in to say that tea and coffee would be brought in soon, and to offer refreshment. As usual, she said 'Thee' where other people would say 'You'."

"Upon which," broke in Miss Watt, her eyes flashing, "He started up as if he had been stung! Of course one knows that the church looks with disfavour upon Dissenters." Caroline remembered that this lady and the Prices were Methodists, but the others were nominally churchgoers and they seemed equally enraged, nodding agreement when Miss Watt continued, "But dear Mrs Dewsbury!"

Mr Price took up the story. "That anyone could take offence at so pure, so gentle a person, is hard to believe, but the Canon seemed to feel he was polluted by being in the same room as a Quakeress."

"Poor Mrs Dewsbury!" sobbed Mrs Price.

"She of course behaved like a perfect lady and left the room rather than offend," said Lady Lassiter. "Though we all begged her to stay, especially Mr Carpenter."

Caroline was delighted to hear it, and asked how the visitor had reacted to that.

"Badly," said Mr Price. "He even started to read him a lecture, but Mr Carpenter said, 'Not here, Uncle,' and took him off to his own room. The Canon may have been angry, but it is my belief that his nephew was angrier."

"I must say, I would have expected better from my friend Carpenter's son," grumbled Mr Peters. "Fine Christian example of charity! He was not asked to come here, he chose to visit this house so he should have treated the owner with good manners, at least."

Caroline wondered if the Canon had not exaggerated his repugnance in order to make an excuse to see his nephew alone, "But he could simply have requested it," she thought indignantly as Mrs Dewsbury arrived and everyone turned to greet her, with two servants following bringing tea and coffee.

Once the lamps were lit and the curtains drawn, all the boarders gathered round to sympathise with her as she sat and smiled mildly upon them.

"Nay, I am accustomed to that," she said, "Things are a great deal better for Friends these days, I assure you. Why, I remember – Oh, dear, what is happening?"

From behind the closed door to the hall came angry voices, stamping feet, and the banging of the front door. A moment later John Carpenter was in the room, pale with anger and trembling slightly. Immediately he addressed Mrs Dewsbury with contrition. "I do not know how to apologise for my relative," he said. "Believe me, I would never have invited him here, and I am mortified that he should have behaved in such a way."

The old lady smiled at him. "It is what I would have expected," she said a little sadly.

"From a churchman or from a Carpenter? They treated you very shabbily, did they not?"

"Ah, I wondered if thee had heard about that," said Mrs Dewsbury. "Did Penelope speak about it?"

"My mother talked of you as a very dear friend that she had been unable to visit," said John, "But when I was younger she did not explain that she had been forbidden to see you by my grandfather. I think she was trying not to set me against him – or other members of the family. I know now it was only after my father died when my uncles did their best to cause trouble for her. How dared they!"

"No doubt they felt they were in the right, and were saving her from association with people they regarded as ungodly," said Mrs Dewsbury gently. "Remember that her father was scarcely a believer at all. He was a very good man, but even his friends were concerned about him."

"Yes, and they made her chose between him and me!" said John stormily, now seated by Caroline and holding her hand. "I do not know how she bore it, to be separated from one of the remaining objects of her affection when she had lost my father – *he* would not have done that." He looked round the room and said awkwardly, "I am so sorry to obtrude my family disagreements upon you all, I would not have had it happen for the world. However, I think I can safely promise that they will trouble you no more, my uncle has gone away thinking that I am lost beyond recall."

The other boarders murmured something non-committal, possibly unsure whether to commiserate with him or offer congratulations, and Mrs Dewsbury sensibly began to offer tea and coffee so that they dispersed to separate areas of the room, talking quietly and tactfully leaving Caroline and John to sit a little apart, where if they kept their voices down they could converse almost in private.

"How is Dickon? Has he settled after that encounter?"

"Oh, yes," said Caroline.

"Did he speak about my uncle?"

"He told me with great earnestness that he was not afraid of him – you know how he is when he is trying to be brave – but did not want to see any more of him."

"Oh dear – yes!" said John. "It makes me recall so vividly how I felt about Uncle James when I was that sort of age. He is not as tall as all that, but I felt that he loomed over me then. I was very sure that I was afraid! Mind you, he was seldom as affable with me. He would stand and shake his finger at me, and even then I had a sensation that this was aimed at my mother. He has just made it very clear to me that this was so. Would you mind if I told you something of our conversation?"

"If it is not too painful for you," said Caroline.

John gave a short laugh, "I am only afraid that it might be unpleasant for you to hear," he said. "As you may imagine, like my other relations his message was that I should think again before marrying – no mention of how convenient it would be to them all if I did not – he asked what I knew of you – when I already feel closer to you than I do to my own relations! But Uncle James was principally concerned about your spiritual condition. I told him that like me you had been brought up to attend church, and that as I have, you found some aspects of the Established Church unsatisfactory."

"You actually said that? I should have feared that he might explode!"

"He very nearly did," said John, smiling grimly. "It was at that point that he resumed his abuse of our dear Mrs Dewsbury, and told me something I had surmised but never been sure of before, that the Carpenters had more or less forced my poor mother to abandon her friends and family or be exiled from me. He prided himself on having advised his father on that point, and started to vilify my maternal grandfather, a better man than *he* will ever be, churchman though he is." His voice trembled and Caroline remembered how he had spoken of his mother's father to Mrs Dewsbury.

"You sound as if you were fond of him," she ventured.

"I should have been, had I been permitted to know him, they prevented me from seeing him until a little before he died, though my dear mother spoke of him when we were alone. When he was very ill, someone sent for my mother, but she was laid up with a fever, and could not go to him even if they would have let her. I was of age by that time, and a student at Oxford. When I heard from my mother about it, I went to see him, I never spoke of it to Grandfather Carpenter and I do not know if he was ever aware I had done so. My mother was grateful which was all I really needed. I only had a

160

few days with her father and he was dying, but I saw enough of him to regret that I had so little time. He was a fine man, even though by then he had become a complete free thinker – though perhaps not an atheist. But with what pain and distress had he reached that point!

"It cost him his main livelihood, too – he had a small income, and to augment it he had been a schoolmaster and had later taken pupils in his house, which of course ceased. I am sure he would not have tried to influence others even though he could no longer accept the teaching of the church for himself. My mother remained a communicant all her life, though she would not judge other sects as harshly as she was supposed to. I had begun to question things for myself, but it was only because of her that I remained with the church when the attitudes of people like my uncle would have driven me away. *That* was even before I met my other grandfather."

"And your mother was really prevented from seeing her father at all?"

"Yes, was it not shameful? Fortunately my parents were already married when my grandfather left the church, and my father was different from the rest of his family, while he lived she was able to keep up the contact – he had seen me as an infant – but after he died, they treated her shabbily. If my father had not become the heir, I suspect that we would all have been turned out. I do not think my other grandfather ever liked the match very much, my father had been one of the early pupils, that is how they met, but as my father was not then the eldest son, it apparently did not matter so much."

"I did not realise that you had had an older uncle," said Caroline.

"He died of smallpox shortly after I was born. That did make a difference, for though the property is not entailed, my grandfather felt that it ought to go to the eldest son, since my father became that, and I am *his* only child, he regarded me as the heir. We did not always agree, but he knew that I cared more for Coombe Park than his other sons. I am sure both my uncles tried to influence him to leave it to one of them, but I think their efforts merely stiffened his resolve. My Uncle

Edward used to parade his family as being more suitable, which was most unwise, he has two older daughters and when they came to stay they behaved so badly I think I benefited from the contrast. Yes, my grandfather never did like being told what to do, and as you have seen, my uncles can be insistent!"

Caroline nodded. "I only saw the Canon, to speak to, and he was endeavouring to be pleasant to me, but I sensed his antagonism, as Dickon did."

"He no more wishes me to marry than my other uncle does, but I think he found you more to his taste than he expected, once he had met you. I think he would have been an improvement upon my other uncle, had he been able to reclaim us both for the church. But when he learnt that I have practically abandoned it, I fear he thought that this was due to your influence. However, I took some pleasure in informing him that this was a decision I had come to before I had ever met you, at which point he dared to blame my mother! I reminded him what a true churchwoman she had been. So why, he demanded, did I not follow her example? I told him that I wished I could, but she would not have had me be a hypocrite.

"Then I said that though I did not always agree with the Friends, I felt that they and other Dissenters, are more sincere, nearer the true spirit of Christian charity, than his church. And when I added that we had considered marrying at the Friends Meeting House, only it was not practical, he dropped all pretence of friendship. I felt he was sorry he could not call for Bell, Book and Candle! I am so thankful that they do not seem aware that the banns have been called for the last time, I have no doubt that they will make a further effort in a little while, but by the time they do, we will be safely at Coombe Park."

As she prepared for bed that night, Caroline thought over the events of the past few days, feeling relieved that the Carpenter family's attempts to dissuade John had only increased his determination. Though she had spoken so confidently to Nancy, she still found herself questioning her motive for accepting the proposal. One factor was certainly the benefits for Dickon of living at Coombe Park, coupled with the knowledge of how much he liked and admired his future stepfather. The relations might think she was marrying for his money, but he had always been aware that she had an adequate income of her own. She had told him that there was a reasonable sum in trust for her son, she did not doubt that he would have been willing to provide, but was glad that they would not be dependent on his fortune. John had even insisted that she retain control of her legacy, which touched her.

Keeping her background secret did disturb her, but this was the path she had chosen, and the knowledge that neither of them had fallen deeply in love was something she felt grateful for. She had come to like him very much, found him increasingly companionable, and was aware that he both liked and admired her – possibly this was influenced by the similarity with his mother and how she had been treated. Averse as she was to direct lying, she had managed by mentioning certain details of her past to convey an impression of an uncongenial marriage and an escape from the pressures of uncongenial in-laws. Her vision of how the Martin family might have behaved was vivid enough to sound reasonable, and John was anxious to spare her any need to go over it.

"At least," she thought as she got into bed, "I was able to convince him that I was not a runaway wife, if he ever suspected it." The stages by which she had transferred her money away from those who her family might have known, choosing among several recommended by the friends she had made when she left home, and then repeating the process when she left their company, meant that the ones now handling her money really believed her to be a widow.

Part 9

Coombe Park, Wiltshire

August, 1803

"Would you like the paper, my dear?" asked John Carpenter.

Caroline looked up from the coffee pot and smiled. "Not at the moment, thank you," she said. "I will read it when you and Dick have gone out. Would you like some more coffee?"

"Yes, please," said John, passing his cup. The small boy looked up from his plate and made an inarticulate protest, which amused his stepfather. "I know you are anxious to be off, Dick," he said, "But I am going to finish my breakfast first." He turned back to his wife. "Are you sure you will not come with us? It would not take long to order your horse. *Do* change your mind."

As she filled his cup, Caroline considered the offer, but shook her head as she handed him the coffee. "I think not, there is nothing that I would like better, but in the two months since I took up riding again I have been out with you so often that I have seen little of the girls. I really must spend more time with Harriet. I thought I would take her down to the wood. She was saying the other day that she does not go there any more. Nancy prefers to stay on the lawn, you see."

"Nancy doesn't like cows," said Dick scornfully. "She's only happy near the house!"

Caroline frowned at him. "Nancy had lived all her life in London until she came here," she said, "Cows do not wander about near houses there."

"There are horses, though." Dick was unimpressed by this argument. "Nancy is frightened of them, too. She always thinks Admiral is going to bite me!" He gave a superior laugh."

"That will do, Dick," said John firmly. "Nancy is merely concerned about you. We know she need not be, but you must remember that not many females are as good with horses as your mother is."

Caroline chuckled and her husband turned to her eagerly. "Well, you are, my dear," he said. "I am acquainted with many men who have a worse seat on a horse than you have, and know of no other women who are as good."

She was touched and smiled warmly at him. Knowing that horsemanship had been the one accomplishment his mother had not possessed, she valued his praise even though fearing that he exaggerated.

"Well, my dear, I will not press you to ride, I must confess that it had not occurred to me that this might affect Harriet. Dear me, is that the time? I said that we would be at the field they are reaping today by noon." He gulped down his coffee just as a manservant came in to say that the horses had been brought to the front door. Caroline accompanied her husband and son to the door and watched them mount, smiling at the incongruous appearance of the sturdy little pony beside John's large horse, and when they had started down the drive she returned to the house to tell Nancy her plans for the afternoon.

Coombe Park had been built in 1750, and the attic floor was much more spacious than the rooms in Old Manor. The whole of the East side was taken up by the nursery quarters and when Caroline entered it, the big day room was ablaze with sunshine and filled with life.

Harriet Carpenter, with the young nursery maid hanging on to the back of her dress, was standing on a chair by the window looking down at the drive. Nancy was exclaiming at such a procedure, her face turned away from the door as she carried a pile of freshly ironed clothes over to a chest of drawers. The baby was the first person to catch sight of her mother and welcomed her with gratifying enthusiasm, cooing and waving from the wooden cradle that she had so nearly outgrown.

Caroline, as she picked her up and sat down to bounce her on her knee, felt regret that now that she was weaned, Charlotte lived up in the nursery with Harriet. This had been the pattern of her own childhood, and she was sure she spent more time with the babies than her mother had done, but there were times when she thought a little wistfully of the days of Dick's infancy when he had slept in her room and been with her so much more during the day.

Though, she reminded herself, it might have been something of a strain for her son to be so constantly among adults. When he first came to Coombe Park he had not minded spending half his time with toys in the nursery, and there was so much space for him to play, both in and out of doors. With all the responsibility that being the mistress of a household rather than boarding in someone else's involved, Caroline would not have been able to give her little girls the same amount of attention as she had her son. Perhaps they did benefit from inhabiting a well-ordered world of their own.

As a mere visitor to that world, she had to acknowledge that Nancy was its undisputed queen. But how short her reign! Already Dick had been promoted to a room of his own, ate with his elders, and was practically out of nursery jurisdiction. Caroline's entrance must have come to Nancy's notice, even though she had chosen to put her armful of clothes away before greeting her employer. "Nice to see you here at this time, Ma'am," she said, bustling up. "Baby is pleased, too, the lamb! Hasn't she grown, this last month? And look at her hair. Just like Dickon's!"

"Just like mine, too," said Caroline, laughing, as she caressed the red fluff that covered her baby's head. Both women then turned to the window as Harriet became aware of her mother's presence.

"Mama!" she cried joyfully, jumping down, and eluding the little maid came running over, her golden curls dishevelled and her sash coming untied. "I didn't see you come in, I was looking at Papa and Dick. They gone off on horses!"

Nancy, her face suddenly hard, grasped the child's arm and proceeded to brush her hair and neaten her dress, grumbling

166

as she did so at the activities had got her into this state. Harriet pouted for a moment, and then peered at her mother with a grin as the tangles were removed. Nancy's remarks to her were interspersed with sharp comments to the maid, who was tidying the room with scared glances. Bouncing Charlotte on her lap, Caroline looked on with amusement.

Mrs Basset of Islington, she thought, would hardly know her former maid-of-all-work if she could see her these days. Nancy's growth had been permanently stunted and she would never be tall, but some years of country air and adequate food had put colour in her cheeks and substance to her meagre figure. One could never have called her timid, but she now possessed such an air of authority that even Caroline and John would have hesitated to challenge her opinions.

Freed at last, Harriet hurried to her mother and tried to climb on to her lap. Charlotte at ten months old took up far too much of it to leave room for her sister, and the older child protested. "Here, let me take Baby," said Nancy, and put Charlotte down on a rug, while Harriet snuggled up to her mother and gave her an angelic smile. If her blue eyes had not had a glint in them, she would have looked almost too good to be true.

As she plied the baby with toys, Nancy shook her head at her elder charge, "Little madam you are," she informed her. "I don't know what to do with you!" Harriet giggled and buried her face in her mother's shoulder. Nancy addressed Caroline resignedly. "Never know *where* she is – climbing up at that window one minute, down the stairs the next – and that's only indoors. Outside, if I take my eyes off her for a second, she'll be off looking at cows, or trying to get round to the stables!"

Remembering her son's comment that morning, Caroline found it quite difficult to keep a straight face. She gave Harriet a little prod. "Well, what do you say about that, Mischief?"

"Sorry, Nan." The little girl bestowed one of her dazzling smiles upon her disgruntled nurse, who was not proof against it and gave a reluctant twitch of the lips though she shook her head again. Caroline explained her plan to take Harriet out in the afternoon, when she had eaten her lunch.

167

"There, now," said Nancy as the child began to wriggle with excitement, "Aren't you a lucky girl? Would you wish me to take little Charlotte out on the lawn as usual, Ma'am?"

"If you don't mind," said Caroline.

"Oh no, get on with my worsted, I can," said Nancy cheerfully. Since Charlotte could not walk at all and did not crawl very far, she could be left to the nursery maid to supervise, whereas Harriet demanded more activity. Caroline smiled and stayed on with her daughters for a little while before visiting the kitchen to discuss dinner. She then spoke to the butler and by noon she was able return to the breakfast room for some food and a cup of chocolate before walking out with Harriet.

When she had eaten, she collected the paper from the side table where John had left it and sat down in the sun by an open window to glance through it while she sipped the hot drink. Nothing remarkable seemed to have happened, and by the time she had skimmed through the news, she fell back as often before, on the Births, Deaths, and Marriages. What extraordinary names some people had! Fancy a Plover marrying a Peacock. Oh, some poor girl dead at sixteen. Caroline thought of her little sister and wondered how the rest of her family were – Selina had not mentioned them recently... quite a full account of a funeral service of a Martin, of Lincolnshire. Thomas Ainsley Martin, aged thirty-eight. "Mourned by his widow, an infant son, and a daughter, his widowed mother, and his sisters."

Slightly shocked, she looked up from the paper and found the familiar lawns almost an unexpected sight. This could only be the man she had known, Dick's father was actually dead. Close though this man had once been to her she had never regretted that their relationship had come to an end, and having implied his death for the past eight years, it seemed almost indecent to read of his funeral. At least if her son began to ask about his father, she could honestly tell him that he had died.

She thought of the chance accident outside Selina's door, which showed how strange meetings could happen, the likelihood of Thomas Martin reappearing in her life had always been small, but she was glad to think that it could not now happen. Her thoughts led on to reflection about the Carpenters. With the exception of Augusta, who had married and seemed happy to correspond, John's relations had fortunately kept their distance, though she suspected that they took delight in the fact that she had so far given him only daughters. Nevertheless, girls could inherit Coombe Park, which would diminish their satisfaction, but they were probably right to think that he would like an heir to his name as well as to his estate – was it not natural? Caroline thought of her own father, and felt more sympathy for his desire for his name to continue.

The hot sun and her drifting thoughts had put her in an almost trance-like state from which she was roused by hearing the hall clock strike two. Harriet would be ready soon, and she went to her bedroom to freshen up and put on a hat, emerging from the front door just as Nancy and her entourage came round from the back regions. Charlotte was in her nurse's arms, with Harriet trotting by her side wearing a bright straw sunbonnet that nearly matched the curls underneath. Nancy carried a bag but the little maid brought up the rear burdened with rugs and toys for the baby's amusement. Caroline felt a little sorry for the girl, but she seemed cheerful enough, and was at least being paid for what she would have had to do at home for her mother.

It was tempting to stay for a little to watch the baby roll about and suddenly try to pull herself up on the bench near the rug, but Harriet, clutching a small basket, grasped her mother firmly by the hand and dragged her away to the bushes that divided the area from the wider expanse of the West Lawn where she let go and skipped merrily ahead, singing to herself and looking about but not seeming to need entertainment as they crossed the grass, plunged into a shady yew alley, and emerged by an ornamental lake. Caroline's thoughts returned to the piece she had seen in the paper, and she found herself wondering if Thomas Martin had ever speculated about her. Had he been happy with the wife described as "sorrowing?" Caroline imagined her as small and meek, remembering his description of the young woman his father had had in mind for him as a "Silly little thing". Perhaps that would have appealed to him after his experience with a woman of independent ideas. He might not have married that one, but no doubt his family would have found a similar girl for him on his return and she was sure that he would have valued meekness. Thomas Martin in charge of a household, looked up to by his family! The picture almost made her laugh.

A little splash brought her back to her immediate concerns. A small stone had been knocked into the water by flying feet as Harriet raced away towards the wood. She was really a little too near the lake, and Caroline called out to her. An impish smile over the shoulder was the only sign that her daughter had heard her.

"Oh, you minx!" she exclaimed, and abandoning the decorum proper to a settled matron, she picked up her skirts and gave chase, greatly to Harriet's surprise. The child paused when she saw her mother in pursuit, and chortled as Caroline reached her and caught her, swinging her off her feet.

"Oh, Mama! – I didn't know you could run!" she cried.

Caroline began to laugh at the open admiration in her tone. "Why, yes, I think I can run faster than you, love," she said.

"Nancy can't," said Harriet, clearly taking her nurse as typical of the older generation. Of course, with a lame father, she had probably never before seen an adult move very fast.

Caroline put her down on the grass again and remarked dryly, "Well, now that you know I can catch you, don't you go running off again. Especially so near the lake – you might fall in."

"Oh," said Harriet. "Wouldn't I like that?"

"I should not think so. Not only would you get very wet, but we should have to go straight back to the house instead of going to the wood."

"No!" the child clutched at her mother. "I won't fall in, I promise. Will you run after me again, Mama?"

170

"Perhaps," said Caroline, still amused at the result of her instinctive pursuit. Harriet ran forward a few steps and looked up provocatively, but her mother shook her head. "Not now, we are too near the lake. And you will tire yourself out before we get to the wood if you rush about so much." She was aware that it had been because she had been distracted by thoughts of the past that the little girl had tried to attract her attention, and taking the hand that was not carrying a basket, she asked why she had brought it.

"Debbie said there might be blackberries, or nuts. And I could pick some flowers, to put on the table." Debbie was the nursery maid.

"Flowers, yes," said Caroline. "But I doubt if the blackberries will be ripe yet and it is a little early for nuts. We will have to see what we can find."

"Nancy said if there were blackberries I could have them for my supper," said Harriet, hopefully.

"Well, we may find a few, it has been a fine summer, but you mustn't mind if we do not. It is only August, and when I was a little girl we never thought of blackberries until September."

"Did you have a basket?" Harriet asked, admiring hers. It was made of plaited straw and had been bought by her half-brother at the Spring Fair. Caroline could not remember having had anything like it. She thought of the expedition to pick blackberries in her childhood, almost a ritual in which her mother and the babies and the nurses had sallied forth, carrying a picnic on the back of a donkey in baskets which were later used to put the fruit in.

They had now reached the wood, pleasantly cool after the glare of the sun by the lake. Harriet bustled round, exclaiming at every patch of flowers she came to. Caroline sat down on a fallen tree and watched her. Presently she came up looking puzzled, holding up a foot. "Clean!" she said, pointing to her shoes. "No mud!"

"No," agreed Caroline.

"There was lots of mud when we came before," said Harriet. "Nancy was cross."

171

"That was just after it had been raining, I remember. There hasn't been any rain for weeks."

"Where's the mud gone, Mama?"

"It is still there, but it is dry earth now," Caroline explained. "If it were to rain again, you would see the mud come back."

The little girl stamped, sending up a fine shower of dust from the bare ground near an old rabbit hole. "Is that dry mud, then?"

"I suppose you could call it that," said her mother, amused.

Harriet broke into a beaming smile. "Oh, *funny!*" she said. "I'll tell Nancy we found some mud, but it was all dry!"

Caroline laughed and got up from the log. "Shall we go and look for the pond, we might find some mud there."

The pond in the heart of the wood was dark and mysterious, eerily reflecting the trees and bushes round in dark depths. In spite of the dry weather it was quite full, since it was fed by a spring, and the stream which flowed out of it led to the lake, having been dammed to create the ornamental water at the whim of some landscaper for John's great-grandfather.

Harriet found the place fascinating, but seemed a little apprehensive. She held her mother's hand tightly as they followed a path round it, and gave a little gasp as they left it behind and came out in another clearing. "Black in there," she observed. "Not as pretty as the lake."

"No, it is a wild pond," said Caroline, "Just as these flowers are wild, and the ones in the garden tame." Wild, yes, she thought. She had felt something elemental and disturbing about that deep water, it was interesting that the child instinctively shrank from it.

They went on through more scattered trees, and in shafts of sunlight Harriet ran about picking flowers and looking at any bush that might conceivably carry blackberries. She pointed to some dark berries and asked if she could pick them. Caroline did not think that they were Deadly Nightshade but felt they would not be good to eat.

172

"No, love, they are not blackberries, you must not pick them, they might be poisonous."

"What does that mean?"

"Very bad. It would make you sick. You must remember, Harriet, not to pick any berries unless I say they are all right." Caroline did not want to frighten the child, but she spoke earnestly and her tone must have conveyed conviction, producing a sober promise. Disappointingly, they did not find any ripe blackberries, though they did come across a patch of late wild strawberries. There were too few of these to be worth taking home and they ate them there and then.

Harriet gave a sigh. "Oh, that was nice, but I did want some blackberries!"

"In September we might all come, with baskets and bring food," said Caroline, as they emerged from the wood to a stretch of grass leading to the drive.

"Oh, yes!" said Harriet joyfully. She seemed a little tired and was quite pleased to sit on a dry hummock and rest. Her basket was nearly full of flowers, and she began to take them out and ask their names, handling them with great gentleness. This, and her interest, was a surprise to her mother as she searched her memory for names that she had once known well. Surely she had not taken this sort of interest in them when a child? Certainly not at three and a half! At that age, her favourite occupations had been things like rolling in the grass and making mud pies.

But she had been a sturdy little thing, and even when older, her tastes had run much more to boyish pursuits. She had a sudden vision of herself at about ten being dragged out of a game of cricket by a scandalised Miss Yare, which she had joined with some of the village children. Since she had learned to play with the sons of some neighbours, she was still not sure if it were the game, the company, or her age that had upset the gentle governess. Harriet was a much more dainty and feminine creature than her mother had been, resembling Lucy much more than the sister whose name she bore. Yes, the small Lucy had been enthusiastic about flowers at a young age. At about four she had triumphantly made a daisy chain to

173

put round the baby's neck. Visualising this occasion, Caroline found a disturbing picture superimposed on it, of the eighteen-year-old Lucy making a daisy chain in the rose garden. Harriet Randall came upsettingly to her mind for the second time that day. She looked away for a moment in case the pain should show on her face and perhaps distress her child.

"We go on now?" asked Harriet cheerfully, putting the flowers back in the basket. Caroline looked gratefully at her healthy little face, and nodded.

Shortly they came in sight of the drive, and the child gave a sigh of satisfaction. "I have had a nice time, Mama," she said. "I wish you could come out with me every day, but I s'pose you will go out riding again with Papa and Dick.

Caroline felt torn, especially when the child continued by wishing she could ride with her parents and brother. "Nancy says I am too little, but am I?"

"Perhaps not. You will be four in January, and I was about that age when I learnt to ride. We will have to see. I will talk to Papa about it, but don't speak of it to anyone until I have." She could imagine Nancy's horror at the thought, but once it became official, the idea would have to be accepted.

"No, Mama. Oh, look, they are coming!"

"Who are, Harriet dear?"

"Papa, and Dick – look, on the drive." Sure enough, the horse and the pony were coming into sight. Dick waved his hat, John beamed, and they stopped as they drew level, so that Harriet could have a ride to the house.

The library at Coombe Park faced south west. It was long room with big windows looking out over the country side and Caroline and John liked sitting there in the evening, particularly in Summer. Dick had dined with his mother and stepfather and had then been dispatched, protesting, to an early bed after his long ride in the heat of the day. The last rays of the sunlight were still patterning the floor when Caroline and her husband settled down to drink their coffee. She was absorbed in a difficult piece of sewing, but presently looked up to find John leaning back in his chair with his eyes closed, the half-read newspaper lying on his lap. The day must have been something of a strain, but she suppressed the deep compassion that the sight aroused, knowing how much he hated sympathy. After a minute or so, he roused himself and began to read again.

Caroline's needle moved more and more slowly as she watched him, and her concentration apparently communicated itself to him. He looked up, "My dear! Is something troubling you? You did see all you wanted in this paper, did you not?" she said hastily that she was sorry if she had disturbed him.

"Not at all, I simply felt that you were disturbed yourself, but perhaps it is the effect of the heat? I was thinking how much more I seem to feel it myself, than I did when I was young Dick's age. I hope it has not been too much for you."

"No – no. I had a nice shady hat and kept out of the sun most of the time," said Caroline and bent to her work, careful not to look up till he had returned to reading. It was a strange feeling that he might at that moment be reading about the death of Thomas Martin, and it would mean nothing to him. This was how she wanted it, but the thought was rather uncomfortable, all the same. As she worked on she filled her mind with other thoughts, and all at once the nightly miracle broke upon them as the setting sun turned the sky red, pink, soft purple and yellow, and the whole room seemed to be under an enchantment. John laid down the paper and Caroline suspended her needle while they watched the performance until there was only a deep glow on the horizon. Then John gave a sigh. "I never tire of that," he said.

"The promise of tomorrow," observed Caroline.

"What a lovely phrase – where did you hear it?"

"I am not sure. I may even have made it up."

"It is beautiful. The hope of a new day as well as the end of the old one. Some sunrises are splendid, too, but so often they mean rain. And one so seldom has time to sit and look at it."

There was not enough light to sew or read by and until the lamps were lit, they sat quietly conversing about the day's activities John spoke of the harvesting and the pleasure that Dick had taken in being allowed to help. He mentioned how a fellow landowner passing by had spoken of what a good seat the boy had. Caroline smiled, "I thought Dick seemed rather pleased with himself," she said. "He is a little wretch, though."

"How in particular?"

"Why, I was thinking of the way he spoke about Nancy at breakfast. I am glad that she could not hear him, she would have been so hurt – she dotes on him, you know, and he seems quite indifferent."

John looked a little sheepish. "I am afraid that is all too natural. I remember saying much the same sort of thing about my old nurse, and my mother reproaching me! Old Biddy used to run after me as if I were a duckling and she a hen horrified at it taking to the water!" Caroline chuckled and agreed that this was a good description of Nancy. "Oh, Biddy was much worse than Nancy. She had been with us since my grandmother was a bride. She nursed my father and all my uncles, and when I was a child she seemed more important than my grandfather. She was a dear old creature and stood by my mother always. My father had been her favourite and the bride he had chosen must be right. I realised how splendid she was when I was older! depend upon it, Dick will come round in time. He is simply in rebellion against nursery government at the moment."

"Oh, I know," said Caroline. "And I was a naughty enough child myself, I know how Dick feels when she fusses over him. But he must learn to respect Nancy's feelings."

"He respects yours, and mine, I think," said John gravely. "He is really a kind-hearted little fellow. You must not be too hard upon him."

"I will try," she promised, quietly amused at the incongruous rebuke coming from a stepfather. She did not really think that her son was growing callous, but thinking of Thomas Martin had reminded her of aspects of his character that she did not want Dick to inherit. Had that man been taught to consider the feelings of others, when a child. Would his philanthropy have slipped away so easily when he came into his fortune, if his concern was from the heart as well as the head?

"He was in rebellion against his father, but his female relations must have indulged him," she thought with hindsight. "It is a pity Nancy is so afraid of animals," she observed, "That makes things worse."

"Ah, he will come to regard that with indulgence," said John. "Indeed, while we rode I suggested that it was rather unmanly to despise people for their weaknesses. That seemed to have some effect."

"I should imagine that it would, coming from you," said Caroline gratefully. "And it is perfectly right to feel that he must grow away from female influence."

"Oh, but it would never do for him to have no female company!" said John. "That is why I should not like him to go away to school."

"Well, I am happy that he will not have to, thank goodness you are not only able but willing to teach him. He has quite got beyond my little stock of Latin. You had an excellent tutor."

"Yes, I was fortunate, it was one thing for which I was grateful to my grandfather. He was more of a scholar than many people knew, and I think he distrusted the education his eldest son obtained at a public school. I like to teach Dick, it keeps my mind alert and it is interesting to see his mind developing. If I had had to earn my living I might have become a schoolmaster, or a private tutor."

"I wish I could say the same," said Caroline. "I do not mind teaching my own children, but some other mama's spoilt darling would not appeal. No, I would never have done as a governess!"

John smiled, but his mind seemed to be elsewhere, and after a moment he remarked, "Harriet appears to have enjoyed her outing to the wood. Didn't she look delightful with her little basket of flowers."

"She did indeed," said Caroline fondly. "I believe that she is going to be a beauty John."

"And why should she not be? She does not have a plain mother, after all."

Caroline smiled. "It is nice to hear you say so, but I was never a beauty. Harriet takes some of her best features from you, particularly her nose. Mine is not straight enough."

"Is she at all like your sister?" asked John unexpectedly.

With Harriet Randall in mind, Caroline was momentarily startled, till she remembered that when they had been choosing a name for their first baby she had welcomed the chance to speak naturally of some part of her past life without having to explain what had become of her family. John had been touched at the story, and pleased to have a name that had no associations with the Carpenters.

"Our Harriet was fair, but her hair was paler, and though I did not realise it at the time, I think even as a child she was not so robust." Caroline's voice trailed away dismally and John leant over and kissed her gently, saying he was sorry to have pained her.

She took his hand and held it between her own. "No, that does not pain me unbearably, it is simply that I always feel so helpless when I think back, if only there had been something I could have done. I was thinking of her only this afternoon – but there! Who can say she would have had a happy life had she lived? I wish she could have had the chance, but who knows what might have been in store for her."

"Who indeed," said John gravely. "But you are glad to have her name revived in our daughter?"

"Oh, I am." After sitting in silence for a while, Caroline gave a sudden gurgle of laughter, and explained to her disconcerted husband about Harriet's sudden dash away and finding her mother in pursuit. He chuckled.

"I wish I could have seen that," he said. "My mother could run, I remember, but it shocked my relations to see her chase me when I was small. But why should she not? Or you, either."

"Well, I cannot think," said Caroline. "I suppose some people would say that it lacks dignity. You should have seen her face when I caught her up, it was a study. She is a bright

178

child, though. I think I shall have to start giving her lessons soon. Did you notice how she had all the wild-flowers named by heart? I only told her once."

"Oh, she is the cleverest little girl I have ever seen," said John proudly. "She was so delighted when I took her up before me!" His words reminded Caroline of something that Harriet had said to her.

"She wished she could ride, so that she could come with us when I go out with you and Dick."

"My dear, what a wonderful idea. I was thinking the other day that Dick is really outgrowing the pony, it is a trifle slow for him, but a good-natured beast, ideal for a child to start on. But is she old enough, do you think?"

"Very nearly, I was little older when I had my first lesson. It would mean that I did not have to choose between you or the child."

"That would be a great advantage," said John. "Dick is a delightful companion, but one needs adult company sometimes, and I much prefer yours."

Caroline was moved. Her husband occasionally rode out with some of his old companions but doing so tended to leave him feeling irritated, other men did not appear to understand that his injury had had very little effect on his skill once mounted. In spite of the damage to his leg, he could grip as well as ever, and he was naturally annoyed when his friends endeavoured to pick an easy route for his benefit. It was not so much that as a woman, she could allow him to do that without loss of face, since as he had remarked that morning, she rode as well as many men, as the fact that she was not embarrassed by his disability and trusted him to know what he was capable of.

He was happily planning Harriet's riding lessons, "In the paddock at first, of course, then – Oh, dear! Charlotte."

"She is too little to ride yet, except perhaps in a basket on a donkey."

John laughed. "Of course she is! I did not mean that – only that this would mean that she was left alone in the nursery."

"Oh, not all the time, it will be quite a while before Harriet will be able to go far. And Charlotte is a placid child. At the moment her chief concern is managing to stand on her own. She will certainly not miss Harriet, especially if the lessons take place when she has her sleep."

"Ah, no," said John. They had gone to look at the girls in the nursery after seeing Dick into bed and he was clearly envisaging this as he spoke. "She is going to be pretty too."

"Ye-es," said Caroline. "It is a shame about her hair, though."

"It is beautiful hair!" John sounded indignant. "Exactly like her mother's!"

"That was what I meant – poor child having that inflicted on her."

"But I love your hair," he protested. She sighed and said that it had been the bane of her life, and that just about every fault that she had had as a child had been ascribed to it, particularly her hot temper.

"That is nonsense, mine is quite as bad without that excuse. I won't have you abuse yours – it is like the sunset."

"Oh, John, what a compliment!" cried Caroline in delight. "I cannot say I have ever really minded the colour myself, but it was trying to be told I ought to be ashamed of it."

"Because of the temper? People are always ready to blame others for their own shortcomings. I have no patience with it. In fact I think it is downright dishonest."

"The way they refuse to listen to arguments that they do not agree with, preferring to blame it all on temper in someone else?"

"Yes, exactly," said John. "It nearly drove me mad as a child, and it was the worst thing about my relations. Now if *you* disagree, you are prepared to say so, and even admit that you could be in the wrong."

"Reluctantly," said Caroline with a smile.

He laughed, "Yes, but you behave like a human being!"

She understood what he was talking about. His mother had been perhaps too patient, and his grandfather almost totally intolerant. Between those two extremes, the natural impulses of his hot temper must have been constantly frustrated. A meek wife would never have done for John! He needed some one to question his initial reactions. With a meek wife, he might have developed into a tyrant like his late grandfather. No likelihood of that, with Caroline.

PART 10

A house in Bath

September 1807

The rooms seemed suitable enough – surely? Of course, lodgings in Bath would seem cramped after the comfort of a mansion, but as Selina hesitated over the size of the sitting room, a voice from the doorway said, "I am sure I hope your friends will be comfortable here, Mrs Penry," and she turned to find that she was being observed.

Trying not to feel guilty, she stammered out, "Oh, thank you, Mrs Oakley. I only wished to see the rooms again..." This was dreadful. The woman would despise her. Selina drew herself up to her full five feet and hoped she was managing to look impressive. "But of course I cannot say for certain what Mrs Carpenter will think, though it all seems very nice to me," she said rather weakly.

Mrs Oakley surveyed the little sitting room complacently. "Well it's generally been good enough before. I can count on one hand the complaints I've had in twenty years!"

"Really? I am pleased to hear that. Mrs Brewis recommended you very highly, you know."

The woman nodded graciously. "Mrs Brewis speaks well of you, Mrs Penry. She says you are one of the nicest ladies she has had in her house. 'It has been a privilege to have Mrs Penry in my house,' she said to me the other day."

"Oh!"said Selina, taken aback. It would not have occurred to her that her landlady might have given her a good reference to Mrs Oakley.

"You had a very sad loss a little while ago, she tells me."

"My husband?" Selina's eyes filled with tears. "Indeed. We had been married for fourteen years and never a quarrel."

"My word!" Mrs Oakley seemed genuinely impressed. "That's something, that is. Mr Oakley and me, we had our ups and downs, but he was a good man for all that, and I miss him. I know just how you feel."

At that moment, Selina was feeling chiefly bewildered, uneasily aware that she should be suppressing this familiarity, but not knowing how to do so without giving offence.

"Did you say you hadn't seen your friend since your wedding?" Selina couldn't remember having done so, but perhaps she had mentioned how long it had been since she and Caroline had met. "Mrs Brewis said as you had lived in Wales."

"Yes, and Mrs Carpenter was in London till she married and moved to Wiltshire." Selina did not really want to discuss her friend with this woman, but as she turned away to look at Caroline's letter, she found this brought a sort of painful satisfaction. Thinking of the meeting to come occupied so much of her mind that she could not speak of anything else, especially as the conversation had reopened the misery into which she had been plunged into by the loss of a beloved husband.

It appeared that Mrs Oakley was settling down to wait with her, and Selina's heart sank. Afraid that a rebuff might make the woman antagonistic, she wished that she could find some excuse to move to the outside door, and was for once thankful to hear an upheaval from the kitchen which caused the landlady to dash off, leaving the visitor alone with her anticipations. It was difficult to keep up even the pretence that she had merely come to examine the rooms. Caroline's letter had been very precise; she required two or three upstairs rooms for children and nurses, accommodation for a maid and a manservant, and a sitting-room, and bedroom on the ground floor. John Carpenter was having such trouble with his injured leg he would find the narrow stairs of lodgings very difficult to cope with.

This house appeared to have all that was needed, the rooms seemed decent and well kept and what more could one want for a stay of a few months? But until she came to Bath,

Selina had never taken rooms in her life – Caroline, she knew, was quite experienced about this. It was flattering to be asked to arrange it, but fraught with anxiety.

She moved restlessly about the room, afraid to sit down in case Mrs Oakley returned and considered her to be taking a liberty. Besides, she was too nervous to settle. To be seeing Caroline again after all this time, it was like a dream come true. But suppose, despite their regular correspondence, they were to discover that they no longer had much in common. And might her friend be so altered that Selina did not know her. For that matter, would Caroline recognise Selina? Had she changed? She moved to the mirror and peered at her reflection. The small fair-skinned face with large eyes that looked earnestly back at her did not seem any different from her appearance on her wedding day. In spite of her recent bereavement it was remarkably little lined, and the soft brown hair that showed beneath her widow's cap had no grey in it even if she had rather guiltily pulled out one whitened hair a day or so ago.

"But I am thirty-seven!" she thought. "That age used to seem like dotage." Her friend was a few months older. Caroline would now be thirty-eight. With four children! Would she really be the person Selina remembered?

Perhaps she would resemble Mrs Randall – no, she was too much her father's daughter for that. Selina would know soon enough, anyway, it might be better to concentrate on her friend as she had last seen her, the tall lively girl who had brought a ray of brightness to the dull depression of a dutiful childhood, and had returned from London to whisk her away from the terrors of the Coleman's plans to the calm security of a marriage that had only stopped short of perfection by being childless.

All she could bring to mind was a general impression of Caroline, she had never had a picture of her, and she found it difficult to recall her features. The flaming hair could never be forgotten, but were her eyes blue, or brown, or grey like Selina's own? She might not have Lucy's beauty, perhaps, but all the same she made one glad to look at her. Oh, Caroline had once complained that she did not have a nice straight nose, "Like yours." But surely she had been joking. There was nothing unusual about it. Thoughtfully rubbing her own nose, Selina unconsciously straightened a cushion, vaguely aware that the sounds from the basement had ceased.

"Not arrived yet?" Mrs Oakley surged in fresh from a triumphant battle with her cook.

"Er – no, not yet."

"Ah, they'll be glad of their dinner when they get here, I'm sure. Which," said Mrs Oakley jubilantly, "Will be ready – I can assure you of that!"

"Oh, good," said Selina weakly, hoping she would be spared a detailed account of the recent domestic encounter. The woman had taken a deep breath, but something else seemed to have struck her, and a much more kindly smile spread over her face.

"The children, specially. You said that there were four?"

Yes, this had been the most important part of the recommendation, the fact that Mrs Oakley was genuinely fond of children and had willingly accepted ones that Mrs Brewis considered rather spoilt.

"Two of each, did you say?"

"That is so. A boy of twelve, girls of seven and four, and a baby boy." Selina sighed as she mentioned them and the landlady gave a sympathetic smile.

"Ah, that's nice. A nice little family. I had the four myself, you know, but only reared two. Well, well, I suppose that's better than nothing. Bless me, whatever is that girl doing?" The crash had come from upstairs this time, and Mrs Oakley went swiftly to the bottom of the stairs and called out, "Sally? Sallee, come down here at once." The maid did not appear, and with a thrown word of apology, Mrs Oakley charged up the stairs just as Selina heard the sound of wheels in the street outside. Gladly she darted to the front door, pulling it almost shut behind her.

Two carriages had drawn up in the street outside, from the first of which two children were already descending. She only caught a glimpse of a mop of red curls as the boy slipped

185

round to talk to the groom and horses, but the little girl paused on her way to the second carriage, bobbed a curtsey, and gave Selina a delightful smile before running to the assistance of the newly wakened child, who had just been set on her feet by a nursery maid. Her cheeks were flushed and she was rubbing her eyes with one hand while she clutched at her sister with the other.

A tall man was clambering stiffly out of the first carriage using two sticks but sharply refusing the aid of a manservant. She felt nervously sorry for him as she watched him reach the ground and turn back. Lame though he might be, John Carpenter would clearly let no-one else hand his wife out. Selina found herself breathing rather fast as the lady came into view. Tall, the flaming hair she remembered showing under a neat little hat, the main difference in Caroline seemed to be in the changed fashions, and the warm glow of her smile seemed to embrace her friend standing in the doorway.

"Selina! How lovely to see you again!" she cried, and Selina came joyfully down the three steps to greet her. Caroline kissed her heartily and then turned to indicate her husband, "This is John, as you must have guessed. John, this is Selina Penry of whom I have so often spoken."

"I am delighted to meet you at last," said John Carpenter, looking down from his great height and giving a smile that changed Selina's mind about him at once. Pain, and the discomfort of the journey perhaps, had given him such a severe expression that she had almost wondered that her friend could have brought herself to marry such a sombre man. The smile also took years from his appearance.

"Dick, come and be introduced," called Caroline, and the boy tore himself away from the horses he had been petting, giving Selina an impish smile and a little bow before, finding himself almost exactly her height, he gave her a quick peck on the cheek, and blushing slightly, returned to the carriage to collect up some books.

Caroline chuckled. "That is a great compliment, from Dick," she said. "He rarely kisses people without being prompted." Selina was indeed delighted. She watched her

186

friend move to the other carriage and take a baby from the arms of a plump and bustling person who must surely be Nancy. "My other son, Selina. This is our Johnnie."

"Oh, isn't he a love? May I hold him?"

"He is a shocking weight," Caroline warned her, "Only eight months old but he feels more like a year! I think they get bigger every time." He was a heavy baby, but Selina did not mind, it was such a delight to hold the warm bundle in her arms, and look down at the little face with its fine lashes and rosy cheeks. The baldness of his head was just beginning to be relieved by a quiff of downy fair hair. He looked up at the new face in a puzzled way, but evidently decided that she was harmless, cooed, and then began to suck his thumb.

Mrs Oakley emerged, the tear-stained Sally following behind her and Selina introduced the Carpenters to their new landlady. The party began to move towards the house, John, his servant, a maid, Dick, the nursery maid burdened with bundles, and then Nancy who firmly but respectfully relieved Selina of the baby. She stood gazing wistfully after him as he was carried inside, until Caroline took her by the arm and led her over to the two little girls standing hand in hand looking round them in wonder at the buildings around them.

"Here are my daughters, Selina," said Caroline, "This is Harriet, and Charlotte is the one with hair like mine. This is Mrs Penry, children, what do you say to her?"

"Oh, Harriet saw me before everyone else," Selina assured her, smiling at the child. "She has already greeted me most charmingly."

Harriet looked up and gave another peculiarly sweet smile. "How do you do, Mrs Penry?" she said politely. "I didn't say anything, Mama, I only curtseyed. Say how do you do, Charley, and curtsey as I showed you." She gave her little sister a gentle push, but Charlotte seemed too shy, putting her head back she gazed up with big grey-green eyes, the exact shade of her mother's, and only managed a fleeting smile before running to Caroline, who picked her up and petted her.

"Poor love, she is tired," she remarked. "It is the first time she has been on such a long journey."

"Oh yes," said Selina, looking yearningly at the little creature. A small hand slid into hers, and she found Harriet looking confidingly up at her. "Will you show us the house, Mrs Penry?" she asked as they moved towards the front door.

The sitting room seemed smaller than it had, crowded as it was with large people and there was a perpetual ebb and flow between the house and the carriages. Harriet's grip tightened a little, and Selina understood her reaction, she felt small and underfoot herself and was glad when Caroline turned from a discussion with Mrs Oakley and proposed taking Charlotte up to join the nurses and the baby, no, she assured the landlady, her friend could show them the way, she would not keep her from the dinner preparation any longer. They were soon upstairs in the larger bedroom, where Nancy was gloomily unpacking clothes for the children.

"That girl, Ma'am, is a slut," she informed Caroline. "The rooms will do well enough, but I don't think she's done them properly – look at that!" she gestured towards the washstand, where a very plain white jug was in noticeable contrast to the elaborate basin and soap dish. Selina now understood the altercation, and felt almost guilty herself.

"I do, do hope it will be all right," she said nervously.

Nancy looked up and gave her a considering though not unfriendly stare. "Oh, it will do," she said grudgingly. "It's that girl I can't get over. I've been in her position myself, so I know what has to be done, but she – well, never mind." Her attention was deflected as Caroline put Charlotte down. "There, there, poor lamb, she's worn out. Can they have their dinner up here, Ma'am? It is what they are used to, after all, though not at this hour. I daresay it will be a bother to that girl, but just for tonight she'll have to put up with it."

"Yes, I think it would be better," said Caroline. "Harriet, love, would you rather stay with Nancy and the little ones, or come down to dinner with us?"

Harriet, still holding Selina's hand, hesitated. "Will you be there, Mrs Penry?"

"I am afraid not, my dinner will be ready for me when I get home." Selina looked at her friend, "Even without that, I would not like to intrude…"

"We hope you will dine with us, often," said Caroline, "But everything is in such confusion tonight. And you are expected at your lodgings for the meal?"

Selina nodded. Harriet let her hand go and held up her face for a kiss before saying to her mother that she thought she would prefer to stay up with Nancy and the others.

Selina had a faint hope that on the way downstairs she might be able to have a private word with Caroline, but when they came out on the landing, Dick came rushing up carrying things for the room he was to occupy, Mrs Oakley appeared, followed by the Carpenter's servants, bearing luggage. Their progress down was almost like a dance figure, now stepping round the maid, now flattening themselves against the wall to avoid the footman, with Dick on their heels and the landlady behind him.

John Carpenter was already settled in the sitting room with his bad leg resting on a footstool, and his stepson went over to ask him something. Selina turned to find Mrs Oakley was apologising for the shortcomings of her maid.

"A raw girl, Mrs Carpenter, I doubt if she will do, but I've only just taken her on and I must give her a trial. I just wanted to say, the little girls can have their meals up in their room, every day if you like."

"Thank you, but I do not think that will be necessary," said Caroline, the quietness of her voice more effective than the landlady's vehemence. "I can see how difficult that would be. After today, when they have recovered, the girls will be well able to dine with the rest of us and not give you too much extra work." Almost meekly, Mrs Oakley went off to give her instructions, and turning to her friend, Caroline remarked in an undertone, "Anything to keep Nancy and that maid apart as much as possible!"

"Do you anticipate trouble?" Selina murmured back, rather nervously.

"As a Londoner, Nancy is somewhat outspoken, and as she says, she was once a maid-of-all-work in a boarding house and knows how it should be done. Oh, Selina, do not look so distressed! This is a very suitable house, you have chosen well for us."

"Have I really? But – what about Mrs Oakley!"

Caroline laughed. "I can manage Mrs Oakley, don't worry."

"I believe you can," said Selina wonderingly.

"Do not be foolish, my dear. You do not do yourself justice." Caroline checked herself, "Ah, here she comes again."

"Is that the time? I must go now, my dinner will be on the table shortly. I will call tomorrow, if I may? I am sure you will want to take things easy this evening."

Looking back at her husband, whose face still bore that look of strain, Caroline nodded. "Thank you for your consideration, we appreciate it, I am sorry to have so little time with you, after all these years, it is so good of you to understand."

Selina kissed her quickly, nodded to Dick and his stepfather and said goodbye to Mrs Oakley with some relief. To reach the door she had another dance step to take round the footman, but he was nimble and she slight, and they avoided a collision.

She walked back to her lodgings in a bemused state. Images danced through her mind, she could almost feel the weight of the baby in her arms, the way Harriet had clung to her, and the touch of Dick's kiss on her cheek, but most of all she was marvelling at how little fourteen years had changed their mother. There was a difference, though. Selina could not at first think where it lay. Caroline still carried with her the atmosphere of exhilaration that had always stirred and stimulated her more timid friend. Was she calmer? Or quieter? Some of her aggressiveness seemed to have softened. That part of her personality was still there, as her dealings with Mrs Oakley had shown, but she no longer wore it as armour against the rest of the world. And her greeting had been so much more demonstrative. In the past, possibly in reaction to the sentimentality of other women, she had been almost aloof even with friends.

Selina, naturally affectionate, had experienced little warmth from her family, and would have welcomed the occasional hug from her friend, but fearing the sharp tongue so often unleashed upon others, she had been grateful to know that Caroline cared and not asked for more. Now it occurred to her that faced with false emotion, her friend had developed an aversion to all sentiment as a protection. On the very few occasions when both girls had been in company with young child, it had been Selina they had run to.

Yet she had held the baby with perfect confidence, and gathered little Charlotte into her arms as naturally as Selina herself would have done in the earlier days. And there had been none of her old hesitation in her greeting of her friend. "Serenity," thought Selina as she reached her doorstep. "That is what she has gained since I saw her last!"

In the days to come, Selina dined at Mrs Oakley's house several times, walked out frequently with Caroline and the children, and visited the theatre with the adult Carpenters but she seldom managed more than a few words alone with her friend. Sometimes it was all four children, sometimes Harriet and Dick were out riding with the groom and just Charlotte and the baby and Nancy or the nursery maid. It was tantalizing; once she had overcome her awe of John she found him a congenial companion, she adored all the children and to her gratification they seemed delighted to see her, but increasingly she longed for the opportunity to talk freely to Caroline of things that could not be said in company. Not only about the secrets that she alone shared with her friend, she felt that John Carpenter would not be interested in her late husband or her life in Wales.

She wondered if Caroline shared her frustration, with so much to fill her life it was not likely to matter so much, but as they were parting on the fifth occasion that Selina dined with them her friend asked if goes she would care for a walk up to Beechen Cliff the following afternoon. "John goes into the

Hot Bath then, Harriet and Dick will be riding, and Nancy and Debbie are going to take the little ones into Sydney Gardens. I have heard much of that walk and the views one can enjoy of Bath and its surroundings, and I thought it would be a splendid opportunity for us both."

"I should like it of all things!" cried Selina, and the next day she found it hard to wait patiently till it was time to set out, and she was on Mrs Oakley's doorstep a little before the appointed hour, suddenly embarrassed that she might have been too eager as her friend appeared. Was it polite to be so pleased to be without the rest of the family? She almost stammered as she began to express her pleasure, and Caroline gave a gurgle of laughter.

"Stop worrying, Selina, of course you wanted to speak to me alone! I understand perfectly."

"It seems so ungrateful. I have enjoyed meeting your husband, and those lovely children – but..."

"I know, my dear. After all, you have known me so much longer than any of them. Apart from things that cannot be mentioned in front of them, it is often a bore to others when people talk of past experiences they do not share, or people they do not know. Do tell me, have you any news of my family?"

"Not very recently, I am afraid, my only source of information is Georgina and she is not a very good correspondent. You did see the notice of your father's death in the paper?"

"I did. Luckily neither John nor Dick noticed, and I was spared questions about whether he was a relation. It was remarkable, after that stroke, that my father should have lived to be seventy. Would you have heard whether he ever recovered the use of his limbs?"

"I believe he did, to a large extent, but Georgina told me he looked a very old man, the one time she saw him. She was visiting friends in their neighbourhood a year or so after her marriage."

Caroline seemed lost in thought for a moment. "Poor Papa," she said softly, "I do hope he did not miss the Old Manor too much."

"At least he would have had his grandchildren to keep him amused. Georgina spoke of them, when we stayed with her last year, on our way back from consulting the London doctor, but I was so worried about Ifor that I am afraid I had little attention for anything else." Selina was aware that her voice was trembling, and her friend patted her shoulder.

"Of course he was your chief concern," she said sympathetically, "That must have been a dreadful time for you."

"Oh, Caroline! Ifor had always seemed so healthy, it was hard to believe that he had something seriously wrong with his heart. He could not believe it, he refused to rest and to look after himself, in spite of what the doctors said. If only I could have made him take things more quietly! I sometimes wonder, if I had, might he still be alive?"

"Which would you have wanted for him, Selina? Do you think he would have been happy, leading the life of an invalid?"

"He would have hated it. He was so miserable when forced to keep his bed, I found it hard to insist. Do you think that was weak of me?"

"Not unless all you wanted was to keep him alive however it affected him."

"But that would have been selfish!"

"Yes," said Caroline. "It seems to me that you enabled him to spend his last days as he would have wanted to, and that was the best thing you could have done for him. But I can imagine how hard that was for you! I have felt for you, my poor love."

Selina was obliged to stop and wipe her eyes. "Oh, Caroline, I know you do not like people to cry, but when I think of how dreadful that time was, your kindness is almost too much for me. I found it hard to write to you, when it happened, but do you know, I felt that you were the only

193

person who would really understand. Far more so than my own family."

"Did you ever see your parents again?"

"No, soon after Georgina married, they went on a long visit to Frank and his family in Ireland, and my mother died there, as I think I told you. It was quite sudden. My father decided to remain there, and lived on till he died, two years ago. Georgina was most annoyed about that. Her letters were full of how much he was missing, never seeing her children! Still, he was not deprived of grandchildren, Frank has several, and on the whole – I would not wish to be uncharitable, but Georgina's are very noisy, and my father was suffering with his nerves, even when I last saw him in 1798."

"So your brother is quite settled in Ireland now?" asked Caroline. "What has become of the house in Sussex?"

"It has been let, I believe, but it may go to Frank's younger son. After all, his mother, my father's first wife, was Irish."

"I had almost forgotten that. Frank did not always get on with your mother, did he?"

"Not really – though she was fonder of him later than when he was a child."

"And of course she did not have a son of her own," said Caroline.

"If she had, perhaps that would have affected her relationship with Frank, do you think? I never really knew him well, he was away at school by the time I was two years old, and then at Oxford, and then went to look after the property in Ireland. You did not meet him very often, did you?"

"Hardly ever," said Caroline. They were climbing steeply now, and neither had much breath for talking till they reached a bench where they could sit and look down on the pale city of Bath, which gleamed in the sun. After a minute or two, Caroline asked if her friend had heard anything about Lucy recently.

"Well, Georgina writes of her sometimes, she has always admired her, in her way. I cannot help the suspicion that she takes pleasure in calling a baronet's wife by her Christian

194

name! Oh, yes, the last time I heard from her, she mentioned that Lucy had just had her tenth confinement."

"Tenth!" exclaimed Caroline. "My poor sister! I do hope being Sir Charles Carter's wife makes up for all those babies."

"Oh, Caroline." Selina was surprised and a little disappointed at this reaction. "I thought that you liked children now!"

"I understand them better, now that I have my own, but I like children in the same way as I like adults. I do not love all children indiscriminately, as some women appear to do."

Selina sighed. "I used to think I loved all children," she said rather sadly. "But I must confess that I found it hard to care much for Georgina's. They are so badly behaved, and she never corrects them. And she makes so many complaints about the trouble she had, giving birth. She told me that I need not envy her that experience. No doubt it was all very dreadful for her, but I could not help feeling that I would have endured a great deal of pain if I had been able to have just one baby." She thought about what she had just said, and added humbly, "But I have no right to speak of a subject on which I am so ignorant. No doubt that was why you expressed such concern for Lucy."

"Because of my own experience of childbirth? Not entirely, I did not have a very bad time with any of my children, and Lucy, though not as tall as I, is built on similar lines. But only consider what it would be like to have ten children in the, house! Are they all living?"

"Yes, as far as I know."

"Well, you have seen how much time and attention my four require, and they are far enough apart in age not to need the same sort of attention at the same time. Only think what it would be like to have had ten children in about fourteen years! It must be almost like running a school. All the same, I must own to some curiosity as to what they are like, I could almost wish I had a chance of seeing them."

"I would, too," said Selina thoughtfully. "Georgina has met some of them, a while ago. From what she told me, I thought they sounded to be quite well-behaved, she said that the poor little things were so subdued. In contrast to her own, no doubt!"

Caroline laughed. "She did not describe their appearance?"

"Not really, but with such handsome parents, they must be good looking, surely? Mind you, Georgina's children are distinctly plain."

"Oh? She was never as pretty as you, but she does not have bad features and her hair used to be pretty."

"Yes, but her husband is almost ugly. He was very kind to Ifor and me, and I came to like him, more than I had expected to, but he is not good-looking. The worst of it is that the girl take after him more than the boys, it does seem a shame."

"Poor thing," said Caroline. "That is very hard on her. The pity of it is that a lack of beauty in a woman can so easily warp her character and make her even less attractive."

"Like your sister Anna?"

"Anna? No, I was not thinking of her, though she could indeed be unpleasant. But it would not be true to say that it was being plain that made her what she is. She never made any attempt to use the looks she has. I have never understood Anna, she could have been quite as attractive as I am, with a little effort."

"Oh, no, Caroline! She could never have been as attractive as you are. I see what you mean about her features, but that is not everything. There is something about you that she does not have."

"Red hair," suggested Caroline, smiling.

"Well, yes – but that was not what I meant."

"I think I understand you. Yes, poor Anna. I wish I could have liked her more, but we always rubbed each other the wrong way, even as children. No doubt she and my mother are still living near the Carters."

"I imagine so. Georgina has not mentioned them recently. In fact, I gleaned the information about your father from the paper, not from her. Oh, but when we talk about children, Caroline, yours are all so attractive to look at. Especially Harriet! Do you know, I had almost feared to find her too like her namesake, but she is much more like Lucy."

196

"You think that, do you?" said Caroline in a gratified tone. "I wondered if my memory was playing me false. But I think you may have seen almost as much of Lucy as I did, particularly in the years when I lived with my uncle."

"Harriet has a little more of your colouring, I think, but she has that peculiarly sweet smile, and those wonderful blue eyes. And like Lucy, she is so good with younger children."

"Quite unlike her mother!" remarked Caroline. "But both my girls differ from me in that. Charlotte has my hair, but so far no sign of my appalling temper, and she adores Johnnie. She has had the chance to go riding with the other two sometimes, she started to learn a few months ago and is doing well, but she could not bear to be parted from the baby. At her age, I would have done anything to avoid it. I find that surprising, I suppose I do expect her to resemble me more than her sister does."

"But you do not mind that?"

"No indeed. I think her a nicer child than I was, and I have never understood why people expect their children to be exactly like themselves. How many would care to be told that they were a mere copy of their parents? Even if they are devoted to them."

"Very few, I would imagine," said Selina. "I have not heard it put like that before. How clever of you to think of it. But surely you do look for aspects of yourself in your own children?"

"It is difficult not to," Caroline agreed, "But I did suffer, as a child, from the expectations of adults, and I try to not to assume too much about how mine might develop. I have also to remember that they will inherit aspects from their fathers as well as from me."

Her words gave Selina a slight shock. As she was preparing for the Carpenters to visit Bath, she had resolved to be very careful not to even think about Thomas Martin, but since their arrival, seeing Dick on such good terms with his stepfather, she had almost forgotten that Caroline's eldest son was not also John's. She glanced at her friend's profile – incredible to think that she had ever committed what the

197

world would consider a sin. She found that Caroline was still speaking. "No doubt people think Dick is most like me, since they can see John in the others but only I see any aspect of Thomas Martin."

"But is Dick at all like him?"

"Oh, not in colouring, though he had sandy rather than merely fair hair, but the nose and the shape of the head is similar. But some of his attitudes have worried me, and I have feared that they come from his dead father."

Selina recalled that it was really true that Thomas Martin was dead, but she was not quite sure what Caroline had in mind.

"That disturbs you?" she said cautiously. "Surely they would be things you could correct in one so young?"

"I would hope to – but of course I did not know Thomas when he was a child, when some of the aspects I deplored may have developed. Sometimes I have feared some thoughtless or callous behaviour was inherited, only for John to assure me that it was the sort of thing all small boys do. Remember my little brother was under six when he died, and I had known no boy-children till Dick came along. I suspect Thomas, as an only son with sisters, may have been over-indulged to some extent. He did have good points, and when I met him he really seemed to care about helping his fellow men. If he had not known he would inherit money and position, he might not have reverted to the views of his family, especially if he had really had to earn his living instead of playing at it. Certainly Dick has no such expectations. There will be a certain amount of the money my uncle left, for him to inherit, but not enough to live on. He knew that he could not expect Coombe Park, even before Johnnie was born."

"But I thought your husband was fond of him."

"He is, and if we had had no children he might well have made Dick his heir, which I am sure have caused trouble with at least one of John's uncles. Since the property is not entailed, once we had Harriet the relations had to accept that John had a right to leave his property as he pleased. I was glad to give him a son, though. At my age I was not sure that I would be able to have another child. No, Dick understands that he will have to make his own way in the world. I think he does take after me in that, if I had been a man, I used to feel, I would have been eager to earn my own living."

"He is too young to have any idea what he would like to do, surely?"

"Well, he is already showing an interest in the law – John is a JP, you know, and often discusses legal cases in the papers, as part of Dick's education. I must say it would give me a great deal of pleasure if some of my dear uncle's money should go to training someone in his profession."

"Oh!" said Selina. "The law does have a reputation for heartlessness, though, does it not? One hears such tales."

"One does, but any profession is open to abuse by its members, and the law in particular seems to be one where dishonest practitioners tend to give a bad name to all in the mind of the public. Look at the good my late uncle did. And later, I met an Irish lawyer, surly as a bear, who none the less did more for the poor than many clergymen. He was among the reformers that I really admired, so many of those I met were earnest souls, but sadly impractical. I have known this man represent, without charging him, a labourer who had been wrongly accused, save him from conviction, and then make sure he had plenty of work. He seldom had enough money for his own needs, I can hardly say that I would like Dick to follow that example, but my uncle did similar things and still made money. And, Selina, I often think that one reason why the law is sometimes unpopular is that people do not realise that what seems unfair to those who lose, may all the same be just. It can seem impersonal and cold. There are of course unscrupulous men who use the law to their own advantage, but I think they may be exceptions. Look at the number of clergymen who abuse their positions. They are not common, but one has met them. Yet people still respect the office, they do not speak as if that is typical of all, the way they so often do of lawyers."

"I think I know what you mean," said Selina, hesitating. "Certainly the lawyer who with whom Ifor had dealt for years, was kindness itself when he died. He was very anxious that I should receive all that I was entitled to. That is the only one of his profession that I have ever had any dealings with. But as you said, some clergymen are disgustingly unsuitable for their position only no-one likes to say so."

"That was not exactly what I said," said Caroline, smiling. "Though I must confess that I have often felt disgust at the insincerity of men who are supposed to be better than other people."

"But I noticed that you all went to church, last Sunday."

"You may have been surprised, after what I have said about our feelings on the subject, and John and I are afraid we are not quite sincere in doing so, but it is not as if we had not been brought up to it, and living in the country something like that is so very noticeable! At the time of our marriage we did think of joining the Friends – the Quakers, you know – but there is no Meeting House anywhere near Coombe Park, it would have been difficult to arrange. There is also the fact that it is expected of you, I feel that many of our neighbours attend church more out of habit than conviction, being a communicant makes one acceptable. I daresay you feel that I have no right to do so, but I cannot explain that to John."

"Oh, Caroline, I would never say that," said Selina in distress.

"No, because you are too kind hearted. But you probably ought to, as I am aware. Think how shocked our vicar, or the clergyman here would be, if they knew my full story. It might soften them if I were to be repentant, but I am afraid I am not, even though I do not like the necessity of hiding my past from John. I still dislike the way men are treated less harshly by the world if they admit to a lover or a natural child. I cannot regret having Dick though I am not sure I would take the same path now. I merely feel that it is unequal to regard a woman as more of a sinner, particularly if she was seduced, which is not so in my case."

Selina was slightly bewildered. This seemed like a return to Caroline as she remembered her, clever and rather bitter, her brain working too rapidly to follow easily. She seized on one point that had caught her attention, "But to admit it, as some men do, would not have been very pleasant for Dick," she said timidly.

"No, that is what I tell myself. It is the main reason why I could not bring myself to tell John the full story when I married him, the thought of the effect that it might have on Dick. It was not that I felt the disclosure would mean I lost John, I do not think it would have done, and I could have borne it, I was not in love with him then. He would have kept the secret, I am sure, but it would have meant one more person who knew, and it might have made a subtle difference to his attitude to Dick, even if he sympathised."

"But you really do not enjoy having to keep that from him, do you?"

"No indeed. Even more so these days, if I had felt then what I do now, I might have felt differently. But when I could have done so, I did not care enough, and now it is too late."

"I suppose it is."

"Only consider – to discover it after all this time would cause John distress. If I ever do have to tell him, I hope he would forgive me, as I would him in like case, but it seems to me that I should continue to keep my own counsel if I can. It might ease my mind to confide to him something that would give him pain, putting a burden on him that I might have spared him, but it would be indulging my feelings at the expense of his."

"Then you care for him very much," said Selina in wonder. "I thought you did seem fonder of him than I had expected, but that – that seems brave."

"I am glad that you should think so. Perhaps it was selfish of me to marry him in the first place."

"But you did not pretend to be madly in love with him, at that time, did you? I remember your saying so."

"Nor he with me. Perhaps he cared a little more than I did. We liked each other, but he frankly admitted that one of his

201

reasons for marrying was to prevent his uncles from benefiting from the estate. No, our affection has developed over the years.

"You would never admit the existence of romantic love before," said Selina.

"Oh, I knew it existed," said Caroline. "I had seen much that I would have said was mere passion, which can fade to indifference or even to hatred, but I have witnessed enough real love-matches to be sure that it was not just imagination. Yourself, and Lucy, for instance, and one or two others, but I never thought it was something that I would be likely to experience. I did not think I could dote on another human being, since I see people's follies so clearly. I could not believe that one could see and admit the faults of others and still love them. John is far from perfect, his temper is even worse than mine, for instance, and he never keeps things tidy – not that that worries me as much as it might some – he is also inclined to be testy and impatient, which I think is partly due to his accident. But I love him in spite of his faults. I find it very strange."

"Surely that is what is meant by true love? False love crumbles when the adored object is found to be imperfect, true love accepts the imperfections."

Caroline nodded. "That is what I have discovered, but I would not have believed it if I had not encountered it. I am not sure if I deserve it, only think, if I had not left home when I did, I would never have met John. It is hard to regret what happened."

"But you do have regrets?"

"Occasionally, to some extent, when I think of Harriet and Charlotte – but at least as their mother and as John's wife, I have nothing to be ashamed of. I think that many apparently respectable women could not say that."

"I am sure they could not," said Selina. "Not if even a quarter of the gossip is to be believed about some of the fashionable ladies here in Bath! Amours of married women seem to be considered far less shocking than when they were single. I know which I would be more disturbed by! Caroline, when you spoke of women being more censored than men, does that mean that you would still desire rights for women?"

Caroline looked thoughtful. "I still feel that women in general are not fairly dealt with in some ways. For instance, I do not see why we should not vote, when the laws passed by Parliament affect us equally. Nor can I see any reason why females should not be educated in such a way that they could earn their living, as their brothers are. We could become lawyers, doctors, even be elected to Parliament. At the moment the only respectable way for an impoverished gentlewoman to gain employment is to teach, but even that would benefit from an education that laid more emphasis on book learning and less on the frivolous occupations thought suitable for ladies. If I had only received my education from Miss Yare, I should have been less fitted to undertake the education of my daughters. I am so grateful that my uncle saw to it that I had good instructors."

"But will you bring up your daughters to demand their rights?"asked Selina.

"Yes, that is something of a dilemma. I very much doubt if there is any likelihood of such a thing at the moment, and neither of them seem as rebellious as I was at their age. Also, how can I claim that women are ready for independence when I surrendered to matrimony myself? I now feel that each sex needs the other – how many men are truly independent of women? However, I do still feel that some of the laws and social customs press harder on us than they do on men."

"I suppose they do," said Selina as they began to descend the hill. "But I fear that I am not ready for independence yet. I miss Ifor more every day."

"Oh, I am sure you do," Caroline seemed moved. "After so many happy years together, how could you help it? The loneliness must be terrible."

The sympathy made the tears start again, but Selina tried to hold them back as she replied. "Oh, yes, that is the worst. Ifor's place in my heart and in my life can never be filled, but as well as that, you will probably think me very weak, I feel so helpless, so unfitted to make decisions about my own life. In my place, you would not feel lost in that way."

"No, I have always been able to take care of myself," Caroline agreed. "My poor Selina, I was afraid that might be so. I could see that you doubted your own authority in dealing with Mrs Oakley and I was sorry I was too involved to be able to reassure you then. You must not hold yourself too cheap."

Selina shuddered. "Oh, but she is such an imposing woman! It is all very well for you, you are tall enough to impress her."

"But one does not have to be tall, to make an impact," said Caroline, laughing. "Look at Nancy. You have always been rather diffident, but you are not really incompetent to deal with someone like Mrs Oakley. You managed to keep house for Ifor all those years, did you not? He did not complain that you could not control the servants, I am sure."

"I was able to do that, but then I had Ifor behind me, and he would have been very firm if anyone had given me any trouble. Here, in Bath, in rooms, it is all so very different."

"Yes, of course. In every way. You must have hated having to leave the place that had been your home for so long."

"Oh, you do understand!" exclaimed Selina. "I really loved Wales and the Welsh and miss it even though it is not the same with my darling gone."

"The property was inherited by a nephew, was it not?"

"Yes, Gareth Pugh. He is the only son of Ifor's sister. It was not entailed, but he was Ifor's choice of heir. He and I both felt that the property should stay with the family, and Gareth has two small sons."

"I forget – did you tell me if you had ever met him before?"

"Gareth? Oh yes, he came frequently. Often he has spent his holidays with us when he was a boy, his father died when he was at school and he had few other relations. He was left a small property, a farm and some land, but it was let until he came of age. I never saw his mother, she died about the time Ifor and I were married, she was considerably older than Ifor, but he was very fond of her. Gareth is a very nice young man, and I like him a great deal."

"And what about the girl he married?"asked Caroline.

"She is a sweet little creature, not very intelligent, perhaps, but most amiable, and quite a good mother. They have both visited us since their wedding, and brought the first son not long after he was born. The younger one is just over a year old. I am sure they will do very well and the people seem happy to have them. I am glad to think of them and their children living there, though I cannot help also feeling rather sad."

"You must do," said Caroline, "I think it is splendid of you not to resent their being in your place."

"I could not resent Gareth and Mary. They have been so kind to me and never made me feel that I was in the way. I could not have remained even if I had not been ill, have remained, though they would not let me leave until I was strong enough. Mary was such a kind nurse, too. She had just buried her mother and had these young children, it was so very good of her even if she is a little dull."

"I had almost forgotten that you originally came to Bath because you had been taken ill," said Caroline. "You seem to be in the best of health now."

"Do you know, I feel that I am! I never was sick in my life before, even though some people thought me delicate. I was so bad, I feared that my health had broken down completely."

"You knocked yourself up, with the worry over your husband and the strain of nursing him and then losing him," Caroline pointed out gently.

"Yes, that must have been the cause. Of course I am relieved to be fully recovered – and yet, when I thought I would shortly follow Ifor, it was almost a consolation. Now – I have so many empty years to fill…"

"Oh, my dear, you must not talk like that!" exclaimed her friend. "However desolate you feel at the moment, you must not despair, at thirty-seven. There is surely some life ahead for you."

"But what life? I could never marry again – to have another husband when I had known the best, I could not bear that. What is left for me? If only I had had children, something to care about…"

Caroline seemed struck by this remark, and walked on in silence for a minute or two, occasionally glancing at her friend in concern. Selina felt dismayed. It had been such a relief to speak of her feelings to someone she knew would sympathise, she had not thought of it distressing someone who had troubles of her own. "I should not have said so much," she thought. "I must not let her guess how much I dislike living in Bath."

She was certain that Caroline would hate it, but she might not realise how wearying the meaningless round of entertainments and gossip was becoming to Selina. "Even the theatre palls after a while. I do hope she will not enquire too closely. Other widows seem to enjoy the society of the Pump Room, the card parties, the Assembly Rooms. But most of them are so much older than I am."

"Dear Selina, I feel I have not been concerned enough about you," said Caroline. "I do hope you will be able to visit us at Coombe Park, when John is better."

"I should like that very much," said Selina gratefully. "You must not fear that I am too miserable. At least I have enough, more than enough, money. I hope to be able to help others. There are some pleasant people in Bath, and my landlady is very kind. Oh, Caroline, this will amuse you – when I was waiting with Mrs Oakley…" she narrated the story of being given a good reference by Mrs Brewis. "Do you not think that that shows I am not disliked?"

"Of course you are not!" Caroline sounded a trifle indignant. "I suppose it is reasonable enough that these women should discuss their boarders, but I do think that Mrs Oakley might have kept these comments to herself. How very kind of Mrs Brewis to feel that you are no trouble! In your place I think I would feel like giving a little trouble just to show I was there – I wonder what she would say about me? I hope this woman does more than tolerate you."

"Oh, indeed she does. I am sure she would be distressed to know that her words would be repeated to me. We are nearly at her house, so perhaps you would care to meet her? You will come in and take some refreshment before we part, will you not?"

"Most certainly I will," Caroline assured her.

"And you will see how very comfortable I am here," said Selina valiantly as they entered the house.

PART 11

Coombe Park

July, 1818

Caroline found her two younger children waiting by the open windows of the drawing room, which commanded a view of the drive. Tired from her morning's activities, she sank into a chair and smiled at them. "How was your ride?" she asked.

"Oh, delightful, but it was growing too hot out in the open," said Charlotte.

"Harriet is out," said Johnnie, "She has gone for a walk to the wood."

"We offered to accompany her," said Charlotte earnestly, "But perhaps not surprisingly, she preferred to be alone."

"She has the dogs," argued Johnnie.

"They do not talk!" Charlotte countered.

The boy suddenly swung himself up on the window seat and peered out, getting down again to say sadly, "No-one in sight."

"Oh, you are looking out for the visitors," said Caroline. "I did wonder what you were doing in here."

"It is interesting," said her son. "We have never had so many people here at one time. Besides, nobody seems to want us to be anywhere else."

"So we came here. I hope it will be Aunt Selina who arrives first," said Charlotte. "Mama, is it permissible to call Mrs Penry that?"

"She is my oldest friend, and I am sure she will be delighted. In fact, you had begun to do so when you saw her last."

"When did Charley see Aunt Selina?" asked Johnnie, advancing on his mother and flinging himself at her feet, his sandy head in her lap and his hazel eyes alight with interest. "I thought she had never come here?"

"No, we met in Bath," said Caroline. "When you were a baby."

"It was because Papa had a bad leg, we stayed in Bath so that he could have treatment," explained Charlotte.

"I thought he always had a bad leg?"

"Yes, but it was worse then, wasn't, Mama? Of course you would not remember Bath, you were not even a year old."

Johnnie sounded aggrieved. "Oh, I suppose Aunt Selina must have seen me then, and I cannot remember her at all. Did she come to Bath on purpose to see us?"

"Oh no, she was living there then," said Caroline.

"In Bath? I thought she always lived in Wales."

"She had done so for years, but when her husband died and Mr Pugh inherited his estate, she moved to Bath for a while. Mr Pugh was her husband's nephew."

"Did they make Aunt Selina go away? Did they not like her?" asked Johnnie.

"Oh yes, I think so, but she felt that it was their house and that it was not right for her to remain," said Caroline, feeling that there was no point in mentioning the illness from which her friend had happily recovered completely.

"I suppose Mrs Pugh was alive, then," said Charlotte.

"Indeed she was."

"But when she died, Aunt Selina went back again?"

"That was why. Mr and Mrs Pugh had no female relations, and the poor man had no one to turn when she died, leaving two little boys and a tiny baby. Selina was his aunt by marriage, and he had come to know her when he was a boy. So he asked her to return to look after them all, and she has been there ever since," said Caroline.

"Did she like going back?" asked Johnnie.

"Oh yes. She had been very happy in Wales, and loved children but had never had any of her own."

"I remember how kind she was to us," observed Charlotte. "She spent hours devising ways to amuse us. She brought us toys, too. I still have that little china doll I called Matilda, she sits on my mantelpiece. Oh, and she taught us how to play Cat's Cradle, Harriet was very good at it, I took longer – I know I got in a dreadful tangle!"

"You have a good memory, love," said Caroline. "You were under five then."

"Oh, I can remember further back than that," said Charlotte. "But that time in Bath is very clear to me, Perhaps it was because that was the first time I had ever been away from Coombe Park."

"And did Aunt Selina never come here?" asked Johnnie.

"It had been planned that she would come in 1808," said Caroline. "That visit had to be postponed when she was called back to Wales, and what with one thing and another, she has not managed to do so until now."

"Well, she simply had to come this time! "said Charlotte.

"Yes, she would have been very sorry to miss Harriet's wedding," Caroline agreed. "It is fortunate that Mr Pugh had been planning to take his family to London to consult a dentist."

"Poor things!" said Charlotte with a shudder. "I shall not forget my visits to the dentist in a hurry."

"No, my poor love," said Caroline. "You were very brave. Still, now it is over, the removal of those teeth has improved the look of your mouth and cured the way your front teeth were inclined to stick out."

"But I hope the little Pugh children will not have to face anything of the sort. It is bad enough when he has to file the teeth, isn't it, Johnnie?"

"Yes – horrid," said the boy, making a face. "Is that why Aunt Selina can only stay a couple of days? So that she can be with them when they go to the dentist?" His eyes grew round, "I suppose she's like their mother. I should have hated to go to that man without you there, Mama."

Caroline smiled and ruffled his hair. He continued to lean against her knee and gaze meltingly up into her face. She shook her head at him and looked across at her daughter on the window-seat, her hands resting on the sill behind her and her feet stretched out in front. "What has he been doing, Charlotte?"

"I was wondering what he was about to do, Mama."

Johnnie stirred and contrived to look deeply pained, "I was only being a loving son," he protested. "Why should you think I might be up to mischief?"

"Because you so often are," said his sister promptly. "Whenever you are being good, we wonder why!" To Caroline's amusement she then spoilt the effect of this by giving him a doting smile.

He gave a long sigh and said reproachfully, "Well, I really am good, today! I was thinking, Charley, Mama will feel strange without Harriet."

"So shall I. So will we all. It was only to be expected that she would marry and leave us, one day."

Johnnie sat up and looked at her anxiously. "And will you do that, too, when you are older? I don't think I should like you to marry, I should miss you even more than I will miss Harriet."

"How kind!" said Charlotte, laughing, and turned her head to look down the drive. "Oh, look, this must be the Pugh's coach. My, what splendid horses."

"Where, where?" cried Johnnie, scrambling to his feet and running to the window. His sister let him take her place and came over to her mother.

"Nancy said to let her know when they come so we can arrange some refreshment and make them comfortable," she said, "Shall I do that?"

"Yes please, and then rejoin us," said Caroline, getting up and following her to the hall.

There she found the butler about to open the door, and John just emerging from the library. It was unusual for him to be there at that time of day and she wondered if he had been subjected to the same tidying-up process as the children. He made a rueful grimace as he met her eyes, and then asked about Harriet. Caroline had just time to repeat what the others had told her before Charlotte, Nancy, Johnnie, and the visitors all converged on them at once.

Selina came in flanked by the two boys with the little dark girl clinging to her hand, followed by Mr Pugh with a man and a maidservant. Remembering the late Mr Penry, Caroline looked with interest at his nephew. She fancied she could see a resemblance in the sallow skin, dark eyes and strong nose, but his receding dark hair was flecked with grey. His gentle melodious voice was very like his uncle's, but his general manner, no doubt owing to the tragedy in his life, held more of the melancholy often associated with the Welsh than she recalled with Ifor Penry As Selina prepared to introduce her adopted family to the Carpenters, Caroline was delighted to perceive that her old friend seemed held in great affection by all four of them.

"This is Mr Pugh, this is Gary, this Ifor, and here is our little Megan," said Selina, pushing the children forward. Gravely the two boys bowed, and the girl essayed a timid curtsey, but all three seemed almost overcome by the strange country and these tall people. The father was shorter than Caroline, only with a little woman like Selina could he hope to seem imposing. Both her younger children towered over the Pugh boys, though the older one was not much younger than Charlotte and Ifor was about the same age as Johnnie.

Nancy, in welcoming the visitors remarked that refreshments would be brought to the drawing room and would they like to assemble there once they had visited the conveniences. John and his son escorted the males, and Charlotte took charge of little Megan, stooping to her with such gentleness that the child seemed to relax as she was led off to the new cloakroom with a water-closet that John had had installed two years ago, looking trustfully up at her new friend. Selina watched them go with tears in her eyes. "Oh, Caroline, what a lovely girl Charlotte has grown into!" she murmured.

"Hasn't she? Much more attractive than I was. And what do you think of our Johnnie?"

"I find it amazing. Can he really be the baby I carried about when you were in Bath?"

"Yes, he has grown greatly. I think he is taller than Dick was at that age."

"Where is Dick? Should I call him Richard, now?"

"Many people do, but we find it hard to get used to, and he endures Dick from us. He will be here tonight, with Steven. I know it is not the thing for the groom to spend the night here before the wedding but there really is nowhere suitable, since the wedding is taking place at our local church."

"You said that Mr Linton was a friend of Dick's?"

"He is a year or so older, but they met at Oxford and have shared chambers in Lincoln's Inn for eighteen months now."

"And Harriet?"

"She will be here presently," said Caroline, leading the way to the cloakroom when she saw Charlotte and Megan returning. "She is taking a last look round the places she has known all her life."

Selina had clearly been pondering these words and as she emerged and they made their way to the drawing room she looked anxiously at her friend and asked if Harriet was going to miss Coombe Park very much. Caroline smiled, "Oh, she will not lose her affection for her home because she has grown fond of someone who lives elsewhere, but she is looking forward to her life with Steven." Selina's brow cleared, and she smiled understandingly if a trifle mistily.

"And what of my family, Caroline? What do you think of them?"

Caroline watched the rest of the party assemble, Johnnie and the two boys already discussing the rival merits of Welsh and English countryside, their fathers following, and Charlotte showing the little girl some colourful prints. "I was about to say, I think they are delightful."

"Indeed they are," said Selina warmly. She sank her voice to a murmur, though Mr Pugh was far too deep in discussion with John to hear her. "It was one of the most terrible experiences of my life, to return to what had been a happy home when I left it. I never saw a man so prostrated with grief, the poor little boys were sitting on the stairs crying for their mother, and as for Megan! I do not know how we kept her alive. She was quite the smallest baby I ever saw, and so delicate. Thank God she is now quite healthy."

Caroline found this very moving, thinking that the poor mother had had a sad time of it, three children in less than five years, and dying so young. She squeezed her friend's hand as refreshments were carried into the drawing room and placed on a table in the middle. Everyone gathered round it before dispersing to different seats. She found herself placed next to Mr Pugh, and spoke to him having met the late Mr Penry.

He gazed at her in gratitude, "My uncle was such a good man – but, Mrs Carpenter, I think the best thing he ever did was to marry Aunt Selina. You cannot imagine what she has been to us!"

"I think I can," said Caroline soberly. "I have known her since we were both children, and I would say that she would never think of herself if there were others who needed her."

"Oh, she has been – like – like an angel! To give up her comfortable life in Bath to return to Wales and look after us. How can we ever repay her?"

Caroline smiled, "What you have given her is something fate had denied her. She has always loved children and I know it grieved her that she could not have them."

"If she had had children I would not have inherited the property, and yet she never resented that my dear Mary and I should come there," said Mr Pugh. "I do hope we have not been too much for her. Do you think she looks well?"

"I do," said Caroline decidedly. "I was quite shocked when I saw her in Bath after fourteen years apart, I do not think the climate there agreed with her. I think she looks a great deal better than she did then, and very little older."

"I am glad to hear you say that. I wonder that those riotous boys of mine have not caused both of us to turn white!"

"They seem very nice lads to me," said Caroline. "And much quieter than my Johnnie. Hark at him now! Johnnie, stop boasting, do, and show a little respect. Gareth is two years older than you are." Her son grinned impishly, but at his

214

father's suggestion led the Pugh boys outside and they could be seen a minute or so later racing away over the lawn.

John moved over and said reassuringly, "He will bring them back in good time, but I thought it would do them good to stretch their legs a little before they have to continue their journey."

"Very wise. They had been growing restless, indeed, and I am glad for them to expend a little energy. Is your son really younger than Gareth? I find that hard to believe."

"He is about the same age as your younger son, eleven," said Caroline. "Yes, I think he is tall for his age."

"Indeed he is. Of course, you are both tall, are you not?"

"Would you like a short stroll before your coach is brought round?" asked John. Their guest felt this sounded a good idea, and they all strolled out on the lawn, where Charlotte had taken Selina and the little girl to look at flowers in the border. The three boys could be seen in the distance engaged in an impromptu game of football.

Mr Pugh expressed his admiration of Coombe Park, the pleasantness of both the house and the carefully landscaped grounds, as he walked beside Caroline and her husband, his daughter following between Charlotte and Selina, holding a hand of each. By the time they had gone some way round the lake and turned back, the Pugh's coach had been brought to the front of the house, and it was necessary to call the boys in. None of the children seemed keen to leave their new companions, and Megan burst into tears to find that she had to be parted from her beloved Aunt Selina, as well as this tall friendly girl.

Distressed, her father tried to console her with a description of pleasures in store, including the theatre, a circus, some of which were to happen before Selina rejoined them, sensibly making little mention of the dentist. Charlotte seemed relieved to hear that this would not take place until they had their great-aunt's support and Megan was consoled with the promise that they might stay a night or two on their way back, especially when an invitation was extended to her new friend to visit them in Wales one day. As she was put in

215

the coach, she was bravely attempting a smile. Caroline noticed that she was clutching a little wooden trinket box decorated with coloured straws. It had been made by French prisoners of war, and had been one of Charlotte's treasured possessions when she was about Megan's age.

Now that the worst of the heat had gone, it did not seem necessary to return at once to the house, especially as the servants seemed to be everywhere. John, looking slightly haunted, limped off to the stables accompanied by his son, while Caroline took her friend to a seat in the shade of an oak tree, where Charlotte joined them. For a minute or two they sat silent, Selina probably thinking of the Pughs while her hostess enjoyed what could only be a short respite from all the preparations and her daughter dreamily playing with the long curls that hung over her shoulder.

Selina looked up as a young woman came in sight, her sunbonnet over her arm and her red-gold hair gleaming in the sunlight. "Harriet!" she exclaimed in delight, and Caroline watched her elder daughter come gracefully over the lawn, an old pointer ambling beside her and the young spaniel bounding ahead. Charlotte caught him and pulled him up, upon which he flopped down at her feet, panting.

Caroline was not so busy reproaching Harriet for risking a headache that she could not study her friend's expression of admiration and pleasure as she absorbed the change in the little girl she had last seen ten years ago.

"Mama, darling, I have so much hair the sun cannot reach my head!" Harriet assured her, touching her protective top-knot as she turned her attention to the guest. "Aunt Selina, it is so good to see you here at last! How do you do? You look in good health, I do hope that you are?"

"Yes, thank you my dear, I am."

The old pointer thrust his nose into Selina's lap, and Harriet took hold of his collar saying anxiously, "Pinto – come away – I am sorry, he is a foolish animal – but he means well."

Selina patted the grizzled head. "I am very fond of dogs. This fellow is quite an old gentleman, is he not?"

"Yes, we have had him over nine years," said Harriet. "Marmion is much younger."

"But equally foolish," said Charlotte, thumping the spaniel's black and white chest as it waved its paws and grinned, showing a lot of pink tongue.

"He is named after Mr Scott's poem," said Harriet, smiling. "But nobody quite knows why. Aunt Selina, it is such a pleasure to see you again. Neither Charlotte nor I have forgotten the happy times we spent with you in Bath."

"I have fond memories of those days myself," said Selina. "I was so sorry that my visit to you in 1808 had to be postponed."

"We did understand, but it does seem a shame that it has taken so long," said Harriet. "You must find us all much changed."

"For the better, I hope," put in Charlotte.

"Does that include me?" asked Caroline, amused. Harriet chuckled.

"Oh, I meant, Johnnie, Charlotte, and myself," she said. "You do not change, Mama."

"Do I not? Not even for the worse? I feel about a hundred sometimes."

"Oh, Mama, what would you say if I were to exaggerate like that? You only look about thirty," retorted her daughter.

"Oh, Harriet love, do be moderate. Consider that Dick is over twenty-three! If I look no more than forty-nine, I shall be satisfied."

"You certainly do not look that," said Selina. "See how grey my hair has grown – how has yours kept its colour?"

"Not with any assistance from me, I assure you. But you always had light coloured hair, it may be grey as you say, but that does not show."

Selina turned back to Harriet, "Indeed, I see a considerable change in all of you children. Especially Johnnie, though I would have expected that, since he was only a baby when I last saw him. But you have both changed greatly also. You were quite pretty little girls, but I hope I will not embarrass you by saying that you are now quite beautiful."

"Harriet is," said Charlotte admiringly. "My hair is the wrong colour and I am far too tall, Harriet's figure has just the right proportions."

"But surely Harriet is taller than average?" said Selina.

"She is shorter than Charlotte or me," said Caroline. "She would seem tall to many people, love."

"Fortunately Steven is tall," said Charlotte, and Harriet's face lit up with her most irresistible smile.

"I am looking forward to meeting Mr Linton," said Selina. "Do tell me about him."

The girl needed no encouragement to speak of her love. Caroline watched the others, for once in her life very near to tears. Charlotte was playing with the dogs but listening intently, and Selina was aglow with sympathy and enthusiasm. Though Harriet was not quite as fair skinned as Lucy had been, Caroline felt she still bore a considerable resemblance to her sister, and the summer when Sir Charles Carter had proposed came suddenly to her mind.

Harriet was quite as deeply in love as Lucy had been and Caroline felt a pang as she recalled how scornfully she had regarded this. She hoped that she had not shown it too obviously, or lacked sympathy. In spite of being a baronet, he had struck her as such a very ordinary man, hardly worth all the fuss. Apart from having greater tolerance of the effects of love these days, she felt that the object of her daughter's affection was much more interesting. Steven Linton had more than his handsome face and amiable manners to recommend him.

While they had sat there, the shadow of the great tree had spread further across the lawn, which meant that the time must be nearly four o'clock. "I must go in," Caroline exclaimed, "The other visitors will arrive before long and I ought to be there in case they should be early." She got to her feet as she spoke.

Harriet rose also. "I must make myself presentable for Mrs Linton," she said. "This gown has caught on brambles and my shoes are muddy. I only hope that Nancy will be too busy to notice."

"I will come and help you change," offered Charlotte.

"Oh, do not leave Aunt Selina, Charley. I am sure Debbie will be there to help."

"I was thinking that I ought to go in myself," said Selina. "It has been so pleasant here, I had forgotten that I have not seen my room yet. Would it be too much trouble for someone to show me where it is."

"Oh, Selina, I am sorry, how remiss of me," said Caroline. "I will show you at once." But when they reached the house, Nancy called to her, and she had to leave it to her daughters.

By the time the queries were answered and she had checked that the breakfast room was all prepared for the evening meal so that the dining room could be prepared for the wedding feast, Caroline reckoned that her friend might soon be down again. She returned to the drawing room, checked that all traces of the Pugh's visit had been removed, plumped up a cushion, straightened some flowers, and moved to a spot where she could look down the drive.

Footsteps sounded in the hall, and Selina came in carrying a bag with needlework in it, looking round a little timidly until she spotted her friend over by the window. "Ah, there you are, Caroline – can I help in any way? Or would I only interfere with your servants?"

"I am not sure that there is anything left for *me* to do," said Caroline. "Having good servants means they leave you nothing to do once they understand what you want! No, seriously, I have done all I can. Mrs Linton should be here very soon, so come and talk to me until then."

Selina settled herself on the window seat and took out her embroidery, looking eager for conversation. This made her hostess slightly uncomfortable, it would be so easy to let their talk stray into areas better avoided. She trusted her friend implicitly, but had noticed how on first sight of Harriet she had mouthed "Lucy" while Caroline was touched, and no one else would have seen, it was a little alarming. To avoid the subject she asked if Selina was comfortable in her room, a natural enough query but it sounded a little chilly to her own ears and she was afraid she might have distressed Selina.

Hastily she apologised warmly for not being able to take her there.

"But the girls did it so most charmingly! I was so pleased that you had remembered how much I like yellow roses. It was you that placed them there, was it not?"

"Yes my dear, it was. But Charlotte picked them."

"Dear child – she and Harriet accompanied me into the room to make certain all was well, and I had everything I needed. Caroline, they are such delightful girls, how proud you must be of them both. It is lovely to see how attached they are to each other, this does not always happen with sisters."

"Indeed it does not," Caroline agreed.

Selina sighed, "I wish I had known what it was to have a good friend in a sister – I found it so very difficult with Georgina."

"Oh, I meant to ask – how is your sister?"

"As far as I know, she is perfectly well, but we do not communicate very often these days. I think she enjoyed the idea of visiting me in Bath. She has never forgiven me for leaving the city and returning to an uncivilised place like Wales!"

Selina spoke with unusual asperity. Caroline sympathised with her, but her attention was caught by the sight of her husband and son coming from the stables and heading off down the drive The dogs must have been lying in the shade somewhere, for they ambled up to join the walk, to be greeted absently by John and enthusiastically by Johnnie. Selina must have noticed something in her expression and asked with concern about the injured leg.

"Ah, the trouble that brought him to Bath has not recurred, I do not think his general condition is much worse – does it seem so to you?"

"No, he walks better than he did then, but he does seem older – more so than you do. Is he well in himself?"

"I should have said so," said Caroline. "Of course you are not seeing him at his best at present. No man is at ease when a wedding is being prepared, and I think he is upset at the idea of his little girl marring."

"But surely he has no reservations about Mr Linton?" asked Selina in dismay.

"Oh, no, he is quite happy about that, we both liked him when we first met him, which is some years ago now. It is simply that he does not like the thought of Harriet leaving home any more than I do, however advantageous the match. Well, I suppose it cannot all be rejoicing." Caroline saw that her friend was looking both puzzled and disturbed to hear this sentiment put into words, however people actually felt about weddings, but before either of them could say more, a travelling carriage came up the drive at a smart pace, accompanied by a man on horseback.

"That must be Mrs Linton's carriage, I am sure I recognise her man."

"Oh, you have met her, then?"

"Once at Oxford, when we visited Dick, and more recently in town, while her husband was still alive."

"I had not realised that she was such a recent widow," Selina began, but Caroline could not let her enquire further because she had to go out to the hall to meet the mother of her future son-in-law.

Mrs Linton came through the door like a tidal wave, her arms full of parcels and servants following behind, similarly laden. By the time she swept up to Caroline, the Carpenter's footman and butler were also in attendance. She smiled up from under a monumental cap, all ribbons and lace, holding out a surprisingly small hand in lace mitten. Two of her parcels fell to the floor as she did so, but she simply watched complacently as an already encumbered maid stooped to retrieve them for her. "Take care of that one," she said. "It is delicate. For dear Harriet," she explained, turning back to her hostess. "Oh, my dear Mrs Carpenter, it is really wonderful to see you again. I do trust that you are as well as you look?"

"Yes, thank you, how kind of you to ask," murmured Caroline. "Would you like to see your room at once, or will you take some refreshment first?" Burdened as the guest was, it would seemed most likely that she would wish to take the first option, but large china blue eyes were rolled dramatically and she exclaimed that she was dying for a cup of tea.

"Of course," said Caroline, signalling to Nancy, who sent a maid off to the kitchen and then came forward to escort Mrs Linton's personal maid up to her bedroom. The visitor handed her cloak on to this woman, and beamed round the circle of servants before unloading the rest of her impedimenta on the other maid, retaining only what appeared to be a fur muff until it snuffled and whined, proving itself to be a tiny dog. A fondness for pets also manifested itself in the cage carried by the man, which contained a large green parrot. She directed that this should be placed in her room along with her more orthodox luggage, and tucked the hand not clasping the dog into Caroline's, so that she could be led into the drawing room.

Selina had been quietly working at her embroidery but rose at their entrance and stood looking quizzically at the newcomer, who peered at her while they were introduced and then exclaimed, "Oh, how charming! So you also have just arrived. No, no, please sit down again, do not stand on my account, I beg of you." The animal in her arms gave out a plaintive cry and she looked down at it in concern, "My poor Didi – is he thirsty too? Dear Mrs Carpenter, could the poor sweet have a saucer of milk and water, do you think?"

"Why, certainly," said Caroline. "Thomas, would you be so kind as to ask for that to go on the tea tray?" As the footman left on this errand, Mrs Linton found herself a chair, sank into it and placed Didi on the floor beside her. The little creature took a few apprehensive steps, hesitated, and scuttled back to its mistress's skirts, where it peered out. Caroline tried not to think what would happen if it came to the attention of Pinto and Marmion.

Mrs Linton had chosen a chair some distance from where Selina and Caroline had been sitting, and they joined her, now able to make a more leisurely appraisal of the new arrival. Caroline wondered if her friend was feeling as overwhelmed as she was. Steven's mother as she remembered her had certainly been attached to rather frilly garments, but she had stayed quietly in the background when encountered, looking admiringly up at her tall clever son and large cheerful husband, both of whom were inclined to treat her with the gentle indulgence one might accord a favourite child. She had not seemed to resent this, but was she really as ingenuous as she appeared? Listening to her conversation while they waited for the tea, it was surprising that she avoided seeming totally ridiculous, considering how much her manner and way of dressing conflicted with her age.

"My dears, it has been such a journey, you cannot imagine!" she began, "The poor horses, on the hills, I would have liked to get out and walked to spare them. I always did want to, you know, but my dear husband would never permit me to do so."

Selina inquired about the late Mr Linton, to which his widow replied with warm enthusiasm, "Oh, such a dear man. He always took such good care of me. Have you also lost your husband, Mrs Penry? I beg your pardon if that is rude of me, but I could not help seeing that you appear to be alone?"

"Yes, my husband died nearly twelve years ago," said Selina sadly.

"So long? You poor dear. Ah me, I had mine till two years ago. You recall him, I am sure, Mrs Carpenter?"

"Indeed I do. I thought he was a very fine man."

"Oh he was, he was. By the way, where is Mr Carpenter? Is he well?"

"Yes, thank you." Caroline was relieved that her husband and son must have left the drive for the fields before Mrs Linton's carriage arrived.

"And your children? Your little boy must have grown. How is dear Richard? He is such a delightful creature." Mrs Linton turned eagerly to Selina, "Such a good friend to my Steven! You have not met my boy, I believe?"

"Not as yet, but I have heard a great deal and I am looking forward to meeting him." Mrs Linton beamed.

"I know I am prejudiced," she said, "But to my mind he is one of the finest youths to be found anywhere. Ah, here is the tea, and the saucer for Didi, how kind."

While Caroline poured out the tea and passed bread and butter and cake, Selina questioned her new acquaintance about conditions in London. Mrs Linton cocked her head at her, looking surprised. "Oh, my dear, I have not been there this age! When I was bereaved, it seemed best to let the house until Steven had need of it – it has just been completely refurnished. No, I have settled in Bath, which is where I have come from today. Are you familiar with that city?"

Caroline avoided looking at her friend, but admired the gravity with which Selina replied that she had lived there for a time after her husband's death but had had to return to Wales, narrating the tragic events, which had brought this about.

Mrs Linton murmured sympathetically about Mr Pugh's loss, but her chief concern appeared to be the effect upon Selina. "My dear, how dreadful for you! Of course you had to do your duty by your relations, but how sad you must have been, to be forced to leave Bath!"

"You find it congenial?" asked Caroline.

"Oh, indeed. It is a most delightful place – there is such nice company to be found in the Pump Room! One seems to meet half the world there! The Assemblies, too. I enjoy playing cards, and it is so pleasant to watch the dancing, especially the young people." Mrs Linton heaved a comfortable sigh, "I never cared to dance myself, I found it so hard to remember the steps, and my husband was indifferent to it. But I love to watch others. Oh, my dear Harriet – there you are! Come, you must not be afraid to meet your new mama-in-law. Come and give me a kiss. I am so pleased that my Steven has chosen such a beautiful bride."

Harriet advanced into the room, smiling. Her mother noticed the pink flush now fading from her cheeks and thought she probably had been a little apprehensive, while Charlotte coming behind her had her hands clenched anxiously. The flow of talk seemed to reassure them both.

Didi yapped as his mistress rose to embrace Harriet, who looked in surprise for the source of the sound. "This is my dear little dog," Mrs Linton held him up. "Is he not sweet?"

"Er – yes," said Harriet, gingerly patting the small animal as if it were made of porcelain.

"I should so much have liked to give you one just like him for a wedding present, but that bad Steven is so very rude about him that I feared he might object. I am so sorry!"

Harriet made the proper murmurs, but the look she cast at her mother expressed her relief at that her fiancé had taken a firm line. Mrs Linton in the meantime had noticed Charlotte standing quietly behind her sister and exclaimed, "Why, this is never the little redhead! How you have grown. You are very pretty too. We shall have someone coming to marry you, soon."

"We hope not for a while," said Caroline. "Charlotte is only fifteen."

"I was married at fifteen," said Mrs Linton unexpectedly. "Just two days after my birthday, in fact."

"Really?"said Caroline.

"Indeed," the lady looked at them thoughtfully. "I fear that might have been a sad mistake, now I consider it, but dear Mr Linton was always so kind. I think you are wise not to wish your daughter to marry too young, if Heaven had blessed me with a girl, I hope I would have felt the same." She glanced at Harriet and her sister, and clutching her little dog, prepared to rise.

Harriet held out a hand and looked at Caroline. "May I show Mrs Linton to her room, Mama? You would not mind?"

Mrs Linton beamed. "My dear, that would be delightful. I have some parcels for you, and for your sister. I am sure you have other calls on you, Mrs Carpenter."

Caroline admitted that she had other visitors to prepare for, and watched in amusement as the three of them left the room, the two tall girls flanking the not inconsiderable figure of Harriet's future mother-in-law.

Waiting until they could be heard ascending the stairs, Caroline caught Selina's expression, and found dancing eyes and a quivering lip. She chuckled, and they laughed together almost as they would have done in their girlhood.

"Oh, Caroline, no!" said Selina after a minute, "It is not kind to make fun of that poor woman."

"I do not think she would mind as much as you think. I had the impression that she was enjoying the effect that she produced."

"Did you? I could not help feeling that she was rather pitiful."

"But then you have a kinder heart than I have! But all the same," said Caroline reflectively, "I do not think she is to be pitied."

"You saw her in company with her husband. How did she seem to you in those days?"

"Much less voluble, but then I did not spend much time in her company without our husbands and sons."

"And you would say that they were a happy couple?"

"I would not say that their relationship was such as you or I would have wished for, but it seemed to suit them. He was clearly more than ten years older than she was – if she was only fifteen when they married, it probably explains a good deal."

"Mr Linton was inclined to treat her like a child?"

"Did you deduce that from her conversation? That was clever of you, Selina. It seemed so to me, but she appeared content. He was devoted to her."

"But I would not have thought that Harriet would care to be treated like that," said Selina a little anxiously.

"You are thinking of her son? He does treat his mother much as his father did, but he obviously does not expect all women to be the same."

"But did his father?"

"He may have done. I remember that he was somewhat disconcerted to hear John ask my advice on some matter, as this was a novel idea to him."

"One cannot help liking Mrs Linton, though," said Selina.

"Oh, she is a most endearing creature! I should not think she has an enemy in the world?"

"Of whom are you speaking?" queried John, entering the room.

"Mrs Linton, who arrived just after you and Johnnie went down the drive."

John looked slightly guilty. "I did wonder if I heard a carriage, but I did not see it – she was not offended? No, she would not be. And is she well?"

"In high spirits and full of praise for Bath."

He grinned. "Is she, now? I cannot say that I admire her taste."

"Why, Bath is a beautiful city," said Caroline.

"I never said that it was not, my love. You know that I did not refer to the architecture."

"Nor did she. Poor Selina did not know where to look when she found herself being commiserated with for having to leave all its pleasures."

Selina choked and looked reproachfully at her friend, "Caroline, you must not set me off again! Because *I* did not enjoy Bath does not mean I despise it. What will your husband think of me?"

John merely grinned again. "I think you a woman of sense," he said.

Their son could be heard approaching the house, accompanied by conversational barks, and Caroline looked dismayed. "John, we shall have to keep the dogs out of the house while Mrs Linton is here, she has a pet dog – so tiny. Pinto would likely mistake it for a rat."

"Well, the dogs are not really supposed to come into the house, especially if there are visitors, are they?"

"But you know how often they do."

"I do indeed. Let us hope that this prohibition will not cause Johnnie to resent our guest."

"So do I," said Caroline. "She is full of good will to all. I do not suppose that she has any notion of how her 'Didi' would affect Pinto and Marmion."

"Is that what she calls it? Good Heavens!"

"I know, it is rather pathetic, but she clearly adores it."

"I find it distressing that they breed such small dogs," observed Selina. "I wonder how – and why – they do so."

"I agree," said John. "It seems an insult to Nature. Well, I must go and secure our dogs. Caroline, surely Augusta should be here soon? They are only bringing their three older children, are they not?"

Caroline nodded.

"That is as well, or they would be later still. I am fond of Augusta and have always liked James, but he was never one for being prompt." John limped out of the room, and Selina looked inquiringly at her friend.

"Did I gather that Augusta is a relation?"

"Yes, John's cousin, and the only Carpenter to welcome our marriage."

"I thought there was a complete breach with them, but it has healed?"

"Not really. Augusta is the only one to maintain contact. She is married an old university friend of John's – not entirely to her parent's satisfaction – and was glad to renew the connection. They visit now and again, and her two older daughters are to be the little bridesmaids, Emily is eleven and Margaret eight, the other two girls are little more than babies. As the Lawrences will only be staying a couple of days, they and their baby brother will stay in Shropshire with the nurse. Jamie, the oldest child, is a little younger than Charlotte, but he and Johnnie are quite good friends. They will dine with us, but the girls will have supper in the nursery. As John said, it would be as well for them to arrive fairly soon with all that will have to be arranged."

"I begin to understand why John was relieved that only half the family are coming," said Selina, amused.

The Lawrences were indeed late, and everyone else was ready to eat before Augusta, James, and Jamie joined the company in the crowded breakfast room, making for an uneasy meal. The proportion of males to females was uneven, too, especially since the boys were too young to remain behind with their fathers and the port, and had gone out to comfort the exiled dogs when the ladies retired to the drawing room.

This session with the ill assorted females was the most trying time of the entire day for Caroline. Mrs Linton absorbed the full attention of both girls but kept appealing to their mother and at first she was afraid that Selina and Augusta would have nothing in common besides herself. Fortunately Charlotte had mentioned the Pughs and how Selina had taken the motherless children under her wing, and kind hearted Augusta had been moved to hear about it and compared notes happily enough while Mrs Linton rambled on to her hostess. Not long after the gentlemen joined them Charlotte slipped off to bed and Harriet followed quite soon. When tea was brought, most of the guests were feeling the effects of the long day, Augusta and her husband did not keep late hours and Selina had had a tiring journey. By eleven Caroline took the opportunity of saying that only she and John need wait up for the young men. Predictably, Mrs Linton was anxious to see her son, but the other guests were happy to retire to their rooms.

Caroline looked at the clock on the mantelpiece and suppressed a yawn, "It wants less than half an hour to midnight," she thought. Richard had warned them that he and Steven might be late, but at what point need one start to worry? She looked at her husband and Mrs Linton. The lady was frankly sleeping, with Didi on her lap, an untroubled smile on her plump face, but at least she was not starting to fret. John made a nervous grimace and shifted his lame leg uncomfortably. Selina's remark that he looked older came back to her mind, and she acknowledged that the changes in him had been so gradual that they were only now apparent to her. Though his hair had receded very little, it was very much greyer and the lines etched by pain no longer looked as out of place as they had on the youthful face she had first known.

Mrs Linton stirred in her sleep and made a little bubbling sound before starting to snore gently. John looked irritated and rose stealthily to his feet, moving haltingly to the window where he pulled back the curtain enough to see down the moonlit drive. Their guest was clearly not in need of her company, and Caroline went to join her husband at the other end of the room. He looked round at her approach, smiling wearily, and put his arm round her. Following his gaze she said quickly, "I do not think we need worry until midnight."

"I was not worrying exactly, and not only thinking about the delay to those lads." He sighed, "My dear, I do hope we are doing the right thing, allowing this marriage."

"Harriet seems to think so."

"That is true, bless her. But she is so young! You were not married at her age."

"No, but many women were. I was perhaps unusual. Do you know, Mrs Linton was married just after her fifteenth birthday."

John cast a look over his shoulder at the guest, and lowered his voice carefully. "Good Heavens! – Oh, but that is too young."

"Yes, I agree. I think she is now aware of it. She is not quite a fool, you know."

"I do know. I frequently had the feeling that Linton was unaware that she had a mind of her own. I suppose if he married a schoolgirl, he found it natural to direct her actions, and he was really devoted to her. But what can her parents have been thinking about to permit that?"

"Marrying her off to the best advantage, I imagine," said Caroline dryly. "Mr Linton was a very rich man."

"But quite without property," said John.

"Ah, there speaks the landowner!"

John laughed, "Well, were we trying to marry Harriet to the best advantage, we would not have chosen a man who had money but no estate."

"Yes, but I do not think her family would have possessed either," Caroline pointed out gently.

"I daresay you are right, said John with another sigh. "It still seems a poor decision on their part. Fortunate that in Linton she had someone who was good to her. I was looking at those diamonds she brought for Harriet. They will become her very well, but it is not to my taste for a young girl."

"Nor to mine," agreed Caroline. "But a wedding present is something to last beyond youth. What would be more suitable for Harriet now might look very foolish in years to come."

"Not if she keeps as young-looking as you do, love," said John, pressing her fondly against him. Caroline was both touched and amused.

"Selina and the children said something like that," she said. "I cannot understand it, I make no effort to look younger than I am. Do you remember poor Mrs Price, in Hampstead? But the strange thing is that I never did look as young as Harriet does. Even when I was fifteen I was frequently taken for about twenty."

"You would have been fitter to marry at fifteen," remarked John, glancing back at their sleeping guest.

"Perhaps," said Caroline, "I was bright enough, but no more suitable." She thought back to her girlhood, and leaning against his shoulder compared it with that of her daughters. She felt that she had a better relationship with them than she had had with her mother, but then her parents had not been the only people in her life to guide her. She suddenly wondered what Charles Randall's influence had meant to his sister-in-law. Having enjoyed her time with him and her aunt so much more than the regime at home, she had felt that he was right and her mother wrong, but however grateful she was for the superior education he had provided for her, she now perceived it as an affront to her mother, and felt distressed for her.

Again her mind went back to how boring she had found the preparations for Lucy's wedding. Of course, Harriet's was a much simpler affair – Mrs Randall had brought off a social triumph – but she felt the whole thing had imposed a great deal more strain on the household. Having escaped the culmination of all those weeks of labour, she found herself wondering what her mother's thoughts had been as her father walked Lucy down the aisle. Self-congratulation, no doubt, but had she had twinges of anxiety about this being the best thing for her daughter? She knew that her sister been happy in her engagement to Sir Charles, who had apparently made her an excellent husband, but what if she had changed her mind?

"Ah, at last," said John in tones of relief as lights appeared at the bend in the drive and a carriage swept up to the front to be illuminated by a yellow glow as the waiting footman flung open the door.

"What has happened?" Mrs Linton jerked awake, making a grab at her little dog as she struggled to rise. It eluded her and leapt to the floor, "Oh, have they arrived?"

"They have indeed," said John, politely coming to her assistance while Caroline retrieved the animal and they moved to the hall.

All the female servants had been given permission to retire to bed, but one at least had ignored this, and as the carriage was driven round to the stables and the two occupants entered, a stout little figure watched the footman shut the door and marched firmly up to greet them.

"Nancy!" said one young man in tones of mild rebuke. "What are you doing up at this hour? You should be getting your beauty sleep for tomorrow."

His old nurse snorted. "Oh, indeed, and how much sleep do you think I'd have had, till I knew you'd got here all right, young Dickon?"

The use of his childhood nickname appeared to leave Richard quite unmoved, "Go on, don't tell me you were worried."

"Wasn't I, though? So was your mother, I'll be bound."

"We will have to explain, Richard," said the other young man with a chuckle.

"Steven!" cried Mrs Linton, peering up through sleep-dazed eyes. "There you are, my darling."

Her son turned and bent to kiss her, "Yes, here I am, dear," he said gently. "And very sorry that you have all been kept waiting so long. Good evening, Mrs Carpenter, good evening, Sir."

"Good morning!" responded John, somewhat grimly.

"Oh, my," said Steven. "Richard, look at that!"

Richard examined the face of the hall clock and laughed. "I said your watch was slow!" he remarked. "Nancy, we are starving!"

"Are you, now? And whose fault is that?"

"Not mine, I assure you."

"Well now, I'll see what I can do. I made that Ellen stay up, I thought you might be hungry when you got here – knowing you!"

"Could you order some wine for us all, Nancy," said John, "I feel some refreshment is called for."

Nancy nodded and gave a little bob before vanishing to the back area, and Richard moved forward to greet his mother and stepfather.

"Poor Mama, poor Papa," he said cheerfully, "I really am sorry that we are so late."

"But it was not your fault," intoned Steven cheerfully.

"I am sure it was not yours, my darling," cried his mother loyally.

"Well, no – not exactly," Steven put his arm round her as they made their way to the drawing room. "It is true that I was driving when we lost our way, but then I am not as familiar with the country round here as Richard is." He grinned at his friend.

"You lost your way?" said John, looking quizzically at his stepson.

Richard's eyes twinkled. "Yes, wasn't that dreadful! The thing was, I was up very late last night so we could not get away as soon as we hoped. We had an early dinner on the road, and when we continued, I am afraid my lack of sleep caught up with me. Poor Steven, good fellow that he is, did not like to wake me just to ask the way, and took the wrong turning, which landed us up in a farm-yard. I awoke to find a cow looking mournfully into my face and started to wonder if I had drunk more than I thought I had!"

"Portsman was busy trying to direct me away from a haystack," Steven continued, "I got him to soothe the horses, who not unreasonably took exception to the whole affair."

"In the middle of this, the farmer appeared looking furious and tried to claim that we were damaging his property," said Richard, "He threatened us with the law."

"'We are the law,' says Richard," Steven put in. "And reads him a lecture about the state of his roads. I doubt if the poor man understood a word of it!"

"In the end, Steven paid him to direct us back to the toll road," said Richard, "And we got away. But we had strayed from the part of the country I know, and it was not until Steven's watch pointed to quarter past ten that we found ourselves back on the right road."

"I guess it must have been after half past by then," said Steven. His mother, who had been clasping his hand anxiously throughout this account, seemed near to tears.

"Oh, my darling boy. Thank goodness you are both safe!"

"Oh, foolish Mama, of course we are," said Steven. "Farmers hold no terrors for us!"

"Oh, but you might have met with highwaymen! Ah well, all is well that ends well."

"I will just go upstairs and see that your rooms are ready," said Caroline, "Before Nancy comes back." John gave her a slightly puzzled look as she left the room, but he said nothing, and she felt sure he would soon understand her real motive.

As she had expected, Harriet was standing, a slim pale figure, just inside her door. She put her finger to her lips, indicating the sleeping Charlotte, and crept out on to the landing, whispering, "Oh, Mama, is he come?"

"Yes, you bad creature – what do you expect to be like in the morning, staying awake in this way?"

"But I could not sleep until I knew he was here," protested Harriet. "I kept fearing that something terrible might have happened to them both! I do wish I could see him."

"Never mind, you will soon be together all the time," said Caroline, urging her back to her bedroom.

"Oh, I know. Oh, Mama, is it wicked to be so happy?"

"Wicked? Don't talk nonsense, child."

"But – leaving you and Papa, and the children. I feel that I ought to mind more."

"It is kind of you to mind at all," said Caroline firmly. "I should be seriously worried if you were more concerned about that than marrying Steven."

"I know you do not like to talk about your parents," Harriet said cautiously, letting herself be led back to bed and lying down, "But did you mind leaving them?"

"As I think I may have mentioned," said Caroline evasively, "I was really a great deal closer to my uncle and aunt, who had already died." She wished she had not had to convey a false impression of her early background – without really deviating from the truth she had made it seem that she had had an unhappy childhood except for her time in London – but it still saddened her. Her daughter was obviously afraid that she might have distressed her, gave her a penitent kiss, and snuggled down on her pillow. She seemed to fall asleep almost at once, and Caroline waited a minute to make sure and quietly left the room, closing the door softly.

"And were the rooms all right?" asked Richard wickedly as she rejoined the company that had gathered round plates of food and glasses of wine.

Caroline regarded her son with steady eyes, "Perfectly – when I saw them this afternoon," she said. The guests did not seem to have heard, but John and Richard looked at her with understanding.

Steven had just established his mother in a chair and was plying her with food, which caused the little dog to wake and yap enthusiastically. He groaned, "Oh, my dear. Have you still got that creature?"

Mrs Linton looked up reproachfully, "You naughty boy," she said. "I told Harriet how rude you are about my little Didi. I told her I would have liked to give her one just like him but I was afraid you would not permit it."

"If I really thought she wanted it," said Steven, "I would endeavour to endure it. But I think she might prefer a larger dog, a spaniel, say."

When Steven had escorted his mother upstairs, Richard regarded his mother and stepfather thoughtfully, leaning against the mantelpiece, his handsome head alert and his grey eyes for once serious, "My dears," he said. "I know how you must be feeling. In a way, I suppose I am responsible."

"Do not flatter yourself," said Caroline. "If you had not brought Steven here, Harriet would have met someone else."

"Well, old Steven really is a good fellow. I know he will make Harriet happy, and believe me, I would not say that if I were not sure. He is a better man than I am!"

"Is he, love?" asked Caroline, smiling.

"I certainly wouldn't recommend myself as a husband, not at the present time." Richard gave a sardonic grin. "Of course, he is a bit older than I am. But he is – steady."

"Not too steady, I hope," said John. "That would make him a dull dog"

"Oh, he is not that. But he keeps regular hours, and drinks moderately – whereas I myself…"

"We all know you are a dreadful creature," agreed Caroline cheerfully. Richard was moved to put his arms round her and lean his cheek against her forehead.

"Oh, Mama, I am not sure it is quite a joke," he murmured. "If you knew everything about my life…"

"It would not make any difference, love," said Caroline quietly and perhaps more sincerely than he realised. He kissed her, grinned at his stepfather, and said, "Well, I must go to bed. I really was up late, working on a brief."

"Do not worry," said John as they were left alone. "He is not really as bad as all that!"

"I know. And he is still my son." He kissed her, and then brought up the topic nearest to his heart.

"Did you find Harriet still awake?"

"Yes, foolish girl. She is asleep now. Harriet was indeed slumbering peacefully when they looked in upon her on their way to their bedroom.

PART 12

Hyde Park, and the Lintons' house in London

Summer 1824

"This *is* where Johnnie – sorry, I must remember to call him John! – is going to meet us, Mama?" asked Charlotte. "What a very pleasant lake."

""I have always liked the Serpentine," Caroline agreed, thinking walking there with her uncle and aunt. When she had kept house for Charles Randall, he had preferred to drive out to Richmond. She sighed, and her daughter looked at her with concern.

"Oh, Mama, I have tired you," she said self-reproachfully, and looked about her. "There is a bench over there. Come and sit down. He will see us there quite easily."

"I am not in the least tired," Caroline protested as she was gently urged towards the seat.

"Oh, Mama, think how much walking you have done today, and in London, too."

"My dear child, I lived in London before you were born."

"But it is all changed now, you said so yourself. And don't forget that Dick and Sarah are coming to dinner tonight. Harriet would never forgive me if I let you get exhausted!"

Caroline sat down obediently, "Very well, dear, if you will sit down as well. I have to admit that I am more tired than I would have been forty years ago, when I last saw this place.

"Forty years?" asked Charlotte, arranging her apple-green skirts carefully as she seated herself. "Really? I thought you lived in London when Dick was a baby?"

Caroline explained how far Islington was from the area they were in now, and Charlotte listened with interest and understanding. Looking at her down bent head with its beautiful profile, her mother felt again the helpless anger she had a few months ago. "That wretched young man!" she thought. As if reading her mind, Charlotte looked up and perhaps deliberately pursued the subject of her old nurse.

"Was it in Islington that you first met Nancy? She was Dick's nurse, was she not? Did you employ her for that when he was born?"

"No, that came about almost by accident. She was the maid-of-all-work in the house where I boarded. But she had helped to bring up a younger brother and sister, and was so helpful, whereas I had had no experience of babies at that time."

"And now she has gone back to London," said Charlotte. "It was such a surprise when she decided to leave Coombe Park. I thought she was a fixture there. Of course, Dick was always her favourite, wasn't he? I suppose now that he is about to become a father she feels he needs her more. Do you think Sarah minds the way she talks about his as childhood?"

"Sarah is a sensible young woman," said Caroline. "I am sure she can make allowances, especially as Nancy seems to have taken her under her wing."

"It is a mercy that she likes Sarah, don't you think? I like Sarah myself, very much."

Caroline agreed, refraining from expressing too much pleasure that her elder son had finally found himself a wife, in case it seemed a callous reminder to Charlotte of her own disappointment.

"Dick, and Harriet, both happily married," said her daughter at once. "You should be content with that, Mama, do not worry about me."

"But I do!" said Caroline unhappily. "I am very distressed for your sake."

"I wish you were not. I am not miserable, I never expected to marry, and at least I know that I am not unattractive, since Mr Perceval was distracted from his duty by my face. That is something, Mama. Some women never have that."

"Oh, love," said Caroline, watching her attempt at a smile.

Charlotte shook her head and said briskly, "But that is enough about me. I wonder how Nancy likes being back in London."

"Probably she does not think of it as being 'back' they live in such a different part of the city," said Caroline.

"I expect we will hear all about it this evening – Oh, there is Johnnie. Has he seen us?"

"Yes, he is waving." Caroline watched her younger son make his way over the grass from the direction of Piccadilly. Tall, and already losing the gangling appearance of adolescence, he did not look to be under eighteen, particularly in the assured way he moved among the other visitors to Hyde Park.

Charlotte watched him approach lovingly, "To think our little Johnnie will be going up to Oxford soon," she said. "I expect it seems even stranger to you! He will really get ahead of me then." She looked almost wistful, and her mother regarded her thoughtfully. Apart from Richard, Charlotte had profited most from her father's classical education.

"Would you have liked to have gone to Oxford?" she asked, remembering her own longings while studying at her uncle's house.

Charlotte laughed. "Oh, what an idea, Mama! A female to be studying at the university – whatever would they say? It would be nice it if were possible, but of course it is not."

"I wonder," said Caroline. Her uncle had sympathised with her and had prophesied that one day the universities would open their doors to women, and she thought her daughter was perhaps more intellectual than she had been. But Charlotte was no rebel.

John had now come up to them. "So there you are," he said. "I am glad you were able to find a seat. How are Harriet, and Steven, and the children?"

"All very well," said Caroline. "Stevie and Maud keep asking when they are going to see Uncle John."

"They seemed very disappointed that you are staying with Dick and Sarah, instead of at their house," said Charlotte.

John was amused. "I expect that Harriet feels Stevie is bad enough without my encouragement! I hope they missed Papa, too?"

"Oh they did," said Charlotte, "Quite upset that he had not come. We promised them a visit to Coombe Park in September, but at their age that is not really a consolation. How are Dick, and Sarah – and Nancy?"

"All in excellent health. It was good to see Nancy again, she is wonderful the way she has everything organised. Oh, do you know, she had a visitor the other day, from a nephew and niece, Sarah was telling me. It seems that Nancy has a married sister living not too far away. Did you know about that, Mama?"

"I knew of the sister, but I had no idea where she lived. There was a brother as well, who had a shop in Holborn, but I think he died."

"Of course, she came from London, I had not really appreciated that until now," said John. He had not seated himself and now consulted the watch he had recently been given. "You said that you wanted to see that statue, Charley?"

"Yes, I did – but, John, Mama is rather tired. I do not think we should go any further."

"Charlotte, I keep telling you that I could walk a great deal further," said Caroline, and paused.

"But?" said John, grinning.

"Mama does not really care about the statue."

"I must confess I am not very eager about it," Caroline agreed. "I admire the Duke of Wellington – in moderation – but since this is only a tribute to him and not a likeness, no. I can manage perfectly well without seeing it. If you and John are worried about me, why don't you go and see it without me? I will be quite happy sitting here until you return."

Charlotte looked doubtful. "Are you sure, Mama? I must say, I would like to see it, and I do not want you to tire yourself – but I am not very happy to leave you alone."

"Oh, go along with you!" said Caroline. "I have said I will be all right. John, take this foolish creature away. I can assure you both that I have not yet reached the stage where I need to be looked after."

Charlotte permitted herself to be led off, and Caroline sat gravely watching the tall pair as they made their way towards Hyde Park Corner and became lost in the crowd. Her heart was still wrung as she contemplated that deplorable affair last November. The fact that it was difficult to find anyone to blame to did not prevent her feeling that the young man in question was more at fault than Charlotte would permit anyone to say.

"Why could he not have said he was considered engaged from the first? Did he have some hope that the Ashwood family would not press him, or had he fooled himself that he was not being serious in his approach to Charlotte? He was exactly the type to take her fancy. If only he had mentioned that wretched young woman from the start, Charlotte would have tried to curb her feelings before she had a chance to fall so deeply in love."

As it was, it had been she who had insisted that he should not to turn his back on the match that had been arranged for him. Mr Perceval had seemed grief-stricken, but Caroline had little sympathy for him, and had found it hard not to wish that his marriage would be unhappy. She restrained herself because it distressed her daughter so much. Charlotte would not hear a word against him, and Caroline contrasted her behaviour with how she might have felt in a similar situation. "I think I would have let him repudiate the engagement," she thought, "If such a situation had arisen when I was her age." Her younger daughter might resemble her in looks, but in this she was very different. Charlotte was not meek, but the hot temper that flared up in both her parents seemed to be transmuted into a sustained endurance. Her will to overcome her misery was formidable, and her mother felt both awed and humbled by it. Only those who knew her well would realise how deeply she was hurt, and Caroline was afraid that she would never change. How far she herself had come from the attitudes of her youth, she thought, when she could sincerely grieve that a bright intelligent girl might be denied a happy married life!

She had been idly watching three people coming in her direction for a minute or two, and now realised that they were aiming for the seat she was on. Even before she was close enough for Caroline to see her features, the taller of the two girls accompanying a plump middle-aged woman had made her think of her youngest sister. A fair, flower-like creature with very fair hair, she was at least eighteen and looked healthy, but the nearer they came, the more she resembled Harriet, how strange. Though the other girl was smaller and dark, with twinkling hazel eyes, they were obviously sisters, and this was plainly their mother even before the shorter girl remarked, "There you are, Mama, I am sure this lady will not mind your sitting here."

The other girl addressed Caroline, who was making room on the seat. "My mother feels the heat very much, it will not inconvenience you if she rests bedside you?"

"Of course not," said Caroline, turning her attention to the stout mother for the first time. In spite of the large shady bonnet on her head, her face was red with exertion and heat, but it was still comely. It was amusing to hear the two girls fussing over her, blaming themselves for overtiring her. No, she assured them in a sweet clear voice, she was not exhausted.

"Perhaps not, but you cannot go any further," said the fair girl in blue, firmly.

"Oh, my dears – I must! I know how much you both wish to see that statue. If we wait until Edward comes, perhaps I shall be rested."

"Edward! He think it is very foolish that females should have contributed to a monument," declared the other girl with her small nose in the air. "I do not see why Olivia and I should not go together on our own, to see what we have helped to pay for. We do not need Edward to escort us."

"Oh, Elinor, we cannot leave Mama!" exclaimed her sister reproachfully.

"Of course you can," said their mother. "I will certainly be rested by the time you have made your way there and returned." She turned astonishingly blue eyes on Caroline and said with a peculiarly attractive smile, "As long as I am not disturbing this lady?"

"Not at all," said Caroline. Hearing her voice for the second time, the woman looked puzzled as she turned back to her daughters.

"There! You see, girls? Off you go, now, or Edward will be here before you know it."

Reassured, the girls went back in the direction that Charlotte and John had taken. Caroline gazed at her companion with a mixture of pleasure and dismay, and the recognition appeared to be mutual, the heart shaped face surprisingly unaffected by the increased weight, the blue eyes swimming with the familiar tears. She gulped, and said in a small voice, "Caroline?"

"Yes, Lucy, it is I." The tears brimmed over, and in the pause that followed, Caroline wondered if her sister had now realised that she ought not to be speaking to an outcast. Since they were both pledged to remain where they were until claimed by their respective children, this might prove awkward. But Lucy had only been mopping her eyes and collecting her thoughts, and as she turned she gave another of the lovely smiles that had always been characteristic of her.

"Let me look at you! I knew your voice as soon as you spoke, and I had just been thinking of you. You really have not changed very much, even your hair has kept its colour." Something about these words made her frown thoughtfully, but Caroline assured her that she certainly had quite a few grey hairs. "But I am sure you did not know me, at first. I have grown so fat!"

"Oh no, just comfortable."

Lucy gave her clear laugh, "Well, it is comfortable, you know, but not very attractive."

"And your face is unchanged," said her sister. "And after having ten children…"

Lucy looked surprised. "Oh, how do you know that?"

"Selina told me, she heard it from Georgina."

Another tear fell. "I only have nine, now," said Lucy sadly. "My third son died three years ago, but I have lost touch with Georgina, so perhaps Selina had not heard."

"I am so sorry," said Caroline gently. Her hand was grasped and pressed.

"Yes, that made me understand how Mama felt when she lost little Dick, and Harriet. I had always sympathised, but somehow, when it happens to you it makes it so much more poignant. But I still have nine, in good health. Those girls are my youngest."

"I thought they seemed delightful," said Caroline. "When I first saw the one in blue, she reminded me so much of our sister Harriet."

"Ah, you noticed that? It made Charles very worried, till she passed sixteen – and as you can see, she is the picture of health." Lucy played with her wedding ring, glanced at Caroline's ungloved left hand, and then turned eagerly, "Oh, Caroline, I know why I was thinking of you, we passed a girl who was the image of you. But even if I could have spoken of it to Olivia and Elinor, they were fussing so it almost drove it from my head. Could she be…?"

"My daughter Charlotte has just gone with her brother to look at the new statue," said Caroline. "I was not particularly interested and they were afraid I'd get tired, so begged me to sit here and rest."

Lucy laughed softly. "I see I am not the only one with firm children," she said. "Um – you did not marry Mr Martin?" it was more of a statement than a question, and her sister's negative did not take her by surprise. "But you are married?"

"Oh yes," said Caroline.

"And that was your son? What a handsome boy. Do you just have the two?"

"No, I have four. The two eldest are married."

"And are you a grandmother? I have a number of grandchildren, as you might imagine."

"Yes, I have four, all the children of my elder daughter. My son did not marry until last year, but he is shortly to become a father." Caroline felt that mentioning Richard might evoke

244

memories of Thomas Martin and changed the subject, asking about other members of the family. "I saw the notice of Mama's death in *The Times* last year, but I imagine that Anna is still alive?"

"Oh yes," said Lucy a little bleakly. "She and Mama came to live with us, after Papa died, they only rented their house in Hertfordshire. I suppose Selina told you how they leased out the Old Manor and came to live in the next village?"

"She did." Caroline could not help a grim note finding its way into her voice.

Lucy gave the ghost of a sigh. "It was very pleasant having them so near, but I think Papa missed Sussex once he recovered from his stroke enough to walk out."

"Oh dear, I did wonder about that. And did he leave the property to Anna?"

"That was what he did, for her lifetime, but it was to go eventually to my second son, Hugh, who was only six when Papa died. Anna was forty then, he did make the proviso that should she marry she could leave it to any child she had, but there was little chance of that happening. She has been very generous" – Lucy made this admission almost grudgingly – "she insisted on making the place over to him as soon as he was old enough, he married young and now lives there with his wife and baby son."

"And Anna still lives with you and Charles?"

"Indeed. She has a suite of rooms in the East Wing. I think you would recognise her at once. Her hair is greyer, but otherwise she looks much the same."

"Yes," said Caroline thoughtfully. "Anna was made to be elderly, I always felt – it was getting through the intervening years that she found difficult!"

Lucy may have meant to look disapproving, but failed completely and chuckled, murmuring faintly, "Oh, Caroline! No one but you says things like that." To her sister's dismay, and secret irritation, she then sat weeping silently, dabbing at her eyes with a wholly inadequate handkerchief. "It has made me so unhappy when I thought about you! Not knowing what had become of you, even if you were still alive. And except to Mama, I could not even mention you."

Caroline was startled. "Mama?" she echoed.

"Oh, yes, after Papa went, she often talked of you. Only when we were alone, and to me, never to Anna. I believe that she thought I would sympathise, as a mother myself."

"Poor Mama, I was a sad trial to her," said Caroline gravely. "Now that I have daughters of my own, I can understand why she was so out of charity with Uncle Charles."

"At the end, she spoke quite kindly of him, I think she perhaps appreciated him more," said Lucy. "Her mind never wandered, as dear Lady Carter's did, poor soul, but she became more – mellow, could one say? Especially about you and Uncle Charles. I had the feeling that this had been discussed often with my father. She sometimes wondered if she had been wrong, when my uncle died."

"But Mama was always so confident that what she did was right!" exclaimed Caroline.

"Yes, it was after Papa died that she began to express different ideas, I used to feel that she was almost speaking to him. She was very low at that time and we never thought she would live another sixteen years." Lucy hesitated. "I do not wish to offend you, Caroline, but she spoke also of Mr Martin and the effect he had on you. She was convinced that it was not simply his intellect that appealed to you, whatever you said."

"She may well have been right," said Caroline guardedly.

"She said something strange, too, she did not feel that he was really intelligent enough for you. I myself…"

"Yes?"

"I did not dislike him, the little I saw of him, but I did not think he was really the sort of man that Uncle Charles would have rated very highly." Caroline was impressed with this perception but had no desire to recount her own disillusion with the man, and was glad when her sister concluded by saying, "I do think she would have been glad to know what had become of you."

Caroline pondered this. Would Mrs Randall have really liked the idea that her erring daughter had had a happy life with a husband and a family, albeit with a secret that must be kept? There must surely have been a side to her she had not shown when her daughters were younger, and she remembered how she had occasionally felt that it was she, rather than her husband, who had the greater intelligence. Lucy was sitting gazing dreamily at the Serpentine, there seemed a real danger that they would both become too concerned with memories, when they probably did not have very long together. She broke the silence by asking how Sir Charles was doing.

Lucy gave a loving smile. "Oh, he keeps very well. He has grown even stouter than I have. We are as fine pair! He and I and our three youngest children have come to town for the christening of a grandchild, my eldest son's first son."

"An important young man, then," observed Caroline.

"Indeed he is. Today Charles is visiting his bank and seeing his attorney. Caroline, do you live in London?"

"No, in Wiltshire. I am visiting my married daughter."

"And is your husband with you?" asked Lucy a little anxiously.

"No, he has been lame since an accident when he was younger, he finds long journeys in a coach constricting. He found it very painful last time he came to London. He prefers the country, in any case. So Charlotte and Johnnie and I have come without him. Tell me about your family, Lucy – Selina only knew how many you have. She said your eldest was a girl but that you had a son the following year."

"That is so. We had four sons altogether, Charles, Hugh, James, and Edward. Hugh was given Papa's second name."

"I realised that," said Caroline. "Why not Richard?"

"Charles felt that it would be unlucky, because of little Dick."

"But any name might have been given to a child that died," said Caroline.

"That was how I felt, and not being called Richard did not prevent my dear James dying at the age of fifteen," said Lucy.

"Still that was how Charles felt and I would not have distressed him for the world. I was prepared for that when Hugh was born, because I had wanted to call my first baby after Harriet, instead of giving her my name, and Charles told me what he felt then." It was almost a shock to Caroline to realise that her sister had been pregnant when she was expecting Richard, but she had no chance to think about it because Lucy was continuing almost wistfully, "I was pleased to have a girl first, it seemed as if we needed one to fill the space Harriet left. Not that Lucy resembled her in the slightest, she was born with dark hair and has always looked a Carter."

"And you had a son the following year?"

"Yes, Charlie was born in 1796. Then we had two more girls, Anne, for Mama, and Cecilia after Miss Carter. Hugh came next, and then Clarinda, which is a family name of the Carters. Charles has a great friend called James, and then we had Edward, for his uncle, our vicar, if you remember?"

"And where did the names for the two youngest come from?" asked Caroline with interest.

"They were simply names that appealed to us, we seemed to have exhausted most of the family ones."

"I am not surprised," said Caroline.

"No – ten is a large family, is it not? "Lucy sighed. "I always seemed to be pregnant in those days. Many women sympathised with me, but you know I really did not mind."

"No? I did feel some concern when I heard."

"I suppose I was fortunate, my babies came easily, and I experienced very little pain. I think other people may have had a worse time. One of my elder girls, and Charles's wife Sophia certainly make a great commotion about their confinements. But perhaps you agree with them?"

"I think my experience has been much like yours, I had little trouble, and nor has my daughter."

"Ah, your elder daughter. Caroline, you have only named two of your children to me – what are the others called?"

Caroline smiled. "Harriet, and Richard," she said.

Lucy's face lit up, "Oh, Caroline, I am so pleased to hear that. Particularly about Harriet. Does she look like our little sister?"

"No, she is more like you."

"As I was, of course. Fancy! Do you know, not one of my daughters really resembles me – not in the way yours looks like you. Is she going to marry?"

"Charlotte? I am very much afraid it is unlikely. Caroline sighed, "It is something that distresses me." She gave Lucy love as brief account of her daughter's unhappy experience. "She is young, I would hope she would change her mind, but she is determined that marriage is not for her."

"As you were," Lucy reminded her.

"Yes, indeed," said Caroline. "But although Charlotte may look like me, she has a very different character. I was simply against the idea of marriage, I had not had any reason to feel I could not have a man I loved."

"You have surely altered your opinion on that subject?" said Lucy eagerly. "You have been happy with your husband?"

"I have. John and I are well suited, and I think we care more for each other the longer we are together."

"Ah!" said Lucy in a pleased tone of voice. "I would say that is how Charles and I feel, too. We like the same things, you know. But I have noticed that some people appear to become strangers, leading separate lives, once their children have grown up and left home. It is almost as if only that common interest kept them together."

Caroline was glad to know that the Carter's affection had survived ten children and that her sister's initial infatuation had grown and deepened. "Children do affect a marriage," she observed. "But their absence need not matter, if the affection is there. You recall Selina? Her marriage to Mr Penry was childless, but they were a devoted couple."

"They were? Oh, I am so glad to hear that. Georgina spoke of her being unfortunate in not having children, and then being widowed, but it was almost as if she resented her sister being free of ties. Poor Georgina! She never seems content with what she has – nothing is ever quite right. Are you still in communication with Selina?"

"Certainly. Did Georgina tell you that she returned to Wales to look after her husband's nephew, whom she had known as a boy, when he was tragically left with three tiny motherless children?"

"She did," said Lucy. "That was something else she resented, that Selina should go back to what she called that barbaric country when she had got away from it, when she could have come to live with them. Charles said she must think there would be money in it for her and her family, which was naughty of him, but I am afraid I could not feel it was unjust."

"I suppose Georgina felt rebuffed," said Caroline. "But it is suspicious that she should suddenly discover affection for Selina – there was little enough of that for her when she lived with her family. It is hardly surprising that she turned to those who cared for her and needed her."

"I do not think poor Georgina ever loved any one very much," said Lucy gravely. "Possibly not even her husband or her children. Before her husband died they lived near enough for our two families to visit occasionally. I felt that she was for ever comparing my children with hers, of course I felt that mine were superior, but I would never have said so. Hers were over-indulged when younger, and then the poor girls were so plain – she constantly boasted of their accomplishments. No, I was not sorry to lose contact with her!"

Caroline was sympathetic, but she had caught sight of Charlotte and John in the distance, and began to rise to her feet. This dismayed Lucy, "Oh, you are not going?" she cried. "Can you – not – stay – until – my girls – come?" her voice faltered, and she looked piteously at her sister.

"But to what purpose, my dear? You could not tell them who I am, could you? How would you introduce me? I am sure that they have no idea that I exist."

Lucy looked up at her unhappily. "You are correct," she said sadly. "But now that you are married, surely it is different? I should so much like to meet your children…"

"Oh, Lucy dear, cannot you see that the same consideration applies in my case? I could not introduce you to them. They know that I had a sister who died, for whom Harriet is named, but when I met my husband he thought me a widow with a little boy."

Lucy had gone pink. "Oh!" she said. "Yes, I see. Oh, Caroline, if only you had never met Mr Martin and left home."

"I should still have gone, my dear. I will admit that Mama may have been more perceptive than I was about what I felt for him, but it was partly because he made such a convenient excuse. I could no longer face life with my parents, and – Anna! It would have driven us all mad!"

The mention of their older sister caused Lucy to nod understandingly. "Even before I was married, I had begun to realise what she is like – I suppose she means well enough, but, oh dear!"

Caroline glanced at her children, who had paused to talk to a family with two dogs, and bent to kiss her. "Well, Lucy, at least you know what has become of me."

Lucy held on to her for a moment. "I shall say nothing of it, even to Charles, but it will be a great comfort to me to think of you now. Ah, here come your children."

Her sister indicated to Charlotte and John that she would join them, and remarked, "I see your daughters, with a young man, only a little further off."

"That is my youngest son, Edward," said Lucy. "He is to be ordained next month." She sounded so unenthusiastic that Caroline wondered if the serious-looking young man was inclined to preach at his parents. She disengaged herself and walked swiftly away, resisting the temptation to look back.

As they moved off in the direction of Steven and Harriet's house, Charlotte said casually, "So the large lady did come and sit beside you, Mama." Her tone was not unkind but Caroline found herself wincing. It was somehow painful to realise that her sister might have appeared ridiculous to strangers.

"We did not think she would get any further than your seat, she looked so knocked up," said John. "Still, it was someone to talk to, I suppose."

Clearly neither of them had seen her kiss Lucy, but Caroline still found herself totally unable to reply, and her expression caused her daughter to cry out with dismay, "Oh Mama, what is the matter?"

"Nothing, really." Caroline attempted a smile, "That lady happened to be someone I used to know, you see. It was a shock, she had changed so much I hardly knew her at first." And half to herself, she added, "She used to be so lovely."

"I thought she had a very attractive face," said Charlotte anxiously. "I am sorry if I hurt you by the way I spoke of her."

"No, you were not to know she was not a complete stranger, I was saddened by the alteration, that is all." Caroline found that not only did she not want to discuss the meeting with her children, she could not examine her thoughts at that moment, and to distract them, she brought up the subject of the statue, which had been up for nearly two years, but which only her older children had seen till this afternoon. "What did you think? Did you like it?"

Charlotte hesitated. "Well, it is certainly very noticeable," she said. "Big, and black."

Caroline laughed. "Is that all?"

"It is interesting, being made from cannon that has actually seen action," said Charlotte, "But I find it interesting rather than beautiful."

"It is not that Charley minds it being so naked," said John, grinning.

"After all, one might expect that of Achilles! Though do you really think that at the siege of Troy even Greek soldiers would have fought like that?"

"Well, the Spartans might, but in general they would surely have had the sense to wear some sort of protective armour," said John. He turned to his mother. "I gather that some people were of the opinion that for a monument subscribed to by females, a little more clothing would have been appropriate."

"Dear me, how very proper," said Caroline, smiling. "And how did you like it?"

"I do not know as much about art as Charley does," said John. "But I could not help feeling that the cannon in their original state would have made a much better monument to Waterloo. I suppose that would not have done."

"I doubt it," Caroline agreed. They were now out of the park, and John and his sister looked at each other with concern and asked if they ought to try to hire a carriage for the rest of the journey. "That is ridiculous! By the time you had located one, we would be there."

"Harriet did suggest that we went in the Barouche," Charlotte added, "But it seemed so near and we felt we would benefit from the walk, Johnnie."

He made a face at her use of his old nickname, but nodded at his mother. "We did not anticipate that the day would be so hot, did we? I came further, from Dick and Sarah's. No, we are not really far from the Lintons' house."

As they reached the gate, a small boy and his even smaller sister rushed to greet them, calling back to the house so that by the time they entered, Harriet was coming to the door, a baby in her arms, and a tiny girl peering round her skirts. Charlotte and her mother had been staying for some days, but it was John's first visit since early spring, and the children seemed to feel that he ought to be greeted with more ceremony.

"This is Caro," said Harriet to her brother, holding out the baby. "She has acquired some teeth and hair since you last saw her."

"An improvement," agreed John, gently stroking the baby with one finger. Pretending to ignore the older children, he stooped to the smaller girl and said, "And is this Maud?"

A delighted shriek corrected him, "Oh, silly Uncle John! That's Edith. *I'm* Maud!" and the young lady in question bounced up to him with the assurance of nearly four years old. She and her older brother led him off to see something in the small back garden.

Harriet rang for tea, remarking that even if the gentlemen would not be dressing for dinner, her mother and sister would probably like to change into clean gowns. By the time everyone had refreshed themselves, she declared it was getting late for the children and they must return to the nursery.

"I hope they won't be banished entirely," said John, coming up with Stevie clinging to one hand and Maud to the other. "I know Sarah would very much like to see them."

"Oh, Stevie and Maud will come in after dinner," said Harriet, handing the baby to her nurse and picking up the smaller girl. "Caro and Edith will be in bed by then, but we can go up and see them before we have coffee if Sarah would like that. No, Maud, Aunt Charlotte will not carry you upstairs! Do not encourage her, Charley – she is perfectly capable of walking."

To Caroline's relief, neither of her younger children had mentioned the encounter in Hyde Park, it had probably made little impact on John, but she thought Charlotte had some idea that she had been disturbed and was carefully refraining from what might be giving her distress. She found that she had been more affected than she realised, when she sat down to dinner she felt as if she were seeing the table, and those gathered round it as if they were at a distance and she a mere observer. She heard herself joining in the conversation mechanically, part of her mind preoccupied by the unexpected meeting with her sister.

She decided that it had been more of a shock than she had realised, imposing a very different image over the one she had carried for nearly thirty years, of the eighteen year old Lucy, so fair and flower-like. In a rare poetic impulse, Sir Charles Carter had once compared her to a golden rosebud, and trite though this was, it had described her very well. But Caroline suddenly thought that of all flowers, the rose was at its best in youth, tending to an overblown maturity.

She looked down the table, wondering if a similar fate awaited Harriet, but the bearing of four children did not seem

254

to have increased her girth. Had memories of Lucy been overlaid by impressions of her daughter at the time of her marriage? It was the differences rather than the similarity she saw now. Caroline had not watched her sister move from bride to young matron, it was the contrast between slim youth and very stout middle age that had been so disconcerting.

In some ways she might almost have wished to been spared the sight of this metamorphosis, especially as the pleasure of hearing about the rest of her family was blended with the consciousness of all she had to hide, yet it had been good to know a little more than she had been able to glean from Selina. Lucy's information about her mother had really shaken her. Harriet was giving the signal for the ladies to ride, and Caroline had not taken in a word, not one word, of the conversation.

They went up to look at the babies, and returning to the drawing room found Stevie and Maud, very neat and subdued, waiting under the sharp eyes of a nursemaid. Caroline wrested her mind away from the encounter of the afternoon and concentrated on the children, her daughters, and most of all, her daughter-in-law, who still seemed a little in awe of her and might think that her absorption reflected a disapproval that she was far from feeling. It did not seem as if those who knew her best had noticed much, so perhaps she had appeared to participate in the conversation after all. At first the children absorbed all the attention of all four adults, but presently Charlotte embarked on one of the stories that made her so popular with her nephew and niece, Stevie leaning against her and Maud on her mother's lap, which enabled Caroline to smile encouragingly at Richard's wife and get her to sit down a little way apart.

Sarah Randall lowered her by now considerable bulk on to a chair and made a little gentle sound through her nostrils. Caroline smiled sympathetically and patted her hand. "A trying time," she observed.

Sarah turned eagerly, her long pleasant face lit up with a wide smile. "It is generally so, is it?" she asked. "This is all so strange to me, I wondered if it were my imagination. And not having a mother myself..."

"Yes, that is so sad," said Caroline. "Do you really not remember her at all?"

"No, I was not quite two years old when she died. And then my father was such an eccentric person, he brought me up in a world of books and his fellow scholars and taught me himself, I never had a governess. I seldom spoke to another female apart from my old nurse who kept house for us. But you will remember Papa, of course."

"I only met him a few times," Caroline began, thinking particularly of the sick old man entertaining the Carpenters on the occasion of Richard becoming engaged to his daughter. "But I liked him very much."

"He liked you," said Sarah earnestly. "It was not simply gratitude." No, old Mr Joseph had not been the sort of man to flatter Richard's mother merely because her son had been the means of saving his small fortune from a grasping claimant, it had been genuine liking that had attracted the unworldly old man to the young lawyer.

"After the first meeting, he said to me that you were the first sensible woman he had met since my mother died. He seldom spoke of her, but she must have been a remarkable person, to come between him and his books long enough for him to fall in love with her. He was fond of me, but unless I attracted his attention, he only noticed me on matters to do with books! I was very fond of him, and I do not think his methods of education did me any harm, except in so far as they made me shy of talking to other women. Not that I was kept away from them, but on the rare occasions when we dined in company, I felt as if I were in a foreign land. Especially if there were daughters! I had no knowledge of the things that were supposed to make up a young girl's life, and very little interest, either."

Caroline had a strong fellow feeling, since even with a mother and sisters she had frequently found other young women incredibly boring, but felt this was not the moment to pursued the subject. "What became of the old nurse you spoke of?"

"She died when I was fifteen," said Sarah. "As I said, she was supposed to be our housekeeper, but she was not very efficient. She had no sense feeling for figures – I kept the accounts from my tenth year. My father did not care to employ a stranger, and as we had no relations to scold him for permitting it, I took on the housekeeping from then on."

"And now you have Nancy to do it for you," Caroline commented.

Sarah laughed. "I did not say I enjoyed it!" she said, "I still keep the accounts, but for the rest I am very glad to have her advice and assistance. And in the matter of this baby – that is another foreign country." She glanced at Harriet, Charlotte and the children. "But that is one I am anxious to learn how to live in. Indeed, I shall have to! Not that I have any objection."

"No?" said Caroline, amused.

"Oh, you must not think that because I was brought up by my father I am devoid of normal feminine feelings for infants," said Sarah, a shade too emphatically.

"I do not," Caroline hastened to assure her. "But it would be no shame if you did not dote on them. Why should it be assumed that all women must love children?"

Sarah was looking at her sisters-in-law again, "But are you not shocked if they do not?"

Caroline followed the direction of her glance. Maud was half asleep on her mother's lap, and Stevie was sitting at his aunt's feet with his head on her knee. She smiled. "I assure you I am not at all shocked. In fact, even when they were tiny girls, mine amazed me by the depth of their feeling for babies. They do not take after me in that respect. When I was young I found children a bore, and certainly had no female feeling for infants."

"Really?" said Sarah. "But surely when Dick was born it was different?"

"Oh, indeed it was. But I had to learn to love him, and felt no special tenderness towards the baby I was expecting. I

257

quickly came to love him as a person in his own right once I knew him."

Her words seemed to have relieved her daughter-in-law. "I am glad to hear that – I mean, I had begun to wonder if I were quite feminine in the way I feel about becoming a mother. I never thought of your feeling like that."

Caroline smiled. "I suppose Nancy has been telling you that I was a wonderful mother, especially to Dick?"

"Yes, she has. Particularly to him, in fact, just as you said."

"Well, it is true that when he was small I had no one else to absorb my attention," said Caroline.

Sarah looked dismayed. "Oh dear, yes – you were a widow then," she said, "That must have been dreadful for you, to be in this condition without the support and affection of a husband."

As so many times before, Caroline felt a pang of guilt at receiving undeserved sympathy, yet when she compared her first pregnancy with later ones, she realised that she had been lonely. She patted Sarah's hand again and might have spoken but the coffee, followed by the three men, arrived at that point to distract attention.

Charlotte had just finished her story and the children were half asleep, they roused to greet their father and uncles, but Harriet saw to it that things did not get too boisterous, and within a few minutes Charlotte and the nursemaid took them off to bed, John obligingly accompanying them as their mother started to pour the coffee, her husband sitting beside her ready to hand the cups round.

Richard joined Caroline and Sarah, grinning at his mother, and regarding his wife with anxious solicitude. As he fetched them a plate of little biscuits he exchanged an intimate glance with Sarah, and Caroline noticed a similar affection pass between the Lintons. Charlotte's words still pierced her heart, but she had to acknowledge that she was fortunate that two of her four children were not only married, but happy with a partner truly congenial to their temperaments.

Harriet and her Steven seemed as much in love as they had been six years ago, of course they had health and wealth to cushion their existence, but how many people seemed able to take as much enjoyment from their home and their children as they did? No, she had never worried about her elder daughter.

Richard, on the other hand, had caused considerable concern in his early years in London, though working hard, he also seemed to find time to dine out, visit the theatre and other entertainments, and Caroline and John suspected that he drank rather more than was good for him. He was very reticent about his life, but Harriet, seeing him more frequently, occasionally expressed her dismay about the company he kept. It was from her through her husband that the Carpenters learned about an association that they considered disastrous, with an older, married woman, who had played with the affections of the handsome young lawyer till it suited her to bring the affair to an end.

Richard had been so deeply hurt that his mother had feared his nature had been permanently embittered. She was determined not to interfere, but she had agonised over him. Harriet's attempt to find some girl who would charm him out of this mood had been fruitless and nothing about the brief he had been given to defend Philip Joseph would have led anyone to imagine that he was about to find a wife.

He had described his client's daughter rather scathingly on one of his rare visits home to Coombe Park, as pleasant enough to look at but not a patch on his sisters, and rather blunt in manner. "She is intelligent, but no more so than Charley," he had remarked to his mother, "And she does not make the most of what beauty she has." Now that she knew more about what Sarah's life had been, Caroline wondered if it had ever occurred to him that a girl reared in that way would not know how to charm a man.

All the same, the fact that he found her so irritating had suggested that he was not totally indifferent to her, and he had possibly been piqued by the fact that unlike most females he met, she had not tried to flirt with him. His genuine liking for her father had caused him to visit them often, and even before the old man's health began to fail, he had begun to revise his opinion of this unusual girl, and the match had clearly delighted Mr Joseph. Caroline felt that it was as well that the money he had been instrumental in saving, though enough to make the young couple comfortable and allow Richard to be selective about the briefs he took, did not amount to a fortune and he had no need to feel guilty at profiting from it.

"Mama, you are very silent," said Richard. "Is anything the matter?"

Charlotte, who had just come downstairs, looked anxiously as she moved to take her coffee, was she recalling the afternoon's encounter? Hastily, Caroline smiled at her two red-heads and said cheerfully, "No, no, I was simply thinking. I do that sometimes, you know."

PART 13

The Dower House, Corwood Hall, Hertfordshire

Autumn, 1830

The original mansion had burnt down in the early part of the eighteenth century, and the building Sir Charles Carter had inherited from his grandfather was a fine Georgian house, designed with care by an architect with a passion for symmetry so strong that he had insisted on the undamaged Dower house being pulled down and replaced with a miniature replica of the Hall. Every feature, including the terrace, was scaled down the size of a cottage, but perfect in detail. This was a charming fantasy and Lucy had liked the place whenever she visited her mother-in-law there in the early years of her marriage.

The late Lady Carter had been a dainty little creature and the proportions of the building had suited her well. She had seemed placidly content with the small rooms, sitting there dressed in the fashions of the previous century, her snow-white hair piled high on her head in the style of her youth, but having occupied it herself for nearly eighteen months, Lucy had begun to wonder how her predecessor had really viewed it. Surely she must have missed the spaciousness of the Great House? It would have been more cramped in an actual cottage, no doubt, but the resemblance of these rooms to the ones she had lived in for nearly thirty-five years frequently affected Lucy with an almost giddy feeling. Entering the breakfast room after a disturbed night she reflected again that the furniture looked rather foolish. It was smaller than that in the main building, but still out of proportion. If it could have been scaled down in the same way, it would have been useless for normal adults.

The breakfast room was empty, but the manservant came in from the other door just as Lucy arrived. He had come to check on the fire, and she waited while he put coal on before asking if her sister had come down yet.

"Oh yes, my lady, Miss Randall has gone out to speak to the gardener."

Lucy had a sudden stab of irritation and had to repress an inclination to enquire why. She hoped her face was not too expressive, the discussion the night before had become acrimonious, and she was sure that the staff had been aware of it. Particularly this man, to whom she had spoken after her sister had gone up to bed.

"Oh, Parker, did my letter reach this morning's post?" she asked.

"Yes indeed, my lady. I took it out first thing, and saw the mail coach leave with it."

Lucy had a feeling of relief as she smiled and thanked him, becoming aware that he was looking behind her. She swung round to find her sister coming in and looking at the man so sharply that Lucy thought for a moment that she had overheard those last words. She gave no sign of it as she moved to the table and Parker beckoned in a maid with tea and coffee. No, it did not look as if Anna was aware of what her sister had been discussing, even if she was going to have to learn of it soon enough. Thank goodness the letter to Olivia had gone irrevocably.

After the disagreement of the night before, Lucy felt slightly awkward in her sister's company, and she was still shaken by the anger she had discovered herself capable of. Anna however, sat calmly eating her breakfast as nothing in particular had happened. The conversation during the meal touched on no subject unsuitable for the maid who waited upon them.

They talked chiefly about the weather, which had turned fine after a series of dull damp days, and about the garden. Anna took no interest in the plants, but hated the grounds to look untidy, when questioned she admitted that her purpose in going out so early had been to direct that the leaves be swept up in front of the house. Lucy was disconcerted.

"But, Anna, he does so almost every day," she said rather sharply. "With only a young boy to help him, he has a great many other things to do. We hardly see the leaves from the drawing-room or even the dining-room, and only yesterday I gave him permission to let them lie until he had finished some more urgent tasks."

Anna pinched her lips together. "You are too easy with the servants," she said sharply. "I suppose that was why the fellow had the impudence to say he did not have to do that yet. All the leaves ought to be swept up at once, or the garden will look neglected."

Lucy sighed, recalling how her children had enjoyed the crackle the leaves made when they walked among them, and felt like saying that she thought the carpet of russet, yellow, and brown looked rather pretty. Anyway, she thought mutinously, was it for her sister to contradict her orders? She regarded Anna as she sat there in a dark stuff gown with her hair hidden under an unbecoming cap. Just so had she appeared when she accompanied her parents on the move from Sussex, her face was perhaps a little more lined, but she seemed strangely ageless. Even the style of her clothes was almost unchanged, waists had risen and fallen, skirts had narrowed and were now spreading again, and sleeves were getting fuller, Anna dressed in severe, plain garments that would have caused a stranger to imagine that she was a poor relation. Not for the first time, Lucy wondered why.

When breakfast was over Anna looked around to make sure that there was no one in earshot, and said earnestly, "Now, Lucy, we must speak of this letter from Olivia."

"I thought we had discussed that last night," said Lucy.

"We spoke about it, certainly, but you became a little overwrought," said Anna, almost indulgently. "After a good night's sleep, I am sure you will agree to the need to consult Charles and Sophia before taking any further steps." She seemed so confident that Lucy found her irritation returning, especially as her sleep had been anything but peaceful.

She hoped this did not show on her face, and turned away for a moment to gain time. How long had her sister been treating her almost as a child to be humoured? Overwrought, indeed. It had only been when Anna's agitated objection had made itself felt that she had even raised her voice. And as soon as she did, she was accused of being unreasonable, "delirious", in fact, and told soothingly to leave things till the morning. Very conscious that she had done no such thing, she found herself increasingly aware that her sister's behaviour since Sir Charles's death had become irksome.

It was true that she had contracted a fever after the strain of nursing her sick husband, and she might well have rambled for some days, but delirium? For a year the loss of someone who had been so dear had made her so miserable she was barely aware of what went on, but the numbness was beginning to wear off and she was finding Anna's protective solicitude almost stifling. She was starting to realise that any comment that her sister did not agree with was likely to be dismissed as Lucy getting over emotional, and until now it had been easier to give way. But not this time. It was almost with satisfaction that she informed Anna that she had already written to Olivia, asking her to come and live at the Dower House.

Anna looked horrified. "You have written?" she said in dismay. "Without discussing it further?"

"But I told you I intended to do so," said Lucy. She remembered exactly what she had said as they parted overnight. She was sure that her words had been heard, but her sister had clearly decided to ignore them. It was infuriating not to be taken seriously.

"I would like to see this letter," Anna's comment was practically a demand. "Where is it? You will show it to Charles, will you not?"

"Unfortunately, it has already gone to the post. Parker took it out at first light."

Anna seemed aghast. "Ah, Lucy, Lucy," she cried, "Whatever has happened to you, that you should take such a step without consulting Charles and Sophia? When your husband was alive, you would never have done such a thing."

This was the first time Lucy had heard a reference to her lost love without dissolving into near hysterical tears, it occurred to her that on occasions when they had disagreed Anna had mentioned him and then produced soothing words and exhortations to rest. Her eyes filled with tears, but she blinked them back and said sharply, "If Charles were here, I would certainly have had no need to consult his son and daughter-in-law on a matter that does not concern them." Young Sir Charles, she thought, might own the Dower House, but it was hers for her lifetime.

Anna became agitated again. "It must concern them! For one thing, their feelings will be hurt, and you have clearly given no thought to how what you propose would affect everyone else. What about the servants?" Considering how she usually regarded the servants as almost pampered, Lucy found this risible till the frantic way her sister rushed from the room exclaiming, "Oh, Lucy, I can hardly believe it!" chased away amusement.

Lucy had been bracing herself for more reproaches, and was surprised that her sister had responded as she had to being confronted. Her placid nature would normally have shrunk from causing Anna distress, but now her main feeling was of gladness that she had obeyed her instinct to act so promptly over the letter to her daughter. She became aware that Parker had returned, probably he had heard the latest argument, but he showed no sign of it as he indicated a female figure behind him, "Mrs Old would like a word, my lady," he said respectfully.

Lucy inclined her head and the woman who had been her personal maid since she had arrived at Corwood Hall as a bride, came quietly into the room and stood looking at her mistress almost sadly. They had had a close relationship from the start, as this former servant of old Lady Carter had been widowed young and had been forced to leave her little boy with her mother and return to work. Her manner when Sir Charles died had been rather a disappointment, she had never mentioned his name and had seemed almost embarrassed, and Lucy had felt hurt that their closeness had seemed to diminish.

"Oh, my lady – I know you would prefer that I do not mention my own situation, but I feel I must say something about poor little Miss Olivia, Mrs Brandon, I should say, to think of her being left a widow at her age, and with that little baby."

"Yes, of course, you would understand," said Lucy softly. "I remember so well your situation when I first met you. Do tell me, how is your son doing as a carpenter?"

"Very well indeed, my lady. You know he is married, now?"

"No, really? When did this happen?"

"A little over a year ago. I did tell Miss Randall, but she said you were not to be troubled." This had clearly distressed Mrs Old, and Lucy did not blame her. Had Anna for some reason discouraged this woman from offering commiserations over Sir Charles? She could hardly ask her that outright, but she could surely make it clear once and for all that she would welcome the sympathy.

"I do not know if you have heard that my daughter will have to leave her house," she said. "That is needed for another curate, so she has lost her home as well as a dearly loved husband. I am asking her to come here, with baby Janet, probably with a nurse, though that is not certain. I do hope this would not make too much work for you and the others?"

"Work? Why should it?" Mrs Old was indignant. "There are servants enough in this little house, even if she does not bring a nurse for the baby. Many of them have not enough to do, if the truth were known. And where would the poor thing come, in her desolation, if not to her mother?"

Yes, at least part of the loud discussion of the previous night must have been overheard. A little tearfully, Lucy smiled at her old friend, thankful to realise that her apparent coldness might have been due to Anna's interference. She suggested that they go upstairs and decide which bedrooms would be suitable for the newcomers, and tried to push the overnight dissension to the back of her mind as they went. It was an added irritation that Anna should have apparently used Lucy's illness to separate her from someone who had seen her through over thirty years of marriage and the birth of ten children, who had in fact been more congenial in many ways than her sister. Had Anna sensed this and been jealous?

There were as many bedrooms on the first floor as in the Great House, but they suffered even more than those downstairs from the smaller space available. Lucy would have liked to place her daughter close to herself, which would let Olivia have a room with a connecting door for the child, but upon their moving to the Dower House, Anna had occupied the bedroom next door to her sister, and the room that would have been best for little Janet had somehow come be the one where she did some of her sewing for the poor, and to house all the materials she had acquired for this. Any proposal that she should alter this would certainly increase the grievance that she already felt!

Lucy reflected, as she made her way back to the staircase, that it would not have been her choice to have her sister next door, and recently the constant solicitude had begun to irk her. It was almost surprising that she had not been urged up to bed the night before, but her disinclination to give way had caused Anna to stalk out coldly. Had she intended this mark of displeasure to subdue her sister? It had rather fuelled Lucy's desire to write to her daughter at once. She wondered if her maid had noticed how stealthy she had been in undressing and going to bed.

Coming down about noon and planning to summon some refreshment, Lucy found her manservant admitting the new Sir Charles and his oldest son, infrequent visitors that she would generally have been pleased to see. At this moment she was not very eager, though she greeted them warmly and led the way into the drawing room.

Little Charlie was full of his own exploits in having ridden down to the Dower House. "I ride every day, now, Grandmama, and I have only fallen off once!" he said proudly.

"And that was because you would not heed what I told you," said his father sternly. The child looked suitably repentant, but did not seem greatly cast down, almost immediately he was prancing round the room, up to the French windows, gazing out at the lawn, turning round to examine the room as if to check something, and then saying, "Oh, Grandmama, this house is like ours, only smaller, even this room. Why is that?"

"The same man made both houses," Lucy told him, smiling.

"Made them – all by himself?"

"No, no, Charles," said his father. "Do not be foolish. Have you never heard of an architect?"

"No, Papa," said the little boy, puzzled. "What is that?"

Sir Charles clicked his tongue and began to explain about plans, and how workmen would build to the architect's design. Lucy watched with interest as Charlie listened intently, showing intelligence in the questions that he put to his father. Her customary good humour began to return. The child amused her in himself, apart from the feeling that her son would find it difficult to introduce the subject of Olivia, if that had been what had brought him to her house at this moment.

She had not formerly been aware that her eldest son irked her, but comparing him at the age of seven with the lad in front of her, she was conscious of how dull he had been. Charles, even as an infant had been a foretaste of his adult self, large, smooth, good-looking and complacent. He had seldom been mischievous, but it had been equally rare for him to express spontaneous affection or kindness. As a young mother, Lucy would have felt it a disgrace to admit to a lack of affection for any of her children, but it was hard not to care more for some than others. She had adored little brown Lucy, who had come to her almost as a consolation after the loss of Harriet, and the advent and arrival of Charles had interrupted the relationship she had had with her first baby. Perhaps if he had been more like the next two sons, she would have delighted in him more, but it was difficult to feel more than mild affection with a child that seldom cried and showed only a placid response to being cuddled.

Lucy studied him as he continued to hold forth, becoming rather too technical for so young an audience. Charles had been very conscious of his own dignity all his life, however good humoured he seemed at the moment, it would only take a suspicion that he was not being taken seriously to arouse crushing irony. Could he have been laughed out of it in childhood? It was hard to find fault with his behaviour, then or now, and she knew most people had regarded her as fortunate to have such a perfect eldest son.

The entrance of Parker and a maid bearing refreshments interrupted the lecture on house construction and Charlie was taken off to be amused and refreshed in the kitchen. Wryly, Lucy realised that this would enable her son to speak his mind about Anna, who must surely have gone straight to the Great House after breakfast.

"Well, Mama," he said earnestly over a glass of wine. "I am glad that I find you recovered."

"Recovered?" said Lucy a little coldly.

"Ah – Aunt Anna said that you were unwell last night. But on the whole, you look in better health than when I last saw you, Mama."

"Charles, I can assure you that I feel fine this morning, nor have I been ill." She realised that her son had probably not intended a compliment, but she was suddenly pleased that she had lost some extra weight and was nearer to how she had looked when younger. He seemed taken aback by her response.

"But Aunt Anna was most concerned, she said you were not at all yourself," he said awkwardly.

"Your aunt was in error," said Lucy dryly. Her son seemed shocked at the suggestion that Anna could be mistaken. "I am perfectly in control of my senses, thank you Charles." She wondered how he would react if she told him she had been angry, this was not an emotion he associated with his mother, especially in her dealings with his aunt. He must have prepared a speech about her being unwell, and before he could collect his thoughts, she took the initiative and asked exactly what her sister had said to him.

"Oh, she said you had had a letter from Olivia that upset you. It is of course a great shame about Brandon dying so suddenly, I realise that you found it distressing. Poor fellow," Charles added after a pause.

"And poor Olivia," said Lucy sharply.

"Yes, of course – very distressing. But, Mama, my aunt tells me that you were talking about having her and her child to live here. Have you considered what that would mean, having an infant in the house?"

"My dear boy, I have had ten children." Lucy reminded him quietly.

"Oh, I know, but that was years ago." Sir Charles frowned and muttered something about the Walcots.

Lucy frowned as well. "You are referring to the fact that they took Cecilia and her little boy into their home when Mark Walcot broke his neck in a steeplechase? The cases are not the same, Mark was the only son, and heir to the estate. Mr Brandon has a second wife and a young family, and Lionel was the third child of his first marriage. Olivia says they have been very kind, but it is not to be expected that the Brandons should add to their responsibilities if there is an alternative."

Charles ignored this remark and returned to his previous argument. "I still think that this would be more of a strain than you realise," he said stubbornly. "It is not as if you had so much space here, after all."

"Your anxiety for my welfare is very gratifying," said Lucy coldly. "But do please allow me to know my own powers of endurance, Charles."

He rose and began to walk about the room, narrowly avoiding some small tables as he did so. Lucy found this irritating, it was so like and yet so very unlike his father's way of working out a problem. Finally he turned to face her squarely. "Mama, you – I mean, are you not forgetting about Aunt Anna?"

"Now, how could I do that?" said Lucy. Her son did not seem to catch the bitter note in her voice, and took her hand eagerly.

"I was sure you could not have done. But perhaps you have not considered what a strain it would be for her, having a child here? She is some years older than you, is she not? Do you not think that it is asking too much of her?"

Lucy felt like replying that while Anna was able to walk daily to the Hall, and down to the village two or three times a week, she could hardly be thought in need of such solicitude, but restrained herself. It was becoming increasingly apparent to her that her son and his wife held her sister in greater esteem than she did. Once she had married and left Anna behind, it had been possible to ignore her behaviour just before the wedding, but she had never forgotten it completely. When her parents and sister moved from Sussex, she had not been entirely happy, partly because she had doubted if that was really what her father wished for, and also she had not been eager to see more of Anna.

At least the house they had taken was a mile of so away, and even when Mrs Randall and Anna moved to Corwood Hall, they had had their own suite of rooms and did not participate in the social life of the Carters to any extent. She had never attempted to disillusion her husband in his view that his sister-in-law was to be pitied for her single state, but though he tolerated her presence in his house Lucy knew that he found her company trying for long periods. Yes, she had done a good deal for the older children when the younger ones occupied their mother's time, in addition to all her work for charity, and her generosity over Old Manor had meant in effect, that the Carters had two oldest sons, but it had been a relief to both of them that on the whole even after her mother died she had dined with them infrequently and kept to her own rooms and activities much of the time.

It was not unreasonable that Charles and Sophia should see Anna in a different light, but their concern for her did take Lucy by surprise, did they really expect her to put her sister's needs before those of her young daughter? She was visited by a more than usually strong longing for the warm open-heartedness of her husband and a corresponding indignation with his eldest son. He was looking at her expectantly, but before she could frame a reply, young Charlie was restored to them, bouncing in joyfully to ask if it was time to leave. His father frowned upon him and said repressively, "Hush, Grandmama will think you do not like to come here."

The little face crumpled and the child came up to Lucy saying with a sob, "Grandmama! I do like coming here. I wish I could come every day." She kissed him and he flung his arms round her neck. Over his head she faced her son, tears in her own eyes, and the large fair man looked suddenly sheepish. Abandoning the topic of his sister Olivia, he was unusually patient with Charlie as they mounted and rode away.

Their departure coincided with the arrival of the post boy, and when she had taken further refreshment Lucy settled down in the drawing room to read letters from several of her children. She was still engaged on this when she heard the sound of horses again, and realised that Anna must be returning in the Carter's carriage. From where she sat she could see that her sister was accompanied by the present Lady Carter and sighed. Sophia seldom honoured her mother-in-law with her presence, and her doing so at this juncture seemed ominous. She rang for Parker and alerted him to the new arrival, asking if he could arrange for tea to be brought, and as an afterthought, could he request Mrs Old to be within earshot in case she was needed.

The bell sounded, and she watched the groom who had pulled it return to assist the ladies down, Anna holding herself stiffly but descending nimbly, Sophia slow and ponderous. The latest addition to the family was expected early in the New Year and she tended to be more cumbersome than many women. Anna, looking anxious, took the younger woman by the arm and they disappeared from Lucy's sight as they reached the steps.

Parker returned to announce the visitors, just as she finished stuffing her letters into her work-bag. She took up some sewing, feeling unwilling to answer questions about

272

Hugh, Elinor or Clarinda. She rose as they came in, and moved to greet her daughter-in-law. Sophia, looking exhausted, pecked her on the cheek and permitted herself to be led to the sofa, while Anna fetched her a footstool.

Taking up her sewing, Lucy remarked that she had ordered tea. "I thought you might need some?"

"Oh, yes, indeed," said Sophia, sinking down gratefully, nevertheless frowning a little. She was never averse to having her delicate condition acknowledged and to be pampered, but embarrassed if it were referred to directly, something that Lucy always found tiresome. Anna placed herself on a hard, high-backed chair that enabled her to be near the sofa and yet see her sister. She too began sewing, one of her endless garments for the poor. Her austere expression made her face look like an ivory mask.

Lucy decided to introduce a topic likely to distract her daughter-in-law, and avoiding Anna's eye, asked after the children. Were they well? Was Sophia's cough better now?

"Oh, yes," said Sophia. "Dr Archer does not fear for her lungs. Were you aware that Lucinda has had trouble with her eyes? Fortunately they are improving, but she was forbidden to do close work for a time."

Anna looked disturbed. "I am glad to hear that is over," she remarked. "It is such a check to her progress, to have to neglect her needle."

"That surely will not do much harm, at eight years old!" exclaimed Lucy. Sophia looked shocked that her mother-in-law should treat the subject so lightly.

"It will not be irreparable," she said stiffly. "But it will have set her back considerably."

"And little Sam? How does he do?"

"Oh, he is well enough," said Sophia, putting her hand to her brow. "But he makes such a noise I can hardly bear him near me at present. The girls are all very well, but Sam and Baby are too much for me."

"Did I hear that the baby has grown some hair at last?" said Lucy, recalling that the last time she had seen the child, that even on her first birthday the child had had only a faint down in her head.

"She has," Sophia sounded rather grim. "It has been a shock to me, I must confess."

"Oh?" said Lucy, taken aback, "Why is that?"

"I do not care for the colour."

"It may get darker, in time," said Anna. Sophia shook her head.

"I fear not, it is a very bright red."

"Oh, how nice," said Lucy, and saw that this had caused surprise in her daughter-in law. None of her children had inherited that colouring, and only knowing their mother and aunt, would have had no idea it ran in the family. Anna gave her a frown and she realised that it would be as well not to refer to having had a red-headed brother and sister. "I think it is a delightful colour," she persisted. "My – my dear father had hair like that until it went white."

"Oh, is that where it comes from? There is none in my family, and I thought that the Carters were dark."

"They are, but my family have red hair as well as fair," Anna had half-relaxed, and Sophia was clearly concerned that she might unwittingly have given offence, and said graciously that if little Susan was going to resemble her great-grandfather, that would be a different matter. "I do not ask after Charlie, as I saw him this morning. What a fine child he is growing into," Lucy concluded.

Sophia usually responded favourably to praise of any of her children, but she shook her head at this. "He grows tall and sturdy, but I fear for him. He behaves appallingly at times, he is noisier than Sam, and though he is not stupid, he has no application. It is very difficult to get him to study."

Lucy thought of the little boy listening with interest to his father that morning, but after the way her comments upon Lucinda had been received, refrained from pointing out that since he had only just turned seven, it would be more remarkable if her grandson took eagerly to study. It was a relief to have tea brought in at that moment. Once Parker and a maid had placed trays and arranged tables, it was possible to take refuge in the ritual of filling cups and offering cakes. Passing some round, Lucy could not help thinking of other occasions when she had sat on the very sofa, enjoying a comfortable chat with her mother-in-law, often in the condition Sophia was now.

Both her companions seemed unwilling to make casual conversation, they seemed tense and she felt uncomfortably feeling that they were conspiring against her, especially when Anna remarked that she had promised to show Sophia some patterns.

"Patterns?" murmured Lucy.

"Yes, to make clothes for the school children," explained Sophia condescendingly. "The teacher has been lamenting the condition of their garments, some of the village people even make that an excuse for keeping them at home. Therefore we intend to provide them."

"I know I have those patterns," said Anna. "But I fear that I may have put other things on top, so it might take me a while to find them." She departed, leaving Lucy alone with her son's wife.

Sophia settled herself more comfortably, clasped her hands over her extended stomach, and looked at Lucy, who continued to sew, visited by a sudden intuition that she was expected to make more casual conversation that would be broken into so that the young woman could introduce the subject uppermost in her mind. Why should this be made easier for her? Her head bent over her work, Lucy avoided a couple of fabricated coughs, and was eventually addressed directly. "Ahem. Charles told me about his visit this morning."

"Yes, I mentioned that I had seen him and Charlie," said Lucy. "It was very pleasant to see them both."

Sophia's tone was reproachful, "What I was about to say is that he told me about the conversation he had with you. He seemed uncertain what you were going to do about Olivia's letter."

"I thought I had been perfectly clear, to both him and my sister, that I have written to my daughter asking her and her baby here."

"But you could change your mind," Sophia urged. "Charles was quite sure you have not fully considered what that would entail."

"Oh, but I have," said Lucy, smiling at the maid who had come to clear away. "I can assure you of that." The girl gave her a scared look and then as she went out glanced back from the hall where she could see Mrs Old hovering. At Lucy's nod the personal maid slipped in and took up an unobtrusive position, apparently unnoticed by Sophia.

"But have you really? The noise, the upset to your routine, the strain, at your age, to yourself and your sister?"

"I have indeed," said Lucy coldly.

"But you surely, surely have not thought about it rationally. Dear Aunt Anna was concerned that it would be a great deal too much for you."

"Perhaps it might be too much for her," Lucy agreed. "But I do not think it would be for me."

Sounding shocked, her daughter-in-law cried out that that was not what had been meant. "Aunt Anna was simply concerned for you, especially considering what you have undergone this last year or so. She had no thought for herself, none at all. But I feel bound to say that Charles and I both feel that it would indeed be too much for her."

"He said something of the sort to me," said Lucy, trying to contain her unaccustomed anger. The effort not to snap at Sophia brought tears to her eyes, and the sight appeared to make the younger woman soften.

"There, I did not mean to distress you," she said almost complacently, and this seemed the final straw.

As if from a long way off, Lucy heard herself saying, "Did you not? You have certainly succeeded." It was a relief to see Mrs Old give her a bracing but approving glance, and she felt that she had herself in hand again.

Her large pale eyes open wide, Sophia clasped a hand to her heart. "That was not kind," she said in a small voice. "How could you say such a thing?"

Lucy felt that she ought to appear concerned. "Perhaps we had better not continue this conversation, my dear, in case it has an effect upon your child."

The young woman shrank away, covering her face with her hands, and Lucy was exasperated to realise that the reference would have affronted her sense of decorum. "Grandmama!" she protested. Since becoming Lady Carter herself, Sophia had adopted this form of address to her mother-in-law. Coming at this moment it roused a dormant wit in her listener.

"Oh, Sophia, really!" she began, "Please do not be so – shocked."

Sophia sighed, "I suppose that it was different when you were younger," she said. "You did not mean to be indelicate."

Lucy could not really see that she had been. Some people these days appeared to think that those born in the last century were accustomed to cruder language than was now in use, but to be expected to ignore the evidence of her eyes and pretend ignorance of the facts of life seemed to her to be carrying delicacy to extremes.

In the short silence that followed, Lucy exchanged glances with Mrs Old, who continued to wait quietly. If Sophia noticed her presence, she gave no sign of it, and did not ask for her to be dismissed from the room. But her next words made it clear that she had no intention of leaving the subject of Anna alone.

"I really did not intend to say something that would distress you, Grandmama," she said. "I am aware that you have a very tender heart, and I am sure you would never be neglectful of Aunt Anna."

Lucy looked at her almost sorrowfully. "Anna, Anna, Anna!" she thought. That seemed to be their main concern. How could she make it clear that it was not her own? "I do not think you understand. However fond I am of my sister, if having Olivia and little Janet here will make her unhappy, I am sorry, but I cannot to consider her above my own daughter.

Neither you nor my son could really expect me to choose between them." Sophia seemed to be contemplating this, and Lucy pressed the point. "I quite understand that you and Charles could not have them at the Hall – I would not expect that, do not worry – but where else could they go? If it were your daughter, would you not feel she needed you more than a sister?"

"You know I was not fortunate enough to have a sister, only brothers," said Sophia rather plaintively. She clearly regarded the relationship as something very special, but did not pursue this line, returning instead to respond to Lucy's remark. "I was not aware that anyone was asking you to make a choice in this matter. All that we are concerned about is that what you propose might be too much for you."

"But when I assured you that it would not, you introduced the subject of my sister," said Lucy. "I can imagine that it might not be a welcome prospect for a spinster in her sixties. But why could she not say that?"

"She would not be so selfish!" Sophia protested loyally.

"I am not sure that it would be selfish," said Lucy thoughtfully. "It might well be natural for her to view it with alarm. But I still do not see that it is anything to do with my decision. I feel that my duty is to my child, and I would be failing that if I left Olivia alone in her sorrow."

"And is that all you have to say about your dear sister? After all she gave up for you!" cried Sophia, rising with an effort and waving away Lucy's assistance.

Lucy was slightly puzzled. "I realise that she was very generous over Old Manor," she agreed, "I do not quite see how that affects the present issue."

"Oh, of course, she was so noble about that!" Sophia seemed taken aback. "That was not what I had in mind. Your sister need never have left Corwood Hall when we moved in, Charles and I begged her to stay, but no, she could not let you come here alone." She looked suddenly less confident, and pressed her hand to her head again. "Oh, I should not have said that, you were not supposed to know." She swayed slightly, and Mrs Old moved swiftly to her side and urged her to sit down on a higher chair.

Lucy gazed at her daughter-in-law almost incredulously, and noted that even as she accepted the ministrations, Sophia seemed to become aware that her words had been heard by a third party. She wrung her hands almost frantically and dissolved in tears as Anna returned to the room, dropping her armful of patterns and materials and rushing forward, casting a reproachful look at her sister and waving Mrs Old away. Sophia took refuge in a handkerchief but cast an anxious eye at the other inhabitants of the room, apparently worried about her own indiscretion. "I – I think it is a trifle hot in here," she murmured, gesturing at the pile of stuff on the floor. "Perhaps I could take those with me to examine at the Hall?"

Lucy had already summoned Parker and told him that her ladyship's carriage would be required, and Anna took charge of the proceedings, insisting on returning to the Great House with the distraught young woman, and continuing to look indignantly at her sister. The front door closed upon Sophia begging her to stay to dinner, and as Parker withdrew, Lucy and Mrs Old were left regarding each other speechlessly.

There seemed nothing to say that would be safe to discuss, and Lucy was very grateful to think that she could trust her personal maid to be discreet. She felt suddenly rather tired, and Mrs Old urged her to sit down and take a sip of wine, saying, "Would you like to have dinner in your room, my lady?"

It was tempting, but even if Anna not only dined, but stayed the night with Charles and Sophia, she would be bound to find out that her sister had retreated upstairs, and accuse her of not being well. It felt strange to sit in solitary state at the table, but Lucy had to admit to herself it was a relief. She thought back twenty four hours to when she had told Anna of her intention to offer her daughter a home, she had not be expected it to be received with enthusiasm, but she had hardly anticipated the emotion with which her sister had greeted the information. It made her realise how much Anna had assumed authority since their move to the Dower House, up till now it

279

had been easier to let her take charge, but it seemed too much that she expected to raise objections in this instance.

Lucy's determination to get the letter written and out of the house had been instinctive, but the day's events had shown that this had been a wise decision. The attempts to make her change her mind had only stiffened her resolve even though they had left her feeling rather as if she had been buffeted by a strong wind.

When she was in her room, she thought, she might have leisure to think about the various encounters she had since she came out of it that morning, but as she was finishing her meal, a similar impulse to that which had decided her not to delay the letter overnight caused her address the manservant with a query. "Parker, I believe that Dr Weston is now quite recovered from his carriage accident, and taking a few patients. I shall be writing him a note while I wait for my coffee. Would you be so good as to see that he receives it?"

"Certainly, my lady." Parker was as usual perfectly correct in his manner, but did she imagine a touch of anxiety? Once the note was gone, she wondered a little what had impelled her to write it. Almost certainly Dr Archer would be sent for to attend Sophia and she thought of how both her sister and her son had interpreted her determination as a symptom of illness. She had had to be attended in her fever by the doctor the younger Carters had chosen, instead of the man who had attended her ever since her marriage because he had been injured just before her husband's death, but she had not really taken to the younger medical man.

Anna had not returned by the time Lucy retired, and she felt some relief as Mrs Old helped her to prepare for bed. Of all the happenings of that eventful day, the restored relations with her had been the most positive, and she felt calmed and comforted by the time the woman left. Anna had seemed less than pleased to see who was assisting Sophia – her cold manner to her sister's personal maid had surely confirmed that she disliked her even if she did not resent her. Lucy found the estrangement hard to forgive, and as she settled for sleep she pondered on the revelation that her daughter-in-law apparently regretted making. She was too tired to examine her feelings about her sister in any detail, but the whole confrontation seemed to have opened her eyes to aspects of Anna's character that she had almost forgotten.

A much better night's sleep sent Lucy down to breakfast in a more relaxed mood, and she discovered that her sister had indeed spent the night at Corwood Hall, but had returned early and was sitting in her usual place eating her meal, looking sternly at Lucy while maintaining a discreet silence in the presence of the servants. Once they were alone, Anna said coldly, "I am pleased to inform you that Sophia is in no danger, though Dr Archer advised that she rest in bed for a few days."

Lucy said quietly that she was glad to hear it, but resisted the temptation to point out that most of the distress had come about because her daughter-in-law had let herself become agitated. It seemed to her that both Anna and Charles shared responsibility since they had permitted the young woman to come to the Dower House in the first place, and she had no intention of accepting responsibility for the upset.

"Lucy!" said Anna reproachfully. "Charles is concerned about you, as well as his wife. He thinks that we should ask Dr Archer to visit you as soon as possible."

"I do hope he will not do so without consulting me," began Lucy.

Anna almost snapped at her. "If Charles had consulted me," she said. "I would certainly have advised sending for him at once, but he asked me to speak to you first. You would not have any reason to object."

"Oh, but I would," said Lucy quietly. "It would have pained me to be uncivil, but if Dr Archer were to come to this house, I would not see him. Before you say anything else, I must tell you that I have requested a visit from Dr Weston."

Anna seemed disconcerted. "I thought he had retired," she said.

"No, he does not do much but he still sees some patients."

"But, Lucy, Dr Archer was so good when you were ill and Dr Weston an unfit man himself. Why change again?"

"You forget, I had no choice in the matter, I was taken ill just after that accident. No doubt Dr Archer is an excellent physician, but Dr Weston has attended our family for over thirty years and I prefer to see him. Now, if you will excuse me, I have to speak to my maid." She walked out of the room, not looking back to see how her sister reacted. As she expected, her son arrived quite soon, ostensibly to reassure her about his wife, but also to express concern about Lucy's health. He was clearly displeased at what she had to tell him, he appeared to feel that Dr Archer was to be preferred, but had to admit that the other man was an old and trusted friend.

Two weeks later, as she checked yet again if the rooms were ready for Olivia and little Janet, Lucy recalled the effect that Dr Weston's visit had had on her household. His robust response to the idea of her taking in her daughter and grandchild had not been what her son had hoped for. The doctor had congratulated her on her restoration to health, and declared that fresh interests and new life would be the very thing to complete her recovery. Both Charles and Anna had greeted this pronouncement with dismay, and had continued to insist that it would be a strain, even citing Dr Archer's opinion, but Lucy had found it easy to ignore them. Her son had reiterated that her poor sister would suffer, and Anna had renewed her objections on the grounds that Lucy would not be able to cope, and had become almost hysterical the nearer the prospect came. Surely the Carters must see that she was considering her own comfort in this matter? Lucy still did not blame her, but wished she could be honest about it.

Though her indiscretion had subdued Sophia to some extent, she had joined the reproaches to her mother-in-law, and apparently it was on her behalf that Anna agreed to abandon her sister and return to the rooms she had formerly occupied at Corwood Hall. Lucy was given a strong impression that she was being taught a lesson by her son and daughter-in-law; that by depriving her of her sister they were condemning her to a harsher existence.

She looked at the room her sister had occupied, now available for Olivia now Anna had swept away all her possessions. The sensation it produced in her was relief rather than desolation, and she realised that there was less tension in the whole building. The servants seemed to grumble less without Anna constantly chivvying them, even though all these preparations had made rather more work for them to do.

The clock struck two, and though she knew that there was at least an hour before she could expect the carriage, she glanced out of the landing window, wishing she could go into the garden for a little. But it was not only dull, there was a hint of snow in the air, the idea was impractical. She sighed, and Mrs Old who had been hovering at the top of the stairs, looked at her anxiously, "My lady, everything is ready now," she said.

Lucy smiled, "I hope I have not seemed to fuss too much," she remarked. "It is simply that I have been concerned for them."

"Of course you have, we all know how you must feel. But you have had a tiring time these last few weeks. Why don't you go down and rest, and let me get you a nice warm drink."

Without being tired, Lucy became aware that she had been on her feet for quite a while, and that a cup of chocolate would be very welcome. She said so and made her way to the drawing room, thinking again of her sister Anna and how her presence had seemed to cast a cloud over an entire household. And it was almost as if she were only now starting to mourn her husband as she wished to. Her sister had laid emphasis upon the consolations of religion, but her idea of consolation had taken the form of protecting Lucy from any involvement in running things, and as the numbness began to wear off, this had not only become trying, it done nothing to alleviate her loneliness. After her cheerful husband, Anna was a dreary companion, and reassurances that his spirit would continue was a poor substitute for his presence. What she had to accustom herself to was the blank made by his removal from her life, and occupying her time with activity had been of considerable assistance.

A maid came in with her drink, and seemed gratified that Lucy recalled her Christian name, something else Anna had regarded as pampering servants. Anna, she thought, for all her earnest work for the poor, did not really seem to think of them as having feelings. Looking back over the years it occurred her that her sister was totally lacking in the sort of cheerful enjoyment of life she and Sir Charles had had. Images came to her mind, of poor little Harriet, smothered with her sister's care but seeming almost cowed. Then she thought of their father. In the midst of her preoccupation with her young family, she had not seen a great deal of him, especially in his last illness, but she had a sudden vision of him on one occasion, enjoying the companionship of her husband and three of her children and Anna attempting to hush them up and hurry them off. Mrs Randall had checked her that time, and Lucy could now see that she had protected him from their eldest daughter's solicitude. "Poor Mama," she thought, recalling the years that her mother had shared rooms with Anna in their rooms at Corwood Hall, "I know now why she sought me out so frequently even if I could not always spare her a great deal of time."

If the argument about Olivia had not happened, it might have taken longer for her to realise how difficult it was to live in harmony with her eldest sister. It was surely no wonder that Caroline had been unable to face the prospect, something Lucy had suspected at the time she left and had confirmed at that one meeting which she still cherished. But at that time, with Sir Charles happily still alive she had assumed that it was the antipathy between the older girls that would have made it so dreadful, though she had recognised that Anna, rather than Caroline, would have been the discordant one.

She gratefully finished her chocolate, just as the maid returned to see if she needed anything more. "Thank you, Margery," she said, and noticed that the girl had a small pile of papers in her hand. "Is that the post?"

"Yes, my lady, Mr Parker said to apologise that it was so late arriving." Lucy thanked her and took the letters over to the window where there was more light. Several from her children, which she approached rather nervously. She had had some rather unpleasant missives from one or two of her family about her invitation to Olivia, several of them seemed to have heard from Charles before they got her letters, and had written disapprovingly, under the misconception that she had wantonly forced her sister to leave. Anne had written angrily in defence of her godmother, but it had been Edward's self-righteous comments that she had found most upsetting, as a clergyman he should surely have been kinder about a fellow curate who had actually been a student at the same college but because Lionel Brandon had been less evangelical than he was, he had written as if his late brother-in-law had somehow been a failure, and he obviously held his mother to blame over his aunt.

To her gratification, she had nothing this time but sympathetic interest from Lucy and Clarinda, a slightly plaintive one from Cecilia asking why the Brandons could not have helped her sister as her late husband's family had helped her, and finally, Octavia Carter, Hugh's wife, had written to reinforce the loving offer of help that she had received from her second son in Sussex. She had a faintly guilty wish that it was this daughter-in-law that lived closer. Oh, no, there was yet another note that had slipped under the pile. Dear Elinor had remembered that this would be the day that her sister came and she wrote from the north to say how much they were in her thoughts. She had just recovered from her first confinement and had already expressed her distress to her mother as well as Olivia. "Oh, my darling," thought Lucy remembering how close the two girls had been all their lives. There had been real sisterly affection, surely? Did some of the family imagine that she had a similar feeling for Anna? None of the other girls had been particularly close, after all.

Her other sisters came to mind, had Harriet lived she might have been a friend as well as a relation, and Lucy still thought lovingly of Caroline. That quarter of an hour in Hyde Park was a precious memory to her, even though it were one of the few things she had ever kept secret from Sir Charles. "What ever would Anna say if she knew of that!" she thought, feeling thankful that her sister would never know. It would have given her a certain amount of satisfaction to inform her that this sister had not met with retribution but had a happy family life, but suppose Anna, even now, tried to find some way of making trouble for Caroline?

It might be wrong of her, but Lucy could not find it in her heart to judge Caroline harshly, even if she had sinned in the eyes of the world, and she remembered how her mother had spoken of her. Almost as if both her parents had felt at fault in some way. She was aware that Anna would be thought of as the good daughter, Caroline the erring one, but when she compared them it was not the older sister, almost repelling in her rectitude, who appealed, but the younger one with her sheer vitality.

She wondered how Caroline was doing now, had that attractive redhead found love after all? Had she more grandchildren. "I do not even know her married name," she thought sadly, but took some comfort from the last glimpse she had had of her sister going off across Hyde Park between her two tall children.

And Caroline had particularly noticed Olivia, had seen the resemblance to Harriet, something that Anna, curiously enough, had never mentioned. Of course Olivia was a much more cheerful person than the sickly little creature unfit to attend Lucy's wedding yet while she was healthy Harriet had surely had much in common with the niece she was never to meet.

One of her children had pointed out that Olivia might well marry again in a few years, and leave her mother alone but the late Lady Carter had seemed perfectly content, with her endless embroidery and her interest in new netting stitches. And during the sorting process, Lucy had come across some of her old paintings and the paints and paper she had used. She had really had little time for it with her large family, but why should she not take it up again?

The blustery wind blew sleet against the window, but did not hide another sound, that of a carriage driving up to the door. Lucy almost ran to the hall in time to see Parker admitting the new residents to the house, and clasping her pale tired daughter in her arms, she saw Mrs Old take the wrapped-up baby from the nursemaid and joggle it till it cooed. The Dower House seemed suddenly to have sprung to life.

PART 14

Coombe Park, Wiltshire

Christmas, 1859

Caroline paused at the top of the stairs and looked down at the activity in the hall below. Greenery was heaped there, branches of holly, trails of ivy, all awaiting the ministrations of servants who were busy with stepladders and string. There was a thump on the front door causing all heads to turn and a maid who was near the window peeped out and exclaimed, "It's the tree!"

The front door was flung open and Caroline caught sight of her younger son and two gardeners manhandling an enormous conifer into the house. It was planted in a wooden tub, and when safely in the hall, reached nearly to the foot of the stairs. Raised vertically it would nearly touch the ceiling, and as they manoeuvred it in the topmost branches set the glass brilliants of the chandelier jingling. From her elevated position she could see that there was no danger provided they lowered the tree a trifle, she nearly called out to that effect, but the man up the stepladder called out directions and the wooden tub was eventually taken in to the destined place in the drawing room.

Caroline decided that it was time she went downstairs and moved forward. One of the maids noticed her and ran up to offer assistance, calling for some of the evergreens to be shifted to clear a path for her in the hall. Holding the banisters, she needed no other support, and though she expressed her gratitude to the girl for offering her arm, she had a stab if irritation. It was kind of them to show such concern, but also annoying to be treated so cautiously merely because she was old. Oh dear, they were all watching her so anxiously! Smiling ruefully, she passed through the hall to the drawing room, where she found John regarding the Christmas tree with a quizzical expression. "It is getting a trifle too tall," she observed. He swung round and moved hastily to her side.

"Mama, I did not hear you come in – where were you? Come and sit down." He tried to take her arm, but Caroline stood where she was and laughed at him.

"Oh, John, not you as well!" she begged. "The servants have just been regarding me as if I were made of porcelain. When have I shown signs of decrepitude?"

"Well, I must admit, never," said John reluctantly. "But you are nearly ninety, after all. A fall down the stairs would be – dreadful."

"You mean it might be fatal," said Caroline crisply. "Very possibly, but I like to feel that I am still able to come downstairs and over to a chair without assistance." She seated herself and smiled at him. "I begin to understand why children get so frustrated when people insist that they cannot do things for themselves. I am not come to that yet!"

"No, no," said John hastily, "Of course not."

"And do not say that I am wonderful for my age, please."

He protested, "But you are, Mama! I suppose it is not very original to say so." Sitting down beside her, he looked consideringly at the large tree and said, "Well, we got it in here, but I think it will probably be too big next year. Did you see it come?"

"I did," said Caroline, taking up some sewing. "I nearly called out to you that the chandelier was safe as long as the tree went no higher."

"Yes, we will have to look for a smaller one. I was thinking, how strange it is, that the custom of bringing a fir tree into the house has taken hold?"

Caroline smiled, "Chiefly due to Prince Albert, I suppose. Still, some of our old traditions were dying out. Think of the Yule Log in an open hearth."

John glanced at the fire in its neat enclosed grate. "Yes, that would be difficult to have in here. You have been upstairs, Mama?"

"Indeed – tying up presents – I may not get another chance before the visitors arrive."

"Is Annie up there?"

"She was on her way to the nursery when I last saw her," said Caroline. "Making certain that the rooms had been made ready for Joe's children."

John smiled fondly. "And she would be just as pleased if it was only Dick's grandchildren coming, you know," he said.

"I know," said Caroline. "But it is lovely that she will have one grandchild of her own this year."

Her son looked thoughtful, "With all the grandchildren and great-grandchildren you have, you must think us rather foolish over our one."

"No, dear," said Caroline, thinking of the babies he and Annie had lost. Their surviving son was happily strong and healthy, but their chances of grandchildren were slim in comparison with Harriet's five children, or even Richard's two.

This thought was probably on his mind as well, his good-natured face was grave as he looked into the fire. At times like this he resembled his father more than usual and Caroline was moved. "Jack and Mabel and the baby will be here this evening rather than tomorrow, will they not?" she asked. He looked up in surprise.

"Oh, yes, I thought you knew. Did Annie not tell you?"

"She said they would probably be coming, but I was not quite sure at what time."

"They hope to catch the train that arrives about five o'clock, yes, I must remember to order the carriage to meet it. But you usually know it all, Mama."

Caroline made a face. "Too much," she said quietly.

"Too much for you? I cannot believe it."

"No, I interfere too much, I am resolved not to do so, this Christmas."

"Oh no, Mama. You never interfere."

"Do I not? I was afraid Annie might think that I take too much for granted in ordering the household."

"Oh, nonsense, Mama. She has always been grateful for your help. Yours and Charlotte's."

She sighed. In the twelve years since she had lost her husband, she had several times endeavoured to hand her responsibilities to her daughter-in-law and slide into the background, but it had been hard to lose the habit of years, especially as the servants tended to look to her for orders, and Annie so reluctant to take command that if Caroline was not at hand, she turned to her sister-in-law.

"And with Charlotte away just now," said John. "She is doubly grateful for your assistance and advice.

His mother nodded. "Well of course I am always available," she said, amused that a few minutes before he been treating her as a fragile old lady.

The door opened softly and the person they were speaking of joined them by the fire. Caroline looked at her affectionately, thinking how little she had changed from the shy little creature John had brought home nearly thirty years before. Small, with the reddish hair she had inherited from her Scottish father, she was by no means unintelligent, but she still had very little confidence in herself and now sat twisting a scrap of handkerchief in her hands, while her husband patted her shoulder encouragingly. She looked up at him and her pale little face lit up with an almost worshipful delight.

"Oh, the tree!" she exclaimed as she caught sight of it. "I am so glad that you managed to bring it in again, the children will be pleased. Will they be old enough to decorate it themselves this year, do you think?"

Caroline thought about this. "Possibly Arthur, but he may consider himself too old."

"What, at fifteen?" exclaimed John. "Surely not."

"Perhaps not, being Arthur," Caroline conceded. "Joe's children will be eager enough, but they are rather young."

"But Sarah is over six now," said Annie hopefully. "It is a shame that Harriet's other grandchildren will not be able to come. I know Rose lives too far away, but Maud's came last Christmas."

John smiled at her warmly, "I am very fond of my niece, but the Blakes must want to see their grandchildren as well, it is only fair."

"Still, dear Harriet will be here tomorrow, with Stevie and Arthur," Annie smiled at the thought.

"And Caro? She will be back from Scotland?"

"Yes, of course – oh, no, she wrote that she was going to Rose's family for Christmas."

"Caro is nearly as much in demand as Charley is," said John. "I do not know how we managed without a maiden aunt – oh, Mama, I am so sorry, I forgot about your sister."

Annie looked surprised and said shyly that she had not realised that Caroline had ever had a sister. "No, my dear, she died a long time ago. Her name was Harriet."

"Ah, is our Harriet named for her?

"Yes, she was named in memory of my sister." Caroline had never forgotten Harriet, but it was a shock to realise that it was over sixty years since her death. She smiled reassuringly at her daughter-in-law and turned to John, "But she was very young when she died, she might not have been a maiden aunt, she might have married."

"And Charlotte *should* have married," said John. "Even poor little Caro had those few months of marriage. I am so grateful for all that Charley does, I think we all depend upon her, but I do so wish she could have had her own family."

"It is hard to see that she would have been any happier," said Caroline. "You, and Richard, and Harriet have been so fortunate in your marriages, but not everyone is."

"Do you think, if things had been different, that fellow Perceval would have made her happy?" asked John. "I was only a lad at the time he was courting her, but I never thought he was good enough."

"Still, he acted honourably," said Caroline, concealing the fact that she had often felt the same about the man she suspected Charlotte still cared for deeply.

"Who is Mrs Nelson?" said Annie suddenly. "I mean, I know about the relations Charlotte goes to stay with, but Mrs Nelson is not a member of the family, is she?"

"She is Aunt Selina's niece," said John.

"Great niece," corrected Caroline. "Her father was Selina's nephew by marriage." She turned to Annie, "Selina was my greatest friend from childhood. I think you met her once, not long after you married John."

"Oh, yes, I do remember her now. She died not long after your dear father, John, did she not? I think I had the idea that she was a relation."

Caroline gave a sigh and caught a concerned glance passing between John and Annie, and with a slightly bitter humour felt sure that they were seeking a more cheerful topic to discuss with an old lady.

Annie finally said encouragingly, "I am so glad that Charlotte will be here tomorrow, I have missed her! Almost everybody will be here tomorrow. It is only Jack and Mabel and the baby who will be coming tonight."

"Which reminds me, I must go and order the carriage," said John, beaming at his wife and mother, and left the room. Annie followed him with her eyes, and turned anxiously to Caroline.

"Do tell me, am I doing the right thing to put the baby and his nurse in the room next to Jacky and Mabel?"

"But that was where they were when they came last summer," Caroline reminded her.

"But the nurseries were not in use at that time…"

"True, but it is probably better to do it this way. Joe's four will occupy much of the space and two nurses might well disagree."

"Oh, yes, I had not thought of that. I can see it could be a problem," said Annie almost gratefully.

Next day, Charlotte came home just before noon, taking a fly from the station. Caroline watched from the drawing room window as this drove up. She heard her daughter's voice in the hall, and presently saw her come in looking a little anxious.

"Mama!" she cried, skilfully manoeuvring her wide skirts round the chairs, as she crossed the room. "How are you, love?"

"Very well," said Caroline, smiling.

"Really? Are you sure?"

"Of course, my dear. Sit down, do."

Charlotte took a seat beside her and continued to look concerned. "It is so unlike you to just sit in here sewing at this hour of the day," she remarked. "I expected to find you with Annie."

"Mabel is here," said Caroline quietly. "They came a day early." Charlotte gave her a look of understanding and relaxed.

"Oh, I see. In that case I need not worry that you might be ill."

"No, please do not do that!" said Caroline promptly, and her daughter laughed.

"I had been feeling that Annie might need me, but in that case I can sit and talk to you with a clear conscience. And how is the baby?"

"He looks fine now, he has gold curls and pink cheeks. Oh, thank you, Polly, coffee is very welcome."

The maid who had come in with a tray laid it down and asked if Charlotte would like Mrs Carpenter to be informed of her return.

"Where is Mrs Carpenter? Upstairs?"

"No, Miss, she is walking in the garden with Mrs Jack."

"Oh, if that is so, please could you tell her I am here when she comes in, no need to bring her in especially, thank you, Polly."

Polly bobbed a curtsey and departed. When the door had shut behind her, Caroline said dryly, "Annie would not mind."

"No, but Mabel would. She would resent the interruption – she does not care for me, you know. Perhaps I deserve it, since I do not like her very much either."

"Nonsense, my dear. When do you take a dislike to anyone?"

"I must say, I did my very best to like Mabel, but it was the way she seemed to have taken an aversion to you that I found hard to endure. Why does she dislike us so, Mama?"

"I think she resents the fact that Annie relies on us. She may even imagine that we are unkind to her."

"How could anyone be unkind to Annie?" demanded Charlotte.

"Mabel may think that we dominate her, and prevent her running the household."

"She does not know Annie, then," said Charlotte.

"She herself would be capable, in Annie's place – it possibly does not occur to her that not everyone is like that."

Charlotte shook her head, "Poor Annie, I hope Mabel will not make her feel guilty at asking our advice. What made Jack choose that girl? He was a nice enough boy."

"He is a nice enough man," said Caroline thoughtfully. "I suppose to marry the daughter of a judge was a great advantage to him, and she is really quite pretty."

"She has a sharp nose, in more ways than one. As for an advantage, Jack does not need the connection to do well at the Bar. Isn't it strange that he should be so eager, when his father…"

"John was always too kind hearted to make a good barrister," said Caroline. "Running Coombe Park was much more to his taste. Jack is more ambitious."

"Parliament, I presume." Charlotte paused, listening, "Ah, I hear him in the hall, with John."

"In that case, perhaps it would be as well for us to change the subject – I really would like to hear about Megan."

Charlotte chuckled, and then sobered. "She is still poorly, this rheumatism plagues her dreadfully. But her husband and children take such good care of her."

"Do you know, I still find it difficult to forget that first time we met her, when Selina came for Harriet's wedding, such a shy little creature."

"She is not so shy, and of course she grew a little taller, but I do not think she looks very different from how she did then. She is still so sweet. Very like Aunt Selina, I feel. It is hard to realise that they were not actually related."

"It is surprising how people do catch the characteristics of those who bring them up." Caroline thought for a moment of the many ways that her elder son seemed to take after his stepfather. "How are Megan's brothers?"

"Poor Ifor had a bad year on his farm, but I think his prospects are better now. Gareth was the one they spoke about most. He has been elected for Parliament, for his local constituency."

"Oh, well done, Gareth," said Caroline. "I wish Selina could have known that. Her husband stood once, though it was against his nature, but she was so proud of him."

"Yes, old Mr Pugh was speaking about it. He arrived a day or so before I left the Nelsons. I think he prefers to spend Christmas with them. In fact, I have a feeling that he is happiest with his daughter's family than in his own home. Gareth's wife is rather gay – always giving parties."

"Oh dear," said Caroline. Her daughter nodded.

"It is his property, but I think he has practically made it over to his elder son. He seems to feel that his life is past."

"Why, he is more than thirty years younger than I am."

"I know, but you know how it is with the Welsh if they are melancholy..." Charlotte broke off as the door was opened and her brother looked in, accompanied by his son, a tall wiry lad with russet hair and whiskers to match. Jack seemed surprised to see his aunt.

"I had not realised you had come home, Aunt Charlotte. How are you?" and as an afterthought, "How is the friend you were staying with?"

"As well as rheumatism will let her be, and in no need of legal assistance," said Charlotte crisply. Jack flushed.

"Oh, Aunt – I did not intend to sound as if I was interested in that way."

She laughed, and told him not to be a silly boy. "I know you didn't! Can't you take a little teasing?"

"Oh – er – Ha!" said Jack. He turned away, smiled at his grandmother, and left the room, closing the door rather firmly be hind him.

John regarded his mother and sister ruefully, and sighed. "There are times when I think we spoilt that boy," he said.

"Well, he was your only one." Charlotte looked conscience-stricken. "I am sorry, John, I do not know what

296

comes over me sometimes, with Jack. I have an irresistible urge to tease him, I am afraid."

John shook his head, clearly inclined to blame his son. "A sense of humour would do him no harm," he commented.

"Possibly he does not like being teased by a woman, and an old aunt at that," said Charlotte. "Perhaps I hurt his feelings by calling him a silly boy."

"And perhaps he could show some manners!" retorted John. "You and Mama still say that to me, after all."

"But you are not really a boy," said Caroline quietly.

"You mean, Jack still is one, in spite of having a wife and child? I agree," said John. "And that is the reason why he did not appreciate your joke, Charley. He is a trifle too eager in his pursuit of forensic success to take it as such." He sighed again. "We did spoil him. Oh, did you need me, Archer?"

"Yes sir," said the butler. "Concerning the carriage, you asked to see Porrit before he met the train."

"Oh, so I did. In fact there will be two trains to meet, one shortly and one just before five. I had better go, please excuse me, Mama, Charley."

"Oh dear," said Charlotte sadly as he left. "Sorry about Jack, I did not mean to cause trouble."

"Now you are being silly," said Caroline, laughing. "Jack should not have taken offence. I was sorely tempted to be far less kind. That boy is altogether too full of his own importance."

"And John is generally so mild about him. He hardly ever raises his voice to him, even. Still, it his son, I should not criticise."

"He has an equable temper, but in dealing with Jack, I think he has always tried not to raise his voice because it is so distressing for Annie."

Charlotte looked thoughtful. "All the same, Jack never seemed to mind my teasing him when he was a child. Do you suppose his response just now has something to do with Mabel?"

"Oh yes," said Caroline. "She feeds his self-importance because she likes to feel that he is a somebody. She sees him

297

as the son of the house. I daresay she feels we do not treat him with enough respect."

"Oh, Mama! Yes, I think you have something there. Her husband must be all-important – and to do her justice, she does look up to him as well as push him forward. She probably does not realise that in this family he is just one of the grandsons."

"Exactly. And because John is so modest, we all tend to treat him as a younger son, which of course he is not as far as Coombe Park is concerned."

"That is very true," agreed Charlotte. "*He* still regards Dick as the head of the family. Dear Johnnie! Well, Mama, I must go and unpack before the rest of them arrive." She stooped to kiss her mother's cheek and moved gracefully from the room. The sun broke through as she did so, and Caroline was aware that the carriage had gone to fetch Harriet, her son and grandson, and Richard and Sarah.

She picked up her sewing just as a sunbeam illuminated a painting on the wall. It was one that John had commissioned just before Harriet's wedding, and it always seemed to her that the artist had captured her remarkably well. On the table beneath it were several framed photographs of other family members, which were said to be remarkably like their sitters. The camera, she was often assured, was so much more accurate than a mere drawing or painting, but Caroline was not sure if she agreed. The portrait seemed to have more animation than the stiff poses of the photographer's studio, quite apart from showing the sitter in colour. Still, the whole process was a remarkable innovation, and contemplating the changes she had seen in her lifetime she almost forgot to sew and was taken by surprise to hear the carriage returning.

Normally she would have left the drawing room to greet the new arrivals, but hearing Mabel's voice as well as Annie's in the hall, she hesitated. Poor Annie was anxious enough without a confrontation between her mother-in-law and her son's wife, which might have been difficult to avoid if the former spent much time with Mabel. That young woman held the firm conviction that the elderly grandmother should stay

298

in her place as the centre of the house. Thank goodness she was so far an infrequent visitor to Coombe park, "For the festive season I will try to accept the position she wants me to," Caroline thought grimly, but she had enough of her old fire left to resent being reduced to a senility she had not reached.

It caused anxiety, too. Harriet could be heard enquiring for her mother and she came in alone, looking worried and moving cautiously. The muted shades she had worn since she became a widow four years ago generally suited her fair complexion very well, except when as now, she had gone pale.

"Well, Harriet love, how are you? It is nice to see you," said Caroline, hoping that her tone was clear and sharp enough to reach Mabel's ears. "Where are Steven, and Arthur?"

Colour flooded back into Harriet's cheeks, and for a moment she looked almost like her portrait. "They did not like to come in," she murmured, bending to give her mother a kiss. "We were afraid all of us might be too much for you."

"Oh, dear, how foolish," said Caroline. "Are Dick and Sarah holding back as well?"

"That is so. I mean, I have never known you not to come out to greet us. We feared – that you are – are getting old."

"Well, so I am," said Caroline. "After all, eighty-eight is hardly first youth! But I can assure you that I am quite myself."

"Truly? Only that girl Mabel said 'Grandmama is waiting in the drawing room' in such a hushed voice, I was concerned."

"Yes, Mabel seems to felt that that is how she ought to talk about her husband's grandmother. I think in her mind she sees me as a sweet old lady and would like me to use a stick in the house as well as outdoors!"

"Stupid little thing," said Harriet crossly. "Why should it matter what she thinks?"

"I suppose it helps her feel important. And of course Jack will be master here one day."

"I trust I shall not live to see it, then." The door opened cautiously and a head appeared round it, Caroline was momentarily startled by a resemblance to both her late father and her uncle.

"Dick!" she said cheerfully. "Come in. Is Sarah there?"

Her son grinned with relief, "Yes, Mama – come in, Sally, I don't think you need worry." His wife joined him, and brightened as she met Caroline's welcoming smile.

"Are Steven and Arthur still out there?" asked Harriet.

"No, they thought they had better go upstairs first," said Richard. "They did not want to tire you. Are you tired, Mama?"

Caroline kissed them both and repeated that she was in perfect health. Harriet indignantly explained about Mabel.

"Oh well – these Longs," said Richard. "I have often had to go carefully with her father in court. In private life, he is all amiability."

"What a pity Mabel cannot be called to the Bar, then," commented Caroline. Sarah chuckled and Harriet smiled faintly, while her half-brother grinned, shook his head and said he now knew his mother was quite herself.

Before they had been talking for long John came in, greeted his sisters and patted Richard on the back, urging him to come to the library, which produced an amused look as they went.

"John wants to ask him about how Jack is doing," observed Sarah.

"I know," said Caroline.

"He need not worry, Dick says Jack is doing remarkably for so young a man. His progress is extraordinary."

"How does Dick feel about it?" asked Harriet. "He did so well himself, even if it was not as fast."

"Indeed. I am afraid my father would not have been as useful as Mabel's is to Jack, but I think Dick is proud of having got where he is on his own."

"Steven used to say that that was the reason Dick did better than he did, because he had to work for a living. Old Mr Linton left him so well off he could afford not to practise as a lawyer," said Harriet rather sadly.

"But Steven was very clever, surely?" said Sarah.

"Oh he was, but he did not really enjoy taking cases, and he really had no incentive to earn – just like John. Jack seems very different."

"Yes, he would not be content to be a mere country gentleman," agreed Caroline. "And if he were, Mabel would not enjoy it."

"I can imagine that," said Sarah. "When I heard who Jack was going to marry, I sincerely hoped he would be prepared to be pushed."

"You know the family quite well, then?" asked Harriet.

"Oh – as well as one ever does know people like that. He enjoys public life, his wife is very retiring and spends much of the time in the country now that her children are married. Being a QC, Dick sees a certain amount of him, both in and out of court."

"As he said," agreed Harriet. "Oh, Steven darling, there you are. Do come in."

"May I?" said her son, taking a cautious glance at his grandmother.

Caroline laughed and held out her hand, "Yes, come along and sit down, you silly one. Where is that son of yours?"

"Out in the hall," said Steven. "Can you stand to have him in here, Grandmama?"

"Of course I can," said Caroline, raising her voice. Young Arthur followed his father hesitantly. A large gangling schoolboy with a mop of red hair, he was inclined to stammer. In spite of her encouraging smile, he regarded his great-grandmother nervously and did not sit down.

Steven bent to kiss Caroline, who felt the pang his appearance always produced. He remained very like his father, but he was more subdued than Harriet's husband had ever been, and already at forty his hair had receded and his scholarly activities had produced a noticeable stoop in his tall frame. His had been an exceptionally happy marriage, and the death of his young wife giving birth to a stillborn daughter had been a tragedy from which he had found it hard to recover. Devoted to his little son, he had also been a great comfort to Harriet when his father died, and Caroline felt almost as if he were a contemporary of her own children these days.

Arthur came forward to kiss her, treating her almost as if she might break, but as he straightened up he caught sight of the Christmas tree, upon which Annie had draped a piece of tinsel. "Oh, I say, is that the tree we had last year?" he asked eagerly. "Hasn't it grown!"

"Like you," said Harriet, smiling up at him.

"Well, let us hope that Arthur does not grow as much as this has," said Caroline. "It was nearly too big for the house this year!"

"Are we going to decorate it on Christmas Eve, again?"

"Would you like to?" asked Caroline. "You will only have the little Randalls to help you, since the Blakes are not coming this time."

"Isn't it a pity," said Arthur. "Muriel and Charles were so much better than me – I felt that I was rather clumsy. But little Sarah will be able to do the dainty bits, if I help, won't she, Aunt Sarah?"

"I am sure she would love to," said Sarah, kindling at the mention of her eldest grandchild. Having had only sons, she adored her little namesake.

"Your Aunt Annie was hoping you might like to do it," Caroline reassured Arthur. "So you and Sarah and Dick can do that tomorrow morning."

"It will keep them all out of mischief," said Steven ruffling his son's hair.

"I think it is very kind of Arthur to amuse the children," said Sarah, smiling at her great nephew. "I am sure he would prefer the company of cousins who are nearer his own age."

"In a way," said Arthur, "But Muriel seems to be so grown up, these days, and it was difficult to get much help from Charlie – he was too busy reading. That left Addie, Ethel, and Alfred, and they are not much older than Sarah and Dick."

"Don't you like reading, Arthur?" asked Sarah, glancing at Steven, who had picked up a book and become engrossed in it. Arthur reddened, and stumbled over a stool, while his stammer became more pronounced.

"Y-yes, I do, but n-not over C-Christmas, when there are p-people about."

"Charlie lives almost in a world of his own," observed Harriet. "Maud finds it very trying. He is much worse than Steven." Her son looked up, smiled, and returned to his book. Harriet laughed gently. "You see what I mean – one would probably have to touch Charlie to get his attention!"

"Did I hear my name?" asked Charlotte, coming in to the room. "I am sorry I was not here to greet you all, but I have only just come back myself."

"I was actually speaking of Maud's elder boy," said her sister. "But I was wondering where you were. Come and help me unpack, there's a love; it's an age since I had a talk with you. Did you know I am really planning to visit Scotland at last, as Edith has been imploring me to do for years."

"Yes, Caro told me, when she returned from her last visit, she says Duncan Fraser will be delighted, and it is a lovely place." They went off together and Sarah looked after them thoughtfully.

"It must be pleasant to have a sister," she remarked. "Such a delightful relationship."

"If they are friends," said Caroline. "Not all sisters are as close, especially after they grow up. One hears of dreadful family quarrels."

"I suppose it must be so. Being an only child myself, I may possibly put too high a value on the idea of brothers and sisters."

Caroline thought that Arthur looked at her with fellow feeling, but he glanced at his father and did not speak. Sarah caught her eye and they exchanged nods of sympathy. Annie, entering with her usual soft tread, was among them before anyone could find a new topic of conversation. She looked pleadingly at her sister-in-law and asked if she would care to come and see her little grandson. "He is such a darling!"

Sarah rose to her feet and smiled down kindly, assuring her that she would be delighted to do so, and allowed herself to be led away.

As the door closed behind them Caroline rang the bell and asked the maid who answered if she would fetch her cloak and overshoes. Steven put down his book as she got to her feet and regarded her with surprise, while his son moved to her side and hovered uncertainly with one hand out as if ready to take her arm.

"I am intend going for a little walk before it grows dark," she explained. "Will the two of you be my escorts?"

"Gladly, Grandmama, but are you sure you can manage it?" said Steven.

"I am perfectly certain," she assured him.

"In that case, will you take my arm?" Caroline generally took a stick when she went out, but to refuse this offer might hurt his feelings and he was sturdy enough to give her all the support she needed. Unlike some younger people, he did not grasp her elbow but gravely offered his arm when they left the house and she expressed her satisfaction about this as they sallied forth in the last gleams of the sun.

Jack emerged from the house as they returned, and greeted Steven with some deference, since his cousin was fifteen years his senior. "I was hoping to catch you – would you care for another turn in the garden. Arthur, too if he likes." He commented amiably upon Arthur's increase in height, and then looked at Caroline with concern. "Grandmama, you must be exhausted!" he exclaimed.

She assured him that Steven and Arthur had taken excellent care of her, reminding herself that he probably was genuine in his anxiety even if his manner of expressing it suggested disapproval of her being so active. It was infuriating that as she let go of one grandson's arm, the other seized her by the elbow and steered her into the house. Her previous words on this subject caused her to look ruefully at Steven and Arthur, causing Jack to enquire what they were laughing at.

She found the drawing room empty when she entered it, and there might have been no one else in the house except the maid who took her cloak and put coal on the fire. No doubt the other women were still upstairs, and as she took up her sewing she saw her sons pass the window, deep in conversation. The light was beginning to fade, but she saw their earnest expressions quite clearly. John so reminiscent of his father, and Richard again making her think of hers, though surely his hair was greyer? With a shock, she realised that her son was now older than her father had been when she last saw him. No doubt he had eventually gone white, as she had, but it had taken some time for her hair to do that.

Thoughts of her younger days drifted in and out of her mind as she worked. She had been fond of Mr Randall, but her uncle had almost taken his place in her upbringing and her affections. Charles Randall, and her mother had been the people whose authority she respected. Her father had always seemed somewhat ineffectual with his main intellectual achievements being his interest in the history of his family. Yet he had been neither a fool, nor particularly weak – he had simply abdicated from his responsibilities, causing his brother to regard him with the good-natured contempt that had probably coloured Caroline's reaction to him. This characteristic had surely also prevented his wife from relying on him as she should have done. Whenever she envisaged him it was as unobtrusively removing himself from controversy, and looking back, she decided that it was much to Mrs Randall's credit that the illusion of his authority had been maintained as well as it had been.

His distress over the death of his little son, and later of his brother had been, she thought, almost as much for the loss of an heir to carry on the family name. Caroline wondered how he would feel about the knowledge that he did have descendants bearing the name of Randall. She had regarded his obsession with the name, his pride in his book about the family, with indulgent scorn, but the years had brought tolerance, and she found a certain satisfaction in the thought that due to her, there were still Randalls, even though this could never be acknowledged to those who had known him.

Lucy, in that strange meeting in Hyde Park, may have guessed it, but now that Selina was dead, Caroline was the only person who knew for certain. Had her son ever suspected anything? The information she had given him about her childhood and his father had seemed to satisfy him, and it was a source of pride that he had achieved all he had by his own efforts. That his stepfather gave him a stable background must have been an advantage, but he had never presumed upon it. She felt no necessity to enlighten him about the facts that she had carefully kept secret for sixty-four years, no doubt he would cope if he had to know, but why should he?

Something John had said in his last days came into her mind. For the first time he had hinted at suspicions that he had been happy to leave unconfirmed, but assured her that even if it had been so, it would have had no effect on his love for her, or his feelings for her son. She smiled lovingly, and found it really had grown too dark to see what she was doing. About to ring for candles, she realised that though she had not heard the carriages set off on the second visit to the station, they were surely just coming back.

Caroline listened intently, but hearing only servants in the hall, decided that she ought to risk Mabel's displeasure, and laying aside her sewing, went out to welcome the last contingent of family visitors. She sent one maid to fetch lights for the drawing room and another in search of Annie, and joined the butler in welcoming the newcomers hurrying in to the warmth of the house.

First came children and their attendants, a two-year old girl in the arms of a nursemaid, the older ones under the firm control of a stout little old woman. Adults and a younger baby were just emerging from the second carriage. Caroline spoke kindly to the nursemaid, stooped to the children, and addressed their venerable escort. "Nancy, it is so nice to see you again," she said. "How are you keeping these days?"

"Well enough, thank you Ma'am," said Nancy, watching the arrival of the lamps and then casting a cautionary look at her charges. "Should I take these children into the drawing room?"

"Yes, do," said Caroline. "There is a warm fire in there. Alice, my dear – are you frozen? Let me take the baby for you."

306

"He is rather heavy," warned Alice Randall, sounding a little shy. "Are you sure you can manage it?"

"Certainly I can, I assure you I have carried heavier ones."

"But that was when you were younger, Grandmama," said the baby's father, grinning at her and recalling Richard in his thirties.

"Impertinent boy!" said Caroline. "All my grandchildren appear to think me quite ancient, just because they have children of their own now."

"I haven't!" said the last member of the party from behind his brother. "I hope I am expected?"

"I imagine so," said Caroline, leading them into the drawing room and sitting down with the baby on her lap.

"Because if not," said Philip Randall, with an extravagant gesture, "I will have to sleep on the floor. Perhaps there is room in the nursery!"

The older children giggled at this, and their uncle turned to them appealingly. "You would make room for me, Sarah and Dick?" he said, putting an arm round each of them. "I can count on you?"

Nancy shook her head disapprovingly. "Stop it, do," she said. "They will think you mean it. Of course your uncle will have his own room as usual."

"He said he used to sleep in the nursery," said the little boy.

"That was when he was your age, Dicky," said Nancy. "Now he is just being silly."

Philip reached out an arm to include his old nurse in his embrace. "Ah, come on, Nancy," he wheedled, "You know I was always your favourite."

"I know nothing of the kind," said Nancy, putting on a severe expression. "I don't have favourites, and you're a bad boy!"

"Coming here uninvited," said Joseph, winking at Caroline.

"No, Papa, he was asked!" cried little Sarah, running up to him. "He said so, on the train, only he wasn't sure that he would be free to come."

"And here is Aunt Annie," said Philip, "I managed it after all, Auntie. Hallo, Mama!"

Annie, a little flustered, had come in with Sarah beside her, and Mabel on their heels, and before the door was shut, Richard, John, Steven, Jack and Arthur appeared to greet the newcomers. Everyone was talking at once, little Alice began to cry and her baby brother threatened to join her. Caroline concentrated on soothing him, so the exchanges going on round her percolated only intermittently. Annie greeting her guests, tea being brought in, Mabel trying to talk to Alice who had taken her younger daughter on her lap to comfort her, Harriet returning with John and moving to speak to Nancy... And here came Charlotte and the older children ran to her, fighting over which should sit on her lap, Dick won and Sarah looked disappointed till she realised that her grandmother was also sitting down and went to her.

It was impossible to talk to more than one person at a time, and by the time the baby had quietened, Caroline looked up to find Philip seated nearest to her and smiling quizzically, as he looked down at the little crumpled face.

"And how is my young namesake?" he asked, handing her a cup of tea.

"Sleeping, as you see," she replied quietly. Jack's little son began to whimper, and Philip turned his head for a moment to watch Mabel rock him till Annie held out her arms to take him and the baby settled down again. He grinned ruefully at his grandmother.

"The pleasure of family life!" he murmured in mock dismay. Caroline looked at the other males present, especially Jack, who seemed rather pained by it all.

"You do not really mind," she said confidently. "Less so than most men, I should say."

"You know, you are right," he agreed. "I like children, in spite of having none of my own." He paused, and watched her face carefully as he added, "At least, I do not think I have any. Do I shock you?"

"No, dear, I am far too old," said Caroline. "But take care that Mabel does not hear you, perhaps."

Philip glanced coolly at his cousin's wife. "I suppose not," he said. "Though I must say. I would love to shock that woman."

"Now, now, remember it is Christmas!" Caroline was secretly amused but hoped he would not guess it.

"How could I forget? And I shock Mabel quite enough, just by being here. She disapproves of me, you know."

"I do not thinks she cares for red hair," said Caroline solemnly.

"Jack's hair is reddish."

"Yes, but he gets it from Annie's side of the family, it is her Scottish colouring, not so startling as ours."

Philip ran his fingers through his own red curls and regarded his father and aunt as well as the children before surveying Mabel again. "Not quite the done thing," he observed. "It is not only my hair, though. I do not do the right things. She can bear my father, because he is a QC, and Joe is at least a success as a publisher. I have done nothing."

"I thought you had done a great deal," said Caroline, "Studied law, travelled, written a book about it…"

"Helped edit a magazine, organised an expedition to Egypt, and only kept out of prison by sheer luck," finished Philip.

"Really? How dreadful." Caroline smiled calmly at him.

"I may exaggerate a trifle, but there were certainly moments when I feared my debts would outstrip my earnings. Yes, I have done plenty, but where is the evidence of it? Look at Jack – he is five years younger than I am and already doing famously at the Bar."

"Would you change places with him?"

"No, but I can see why Mabel holds me in poor esteem. Why, just at the moment I have no occupation. I daresay I shall end up as a schoolmaster."

Caroline was about to say that this was surely not too bad, when there was a general move to unpack, put children to bed and change for dinner. She had no chance to resume her conversation with her grandson during the evening, but she

309

continued to feel concerned about him even when she was preparing for bed.

Next morning the children were eager to start on decorating the tree, but after breakfast John and their grandfather swept them out into the garden to collect more greenery and have a romp while the sun was shining, and it was not until after two that Arthur Linton and the two oldest Randalls embarked upon the exciting task of bedecking the large fir with tinsel, gold-painted cones, and the ornaments that Annie had been accumulating. Caroline, watching with Sarah, was pleased to see that in spite of his self-deprecating words, Harriet's grandson was deft enough at the work, and very considerate of the younger children. Sarah took some knitting and settled unobtrusively in a corner, and Caroline decided to go for a walk again, now that she had a little more leisure. "Which should also show Mabel that I am still perfectly active!" she thought.

Taking her stick she stepped out briskly on the still frosty ground, but she had not gone far before she heard footsteps behind her and Philip hurried up. "Grandmama, may I come with you? And would you like to take my arm?"

"Thank you, my dear, but I find this stick quite adequate. But I would be delighted with your company. We did not finish our conversation last night, did we? You spoke of becoming a schoolmaster, rather as if it were a last resort. I was about to say that you might do worse."

"I suppose so. If Steven were not so learned I might offer myself as a tutor for Arthur, but I could never come up to his standard."

"Nonsense," said Caroline. "You said you had no occupation at present, but are your prospects really so bad?"

"I was possibly exaggerating, I think I have a chance with a magazine, which would be much more promising than that other one, I'd have to put up some money but Joe says he will help me if it is more than I can afford. It is not something that Mabel would approve of, though."

"Why not?" asked Caroline as they came to the lake. "Is that not a respectable occupation?"

"She would not care for the politics, my friend is rather radical and does not care for the Tories, whom she regards as the only political party worth knowing. Some of us feel that there is a great deal wrong with the way this country is governed, whichever party is in power."

Caroline felt a stirring of interest and questioned him further. He told her of a piece he had written after reading a book Joseph had recently published. "It contained ideas put forward by a man who started off very radical in his youth, and though he mellowed he remained a champion of the poor and of reform until he died in 1840. You won't have heard of him, his name was Ambrose De Lyle."

"I met him," said Caroline unthinkingly, recalling an intense young man full of fire, whom her uncle had prophesied would do great things if his tongue and his temper did not get him into trouble. She had heard him mentioned by the people that Thomas Martin had introduced her to, as someone they admired but who had made London rather too hot for him and been forced to go abroad to avoid prosecution.

Her grandson stood gazing at her in amazement, "Grandmama! When did you meet him, and how?"

"Did I never tell you that I once had an uncle who had progressive views? Mr De Lyle was someone who came to his house."

"I knew vaguely that you had had an uncle, but you have said very little about him. What was his name?"

Caroline gave him her uncle's first two names, since he had been given his mother's maiden name as a second one it sounded authentic. "He was not a public figure but he was very interested in reform in general."

"And what did you think of Ambrose De Lyle?"

"He was something of a hot-head, but very intelligent." She had not been greatly attracted to the man, but had respected his mind, and appreciated the fact that he did not regard women as incapable of rational thought. Philip pressed her to say more about the reformers she had met at her uncle's, and she told him of several long dead men that

Charles Lattimer Randall had admired, some of whom he recognised. Then she sighed and said it was a long time ago, why her uncle had died before the French Revolution had taken such an ugly turn.

As they headed back to the house, her grandson talked of some of the ideas and causes he and his friends hoped to cover in their magazine, and seemed delighted by her response. "You know, Grandmama, I always felt that you, and Mama, and Aunt Charlotte were much more intelligent than most females, but I had no idea about this!"

"Mabel would definitely not approve," observed Caroline, and he chuckled.

"Our little secret, Grandmama?"

"Indeed," Caroline was amused and begged him to keep her in touch with the way the magazine prospered.

Tea was ready when they reached the drawing room, and when it was over Arthur and the children hurried back to the Christmas tree, which they finished just as it was time for the younger ones to go upstairs. Caroline offered to come up with them and once their work had been generally admired, they accompanied her fairly willingly.

The scene in the large day nursery, with Nancy knitting by the fire, the baby gurgling in the old wooden cradle and the younger girl nearly ready for bed was so familiar that Caroline was almost startled, momentarily taken back nearly sixty years to when she had first established Nancy in these rooms to look after the first of her babies to be born at Coombe Park. And now they were both old women.

Sarah ran to tell her nurse how they had decorated the tree, and Caroline prepared to slip away, but Dick clung to her hand and begged her to stay with them, leading her firmly over to another chair by the fire. Nancy was not discouraging, and in response to a question as to how she found the rooms, replied that it could be worse. "Not as it was in my day, but at least it is clean and dry. Not like those rooms we had at Eastbourne this summer. Damp wasn't the word for them, was it, Nelly?"

"Oh, it was dreadful," said the nursemaid, gently easing little Alice towards the night nursery. She seemed to have Nancy's approval, and Caroline felt that though the older woman might instruct and rule, it was Nelly who did most of the work. After all, Nancy must be about eighty by now.

Nancy turned to her two older charges. "So you made the tree look pretty did you? Master Arthur did a lot of it, I'll be bound."

"Oh yes he did," said Sarah admiringly. "He climbed the steps and reached all the high up branches while Dick and I did the ones at the bottom."

"I am very glad to hear it," Nancy fixed them with a mock ferocious look. "Don't let those two near a stepladder, I said to your grandmother, I can just see them falling off. Just like your father, you are. And your grandfather! Naughty wasn't the word for them, when they were your age."

"What was the word for it, then?" said Sarah cheekily.

Nancy snorted, and turned her attention to the little boy who was looking solemn and said anxiously, "Papa isn't naughty, it's Uncle Phil who is that."

"Now what in the world gave you that idea?"

"You said he was, yesterday," Sarah pointed out. "When we got here."

Nancy looked at Caroline and shook her head. "Sharp, these two, whatever you say, they are on to it at once! No, children, I was only joking with him. He and your father were both naughty little boys, there wasn't a pin to chose between them. That does not mean that your uncle is bad now."

"Aunt Mabel thinks he is," said Sarah soberly. "I heard her say to Uncle Jack, 'I don't know why your father has him in the house.'"

Nancy looked disapproving. "Now, you know you should not listen to other people's conversations," she said.

The little girl was near to tears. "I wasn't listening – they came into the room when we were on the other side of the tree and didn't see us." She looked up at her great-grandmother. "She said it was wrong of him to make you go out in the garden, but he didn't *make* you, did he?"

"Certainly not," said Caroline, indignantly. "I went out on my own, he came and joined me for a walk. What did your Uncle Jack say?"

"Nothing. Arthur called out that we were there; I think he was cross with her too. Great-grandmama, I don't think she is very nice, saying things like that about Uncle Phil."

"Yes, well, she does not like him I am afraid," said Caroline, drawing the child to her and putting an arm round her. The little boy looked at her with intelligent eyes and asked if Aunt Mabel liked any one at all.

"'Cos she doesn't like us, does she, Sarah?"

"Now, now, you must not say things like that," Nancy was beginning, but Caroline raised a hand.

"I think we should admit the truth of this, after what they heard," she said firmly, and turned back to the children. "No, Aunt Mabel does not seem to like many people, it is her misfortune – if you like people, they will like you. Perhaps we should really feel sorry for her," she added reluctantly.

"Don't any other people like her?" Dick sounded puzzled, and Sarah asked why they ought to feel sorry.

"I don't!" she said, "She's got Uncle Jack, and the baby, hasn't she? Why should we feel sorry about her not liking people and them not liking her?"

"It is sad that she misses so much," said Caroline. Sarah snuggled up to her.

"I like most people I know," she said, "So why can't she?"

"I suppose it is just the way she is." Caroline was still disturbed at this new evidence of Mabel's sour nature, and changed the subject by asking about the holiday the young Randalls had had in Eastbourne. Had they enjoyed it? She smiled at Nancy, who looked resigned but seemed indulgent at the children's response.

"Oh, we liked it very much," said Sarah, and began to talk about the beach, and the donkey rides, paddling in the sea, and making sandcastles. Dick let his sister tell most of it, leaning a little sleepily on Caroline's knee, but a thought seemed to have struck him.

"Great-grandmama," he said, "When you were little, did you have a holiday at the seaside?"

"I am afraid we did not, not so many people went there then, certainly not to bathe – if they did that, it was in autumn, or winter, for their health."

"That must have been cold!" said Sarah. "Didn't you ever go to Eastbourne, or Brighton?"

"Brighton, yes once or twice. We lived quite near there, in Sussex, you see."

Nancy had begun to bustle about heating milk ready for supper while Nelly fetched the children's night clothes, and turned in surprise. "I never knew that, Ma'am."

Caroline was aware that she had never mentioned the fact before, and was a little surprised that she had done so now. She smiled vaguely and said oh yes but it had been a long time ago and she did not know anyone there now."

"You are very old," said Sarah consideringly, "Grandpapa said you are his mother, and he is old. He says things are different from when he was a little boy, so what were they like when you were little?

"Oh, very different, I was just thinking about it yesterday. Nobody took photographs; for one thing, they did not know how to do that. And it took so much longer to travel, there was no railroad."

"No trains!" said Dick in amazement. "How did people get here, then?"

"They came all the way by carriage or coach. And not nearly so many people travelled far, it cost so much to do so. There were stagecoaches, which people could go on, but they would not hold many at a time, not like the trains. And each coach had to be pulled by two horses which had to be changed on the journey because they got tired – as you know, the engine that pulls the train runs on coal and does not get tired."

"I can see that," said Dick slowly. "Why didn't they have trains, if they are so much better?"

"They had not found out how to make them, just as they did not know how to take photographs. Your papa was nearly grown up before either of those things came along."

"Oh, he never said, did he, Sarah?"

"You ask him about it," said Caroline.

"What else was different when you were a little girl?" asked Sarah.

"Let me see, now. There was no gas, so the streets were very dark, even in London. The towns were much smaller, and there were not many things like furniture and cloth made in factories. You could not buy ready-made clothes, most dresses were made at home, for instance."

"What sort of dresses did you wear when you were my age?" asked Sarah. Caroline thought back to her childhood and recalled the painting of the family done when her brother was a baby.

"When I was very young, a white dress with a blue sash, but grown-up people had very different things. The ladies wore full skirts as they do today, though that changed as I grew up, the dresses were very skimpy for many years. The gentlemen looked quite different. They wore their hair long, tied back and put powder on it. And none of them had a beard, or side-whiskers. Then their suits were not like the ones people wear today, and they wore knee breeches."

"Like footmen?" asked Sarah.

"Something like that, but much more elegant."

"And was Christmas..." Sarah began, but Nancy intervened. "Come along, young lady, and Dicky too. Time for supper and bed. You don't want to be tired for Christmas day, now do you?"

"No-oo," chorused the children dolefully, looking up at Caroline pleadingly. She laughed and kissed them good night, saying that her old nurse had been just like that, particularly at Christmas. Accompanying her to the door, Nancy looked particularly at Dick and said in a low voice, "Bless him, he's just like our Dickon was at that age."

Caroline regarded her great grandson thoughtfully. He certainly shared the red hair and grey green eyes that Richard had inherited from her, but his features were not very similar, and at five years old he seemed more introspective than his grandfather, with more interest in mechanical things – perhaps as a result of living in London. Nancy was looking nostalgic, clearly appreciating the continuity that had seemed apparent when they had come up to the Nursery. "Dear me, that seems a long time ago," she observed, as she said good night to all the inhabitants of the nursery suite, and went downstairs to change for dinner.

When she was ready, she sat for a while by the fire in her dressing room, thinking. The children's questions, coming on top of her earlier recollections, had sent her mind back over eighty years, and she found herself recalling the one time she had been somewhere other than Sussex or London, at about Sarah's age, something she had almost forgotten. "Yes, I was under seven when we went to Cheltenham to see Grandmama," she thought. Why had her father's mother retreated there when she was widowed? Had she perhaps preferred not to remain in a county where she personally had no roots – and how had she got on with her son's wife? Caroline had only a vague impression of the old woman, who she realised with a shock must have been more than a dozen years younger than she herself was now; but she did find the image of a decisive character who possibly clashed with an equally firm-minded daughter-in-law.

"Did I want to ask about her childhood?" she wondered, trying to think if there had been much mention of how things were in the seventeenth century. Nearly as large a gap as there was between her childhood and that of the two she had been talking to a little while ago. Surely there had not been such rapid change? Searching her mind for something she might tell Richard and Sarah about her grandmother next day, an account of seeing the Queen in London one day surfaced. Caroline remembered being fascinated by the idea of there being a queen instead of a king. "If only I had been a little older, I might have questioned her more about that, she would not have been a child when she saw the queen, I know she was sixteen or so when Queen Anne died. I wonder if the children would be interested in that, they have never known a king. In fact, Joseph and Philip can probably hardly remember William the Fourth."

Her conversation with Philip had reawakened memories of her uncle, and of the various radical reformers she had met both with him and with the people she had met when she lived with Thomas Martin. Charles Randall, she thought, would be proud of her grandson, but he and the others would surely be saddened that there was still so much inequality, so many poor people to be concerned about. Though thoroughly urban in his interests, he had shared her father's concern about the enclosure of wide tracts of common land and the effect it had had in many cases of driving countrymen to drift to the towns for work.

Richard Randall had deplored the break-up of the old way of life that he had always known, while his brother worried about the conditions so many people encountered in the towns. But her father had taken good care of his tenants and workers, had he not refused to join in the rush to fence in land many of them relied on to pasture their animals? He had even discouraged several of them from accepting offers that seemed tempting but which would have done away with some of their rights. That had impressed her uncle, she remembered suddenly.

The balance of wealth had shifted a little, there was less money and power exclusively in the hands of the aristocracy and gentry, with tradesmen and manufacturers making fortunes, but how few had climbed out of the working class and then extended a helping hand to those they left behind them? Philip had praised a couple of philanthropists but there seemed few more of them than in her uncle's day.

He had not mentioned if any of his radical friends were concerned with women's rights, married to an intelligent man who respected her mind, she had not felt the inequality so much in later years, but had anything changed there? Impoverished ladies were thrown on the mercy of relations, or could become companions or teach, but there was no other decent way for them to earn their living. "There is a different feeling about it, though," she thought, "Modern young women do not seem quite as contented to accept being treated as inferiors, to be pampered but not taken seriously." Contrasting her daughter-in-law Annie with Mabel, she felt that the younger woman was stronger-minded, even though so much less likeable.

As for women ceasing to be held more guilty than men in affairs outside marriage, attitudes seemed if anything to be hardening. And being extended to men, too. Caroline could not believe that many of them came to marriage as virgins, but this was apparently expected of them. "They think my generation was much more licentious than it really was," she reflected. "Whatever Philip really thought Mabel's response would be, I do not believe he expected me to be shocked by the things he said."

Someone knocked softly on the door and she called out, "Come in," as her elder son turned the handle and stood on the threshold smiling at her. The resemblance to her father still struck her, but now that she was accustomed to the idea that Richard was in his sixties, she was more aware of the differences. His manner, as he accepted her invitation to sit down was very much his own, confident without arrogance, something he probably owed more to the influence of his stepfather than to heredity.

He was also dressed ready for dinner, and she wondered where Sarah was.

"Oh, she is saying goodnight to the children. I looked in, but Nancy seemed to think I might excite them too much!"

Caroline laughed and told him how she had been talking to the older children after they had finished the tree, and of their interest in the days gone by. Richard was a very proud grandfather, and enjoyed this account of their intelligence. But he then said rather sadly, "Oh, I do so wish Phil would marry!"

"Much the same was said of you," Caroline pointed out.

"Yes, I know, but I was a father by the time I was his age."

"Never mind, you already have four grandchildren."

"Oh, Mama, that is not why I want Phil to marry, not the main one, at any rate. I feel that to do so would give him something to work for, settle him down."

"In his place, would you think that a good reason to marry?"

"Not without love, of course, but Joe found a lovely, intelligent girl in Alice, and Phil is popular enough. I worry about that boy, Mama, I really do."

"I do not think you need," said Caroline thoughtfully. "Not while Sarah does not."

"How do you know she doesn't worry?"

"I have seen the way she looks at him. I don't think you are all that concerned about him, either. You only feel that you ought to be because he is not a worldly success."

Her son smiled wryly. "I daresay you are right, Mama. I was not all that happy about Joe going into publishing, instead of pursuing the law, but what would have been the good when he disliked it so much? He takes after Sarah's father in some ways, and his firm is doing well. But Phil could have outshone Jack if he had chosen to."

"He does," said Caroline.

"Oh, in general, he does, I agree, but not at the Bar."

"Well, would you prefer to have Jack for a son?"

"No, indeed. Jack's not a bad boy, but so full of himself. How did a pair of gentle souls like John and Annie come to have a son like that?"

"Perhaps he gets it from the Carpenters, people like Augusta's father and his brother the Canon."

"Oh, I remember the Canon, from when we lived in Hampstead. A big fat man dressed in black, all slimy goodwill. No, Jack isn't as bad as that."

Caroline was impressed that he should have remembered the man so clearly, he had not been as old as his older grandson when they met.

"I remember being really frightened," said Richard, grinning. "And I have heard him spoken of unfavourably by older people who knew him, the servants especially. It is a wonder that Papa was so different."

"I think he got his best qualities from his mother," said Caroline.

"Like me!" said her son, taking her arm as the dinner bell sounded. Caroline felt a glow of pleasure at what she felt was the best compliment anyone had ever paid her.

PART 15

Summer, 1965

(Extracts from the diary of Charlotte Louisa Randall, born 28th May 1947 and living in Mid Sussex.)

24th June, Thursday

This is the fifth time I have begun a new volume of my diary, and I always feel as if I were starting afresh. This one in particular, because I have just realised that it is three years to the day since I began on a diary and kept it up more than a few days. I had always liked the idea of it, but I'd begin one on the first of January and then let it slide somehow. It never occurred to me that you don't have to start then. It was partly because my brother Richard gave me a second-hand copy of Fanny Burney's early diary for my fifteenth birthday that my mind turned to it again, she was only fifteen when she started to keep one, but it was because she wrote a best-selling novel when she was quite young, that he thought I'd be interested. That may have been why I spent some of the W.H.Smith token that Aunt Annabel sent me on a bound book, it helped not having to keep to a page a day! All the same, at that point there did not seem to be anything worth recording till that trip to Petworth House with the school, on the 23rd of June, and the next day I wrote six pages in my first diary, and that started me off. I came to realise that the secret is not to worry if you miss a few days, but just go on from there, writing up anything important if you have time. That's the sort of thing Samuel Pepys did, anyway, and I know Fanny Burney did not write every day.

I've no doubt a lot of people would think me a bit old fashioned, I have never told any of my school friends in case they laugh. Rick doesn't find it funny, anyway, he told me to keep it up. "It will be a valuable document in a hundred years time!" I'm not sure that that's not a quietly sinister remark, but he has been going through all sorts of old diaries and letters for his thesis, so he must know what he is talking about.

So the anniversary is what first comes to mind as I open this new volume, and then I am so happy to record that we had a letter from our grandparents today, saying that they hope to be back in England next week. We are all so pleased about it, they have never been more than a couple of miles away all my life until this last year and I have hated having them out in Australia. I suppose that sounds a bit mean, after all they had never seen their only other grandchildren at all, and couldn't get there till Granddad retired. It was such a shame that they were away when Sue had her baby, he will be seven months old next week. I know they are both dying to meet their first great-grandchild. Sue and Ken are planning to bring David here again in the Summer, but once they have recovered from the journey I daresay Granddad will feel like driving down to Cambridge.

I haven't written anything about what I did today, it was not very exciting, I got in some typing practice, helped Mummy with the shopping, and then got supper so that our parents could go out for an evening meal. I think it turned out quite well, and the boys ate it even if they did make rude remarks about the potatoes being lumpy. Neither of them left any of it, anyway! We are now sitting in the back room, Pat is wildly revising for a Latin test tomorrow, and Rick is buried in a book he picked up in Brighton. It looks old and obscure, you'd have thought he'd have had enough of that sort of thing, but of course History is his subject, he hasn't lost interest even though his thesis is finished. Oh, I think I hear the car. I expect Mummy and Daddy could do with a cup of tea.

4th July, Sunday

The grandparents have been here for the day; it was just like old times. They said they thought we had changed, and though I did not expect them to have done so, seeing them

323

again was a surprise, somehow. They are both very brown, and I think Granddad's hair is much whiter, but it took a little while to feel quite comfortable again. It was a lovely sunny day, and they said they really prefer the climate here – though the weather was pretty unwelcoming the day they got home!

After lunch, we sat in the garden and talked ourselves hoarse. If I tried to write down everything that was said, it would take days, and I'm not sure how much of it I could report verbatim. How Fanny Burney managed to retain and retail such long conversations, I can't imagine. Not only had we news to exchange, but there were masses of photographs to look at, theirs were of course much more interesting, but they were so pleased to see pictures of baby David, and Rick had taken some good ones over Christmas.

We went for a walk before tea, and once it was a bit darker, Rick got out the projector and showed all our slides and then theirs. Granddad really is a very good photographer, his views were magnificent, and even family groups are not so boring if he takes them. I asked him how he manages it, once, and he smiled and said he waited till the people were doing something interesting and not noticing him, and takes the photo then. Even if everyone is consciously posing, he often just pretends to click the shutter and takes the real shot when they have relaxed. There was a particular series of slides taken at a barbecue on the beach that really seemed to bring the Morris family to life.

Seeing Grannie with all these strangers who are yet the same relation to her as we are was very odd, but it made them seem real. Aunt Anne is her daughter, and Uncle Phil is related to us as well, his mother was Granddad's first cousin and her maiden name was Randall. They both look a bit like Daddy, and all have red or reddish hair, like my brothers and me. Is it particularly hereditary, I wonder? Sue is the only one with dark hair like Mummy's, and only Uncle Peter who was killed in the war had Grannie's colouring.

I was especially interested to see Caroline and Elizabeth Morris, as they are nearly my age. They are really identical, Granddad was not sure which was which in the photos and said he had found it difficult to tell them apart when he was with them. Grannie said by the end of the time there she could do so sometimes if they were together, but if she saw only one, it was difficult to be sure. She said Caroline seems more intelligent than her sister, and much more interested in the sort of things Grannie and I care about. Their brother Joseph is almost Pat's age, but he looks more like twelve than fifteen. I gather that he is just as mad about aircraft as Pat, though.

They are the only first cousins we have on the Randall side of the family, though with Mummy having two brothers we have several Weston cousins. It seems that like me, Caroline Morris wants to go to university and she is thinking of seeing if she can get a scholarship to an English one. If she does, she might be able to come and stay with us. There are some Randall cousins in Cornwall that we hope to meet some time, descended from Uncle Phil's uncle, but the only other close relation to the Morris family is Aunt Barbara, she is Daddy's cousin but we have always called her aunt. In spite of her being an important Civil Servant, she is great fun. Goodness, she actually *is* the twins' aunt!

It would be nice to try and put down some of the incidents they talked about but even if I could remember the details, it would take far too long. But I keep thinking of something Granddad said just before they left. He was particularly wanting to know what Rick thought, but included me because he thought I would be interested. He said that now he's retired he wants to pursue an idea that has been interesting him for some time. He wants to find out a bit more about the Randall family, possibly even write some sort of history. Something right up my brother's street. This is a project Granddad has been thinking of for years but never had the time for till now.

He'd meant to talk to Rick about it as soon as he got back anyway, he said, but was even keener after the Morris family expressed interest in the Randalls, he told them all sorts of things they hadn't realised before. Uncle Phil begged him to write down for them all that he remembered, and he'd said he would. "I've made some notes," he told us, "But anything before my time is mostly based on what my father told me." He wondered if it would be possible to trace the family back a little further, what did Rick think? Rick asked how far back Great-grandfather's memory went, when was he born? In about 1853 or 4, he thought.

"I haven't thought about researching our family, but quite often if people try to trace their forebears, they can't get much further than the start of the 19th century," Rick said. "After that, none of them are likely to be literate, they'd be working class, and the census did not come in till the middle of the century."

I asked Granddad what sort of thing his father had talked about, what did that suggest the family had done – how long had they been publishers, for instance. (I know that Daddy is the fourth generation in the firm.) He said yes, it was founded by his grandfather in the 1850s. So literate right back to the start of the early part of the century at least!

"I fear I did not always take as much notice of his stories when I was young," Granddad said ruefully, "And what with being called up and then marrying young, I did not see so much of him except in the firm, we got on very well, but he did not talk to me about the past much. He died in 1942, and now of course, I regret that I did not discuss the subject more as an adult. I have an idea he said that his father was a QC, though."

"Really? Or is that just a family legend?" asked Rick. "He was connected with the law in some way? I mean, he might have been a barrister's clerk or something. But still literate, I'd agree. Are there any documents?" Granddad said he did not think they would have survived; a lot of papers were lodged with the firm and were destroyed in the blitz. Would it be possible to find out? Rick said he was sure of it and he'd try to find out. There was also a family legend of visiting a grand house in the country and meeting a wonderful old lady. We worked out that this must have been the 'QC's' mother, something about her having been married twice and Randall being her first husband's name. But again, as Rick said that could just be the sort of story that family members produce with little or no foundation. Granddad said that he would rack his brains for any other details his father had given him and write them down.

But all this promises to be a very interesting bit of research for Rick and he and Granddad both seem pleased for me to be in on it. If nothing else, I can type things out, how glad I am that I decided to leave school at the end of the Spring term and study shorthand and typing, I was just thinking that might come in useful when I go to university, but the typing at least will be useful at once, and Hooray, I will not be at school when they do any interesting research.

7th July, Wednesday

What with all the friends and relations to visit, Granddad didn't expect to make a start on putting down his memories for several days, but to my surprise he rang yesterday to tell us that a document *has* turned up. On Monday he and Grannie went to Eastbourne to see his sister, our great-aunt Katie. She is a few years older than he is, and he thought she might remember more about things their father said. She was the only one of three girls who did not marry and so saw more of their parents, especially as after Great-grandmother died, when she went to live with her father. She was a teacher in London but changed her job so she could be in Eastbourne. As soon as Granddad spoke of the things her father remembered, she said she was sure he had written some of them down a few months before he died.

She looked them out and drove over with them yesterday, Rick and I were invited to tea and I am going to type them out so it will be easier to consult them, and spare the originals. I shall take a couple of copies, and I might stick one in this volume as a record, I wouldn't want to copy them out in longhand as well as type, and if I just selected bits, I might miss something that turned out to be important. We haven't done more than glance at them, but Aunt Katie is certain he included an account of the mysterious old lady.

It was lovely to see Aunt Katie again; she is always so stimulating to talk to. I'm sure it was more her doing than Miss Willis's that I got keen on English Literature. I don't wonder that the school in Eastbourne were so reluctant to let her go that she still teaches sometimes even if she is over seventy. I feel that she enjoys teaching much more than most of my teachers did, and that rouses one's enthusiasm. She was talking about her early childhood, and mentioned another interesting old lady, who lived with them before Granddad was born. I think I have heard her speak of Great-aunt Charlotte, but is that mainly because I have her name?

I don't think I'd ever wondered who she was. Aunt Katie didn't seem to think that she was a Randall, she was sure she had a different surname. Granddad wished he had known her, how old was she? Auntie said she thought about ninety-five or six. "Now I come to think of it, I don't believe that our grandfather had a sister, so if she was a relation and it wasn't just a courtesy title, she must actually have been a Great-great-aunt," she said. Perhaps there will be something about Aunt Charlotte in these papers, it seems she had been a part of the Randall family for a very long time. Why, she could have been the daughter of the other old lady we want to find out about.

Aunt Katie remembers her as being bedridden, but that she had been spoken of as having been active till she had a fall when she was about ninety. But even after the accident she seems to have kept alert and interested, liking to have small children round her and keeping them amused. And though Aunt Katie was only about four when she died, she got the impression that Aunt Charlotte was not only intelligent, but much better educated than might have been expected for someone born before Queen Victoria. She thinks that when she was a little older she heard some woman who had been to one of the early girls public schools say to her mother that Aunt Charlotte had had a remarkably good brain. If only Aunt Marion were still alive, she was some years older than Aunt Katie and would surely remember more. I begin to see why Uncle Phil felt it would be a good thing for Granddad to put all his memories down now. It is something to have those of Great-grandfather, though.

8th July, Thursday

I have spent much of today typing out these reminiscences. Thank goodness our great-grandfather wrote a nice clear legible hand, without too many flourishes, and it was not too difficult to read. To my surprise, Rick does not seem as enthusiastic about it as I thought he would be, he says it is interesting but not very informative. I found it fascinating, but it is a bit scrappy and rambling, perhaps what he put down were rough notes for an autobiography he did not live to write. Still, we are getting his memories at first hand, not filtered down through his children or grandchildren, and there are a few facts that we might be able to check, such as the name of the big house the family were supposed to have visited. And as he was over eighty when he wrote this, it isn't surprising that he can't always be sure about names or dates. We are going to take the typescript round to Granddad in a few minutes, so I shan't write much more tonight, but by the time I've stuck in one of the copies I made, this entry is going to take several pages! As I said, it is a bit scrappy, but here it is::

MEMORIES OF A MID VICTORIAN CHILDHOOD
Written in 1941 by Richard Joseph Randall

"This hideous war distresses me beyond words, the last one was bad enough, but I was younger then. At eighty-seven I am incapable of any constructive effort to help. I do hope there will be an end to it before too long, but I fear I shall not live to see it. With that in mind, it seems time I followed my children's advice and tried to put down some of my memories of a past that has become history to many people.

"I was born in 1854, the second child of a family of eight, of which I am now the only survivor. For such as we, it was a pleasant time to be born. My father was not rich by the standards of those days, but we were always comfortably off, especially as my parents did not entertain lavishly. We children knew nothing of the misery in which so many of our contemporaries lived, though beggar children on the streets of London were a familiar sight which we took for granted. This though my father was a liberal-minded man, and took up many causes for the relief of the poor. He sometimes impressed upon us that we were fortunate, but I do not think it really sunk in till later. Still, if we did not pity the poor as much as we ought to have done, nor did we envy those who were better off. We were happy with our lot.

"Our house was in Kensington, within easy reach of the Gardens, where as children we spent many happy hours. In those days that part of London was still quite rural, with real country within easy reach, and when we were older my brother and I would go on long walks through areas that are now completely built over.

"We had a large, roomy house and were, I believe, fortunate in that our parents did not follow the practice common to most people at the time, of keeping children in compartments (much as we kept our toys!) to be brought out at specified times. I cannot remember a time when we were not welcome in the rooms our parents inhabited. Though of course we had our part of the house and nurses to look after us. Indeed, when I think of the number of servants it seemed to require to cook and clean and run the house for us generally, and then see my daughter Catherine manage this, admittedly smaller house with one daily woman, and teach in the afternoons, I marvel. Mind you, we now have the advantage of machines like vacuum cleaners and electric cookers, which were not available in those days!

"I mentioned that there were eight of us, starting with my sister Sarah who was born in 1853. She was my earliest companion and friend, and we retained a deep affection for each other till her death in the flu epidemic of 1919, just after losing the husband who had been perhaps doubly dear to her because they had no children. Poor little Alice came next, born in early 1857 – she was never very strong and died at the age of thirteen. Philip, born in 1859, was at first too young to be very much of a companion to me, but as he grew, the gap seemed to narrow and we shared many interests. He was not just a brother; he was a friend and indeed a partner in the family business until his tragically early death in 1898, leaving a widow, a small daughter, and an infant son. Next to him came Charlotte born in 1861, perhaps the prettiest of my sisters, named for a beloved Great Aunt, apparently as a child she resembled her very much, both in looks and in temperament, and she promised to continue to do so as she grew older, but she married in 1882 and promptly emigrated to Australia so though we remained in contact, we never met again and I knew her only from letters and photographs and one marvellous telephone call to celebrate my eightieth birthday.

"There was also the occasion when one of her sons came to visit my wife and myself at our home in Sussex, just after what we used to call the Great War. He seemed a nice lad and I believe did well in Tasmania, but unfortunately since Charlotte's death in 1938, followed by this second holocaust, I have lost touch with them. Of the three youngest children, Joey (1862–1867) and Catherine (1865–1872) were not with us long enough to develop much character; though Cathy was a sweet little creature of whom I was fond – it gave me great pleasure to name my second daughter after her. Harriet, who came between, was born in 1864, and lived till a couple of years ago. As a child she was a strange, difficult creature, not very pretty but enormously intelligent. Thank goodness she was born at a time when it was becoming possible for a girl with brains to have the education that she needed. It was still unusual, but my father was exceptionally enlightened about what a daughter should be taught. Poor Harriet would have eaten her heart out in the expected feminine role of Wife and Mother. She became an excellent teacher and eventually a headmistress, and I reckon for sheer value to society she must have been one of the most impressive people our family has ever produced.

"My mother's parents lived in Shropshire and died when I was quite small, so my paternal grandparents were the only ones I knew properly. I do not think any children could have had better ones. They did not live very far away from us, and we saw them at least once a week. Grandmama was angular and brisk, and although she could be restful for a small child, as I grew older I seldom saw her sitting still until her last illness. She had a lively mind and was interested in everything, and was very unlike most old ladies I encountered. She told me once that she had been brought up by an elderly widowed father, seldom met other girls, and being 'Bookish, did not get on very well with them if she did. That explains why she seemed ill at ease in a roomful of women. With children she was popular, when she talked to us she assumed we would have a fair degree of intelligence and treated us as if we were equals, not the inferior beings so many other adults seemed to consider us.

"Grandpapa seemed more distant, especially when we were very young; I think he was fond of us, but not quite sure what to do in the company of small children. He was a tall man, in later years made clumsy by rheumatism, and I think very small people made him nervous. He had a reputation for sternness, but as I grew older I found him well disposed to conversation with his juniors. He did not go out much after Grandmama died, but I visited him often in his last years and he seemed to enjoy my company. I regret now that I could seldom get him to talk much about himself or his career. It was always 'And what have you been doing with yourself, Dick?' and I would hold forth on whatever subject took my fancy at the time. I have the impression that he encouraged this, prompting me to go on with further questions if I showed signs of flagging. Possibly this was a habit acquired in his career as a barrister – he was certainly skilful in getting others to reveal their minds to him, and I am sure he had a genuine interest in them. It has come to me since that I neglected opportunities to find out more about his life, or even his opinions. I never knew if he was distressed that my father chose to become a publisher instead of following in his footsteps as a lawyer. He may have had hopes of my studying the Bar, but he never tried to influence me. Like my parents, he and my grandmother seemed to feel that people should be allowed to make up their own minds, a policy I always tried to pursue with my own children.

"I was just over twenty when he died; he was approaching eighty and had long retired. And by then life had him some pretty severe blows. There was, for instance that business about his younger son, my Uncle Phil, which happened when I was nearly twelve and Sarah was thirteen. Even now I find it distressing to think about, it was the worst event of my childhood – something that came out of the blue and made all the worse in that it was never really explained. As children we were told not to talk of it, and as I grew older I realised the effect it had had, particularly upon my grandparents. I feel sure it hastened Grandmama's death. I know it had something to do with the political Review or magazine that he edited, concerning a libel suit, I believe, but all we children knew was that a much loved uncle vanished from out lives for ever. Some hint of scandal came our way, I think we were glad not to be able to talk to some inquisitive adults, and I am sure that we soon came to think of him as dead. But if he had been, surely there would have been a funeral? Something my father said once, in his old age, made me feel that he did not think of his brother as dead, but it caused him nearly as much pain as it did my grandfather, and I never liked to press him. I am sure that Uncle Phil had not done anything really wrong, but I have an idea that the paper was very critical of the government, a piece he wrote might have got the magazine into trouble. He was such a splendid uncle, we always loved it when he came to visit, he would joke and tease us and tell wonderful stories. To my father, I now realise, he was even closer than I was to my brother Philip, and they were the only two children my grandparents had, no sisters and no other brothers. Eh dear!

"I have just been for a little walk, and was reminded of my very first visit to this town, at a time when it was in its heyday. This would have been in the summer of 1859, when I was about five. Now I come to think of it, I must have had my fifth birthday there. I can remember having a party on the sands, with donkey rides, and a Punch and Judy show. I think

333

this may have been the first summer holiday we ever had, it was wonderful to feel free of the correct behaviour we had to show when out in London streets. It was not a mere fortnight either; my impression was that we stayed over a month, with my father going up to London by train for some of the time.

"Familiarity with the Eastbourne of today has overlaid my impressions of those early days, but I am certain that it was at that time that I began to develop an affection for Sussex which has only grown with the years. When I finally retired here, I felt as if I were coming home. I have an idea, which I will enlarge on later, that our ancestors may have come from Sussex. Could it be the call of our roots?

"That first journey to Eastbourne was quite a migration, I remember. Even though at the time there were only four of us, we took up a whole compartment and I think a couple of servants travelled separately. It was quite a squash, myself, my sisters, my parents, baby Philip, the nursemaid, and Nancy. When I wrote of the servants, I did not mention that person, who could almost be described as the mainstay of the household. She ruled the nursery completely, although by that time she was very old and getting frail. I felt that she ruled my parents as well, and I do not think it was just my childhood imagination. My father once described her as a benevolent Despot, and I know we all felt a sense of security in her mere presence. I had left the nursery by the time she died, but I know I felt desolated when she did. How to describe her? A little wizened old woman, whose word was law to three generations of our family. Even my illustrious grandfather had been her nursling, and treated her with respect, it is no wonder we treated her with awe!

"Nancy only half approved of Eastbourne, for one thing a seaside holiday was a disturbing novelty to her. She was cautious about the sands, and regarded the waves with suspicion. Nothing in the world would have persuaded her to go on a boat trip! My grandfather told me once that she had lived in the country for over twenty years without really approving of it. 'As a Londoner born and bred, she never quite trusted animals, especially those with hooves. When I, and my half-sisters and brother learned to ride, she resembled a hen who has reared a succession of ducklings but never becomes accustomed to their taking to the water!' he remarked.

That house in the country, I feel dreadful to admit that I cannot be sure of its name, or even where it was situated. Somewhere to the west of London, Hampshire, or Wiltshire, I think, and I am sure the first part of the name was Coombe, but was it House, or Manor, or Park? There ought to be details, somewhere, but I do not feel inclined to seek them out. I do remember the name of the man it had belonged to, my grandfather's stepfather, a Mr Carpenter. We stayed there several times when I was small, when it was the property of Grandpapa's half-brother, Great Uncle John.

"This property had been the home of my grandfather for most of his childhood and youth, and I think he was much attached to it, but we never visited it as a family after his mother, our great-grandmother, died. This was in the early 1860s; the old lady must have been over ninety! I think my first clear memory of her was in 1859, the year we went to Eastbourne, in fact. She must then have been in her late eighties, and though I thought of her as very old, I do not think that she seemed as old as Nancy did. From later impressions I am sure that she was tall and upright, and I think handsome, but at the time I was chiefly struck by the fact that she could speak firmly to Nancy and be submitted to. But of course, since my grandfather once said that Nancy had looked after him from birth, she must have employed Nancy at the end of the eighteenth century.

"It does seem ridiculous that I cannot remember more about the house my relations lived in, but I would have been only nine when we ceased to go there, and I am sure that we were invited chiefly for the sake of my grandfather's connection with it, so that when he ceased to go there, so did we. I have wondered if the scandal about Uncle Phil had something to do with it, but when I consider, I am sure that that happened some years later. I do not think that my grandfather quarrelled with Great Uncle John, they may only have been half-brothers but I feel sure that they were excellent friends, and so were their wives.

"Uncle John's wife Annie was a darling, a sweet little thing, very timid, and no doubt they remained friends with Grandpapa even though he did not visit them. Their son Jack was younger than my father, but though they were cousins, I do not think they were as friendly as the children of John's older sister, my Great Aunt Harriet, were. I remember Sarah and I were a little afraid of 'Uncle Jack' and really disliked his wife, Aunt Mabel. Even at that tender age I think I recognised her as being a shrew, and nothing I have heard since contradicts this impression. I do not think either of them cared for any of the Randalls very much and there was something about her complaining about Uncle Phil. I know that later she was very unpleasant to dear Aunt Charlotte, whom everybody else adored.

"That Christmas of 1859 was not the last time I saw my great grandmother, I am sure we stayed at the big house at least once in the summer, but it is the memories of her then that stick in my mind, particularly on Christmas Eve. I think there was quite a gathering for the holiday with Great Aunt Harriet and her son and grandson. I now know that both she and 'Uncle Steven' had lost their partners and I think they shared a house for mutual consolation. The grandson was called Arthur Linton, and I got to know him well in years to come, when he became one of our authors, but I always remember how kind he was to my sister and me. He was about fifteen, almost an adult to us, we could not understand why Aunt Mabel treated him as a child, but many lads of that age would have scorned children of five and six, instead of letting them think they were helping to decorate the Christmas tree. I'm sure he really did most of it! Oh, that tree, it was one of the largest I have ever seen, brought in from the garden in a pot the day before we arrived. It was a wonderful start to Christmas, to put holly and ivy, painted fir cones, tinsel, and I think glass ornaments provided by dear Aunt Annie, on those dark green branches. Then we were taken upstairs by Great Grandmama, and it is that time in the nursery with her and

Nancy that is perhaps what I remember most vividly. Possibly because among so many people it was a relief to be with the younger children, the nursemaid, and those two very old women, who sat quietly by the fire and talked.

"Even now I fancy I see the expression on our great grandmother's face as we told her all about our visit to Eastbourne, as if she was looking at something a long way away. As she must have been, for she spoke of having lived in Sussex once, something even Nancy did not know. I am sure that is why I have a feeling that the Randalls might have originated in Sussex.

"Looking back, I really feel that it was at that point that I first became aware of historical scale, I know it seems very young for such a conception, but it was when the old lady began to speak of the changes in her life time that I got the idea of how different things might have been. I know my own grandchildren used to marvel at the idea that cars and planes, films and radio had not been around when I was a boy, and when I was five and a half, I was amazed to learn that Great Grandmama must have been old before railway trains were a part of life, that there were no photographs, no gas lighting… I know that at a later date, possibly then or perhaps on another visit, she mentioned that her grandmother as a young girl living in London had seen Queen Anne. This was not something that would have interested me much at the time, but it startles me now!

"When I try to think what my great-grandmother looked like, I am aware that I may be confusing those childish memories with later ones of her daughter Charlotte whom I knew very well when I was an adult and she was a very old lady. I believe there was a strong resemblance, but I still have the feeling that Great Grandmama was not quite as beautiful, and that even in old age she had a forceful personality and would not have suffered fools gladly. I knew both her daughters in old age, I was about fourteen when Great Aunt Harriet died, and I think she was the loveliest old woman I ever saw. I have just remembered something else about that Christmas Eve, there was a painting on the wall of a young girl, seventeen or eighteen, and Cousin Arthur said that it was his grandmother at the time she got married, I don't think I ever saw noticed it after that, but I know it made an impression on me when I was a child."

At this point his memoirs cease, it seems a shame he never said more about his life in London or impressions of things like transport, the theatre, he left a sheet of paper with a few notes on it suggesting he would have gone on to them, but all that remains are a short description of the grounds of the big country house and how his sister said once that being there was "Like living in the middle of Kensington Gardens!"– and a comment that he is sure there are a few photographs dating back to the middle of the 19th century but he can't face climbing up into the loft to look for them.

9th July, Friday

Granddad was very pleased to have the copy I had typed out of his father's memories, but like me, surprised that Rick does not feel that they will shed a lot of light on our present search.

"You see, Granddad, it is not exactly a historical document," he explained. "It was not written at the time, but is his memories of about eighty years before which might be accurate, but cannot be relied on for verifiable facts."

This approach seemed to impress Granddad as being professional, but he seemed depressed that the memoirs were not as valuable as he had hoped. "I was going to put down things about my childhood, as Philip Morris suggested. Are you saying that they would be no use?"

"Oh, not at all," said Rick. "I'm sorry if I seemed to pour cold water on them, they are very charming and they do give a picture of life over a hundred years ago. No, you go ahead, but it would be a good idea to give a fuller account of dates and places. These memoirs would be so much more useful from a historian's point of view if he had given more details that could be checked against other contemporary accounts. For example, he mentions his sisters, but doesn't even give their married names. I'm sure he meant to write more and might have provided more facts, but there is not much to go on there, do you see?"

"I think I do," said Granddad, cheering up. "About the sisters, I know Aunt Sarah was Mrs Tatum, she lived in Finchley and I remember her quite well. But Aunt Charlotte, no. I knew about her, and in fact when we were going to Australia I racked my brains to think if I'd ever heard it, so I could try to contact her children or grandchildren. But I had no success, though I found some letters, which did not give a full address, but there were no envelopes with them, which might have given those details, and she always signed them just Charlotte."

"I daresay we could trace her marriage," said Rick, "But at the moment it might be better to concentrate on things to do with this country. We might try to find the big house, though. It sounds grander than I would have imagined, and might even be on the map. Pity he was only sure about part of it, and didn't know the exact location, but you've got all those Ordnance Survey maps, it would be worth trying." So they both got out the maps, and began pouring over them, while I kept wondering why something seemed familiar in a different context. They came up with a couple of Coombe Houses in Hampshire and Dorset, but the only Coombe Park was in Wiltshire. When Rick said that, I suddenly realised where I had seen the name.

"The National Trust!" I said, "I'm sure they acquired a place called that, quite recently." Granddad said the latest details had come while they were away and they had barely glanced at them yet. He got out the book, and sure enough, they only got the house a couple of years ago, it was open to the public for the first time in 1964. It seems that some of the family still live there, and that the owner was a Mr John Carpenter.

"The name, too!" I said, feeling excited. Rick nodded and though he warned us that that could still be sheer coincidence, he agreed it would be worth pursuing.

"Better not jump in and claim relationship," he said. "But if you like, Granddad, I could write to this John Carpenter, and tell him we are trying to verify a reference to what we think might be this house, would you mind if I said I was doing so on your behalf?" This suggestion met with approval and I offered to type it.

"Perhaps," I said, "Great Aunt Charlotte might prove a link?"

"Yes, and Katie thinks she has seen some photographs of my sister Helen's christening," said Granddad. "Perhaps the ones my father speaks of are with them." Grannie had just come back from visiting a neighbour and made us a cup of tea and as she brought it in, she asked him if he had told us what she had remembered. He said he was sorry, he had not got round to it, and asked her to tell us.

"It was after he and Katie got back here the other night," she said. "We were talking over the memories, especially those of Great Aunt Charlotte and I suddenly remembered something my dear mother-in-law had said, about the old lady injuring her hip? You couldn't think of it at first, could you, Philip? But" – she turned to us – "He did recall it when I reminded him."

"But only my mother telling you at that point," said Granddad, "I don't think it was something I heard as a child."

"Yes, it happened when you were a baby, and your grandmother had come to stay with us. One of our neighbours, an elderly lady, was carried off to hospital with a broken hip. This reminded my mother-in-law of a similar accident, when Great Aunt Charlotte had failed to come as usual to see little Marion and 'Baby Catherine' they had become very anxious and her husband had gone round to her house and found she had had a fall, was unable to get upstairs, and was struggling to cope with the aid of one elderly maid and a young girl. She had not let the doctor or the servants summon her nephew or any other members of the family, but was eventually persuaded to come and live with them, and she stayed for the rest of her life." Grannie turned to Granddad, and continued, "Your mother spoke very affectionately of her, and praised her intellect. She said it was difficult to believe that this was someone who had been born about 1803."

"Yes, I remember that now," he agreed. "My mother had herself had a better education than was usual when she was a girl, but she found Great Aunt Charlotte nearly as knowledgeable and quite as intelligent as she was. She was well grounded in Latin, for instance. It is funny what sticks in your mind most, until you mentioned that, my chief recollection was of my mother saying what a sweet nature the old lady had."

Dear Grannie! She seemed so pleased to have contributed to the memories, it may not be her family that we are researching, but she still takes a great interest.

15th July, Thursday

Richard (I am trying to give him his full name these days, will he take the hint and call me Charlotte?) got a reply to his letter this morning. He and Granddad talked over what he should say, and decided definitely against trying to claim any relationship with the Carpenters, instead he merely said that he was trying to trace a woman who might have lived in the house during the first half of the nineteenth century, who possibly have had the first name of Harriet or Charlotte. He wrote to Mr John Carpenter, but the reply was from a Miss Dora Carpenter, saying that her father had died a few weeks ago, she was now living in the house and had actually been going through a lot of old papers with him before he was taken ill. She had returned to this, and had just come across letters and other things to do with the very period Rick mentioned. She would be willing for him to come and look over them. So he rang this afternoon and is going there on Saturday, it seems that they closed the house when her father died and won't open to the public again till next week.

But last Sunday Aunt Katie came over to bring the photographs she spoke of showing Aunt Helen's christening, and she had discovered others. "I think they may well have been in the loft," she said, "After I moved to the flat, I cleared out a lot of stuff from the loft, but kept things like papers and stored them away in the tiny box-room. I was sure these photos were with them and they were, but before I found them I also turned out things that must have been untouched since the move from London to Sussex over fifty years ago."

We were eager to see a picture of Great Aunt Charlotte, but the ones of the christening were rather disappointing, the old lady in a wheelchair is not very distinct – of course it is the baby that most of the attention is focussed on – you can barely make out the great aunt's features. However, among the other things was a box of odds and ends, which Aunt Katie said she was sure had belonged to her, and an envelope full of old photographs.

Such a shame, there was nothing very special about the possessions, a rather pretty old fan, though with a broken spoke, an old pair of spectacles, needlework tools and an exquisite piece of embroidery, a pair of mittens, some old lace, and a couple of old books, one of them in Latin. "She did have some jewellery, some my mother had, some she gave to us girls, but nothing valuable, I'm afraid. There was a pendant with C on it, which was given to me. You might like to have that, Charlotte. Oh, and the way, the biggest of these photos was in the box as well, but I put it in the envelope with the others," said Aunt Katie as we turned to the photographs.

Richard welcomed the photographs, "Now, these are documentary evidence," he pointed out. "Especially the ones that have names or even dates on the back, but some that are not marked seem to have been taken at the same time." He wants to get them carefully sorted into the right periods, but for now I shall describe them as they emerged from the envelope.

The first two were a couple of those formal studio portraits, with grand details of the photographer, which had been helpfully labelled in black ink. One of a woman of perhaps fifty, very good-looking. Hooray, it was of "Charlotte Carpenter, visit to London 1852." At last we can see her properly, if only we could see her colouring. The second must surely have been taken at the same time, it isn't dated, but the studio background is identical and it's labelled "Richard Randall and his wife Sarah, née Joseph." She is not very good-looking, but looks kind, and also intelligent. Another studio portrait is of a boy and girl about six and seven again not dated, but Grannie who knows a lot about costume and is seldom wrong, thinks may have been taken in 1860 or so. Perhaps it is great-grandfather Richard and his sister Sarah around the time of that Christmas he wrote about. The next two were rather later, not on card; it looks as if some members of the family had acquired a camera of their own by then. "Probably a plate one," commented Granddad. "It is still too early to be a Kodak film camera." The first one shows an older Charlotte, with a much older Richard Randall, in the doorway of a house, and on the back someone has written in pencil "Chelsea, 1871." The other one shows the same doorway, still with Aunt Charlotte, but with a young man instead of her brother. This must have been the same day, but there is nothing on the back. However, another studio portrait, in a leather case, shows this chap with a most attractive elderly lady, and part of a letter (sadly not dated!) saying, "And here, dearest Charlotte, is the promised photograph taken of me with young Arthur. Steven thinks it the best likeness he has seen of us both."

The signature to this letter must be lost, but Granddad and Aunt Katie are sure that 'Arthur' can only be the Arthur Linton mentioned in the memoirs, grandson of Charlotte's sister Harriet. She is quite like the pictures of Charlotte Carpenter, and we could quite see why he wrote that she was a lovely old woman, she must have been quite remarkable.

Finally we examined the biggest picture, an outdoor one surely taken by a professional. It is both interesting and infuriating, for it shows people on the lawn of an imposing house. Judging by the clothes, Grannie thinks it might be as late as 1860, around that time anyway. It shows both Aunt Charlotte and the lady we thought must be her sister Harriet, a younger woman who might be her daughter, several children one of whom is surely Arthur as a teenager, and a tall man whom we have not seen before, who has a very small woman leaning on his arm. He too has a look of the family, and if it is his house, he could be the other son, but this could be somewhere else. In the centre of the group, seated very

343

upright on a garden chair, is an old lady who looks very much in command and fits Great Grandfather's description of his great grandmother. It would be good if we could see her features clearly, and Granddad wondered if we could get it enlarged. Rick is going to take these photographs with him to Coombe Park, but only show them if it really does seem that there might be a connection.

Looking at the pictures, Aunt Katie said rather sadly that she did wish she had known Great Aunt Charlotte better. "But you were only about four," Grannie protested, "I think it is wonderful that you remember so much."

"If only I had been older when she died. Or if I could ask Marion what she remembered, for that matter, she was several years older than me and did talk about her sometimes."

"*She* never wrote anything down, I suppose?" asked Richard.

"Not to my knowledge, but one of her children might know, I was going to write to her daughter Eleanor anyway – I will ask her," said Aunt Katie.

18th July, Sunday

Even though he left early and Daddy let him have the car to go to Wiltshire, Richard was very late back last night, in fact I heard him come in long after I had gone to bed. He didn't get up till nearly twelve, I was longing to hear about what had happened, but since the grandparents and Aunt Katie were coming to lunch, we had to wait till the afternoon for him to tell us. Even Pat was quite interested, but he had promised to go out with some school friends, so we had to tell him later. The rest of us assembled in the sitting room, and he unpacked the things he had brought back with him. I think we could all guess from his face that he had had a successful day even before he spoke.

"As I went up the drive to Coombe Park," he told us, "I became convinced that this was the place in the photo, and when Miss Carpenter met me at the door, I thought she looked a bit like Aunt Katie. And it seems she was a teacher, too. History."

"Is she my contemporary?" asked Aunt Katie.

"No, I shouldn't think she is as much as fifty, but she said she felt she had better come back and help her parents get ready for handing over to the National Trust, and as one of the agreements was that the family would show visitors round, she decided to stay on and assist, her teaching qualifications help make the background interesting. She has two younger brothers, one in America, and the older one in the Army, so neither of them want to return permanently. She had her nephew there, he has just qualified as a solicitor and has been helping her sort things out generally. They were very welcoming, gave me coffee at once and later lunch. I think they had been dying to know why I was interested in their ancestress. "There is a family tradition that she was a remarkable old lady," said Miss Carpenter, "But it seemed unlikely that anyone else would be interested. Why do you want to trace her?"

So I explained about Great Grandfather's memories, and they said, "Ah!" since they knew that the lady in question had been a Mrs Randall before she married Mr Carpenter. But they were afraid that they had no information about the Randalls. I hadn't really expected that they would, but it meant a great deal to be sure that this really was the house Great Grandfather remembered, and I got out the photographs while we had coffee, they actually had a copy of the big one on the lawn, framed and dated 1861, but not saying who the people were. They knew all the ones we recognised, and confirmed that the tall man was John Carpenter and his wife Annie, and that the attractive woman was Harriet Linton with her grandson Arthur, the younger woman, her husband, and their children were her daughter, Maud seems to have been her name. Yes, they had always thought she was beautiful, there were not many other photos of her, but would I like to see the painting of her at the age of eighteen? I certainly would! They explained that it was in the part of the house that is open to the public, and it is always admired.

"As we were making our way there, Miss Carpenter said rather sadly that they seemed to have lost contact with the

Lintons, and Great Aunt Charlotte, not to mention the Randalls, and she had actually begun to wonder if it would be possible to trace any of them. This seemed a bit strange to me, but before I could think what to say, we had come to the picture and I was completely taken aback."

He sounded almost awed, and I think we were all surprised that he was so moved. Grannie asked if the artist was well known.

"Not particularly, but little as I know about painting I could see it was very well done, and Harriet Carpenter must have been exceptionally good looking, but what amazed me was the accuracy of Great Grandfather's description. What he didn't say, though, was that she had golden hair. Yes, honestly, not just fair – and it is apparently really faithful. I asked if I could photograph it, and since it was not a day when there would be other visitors, they decided that they could let me. Miss Carpenter explained that the picture and most of the furniture is on loan to the National Trust. So I took a number of slides, and I hope at least one will turn out good enough to have printed."

After that they took him all over the house, including rooms not shown to the public, and then we returned to their part to have lunch, which had been prepared by a woman who used to be the cook when it was a private house, and still comes in sometimes – she even shows people round. Over the meal, they talked about the family and the things they have been finding out. Miss Carpenter said that recently her father had been looking into the history of what had been a quiet country estate, gentlefolk rather than aristocratic. When he was taken ill, he had just reached John Carpenter, born in 1769, who must be the one our ancestress married, so they really had been about to look at the part we are most interested in.

"She apologised for not knowing much about the Randall connection, in fact it seems, the only reason they knew she'd had an older son was because there was a painting of the whole family, done in 1809, when the Carpenter son John was about two, which they would show me after lunch, it was up

346

in the old nurseries. But they said they hadn't even known that the other son had been a QC Paul Carpenter thought this was odd, since several members of their family had gone in for the law in one form or another."

Richard had taken one of the copies I had typed of the memoirs, mainly to quote from, not being sure if he ought to show them the comments on the woman Great Grandfather called 'Aunt Mabel' but he did tell them the date that the Randalls seem to have stopped visiting Coombe Park and they were fascinated.

"Just this morning we added a couple of letters from the son to his mother to the ones she had written to John Carpenter from London in the 1820s," Miss Carpenter told Rick But before they produced these, they spoke about having few records of Harriet Linton or her family apart from the painting and the photograph.

At this point the nephew said awkwardly that this must have coincided with the difficult time, and Miss Carpenter explained that he was referring to her great grandfather. They worked it out that he would have been the first cousin of Joe and Philip, and the husband of Mabel. He had been a successful barrister, but at quite a young age had managed to get in to Parliament, whereas most of the earlier Carpenters had been content to lead the life of quiet country squires It looks as if his father, the one born in 1807, had tried to follow his half-brother into the law, he was called to the bar, but soon retired to a peaceful life at Coombe Park, Paul said. But Jack was more ambitious, and it seems did well at first. Only apparently he found combining his practice at the bar with success in the Government was more than he could cope with, and he eventually broke down.

"His son, my grandfather, was very bitter about it," said Miss Carpenter. "I was only ten when he died, but he used to talk of it even to me. It seems that his mother – Jack's wife – was unwilling to believe that he was doing too much and pushed him on till his health gave way and for the last four years or so of his life he was a complete invalid."

"And she tried to force her son to take up where Jack had left off, didn't she, Aunt Dora?"

"So I gathered. But my grandfather seems to have been a match for her; he refused to follow in his father's footsteps, and concentrated on getting the estate, which had been neglected, into good order. The nearest he came to legal matters was being a JP, that was probably why my father became a solicitor."

"So that was what they meant about the law," Richard remarked. "It seems that Great Grandmother Mabel made herself unpopular with her children and Miss Carpenter regarded her almost as the Wicked Witch as a child. After that I felt it might be all right to let them read the typed memoirs, and they felt it shed a certain amount of light on what might have happened. They were very taken with the description of Christmas 1859, though – she is hoping to put together a small history of the family, and asked if we would mind that part of the memoirs being included."

"Leaving out the reference to Mabel," observed Aunt Katie.

"Indeed," said Rick. "Anyway, while we were having coffee after lunch, I produced the other photographs, of Harriet and her grandson, of Charlotte and her half bother Richard. And of her at Aunt Helen's christening. They had no idea that she had lived so long, though they had an idea of when Aunt Harriet died. Granddad, they wondered if you would have any records of Arthur, if the Randall Imprint had published him?"

Daddy said that he had already thought of that and had inaugurated a search in the records; did Granddad have any ideas about it? He would be welcome to come and look any time. It is so sweet, since my father took over as head of the firm, Granddad has deferred to him and I think Daddy feels a bit embarrassed about it! I asked if there might be descendants of Arthur, at least. It would be nice if Miss Carpenter could realise her wish to find what has become of them.

"But Richard has not finished telling us about his visit to Wiltshire, Philip," said Grannie. "You have things to show us, dear, haven't you, as well?"

"Yes, I have. They gave me some letters to do with our common ancestress, and a couple of studio photographs taken of her in the 1850s. By that time she had snow-white hair, but the family tradition was that it was red when she was younger. It was then that they gave me the same slightly baffled glance they had when I first got there, and led me up to see the painting they had spoken of, done when she was younger.

"There have been arguments over this," Miss Carpenter told me. "The general feeling is that the artist exaggerated. Some of the Carpenters have been sandy-haired, but never till you came have we seen anything like that." They got me to stand beside the picture and said they thought they had been misjudging the artist all that time. He has certainly got pretty close. Yes, I've taken photos of that painting too. It is not as wonderful as the other, but a nice family group, she and her elder son, and the younger girl have hair just like ours, the older girl golden, the little boy sort of sandy, and Mr Carpenter is fairish.

He showed us the studio portrait of our many times great grandmother, she must be about eighty but very upright, not perhaps strictly beautiful but impressive, and at last we know that her name was Caroline. I quite like being called Charlotte, but I'm not sure I don't like that even better. I remarked that one of the Morris twins is called Caroline, and Granddad said she was named for her grandmother, his cousin, who may have been named for the original Caroline. "Only she was always called Carrie," he remembered. I must have made a face, for he chuckled and said yes it sounds old-fashioned, but it was a very popular abbreviation at that time. I am going to think of Great-Great-Great-Great-Great Grandmother as Caroline!

It was a bit late to start looking through the letters by then, and Granddad asked if they could take them back to study overnight. Richard looked at me, I nodded, and he said, "Charlotte is going to type them out, wouldn't you rather wait
349

till she's done so?" But they reminded us that they are going to visit Grannie's sister for a few days, and didn't want to wait till they get back to see them. So they took them home with them and we'll go round tomorrow morning and collect them before they leave.

19th July, Monday

Oh dear, I was really looking forward to reading those letters with Rick and then typing them out, but we're going to have to postpone it for a few days. We got back just before lunch to find Mummy looking very apologetic. "Cousin Amy!" she exclaimed. "I knew she talked of visiting us this summer, but you know what she is, she never gives us much notice. She'll be here in time for supper." She showed us a letter that had just come. – "And I'll need help from you both to prepare. Oh dear, I am sorry, I know how much involved you are with all this interesting stuff about the Randalls." I think we were both surprised at how disturbed she was, she usually seems to keep very calm. I hadn't thought either she or Daddy were as interested in what we are doing, almost indulgent, perhaps, towards Granddad, but they both seemed quite impressed since Richard went to Coombe Park.

I am not sure if I have said much about Cousin Amy in this Diary, though she must have descended on us since I began it. She is the cousin of our other grandmother, who was killed in an air raid, and I think was a year or so younger. She has a special feeling for Mummy, who I think she looked after when she was little – she still treats her as barely grown up, and I know she rushed to her side when Grandmother died, though Sue was about two and Mummy had been leading her own life for years, and she was very good to Uncle Tim who was away at school then. Even if she was a nuisance, Mummy would put up with her I'm sure, but she is not that. She sweeps in almost like a force of nature, driving a small car, and proceeds to take over our lives, organising outings, making us play games like Monopoly, Happy Families, Consequences…. When I was little I rather enjoyed the disruption, I think, but the last few times she has been rather embarrassing. Rick and

I knew as soon as Mummy said she was coming that we would have to shelve anything to do with the Randalls while she's here. For one thing, she's bound to want to go to places, and then she'd either be bored by what we're doing or throw herself into it with such enthusiasm that it would be difficult to cope with.

Over lunch, Mummy went on apologising about it, "I'm afraid you two will have to entertain her for the first day or so, Pat will be at school and so will I, I don't think she understands that being a part-time school secretary is not something I can just lay aside at a whim."

"Whereas Char and I will be free," Richard agreed.

"She would be so disappointed if no one was available to go out with her," Mum pleaded, "She is such a kind soul, you'll have to forgive her if she forgets that you are grown up."

"As long as I don't have to squeeze into the back of whatever car she is driving," Rick was philosophic. "My legs are really too long for that, these days."

So I may have a chance to have a quick look at those papers, but I won't say anything about it here until I have done the typing.

23rd July, Friday

Cousin Amy departed like a whirlwind after breakfast and we were able to get our breath back and resume our activities, even if she is so disappointed to have missed Grannie and Granddad that there's a threat of her returning later in the summer. Still she is on her way to Hertfordshire to see Uncle Tim, Auntie Annabel, and their children. She was talking of friends in Yorkshire, and then of going to Aberdeen to see Grandfather Stewart and Aunt Mairi and her family. That should be interesting, I know she prefers Mummy and Uncle Tim, and I have a strong feeling that the Scottish relations are less willing to put up with her ways. I am about to start typing and Richard is going up to London to see if he can check on a few things. I will take copies, but not three, Rick is building up a folder of all the papers and photographs and this volume will get a bit bulky if I put everything in here as well. I may quote from a few of the letters – I'll see.

The last few days have been exhausting, especially when it was just Richard and me and Cousin Amy in her little car. She has just discovered the National Trust – what took her so long? – and I must say it was difficult not to mention Coombe Park. (We will have to tell her all about it some time, when we have more facts, perhaps when we have all been. Miss Carpenter wants Richard to come again to help with their papers and asked him to bring other members of the family.)

Cousin Amy was dismayed to find that we had visited so many of the places she wanted to go to, locally, so Rick and I let her drive us to Brighton to visit the Royal Pavilion, and then to Lewes. However, she had discovered a house near the border with Hampshire, called Uppark, and fortunately by yesterday both Mummy and Patrick were free to come too, and we were able to go in our roomy car, and persuade Cousin Amy to let Richard drive. It was really rather a nice place, like Coombe Park still occupied by the family to some extent, and I would like to go again, Mummy was very interested in the old curtains that are being restored, and I know Grannie would love that in particular. If only we could have had peaceful evenings after all these outings, but all of us, including Daddy, were dragooned into playing games till quite late. Since her last visit, Cousin Amy has encountered Scrabble, which she is not good at, but adores. She didn't realise that Richard and I are rather skilled at it, but sweetly praised us when we won. Well, I must get down to this typing; I will try to write some more this evening.

After tea. Before Richard gets home I'll try to comment on some of the things I have been transcribing. When we picked up the papers, Granddad commented that we were no nearer finding out any more about the Randalls, which is true, but as both Rick and Grannie said, it does at least prove the truth of Great Grandfather's story of the great house, and after all, the Carpenters do seem to be relations, however distant.

The nearest to a reference to our family is a clip from a paper, possibly *The Times*, announcing the marriage of John

Carpenter Esq., of Coombe Park, Wiltshire to Mrs Caroline Randall, Widow, "Quietly at Hampstead." With it is a portion of a letter from a friend congratulating her on the event and wishing her well for the future. This woman writes from Wales, and signs herself Selina. There were other letters from the same address, the friend seems to have been a Mrs Penry, but though she seems to have known our Caroline very well, she doesn't refer to the earlier marriage, only asks after the son Richard. Most of these letters are incomplete, as if bits have been cut out of them. There are a couple of rather later ones from the address in Wales, signed by Charlotte Carpenter, but no indication who these people are or how Caroline came to know them. I wondered if this Selina was perhaps a childhood friend, from Sussex, who happened to have married a Welshman. Rick thought this was quite possible, but unless we knew her maiden name it would be very difficult to find out more.

There don't seem to be many letters between Caroline and her second husband, but in 1807 she was writing to him when he was in London for a few days, she tells him about 'Baby Johnnie' and the two little girls, and also how her son Richard is progressing with his studies, it sounds as if he is educating the boy himself, rather than send him to school. It certainly seems as if he were responsible for teaching the girls, there is one from him to her when she was staying in London in 1819. (For the birth of her first grandchild, it seems.) He particularly mentions Charlotte's progress in Latin, which may explain why she so impressed our great grandmother's friends with her learning when she was an old lady.

Then there are the letters from Richard Randall to his mother – the ones that Miss Carpenter had just found when Rick got there. Not just a couple, she found a few more while he was there. Two from Oxford while he was a student, one mentioning how much his friend Steven Linton had enjoyed his visit to Coombe Park "Though I know he has written to you." This must be how their elder daughter met her future husband. Then later he writes from London when he had become a barrister, in one he speaks of the woman he is going

353

to marry, and how relieved she had been to discover that unlike most women his mother did not disapprove of a girl who had been educated to think. "She really is the first female I have met whose brain is equal to yours. It was so good of you both to come and see her father, I fear Mr Joseph has but a little while to live, and he was so happy to feel his beloved daughter would be happy. I was particularly grateful to Papa for making the journey, I know the pain it cost him with his bad leg." My brother Richard said there was some record of John Carpenter having injured his leg when he was quite a young man, which would probably explain why he so seldom travelled far.

The last two letters are quite short, announcing the birth of Richard Joseph Randall, in 1824, and Philip John in 1827. Richard, usually known as Joe, it seems, was of course the founder of the Randalls Imprint, (which Daddy now runs). It was his son who wrote the memoirs, I know I have already said that, but it seems a good idea to tie it in with these letters. But Philip is the mysterious uncle who disappeared from the children's lives when they were quite young. It is to see what he can find out about him that my brother has gone to London today.

Actually, the typing did not take as long as I thought it would, and as Mummy has been busy preparing for some people from the school where she works to come in for drinks this evening, and has some letters to write, I asked if I could help her in any way. She had done the main shopping in the car (Oh, I really must see if I can get driving lessons soon!) but had run out of stamps so I went down to the Post Office and got her some, and accidentally, I think I just might have come across something that might be of interest in our search for the Randalls. I have been getting tired of people asking me the way to some new Housing Estate or other, there must be six or seven that have been built recently, and I hardly ever know where they are. Our local map is so old, it does not even show ones I do know about.

A new map has just come out, showing all the development up to last year, so I bought one and was looking

354

at it over tea. There is a tiny village called Amden a few miles away, and since our old map came out a new estate has been built called "Old Manor Gardens", that is one of the places I have been asked about several times. It's nice to know where it is. But when I examined that part carefully, I noticed something about the names of the roads on it. Randall Way, Randall Close, Randall Avenue. There is no local connection that I know of, and they usually try to choose something that reflects the area.

Like the area near here that was developed in the grounds of a house called Clevelands, the main road is Clevelands Avenue, and where they cut down a coppice known as the clump, that is what that area is now called. (I've just seen it on the map.) So was there in fact an Old Manor, at Amden, and is there some reason to associate it with the name Randall? I will tell Rick about it when he comes home, though he'll probably pour scorn on my idea.

24th July, Saturday

Richard did not get back till just before the guests came, and had hardly enough time to tell me that he thought he had got some useful information. It was quite interesting to meet some of the people Mummy works with and Pat and I were kept busy circulating with snacks and drinks. Rick was cornered at first by people who wanted to know what he planned to do now, publishing or pursuing History? I think Daddy rather wants to know that, too but he is leaving it up to him. I can't see why he couldn't do both, but actually I am more interested in what goes on in the firm than he is, and Granddad at least seems to have noticed. Of course Patrick and I were also quizzed, Yes, I was going up to Oxford next term, to read English, I must have repeated it a dozen times! Pat, looking older than he is, had to keep explaining that he wasn't due to start O levels till next year.

Most of the guests were teachers and had brought their husbands, one had just begun a small specialist firm to publish text books, and wanted to pick Daddy's brains, but the one that we liked best turned out to be an architect with a particular concern for the preservation of older property. If only we could have talked about Coombe Park, but it was all too complicated. What I found surprising was that Patrick suddenly seems to be taking an interest in Architecture, and he was talking about our visit to Uppark. Of course he always did like drawing planes, but now he has apparently added buildings. This chap wasn't condescending to him, and as he and his wife were leaving, I heard him tell Pat to get a small sketchbook and always carry it about with him.

I had hoped to write this before I went to bed, but it was late when I came upstairs – so I am sitting by the typewriter now, waiting for Richard to come and tell me about yesterday, and here he comes, with some notes at least.

Later, after supper. There is quite a bit to tell, and I spent the morning typing out the things that Richard found out, some of it as he spoke about his day, so that it is on record and will help when he come to describe it to the grandparents who will be back tomorrow.

"I didn't discover as much as I hoped," he said ruefully. "But it does look as if Great Uncle Phil had not done anything shameful. I found the Review that he edited, and was able to see the article that caused all the trouble – they were threatened with a law suit. This contributor was probably considered a bit radical, he seems have cared about the poor deal many workers got, and he had accused someone with a reputation for all sorts of philanthropy of hiding his true colours. The man was rich and powerful enough to get the story discounted and withdrawn by the threat of libel, Uncle Phil might have stood firm but the people who put up most of the money apparently took fright – I don't suppose there was all that much cash available. This must be the story that Great Grandfather heard discussed, and I have the feeling that his uncle feared that he had brought disgrace on the family."

I thought it seemed a shame and said so. Surely he was only rash? He must have believed what was written, after all. "Oh, indeed," said Richard grimly. "Uncle Phil had read law, he knew what he was doing, the trouble was that he was up against someone powerful enough to get an obscure magazine

356

suppressed with the aid of influential contacts. But it was eventually proved that the man was guilty of even worse."

"Oh you found out what happened, then? It wasn't in a later edition of the magazine?" I asked.

"Lord, no. It must have been about fifteen years before the truth came out, but eventually the police were able to bring charges that even some pretty important people could not ignore. I didn't have to look it up, I recognised the name as soon as I saw it. It caused quite a stir at the time; he tried to get statesmen, peers, and genuine rich philanthropists, to help hush it up."

I was horrified, "Surely that would have vindicated Great Uncle Phil? Why didn't Great Grandfather mention it?"

"He didn't know the whole truth, remember. And his grandfather would be dead by then."

"Wouldn't you have expected Philip Randall to contact them about it. Oh, no, had he died, and never knew?" I felt very sad about that, but Richard surprised me by saying that this was not the case.

"Perhaps he was out of the country at the time, or up North. He ended up in Berwick." I must have exclaimed, for he nodded and said yes, he had traced Philip at Somerset House, and found that he had died up north, in 1916 – aged over ninety.

"Oh, if only our great grandfather had known that. I don't suppose you have any idea what he was doing there?"

"He may well have edited a newspaper or a magazine, I saw his name in connection with some publication, but dismissed it as unlikely, not knowing then where he ended up. He married a woman of that area in the early 1880s, and I think there were children. So we may have relations up there."

"I do hope he was happy – oh, but why didn't he tell his family then?"

"Well, he would have probably felt unable to face them if he didn't know he had been proved right. All the evidence seems to suggest that he was afraid of dragging his parents and brother into the libel case, at the time. He seems to have been very idealistic, possibly over-sensitive. I really do think that he might have gone abroad; in fact I wouldn't have been surprised to find he had emigrated. He had certainly travelled in Europe and even to Egypt. He wrote a book about it."

"A book? I wonder if Granddad knows about it. Surely we published it?"

"Oh yes, it was under the Randall Imprint. Only a small edition, but rather a good little travel book. They found it for me at the British Museum Library. Perhaps some copies still exist, we will have to ask Granddad."

Once I had typed out these facts and Richard had read what I did yesterday, I showed him my new map and the roads with the Randall name. He was much more interested than I had expected, "Though even if this involves a local family, they are unlikely to be any thing to do with us," he pointed out. "I'd expect to have heard of them. Still, it might be worth looking into." He got out a nineteenth century map of our area and sure enough, there was the village of Amden and a house marked Old Manor. It looks as if there was only one road to it, so it led nowhere, and it still seems like that today. "Probably why we have not noticed it," he said, "We've had no reason to explore it till now. Now where did I put that old book?" He went upstairs and came down with a volume about Mid Sussex about a hundred years ago. It gave the names of many villages with details of the principal properties, together with the owners of the time. Amden is so small, there were only two of them, The Court, (John Sturgis Esq.) and Old Manor (Randall Carter Esq.) could that be where the name came from, I asked. "Randall as a Christian name? Does that sound a likely connection?" Rick thought probably not, but at any rate, it is the first trace of our name in that area.

We have decided to go there this afternoon, and I'll probably tell you all about it tomorrow. The village does have a church, so we can look at the gravestones, and possibly the register.

25th July, Sunday

It looks as if we may have something to show Grannie and Granddad when they come to supper tomorrow. I might have written a bit more last night but there is rather a lot to describe and we wanted to make typed notes of what we had discovered. It isn't very far to Amden, we could almost have cycled. We had to pass by the new Estate to get to the church, didn't really have to go into that, but it seemed a good idea to look at it, Richard thought that the some of the roads may follow old tracks or have field names. On the Victorian map there is a road up to the Old Manor, which is still called The Drive, but it now leads up to an open square, planted with trees and grass, which we were told later was made a year or so ago, when the house was demolished and the estate built.

There were houses round the outside, but two roads out. One was marked as a cul-de-sac, but interestingly, on one side of it was a sort of park, marked on the new map as The Gardens, it looked so well established that it might have been the original garden of the Manor house – we wondered why they should pull that down and leave the garden. At the end of that road was an older housing development, nearly a dozen houses all different and quite unlike those on the main estate. We left the Estate by a road which bore a sign Eastern Avenue, which brought us back to the road to Amden, and drove into the tiny village, whatever it may once have been like, it now has no shops, one pub, and the church. A very old church, it is not often used these days but does still have services. Luckily there was nothing going on yesterday.

Beside the church is a handsome old vicarage, now the home of an archaeologist, which proved very useful for us because his hobby is collecting old and curious epitaphs, he knows all the ones there by heart, and as soon as he saw us looking round, he came to ask if we wanted the key to the church. As soon as Richard explained, he led us to all the graves of people called Randall, which saved us quite a lot of time! For there were definitely a lot of Randalls in that area, dating back to the thirteenth century. This man introduced himself as Archibald Appleby, and told us that he had taken quite a lot of interest in the Randalls, because they suddenly disappear, and by the middle of the nineteenth century it is the Carters who live at the old manor. "I would have thought that they had died out," he said, "but the most recent are the graves of two children, and I cannot find any trace of their parents, mentioned on the headstones. I have been right through all the graves several times and have come to the conclusion that they must be buried elsewhere."

"Did you examine the register?" asked Richard, and Mr Appleby smiled, "I am afraid I tend to simply go on the headstones, I don't have your specific reason for wanting to know more. I could let you in to the church, I have a key, but I think I'd better fetch the sexton who will be able to direct you to the right volumes. He went off and we made a note of some of the more recent Randalls. As he had said, the last two were children and it made sad reading: "Richard, son of Richard Randall and Anne, his wife, born 3rd June, 1773, died 18th October, 1778, aged five years and four months. Sadly missed." The other was of "Harriet, daughter of Richard and Anne Randall, born 12th December 1778, died 17th February 1795. With God." I found it quite upsetting, that they had lost both their children, but Rick said that they might still have had other children. We noted down other Randalls from the 18th century before Mr Appleby returned with the key and the sexton, and practically ordered us to come to the Old Vicarage for tea, his wife insisted! He pointed to the little gate in the hedge and we saw her waving enthusiastically.

I thought it was just as well that Richard and the sexton knew what they were doing; I wouldn't have known where to start looking in the register. It wasn't too hard to find the details of little Richard and Harriet, and they soon discovered that there had been three other children, two older than Richard and one between him and Harriet. Anna, born 1768, Caroline, 1771, and Lucy, 1776. No further trace of the two older ones, but Lucy got married the year before Harriet died, to Sir Charles Carter, Baronet, of Corwood Hall, in Hertfordshire. "Randall Carter!" I exclaimed, when we saw that. "Do you think she was the only one that married? I mean, she would only have been about eighteen."

Richard remarked that girls did often marry early in those days, and he agreed that it did look as if there might be a

360

connection. "It could be that the others married but she was the only one that had a son." He sought for other Randalls that did not match the graves, and copied them out, but only one seemed really promising. The father of those two children had an older sister, Lucy, and a younger brother, Charles, neither of whom are buried there. He felt it might be worth looking the brother up, at least, (the other Randalls were further back.) "Mind you, there are plenty of other places in the area we could look," he cautioned me. "And don't forget, we only know that our ancestress *might* have been born in Sussex and we have no idea of her maiden name."

As we thanked the sexton and made our way to the Old Vicarage, I suddenly thought, funny, Richard, Caroline, Harriet, all names we have come across, but held my tongue in case he pointed out that they are none of them uncommon for that period. We had a very nice tea with the Applebys, she is a sweetie, a bit younger than her husband, and remarked that she too likes digging, but to make the garden attractive. She seems to have made it lovely. "My husband does help," she assured us, "Only he will keep stopping to examine shards of pottery, of which the garden is full."

They were both interested in our search, and begged to know what we find out. I could not help thinking that they would get on well with our grandparents, though I know that just because you like two lots of people, it doesn't necessarily mean that they will like each other. It was from them that we learnt about the old house being demolished. They said that back in the 1930s the owner had to sell off some land for building, and part of the large garden was purchased as a sort of park, which is now maintained by the householders and the Estate people jointly. Mr Appleby said by the time they moved there seven years ago, the big house was considered unsafe and fenced off, so he couldn't tell us what it looked like. Richard produced his Victorian map and remarked on how the two main roads of the new estate seemed to be drives up to the big house, at which Mr Appleby produced an even older map and pointed out that the drive shown on the later one did not exist. "See, what is now the Eastern Avenue was then the main approach to the house," he said. "They cut a new road to the east of here, and this meant the house could be approached from the south."

"But wouldn't that have meant main entrance was at the side?" I asked, and Rick said that he had heard of this sort of thing being done in other places a new road was made, and they probably made a new and grander entrance. We also asked about The Court, the only other property named in the village.

"Oh yes, it is still there," said Mr Appleby. "It is now divided into flats, but before that it was a preparatory school, and then an old people's home." They did not seem to have any idea about the Sturgis family, but there didn't seem any point in pursuing that.

27th July, Tuesday

It seems as if everyone is coming and going at the moment, the grandparents are no sooner home than they are going off to Cambridge for the weekend, (of course everyone wants to see them since they got back from Australia, and this means they'll be able to see Sue). But Mummy and Daddy are going on a business trip on Wednesday, to France and Belgium, and the boys and I will be staying in Herts with Auntie Annabel and Uncle Tim. Still, we managed an exchange of news and information at supper yesterday, Granddad was particularly interested in what Richard had found out about the mysterious Uncle Phil, and he and Daddy are going to see if they can find any trace of the book he wrote. The problem seems to be that a lot of stock and some of the records were destroyed in the Blitz.

We also had some slides to show them, Richard's latest film came back in the morning's post, and we were able to see the pictures he had taken at Coombe Park, including some of the house and grounds. It was interesting to compare them with the Victorian photographs, but the stars of the show were definitely the paintings – they have both turned out remarkably well, and he is going to get prints done as soon as possible. It would be hard to say which painting made the most impression, the one of the whole family was delightful, but the one of the young Harriet was probably the better work of art. Grannie knows more about that kind of thing than the rest of us, and she said she had heard of the artist as having a minor reputation.

"In the mid-nineteenth century, actually," she said, "This must have been one of his earliest pictures, when he was still fresh." Richard was slightly worried about the colour, he thought it was fairly close to the original, but perhaps not totally accurate. Still it shows how good the painting is, and also how very attractive Harriet was at eighteen.

We all liked the family group, though, they look as if they were enjoying posing for it, and I could not help feeling that if you did not know that Richard was only a half brother to the younger three, you would never have guessed it. He and Charlotte had hair that was just the same, and it was really like ours, strange how it seems to have come down through the family. There was so much else to talk about that Rick and I didn't have much chance to talk about our visit to Amden till just before Grannie and Granddad left. They were interested, but I think they felt it was unlikely to be very helpful even though Rick has promised to check on all the leads to the Randalls not buried there, including the younger brother, Charles.

3rd August, Tuesday

Sorry to have missed a whole week; I did take this book with me while we were away, but there never seemed to be time to write much. As we were able to take the car, they were able to show us places we had not seen before – except Whipsnade, which we visited when Pat was even younger than Hamish is now. I was glad to hear that the Stewarts are now thinking of getting a car it seems that Uncle Tim has got promotion and they should be able to afford it. And Auntie Annabel confided that they are going to have another baby in the Spring, quite a gap, since Mairi is now four and Hamish six – still, Pat is nearly four years younger than I am. It is a good thing that we now have a big car, even so it was cramped with us all, and reminded me of outings when I was younger and Sue brought a friend along. Poor old Rick used to get squashed in between the girls, who had Pat and me on their laps. It was Pat who had to be in the middle, this time, but luckily we didn't go very far on any of the journeys.

Richard and I did not mention our work about the Randalls very much, after all it's the other side of the family and I don't think Uncle Tim is even very interested in the Stewarts, who have a family tree going back to the thirteenth century, which Grandfather once showed Rick but which even he rather takes for granted. So we did not really expect to come back with any new information about our search, but we did! It all came about because we were making good time on our way home yesterday and stopped for coffee in a small village. We were coming back by a different route, and looking at the map to make sure we'd got it right, we noticed that the big house we could see in the distance was Corwood Hall. Yes, the home of the baronet who married Lucy Randall in 1794.

As soon as we showed interest in that, the people at the café gave us some information about the family and sold us a book about the village and the house. It is sold in the church as well, we were told but that wasn't always open. The present baronet is Sir Andrew, and the house is open to the public some weekends and on Wednesdays, as a rule. But the family are away and the house being redecorated. Pat was studying the book with interest, and pointed out a paragraph that says Corwood Hall was built in the eighteenth century and has a quaint feature in that the Dower House is a complete replica of it in miniature.

No dowager lives there now, it seems, but the family often use it at weekends, and yes, we could walk in part of the grounds. Pat said he'd like to see the Dower House, and Richard was just asking about the church when a youngish man in black came in to buy cake and the waitress hailed him, "Here is the Rector, he can tell you about the Church."

Richard explained why we had recognised the name of the place, and he looked alert when we told him our name.

"Randall, yes, there are some people buried here called that, an elderly couple and their daughter. Perhaps they are the ones you could not find in Sussex," he said, and when we had finished our coffee he led us to the churchyard, dropping the cakes off at the Rectory on the way. He took us straight to the headstones we wanted, and remarked that one of them had always perplexed him, because it was so strangely worded.

It was clear at once that we had found some of the people missing from Amden, the parents of Lucy, Lady Carter in the first part of the nineteenth century were buried here, he died in 1806, and she in 1823. But the one that the Rector referred to was of their daughter Anna, 1768–1839. It does seem a trifle odd. She is referred to as "Devoted daughter and beloved Aunt and Great Aunt. She strove for others, thinking naught of self."

"You see what I mean," said the Rector, "It ought to be very touching, but it strikes a false note."

We did see. I remarked that it seemed strange that she was not being mentioned in relation to her sister, Lady Carter, almost pointedly ignoring what must surely be the reason for her having moved from Sussex, the fact that her younger sister had married the baronet in 1794. Richard asked if the Rector had spoken of it to the present Carters, and he smiled rather wryly, "Sir Andrew is a generous landlord and patron, but I do not feel that he is the type to relish a discussion of the vagaries of his ancestors, I am glad to have the chance to show it to you, though."

While Patrick did his drawing, I made a note of the inscriptions and those of Lucy and her husband, she lived until 1856 and must have lived in that funny little Dower House for a good many years, how odd it must have seemed in contrast to the Great Hall. One thing I did notice, though, was the fact that there was no sign of the other daughter, either there or in the register as having married there. The Rector showed Richard the relevant volumes, and it was fascinating to note that Lucy seemed to have had had ten children, though one, James, died in his teens.

I think that the Rector would have liked to ask us to lunch, but with the three of us it would have been an awful imposition on his wife, and we really didn't want to be very late home. We collected Pat and Rick took photos for him of the Dower House with the Hall in the distance, and in fact we got back just before our parents did. Even now the comings and goings aren't quite at an end, as Pat is due to go camping with the school on Thursday, which is when Aunt Katie is coming to stay overnight with Grannie and Granddad.

Richard has been very thoughtful since we got back, I thought he might go up to London tomorrow to look up the brother of the man who is buried in Hertfordshire, or at least let the Applebys know what we have found out, but he had just been going through all we have found out since we started this family search.

5th August, Thursday

Well, we certainly have quite a bit more to tell the grandparents and Aunt Katie tomorrow, this morning Richard got a phone call from a friend who works in a second-hand bookshop in Brighton, something had come in he might be interested in, he went in just after lunch and came back with a big slim leather-bound volume, which did not look very interesting till he opened it and I saw that it was entitled *A History of the family of Randall in the county of Sussex from 1590 down to the present day*. Dated 1794, and privately published, it was the work of Richard Randall Esq. Of Old Manor, Amden. "Yes, it's the one we found in Hertfordshire, Char. He had written about his family."

Looking at the way it had been produced, I was quite impressed. Those Randalls certainly seem to have been somebody in the area at that time, how nice it would be to find that we were connected with them. Perhaps that sounds snobbish, but after we had been warned that going back beyond the start of the nineteenth century we would be lucky to discover anyone literate, it had been pleasant to discover that our Caroline seemed to be what was called a gentlewoman. "Do you think we might be descended from his brother?" I asked, but he shook his head.

"I'm afraid not. This makes it clear that Charles Randall died some years before his brother wrote this book." Richard did not seem as disappointed as I would have expected, but he wouldn't say more about that subject, drawing my attention to the subscription "To my oldest friend, Daniel Sturgis, with the author's regards."

"That was the surname of the owner of The Court!" I exclaimed, "But wasn't he called John?"

"Yes, a son or a nephew, I should think." I asked what he thought of it as a piece of history, and he grinned, "Much of it seems to be guesswork and hearsay but it is not badly written, for a country gentleman he must have been a bit of a scholar. He seems to have great affection for Sussex, and I am surprised he agreed to move to Hertfordshire even if it was to be near his married daughter."

We both studied the book till teatime, and I found it fascinating, though I had the feeling that Rick had something up his sleeve. It was rather sad to see that in his final comments Mr Richard Randall wrote that he was the last of his line, When I remarked on that my brother merely looked enigmatic and said, "Wait for this evening!"

6th August, Friday

I think Richard has really taken us all by surprise, it was easy for everyone to see that he was going to produce something new, but I could not imagine what he might have found out. The evening was just as expected at first, with the exchange of news – Grannie and Granddad were delighted with their first great-grandson, and of course Aunt Katie had to hear what Richard has discovered about Philip Randall, especially that he lived on into this century. And she was keen to see the photos, Granddad hasn't got his projector working again yet, so she had to see most of them on the little table viewer, but Rick has now got the prints of the two paintings, which she was really struck with. She had also to be told about our visit to Amden, plus the discovery of the Randalls near Corwood

Hall, and finally the book, with the news that this had ruled out the younger brother.

"So, no connection there after all," Granddad remarked. "Pity – but perhaps it was a bit much to hope, so soon."

"I am not so sure," said Richard. He looked round at us all, but particularly at the three older people. "Would you be very shocked if I suggested our ancestress who married John Carpenter was really a Miss Randall, that her son Richard was illegitimate?" There was a stunned silence, and then Aunt Katie chuckled.

"I am not sure what Helen would say," she said, "but I don't think it would worry me unduly. What made you think of that?"

"Caroline!" I said, "And Harriet, and Richard – I noticed that, but I thought you would say it was just a coincidence." I felt annoyed that he was encroaching on my speciality, with such imaginative speculation, yet he really seemed to believe it. My parents and Grannie seemed almost too stunned to speak, though not particularly upset. Granddad did not look shocked either, but he did seem a little sceptical.

"My dear boy, are you sure you're not jumping to conclusions too hastily? I know it is tempting to think that these people are connected with us, but there must be other areas to examine? Even if our family did originate in Sussex, there are plenty of other places they could have come from. My father only thought that his great-grandmother had known Sussex as a child, no reason to assume that her first husband had."

Richard nodded soberly. "And I am not ruling that out, don't worry. I know you must be finding the whole idea very disturbing, all of you."

They looked at each other, but though they shook their heads, Mummy asked if it wasn't a bit unkind to accuse our Caroline of such a thing on flimsy evidence, and Grannie said surely a girl from a family like that would not have an illegitimate baby?

Richard said that he didn't think the class to which someone belonged had anything to do with it; even Royal

368

Princesses had been known to slip. "But of course it is just an idea. Look, I'll explain how I arrived at it. Like Charlotte, I noticed the way those Christian names were reminiscent – but none of them are particularly unusual. The matter of the rest of the family vanishing from Amden was something strange, four adults vanishing from those records, and it was just a hunch that caused me to look at the churchyard near Corwood Hall. It seemed likely that Mr and Mrs Randall might have gone to be near the married daughter, whatever had happened to the older ones. They might have married and gone elsewhere, for instance. But there was Anna dying single at quite an advanced age, and no sign of Caroline at all."

He held up Richard Randall's book. "This gives the names and dates of birth of all the children, and records the little boy's death, it would certainly have mentioned the fact if Caroline had died elsewhere in childhood. I know it does not give the date Harriet died, but she was still alive when this was printed. Of course I am going to try and trace the Randalls in other ways, but it might be significant that there seems to be no reference to her first husband anywhere. You know, when we started to look into this, I really expected that we would find the family were tradespeople, yeoman farmers, something like that." He looked at Granddad and Aunt Katie. "I must admit that the memories of Coombe Park sounded as if there was a connection there, and so it proved. But all we were able to find out about was the Carpenters."

Aunt Katie observed that our Caroline might have married beneath her and been ashamed of the Randall connection, and he agreed. "All the same, so much reticence often means there is something to hide. Of course I will go on looking, but the dates of this Caroline Randall are remarkably close to what we know of our many times great- grandmother. I think it might at least be possible to prove that she was not the one who was born in Amden, by enquiring of the Carters."

I reminded him that they'd told us that the family were away, and he grinned. "I didn't mean them, I meant the ones from Old Manor, it may be a while since they lived there, but I rather gathered that they only sold it for building in the late

1950s. The sexton said he thought they had moved to Brighton or Hove, just before the war, taking the contents of the house with them. One of them must have negotiated the sale, so perhaps I can find out from the people who built the estate if it would be possible to contact them."

So that is where he has got to today, while the rest of us think about the bombshell he dropped yesterday evening!

8th August, Sunday

It took nearly two days to get in contact with the Carters. Granddad said that if it had been a less common name, we might have tried to trace them through the phone book, but there were at least thirty when we looked, and many of them in Brighton or Hove where we hoped to find them. "For all we know," he said despondently after a glance at the book, "If they were ever there they may have gone elsewhere by now."

Daddy agreed, "We can hardly phone all these people to ask if they once lived in Amden. Especially as we do not know the initials."

So Richard had first to track down someone connected with the estate who could help – rather than give information about the properties now being built. It took most of the morning to find out that the people behind the development were not the ones to whom the Carters sold the property, they had been unable to find the money at that time, though they have since build a smaller estate nearer the coast. They put him on to the man who had handled the sale, and he came up with the Carter's solicitor. Whose offices are in Horsham, if you please!

Therefore he had to drive over there yesterday and see the man in person, saying it wasn't the sort of thing one could do over the telephone. "And even so it took a lot of persuasion," he said when he finally got back. "I saw two of them, and they were not at all keen on giving me a number to contact. It was more difficult than when I wrote to Coombe Park, where we really had some reason to feel that we might be connected. In the end the fact that my name is Randall and they knew a bit about the history of Old Manor made them take me seriously, they rang Mr Carter for me and he agreed to talk to me."

"Did you get his initial?" asked Daddy, grinning, and Rick laughed.

"Yes, we'd have had to go some way through the directory," he said, "It's R! He is Richard Randall Carter. He may have been surprised to get a call like that from a total stranger, but he was quite willing to listen to me."

I was curious to know exactly what Richard had said to Mr Carter when he spoke of Caroline. "You didn't say you were anxious to eliminate her from our enquiries?" I asked. He frowned, and then gave a reluctant smile.

"You make it sound like a detective story, Char, but I suppose in a way, it is a little like that, isn't it? No, I just explained that as a historian I had an interest in the history of Old Manor and wanted to discover some facts about the family there at the end of the eighteenth century. It's funny, when I mentioned the name Caroline, wondering if it would mean anything to him, he said at once that he'd recently come across some books that had belonged to her. He told me he'd be in on Monday afternoon I'd be welcome to come and bring my sister and grandfather if I liked."

"I will need the car then, I'm afraid," said Mummy. Richard rang Granddad, who agreed to come and pick us up. In fact he has offered to take us out to lunch first.

"Mr Carter has a lot of things they took from Old Manor," Rick was saying over the phone, "When I asked about records, he said he needed help in sorting things out."

I am quite looking forward to tomorrow, even if they prove to have no connection with us, it promises to be interesting.

9th August, Monday

I have got so much to put on record, I doubt if I shall be able to finish this entry tonight, but I shall make a start. First of all, it does look as if our Caroline and the one from Amden are the same person – but I will go back to the point when

371

Granddad pulled up outside the big Victorian terrace house in Hove.

Mr Carter opened the door before any of us could ring the bell. I was trying hard not to hope too much that he would turn out to be a relation, but even if I had not had my grandfather beside him to compare, I would have thought he looked a bit like him, and he is about the same age. We already knew that he was a widower, but Richard had had the impression that he lived with a sister, however, he apologised for her absence, telling us that she had gone away for a few days with her daughter and grandchildren. He showed us through a rather crowded hall to a sitting room that seemed much too full of furniture for the slightly austere person he seemed to be, and the first thing I looked at carefully was a framed colour photograph of a boy about Pat's age with the same colour hair. "My grandson," he said, looking first at my hair and then at Rick's, "Mine used to be that colour!"

Our grandfather chuckled, and said so did his. We all introduced ourselves and stood looking round the room and the hall. Mr Carter nodded, and said that we probably thought this was like a fantastic antique shop? "I can assure you, it was much worse when my parents finally moved here! It took the three of us, my brother, my sister, and myself a long time to persuade them that Old Manor was no longer really habitable, and when they finally consented to move, they brought with them just about every thing that had accumulated there in the past three hundred years. If we had not still had some of the elderly servants prepared to remain with them, I don't know what would have happened. Many of the rooms on the upper floor are still packed tight, but after my mother died my father did agree to sell off some of the more hideous items of furniture, large desks and other things full of papers." He seemed to notice my brother's pained expression and smiled. "I know you historians set store by papers," he continued. "Don't worry, we put them carefully into some old trunks."

He still had not asked what we wanted to know about Caroline, but having offered coffee, he asked just what how we had come to know about Old Manor. "I expect you think we were vandals to allow the place to be pulled down, but it was a painful necessity. It had deteriorated too far." He turned to some things on the table beside him, "I thought you might like to see some pictures of it. I have photographs from various periods, but also some paintings."

These were framed, the first, a rather lifeless oil painting, showed a handsome good-sized brick building, more impressive somehow than I had imagined. Mr Carter looked at it sadly, "This must have been done in the mid-eighteenth century, just after they put the new façade on that side."

"At the time they made the new carriage way that is now the Drive?" asked Richard, and produced our map, which Mr Carter examined rather ruefully, saying he had not yet had the courage to go and see what had been done, but he was moved to see the references that had alerted us.

"That was when they turned that part of the house into the front – makes it look grander than it actually was. It had originally been a smaller, timber-framed building, added to over the years, and given a brick coating." We said that Mr Appleby had said something of the sort and told us about the different orientation. "Yes, I think it may have been a mistake, in the long run, to cover up the original structure. The whole place was falling apart inside. Now, this painting is rather sweet." He held up the second framed picture. This was not as professional, but it was a lively little watercolour and quite well done. "This," he said rather proudly, "Is the work of my many times great grandmother, Lucy Randall."

"That was the one who married Sir Charles Carter, wasn't it?" I asked.

He beamed, "That's right. I think she had some talent, don't you? I have found some other work of hers, including pictures of what I think may be the lady you were enquiring about." I felt that he wanted to know what our interest in Caroline was, but was too polite to pry. Granddad, Richard, and I looked at each other, and between us told him of our search and the theory Rick had come up with. Looking from the photograph of his grandson to the colour of our hair, he nodded and seemed to take the explanation philosophically.

The coffee was brought in by a cheerful daily woman along with some small biscuits which she said she had made. While we drank and nibbled, he told us why he was going through the house just now. He said he had been a Discount Broker in the City, living in London with his wife and three children at the time his parents moved from Old Manor.

When his mother died, his widowed sister had come to be with their father but also to be near her married daughter in Worthing. He seemed rather unhappy about the fact that his father had left the house to him rather than to her, but she seemed willing to stay on for a while, particularly as he was on the point of retirement and he and his wife were about to embark on visits to their children in the process of a leisurely trip round the world. "We had a wonderful eighteen months," he said. "And I doubt if I would seriously considered leaving London if she were still with me. Sadly within a few weeks of our return she had some kind of brain seizure and was dead within a week."

We all three made sympathetic noises, which he seemed to appreciate, but he seemed to take comfort in the knowledge that she had enjoyed her last years to the full. As he went on talking, I felt that he was addressing Granddad more than Rick and me, as he explained that his eldest son was a banker who had found himself being returned to England just about the time his mother died. "So it made sense for him and his family to move into our house and for me to return to Sussex to keep my sister company. Fortunately we have Mrs Tidy to look after us, so I can cope when I am left alone here. As I am just now."

Granddad told him about how he and Grannie had gone to Australia for a year, and how they enjoy living so near us, and in return he spoke of his married daughter and younger son who is a political journalist. Rick and I were looking again at the pictures of old manor, both feeling that with his new interest in Architecture, Pat would like to see these. Already it felt almost as if we were being treated as if we were relations, and as I would have done at my grandparents' house, I offered to take the tray back to the kitchen. This gave me a chance to see a bit more of the house. I found Mrs Tidy rather a pet, she seemed to think Mr Carter is in need of cheering up and that our visit was doing him good I didn't know quite what to say when she asked if we were relations, but she appeared satisfied when I said that we might be.

I told her we would try not to make too much mess sorting through things with Mr Carter, but she seemed philosophical about it. "At least he is really sorting – not like his father," she observed as we were washing up. "And it gives him something to do, poor man." Yes, she had known old Mr Carter. "He thought he was going through things, but most of the time he was just being reminded of the old house, he missed it something terrible." She was quite interested to hear what had now been done on the site.

By the time I got back, Mr Carter was putting a little pile of books on the table. "I found these among the stuff I came across the other day," he said. There were French, German and Italian grammars, and unexpectedly a treatise on Political Economy. All the books had the name Caroline Randall written in them, and one could imagine three of them as being part of her education, but that last one seemed a strange choice for a young lady to possess. Richard wanted to look at the signatures from Caroline's letters to compare the handwriting, and it was while he was getting them out of his case that a piece of paper fell out, of the back of the fourth volume. It made a better comparison than the mere names and we all examined the notes and list that it contained with interest. Rick thought that the writing was quite similar to hers, but exclaimed at the things she had written down. "She appears to be applying some of the information in this book to possible ways of improving society," he said. "And look at the books she has listed. Pretty radical. Thomas Holcroft, William Godwin – and Mary Wolstoncroft. Come on, Char, you've heard of her."

"Wasn't she an early advocate of Rights for Women?" I asked cautiously.

"Exactly. If those were her interests, this Caroline Randall was not quite a typical young lady of her time."

Mr Carter now produced a duplicate of the leather-bound book Richard bought in Brighton the other day. "This is the only place I had seen her name till recently, except for a painting," he remarked. "Do I understand that you have acquired a copy of it recently?"

Richard got it out of his case, and we compared them. Different binding, but both dedicated to someone by the author. Mr Carter's volume had been presented to "My Son-in-law, Charles Carter, Baronet, on the occasion of his marriage to my daughter Lucy Randall. December 1794." Under this in another hand was an inscription saying that Sir Charles Carter was passing the book on to his son Hugh on the occasion of his coming of age and talking possession of Old Manor in Sussex.

Mr Carter told us that Old Mr Randall had left the estate to his eldest daughter to be held in trust for his second grandson who was a child of six at the time of his death, but according to all records she never had taken possession but handed everything over to the youth when he reached twenty one. The only difference in the contents of the two books was the section at the back with a family tree, where the details of Lucy's wedding and Harriet's death had been added, followed on the next page by a list of the children Lucy had borne Sir Charles, and separately, the children and grandchildren of Hugh. Our Mr Carter eyed this a little ruefully. "There's my father, Randall, his eldest grandson, but he doesn't seem to have thought of putting any of us, or our offspring," he said, and looked at Richard, "Would you think it would be a good idea if I did that?"

"Well, I've no doubt you have records, but it wouldn't hurt. Look at the names that are printed, it seems as if someone had tried to cross out Caroline."

The name had been scored lightly through, but not very firmly and the ink had faded almost to nothing. I thought it looked as if they had not been very serious about it. Granddad may have thought the same, and when we had finished studying the book he turned to Mr Carter and reminded him that he had mentioned possible pictures of Caroline.

"Yes, I found a portfolio of Lucy's paintings a few days ago. Caroline is also in an early picture showing her with brother and sister when they were children, with their mother. It is a little oil painting which I have known from when I was a child, it hung in the hall at Old Manor. They are upstairs, perhaps you would like to come up with me and I'll show you."

He took us past several objects and papers that Richard seemed tantalized by, to a room containing drawing-room rather than bedroom furniture. "That's it, on the far wall," he began, but Richard had stopped beside a bigger painting nearer the door and asked who it was. We all turned to look at it, a picture of a young girl in a pale blue dress, with long hair hanging down her back that was almost golden. Grannie's knowledge of costume must have rubbed off on to me, because I was sure it was late eighteenth century, (when waistlines were on their way up to the point so familiar in the Regency style) before Mr Carter, a little surprised, told us that it was the girl shortly to become Lady Carter. "I don't think I told you how attractive she was. She is lovely, isn't she?"

Why I should have been so surprised to find that Lucy had been a beauty, I don't know. But she also seemed familiar. Rick had not shown any of the photographs from Coombe Park – no reason why Mr Carter should be interested after all – but he had them with him, and now took out the portrait of Harriet Carpenter. "Yes, she is very lovely," he said quietly. "But apart from that, I was struck by something else. Do look – this is our Caroline's elder daughter, Harriet."

"My goodness!" Mr Carter took the photograph and stood with it in his hand in front of Lucy's portrait. "How extraordinary. The clothes are different, your picture is surely much later, but they are so alike that if I had been told this was Lucy's daughter I should have believed it. It makes it seem increasingly likely that that your Caroline could be Lucy's sister. Now, this is the oil painting that I spoke of, from Old Manor. It must have been painted in the garden; you can see the little plate that identifies them. Mrs Richard Randall with her son on her lap, Anna, and Caroline. When I

377

was small, I knew that little Richard Randall had died young, and as those were my two names, I know I felt a little apprehensive till I got beyond six or seven.

It was rather a joyous little picture; the chubby baby holding out his hands looked so healthy, it was sad to know he had had such a short life. He, and the younger girl playing with a dog nearly as big as herself, had the familiar red hair but the mother and the older girl were paler, almost mousy. Richard produced the picture of the Carpenter family at Coombe Park – was the mother there really the little Caroline grown up? It might be, was all that one could say for certain.

Mr Carter pointed to a parcel lying beside a portfolio on the table. "I found this in the attic, just after this work of Lucy's turned up, I do not think it has been opened in over a hundred years." He looked at the chairs in this room covered with books and odds and ends, and suggested that we could look at them more comfortably downstairs. Rick handed me his case, and offered to carry the other things down.

10th August, Tuesday

I'm sorry I had to break off so abruptly last night, but I was awfully tired and decided I'd better wait till this morning. It is now just after 10.30, and everyone else is out, so I'll hope to do a lot more. There is a lot more to say, though, and a couple of things to type. Like Great Grandfather's memoirs they need to be recorded in full, and when I've done it, I'll stick a copy in this book.

The portfolio of young Lucy Randall's paintings and drawings was really interesting to examine, to be able to have them unframed, and to see the things she drew back in 1793–4 (she has put her name and the date on them all, and usually identified the place or the people). Some of the views are really attractive, I'm sure Grannie would be impressed. Mr Carter recognised most of the places from his childhood, before part of the land was sold off. On the whole, she seems to have been better at scenery than people, but there are some good pencil or crayon sketches, and a couple of paintings of her sister Caroline.

I commented on the quality of the work for an amateur, and Richard pointed out that most young ladies of that period would have been expected to draw and paint as part of their education, and had professional lessons later, if able to profit from that. I was reading *The Woman in White* the other day, and thought of how the young artist who narrates part of the book is employed to teach two young women. I wondered what sort of extra tuition Lucy Randall had. One of the pictures of Caroline was of her reading in The Dell, a figure in the foreground rather than a portrait, but the other is of her in riding clothes, the only thing in the background is the head of a horse which one feels must have been added later. Her red hair is half-hidden under a hat, and we all felt that there was a strong likeness to the mother in the painting of the Carpenter family. The drawings were not so attractive, but it was interesting to see Anna at the piano, Mrs Randall sewing, little Harriet at her lessons – looking quite healthy at that point, the start of a picture of Mr Randall, and another sketchy one of Sir Charles. Had she ever drawn his portrait? I asked, but Mr Carter said he had never seen one.

"Perhaps at Corwood Hall," suggested Rick.

"Possibly, but we lost touch with them some time ago. My brother once visited the area and saw the place, I believe it is sometimes opened but that was not one of the days, and I don't think he liked to try and contact them. I suppose it was inevitable that the two families should have drifted apart, but there is some sort of legend of a quarrel, around 1830." Mr Carter frowned, "I am not sure that I took it very seriously, but one of the things I found quite recently was some correspondence that seemed to give credence, I must look at them again." He looked hopefully at Richard, "I wonder if you would consider helping me with all the accumulated papers? I would pay, of course. My son Hugh, the journalist, has spoken of doing a book one day, but apart from anything else, I am not sure if he would have your patience in reading these old papers, I was most impressed with what you had done with your great grandfather's memoirs – and you had typed them, too."

"My sister Charlotte did that," said Richard, "I think she made a good job of it." Mr Carter looked almost pleadingly at me and asked if I would care to help him too, or would it be a bore?

"I'd love it," I said, liking the idea of not being left out of all this. "But I am going up to Oxford in October – I'd do my best till then."

Mr Carter looked at Granddad, "I would like to think I could involve you all, especially as it seems increasingly likely that we are related."

At that moment Mrs Tidy appeared at the door to say that she had to leave at five, but would we like some tea before then? It was surprising to realise that it was nearly four thirty. I offered to help her, but she said nonsense, she would bring it up just before she left, but if I wouldn't mind washing up she would be grateful. Granddad assured her that we would all help and then asked Mr Carter if he could ring Grannie to say we'd all be a little late back.

We turned our attention to the sealed parcel, which had a faded inscription: "For my grandson Hugh and those who come after him. Anne Randall, 1822." It looked as if no attempt had ever been made to break the seals. "I daresay they just put it away in a safe place and other things got piled on top of it. There was already nearly three hundred years accumulation of possessions by that time in any case," said Mr Carter. Gingerly, he put a sharp paper knife under the seal and began to unwrap the paper, which seemed remarkably thick, and enclosed a further wrapping which contained yet another bound copy of Richard Randall's History. It was in much better condition than the other two, especially Mr Carter's copy. Granddad who in about forty years connected with books knows quite a bit about leather bound ones, looked at it carefully and said it had not been exposed to light and dust as the others had.

"And the binding is particularly fine. I should say this may have been his own copy bound specially, would you agree, Richard, Carter?"

They both nodded, and a note in the same writing confirmed this. There was little difference, but the family tree at the end recorded Lucy's wedding, Harriet's death, and the births of Lucy Elizabeth, and Charles Randall Carter. There had not been an attempt to cross out Caroline's name, but it looked as if at some point someone – Mrs Randall? – had written "Ah, dear Caroline." under that entry. Granddad looked shaken, "The very first sign of some feeling towards her," he observed, and then scrutinised the end paper. "Look at this – the binders appear to have put in a special pocket, this is professional work. The flap has been stuck down with what they called a wafer, I believe."

The wafer crumbled away as Mr Carter lifted it, wondering what it was designed for. Richard suggested to keep deeds in. All there was on those lines was a map of the Old Manor estate, which promised to be of interest to us all, but we were concentrating on two documents, one quite short and one like a long letter, but not addressed to any named member of the family. "That must be for 'those who came after Hugh,'" said Richard as our host picked up the shorter piece of paper. Though the writing was bigger and not so neat, it was recognisable as that of Richard Randall elsewhere in the book. He began to read it to himself, but checked and went back to the start to read it aloud. I am now going to type this out and stick it in here, and then describe the effect it had on us before I go on to the longer letter. I shall have to take care over this, as bits of it are not easy to decipher.

It is simply headed 1806, and plunges straight in with no indication for whom it might be intended:

"To my amazement, after two months as a complete invalid, I have discovered that I am able to write, I can hardly believe it. When I had my first stroke, my right hand was almost useless, but my speech returned quite quickly, and within a year of this move to Hertfordshire, I appeared to have made a good recovery. But this time, I find I can hardly make myself understood at all. The uncouth sounds I make when I attempt to communicate alarm me almost as much as they do my young grandchildren. Nobody has suggested that I put pen to paper, and having discovered by accident that I can do so, I am loath to use this ability simply to answer questions. I tire so easily that I must confess I do not wish to waste what little time I have left on trivial matters.

"Next day. It is so fortunate that young Ben Wright is the only person who is aware of what has happened. It is some months ago that I decided this lad was too intelligent to be a mere boot boy, and began to teach him to read and write. He was an apt pupil, and I was touched, when I was deemed fit to see him, that he wrote of his distress in so clear a hand that I could read it perfectly. He gave me the pen, perhaps to correct his work, and I think we were equally surprised to find that I was able to reply to him. I think it gave him pleasure to realise that I wished to conceal this ability, and as he has been deputed to attend me, wheel my chair, even to feed me, I can seize the opportunity to continue his education, how fortunate that I had already made it clear that he should have the run of my library. He now reads aloud so clearly I can hear comfortably, and an improvement in his speech is bound to secure him a better occupation, perhaps in the local haberdashers, which I gather he aspires to.

"A day or so later. I am not entirely sure what my motive is in concealing this new- found ability to write, but I think it is partly because in a strange fashion I am almost enjoying watching those around me respond to my dumbness. I am certain that most of them are convinced that my mind has gone as well as my speech. My poor son-in-law tries not to appear as embarrassed as I am sure he feels, but he is a kind fellow, and pats me rather as if I were one of his little children. My dear wife, and my daughter Lucy, may not know how much I understand, but they treat me as if I were unchanged, and for them alone I try to speak clearly enough to convince them that I can still comprehend. But others, most of the servants both here and at the Hall, the doctor and the Rector appear to think I am little more than a vegetable, and discuss me as if I were not there.

"Was it yesterday that I last wrote, or the day before? I lose count. But I feel more alert today, and young Ben has taken me out on the veranda of this apology for a house that was taken for us when I let them persuade them to abandon my home. I have set him a task to copy and written a list of books that I hope will be of use to him. Where was I? Oh yes, speaking of how I feel about being treated as if I were no longer here. The person who distresses me most is my daughter Anna, whom others appear to consider the most caring person in the family. I know that she thinks she is, that no one else is capable of looking after an invalid; I recall all too clearly how she behaved towards our little Harriet in her last months, I fear that I found it almost too distressing to bear, and pitied the poor child. Now I am often the victim of the same treatment, and can only be thankful that my dear wife shields me from her determination to take over all my care. I am not a person to Anna; I am an object of her benevolence.

"Two days later. I am looking at those last few lines and wondering how I could apply a word like benevolence to a woman who appears to have no heart. Anna is so pious that she is generally regarded as very good, but I am increasingly aware of something akin to malice in her nature. I think of her attitude to her sister Caroline, someone who undoubtedly had many faults but was impulsive and warm-hearted.

"My dear wife Anne and I have never discussed those two daughters in so many words, but I am convinced that she feels much as I do. For my part, I look back at my own actions with a certain amount of shame. I always preferred to leave everything to do with the household in her capable hands, and I fear that I often did not assert myself as much as I ought to have done. I am more and more convinced that I should have taken a firmer line about Caroline when my dear brother died, not given in to pressure to maintain the conventions and insist that she should return to Sussex."

At this point the manuscript ends, in fact the ink seems to have left a mark as though he had dropped the pen. Had Mr Randall been taken ill again, and did he have time to replace his writing in the pocket of his book? Before we could say anything, Mrs Tidy appeared with the tea, and I think we all

383

felt the need of refreshment. She came back again with a heaped tray; fresh scones and home made cakes, and seemed gratified by our reaction. As she left, Mr Carter looked after her with a smile. "She is a good soul, and takes particular trouble when my sister is away. She will have left me some supper all ready to heat up. You know, I think she likes it more when the family are here to cater for, your visit seems to have pleased her!"

It was difficult to make small talk over the meal, with our minds on what we had just been hearing. I don't know about the others, but I felt as if Richard Randall had reached out to us from the past. The other manuscript was definitely from his wife, and I think we were all eager to see if it gave any explanation of the first, before we discussed it all. Poor Mr Carter had got quite hoarse and suggested that Granddad and Rick might like to read the second piece, he looked at me, but I feared that I would not have been able to keep my voice steady, so they took it in turns. I am now going to start typing this piece (at three o'clock). It's all taking longer than I thought it would.

Mrs Randall's letter is dated November 1821, and as I said, is not addressed to anyone in particular. It starts out "I feel an increasing urgency to put on paper some of the distress I feel I cannot communicate even to my dear daughter Lucy. But it is difficult to hide my feelings and I fear being urged to speak to a clergyman, especially that fool of a Rector who has recently come to this parish."

She states that her name is Anne Elizabeth Randall, now residing at Corwood Hall in Hertfordshire, but apparently could not bring herself to write more for a while. When she takes it up, she puts January, 1822, and begins "When I had got thus far, I was not at all sure if I really wished to continue, and abandoned it during the Christmas celebrations but have been looking through some of my dear husband's possessions, brought here to Corwood Hall after my daughter Anna and I moved from our rented house when he died. Most of these were only removed from Old Manor for safekeeping while that was leased, and now that my grandson Hugh is

384

established there with his young wife, I feel that his grandfather's personal property ought to return there. I had already considered the idea that what I wish to write might go with them, and decided on placing it within the pages of his precious History. That was my main reason for opening this volume, of which he was so proud. I fear I might not have sympathised as much as I might have done with his feelings at the time he brought it out, it was an achievement for him to have done so, and I knew the value he put upon his home and his family name. What I did not know was that he had had this special pocket made, or that he had secreted some writings here.

"I dutifully read the book when the volume came home from the binders, and I found the family tree at the end too painful to look at often. It is still hard to bear the bitterness of losing children, my dear little boy at five, and Harriet cut down by the time she was sixteen, but also Caroline who went out of our lives in 1794 and whose fate I do not know. I wonder if she was aware how fond I was of her, even though she was to some extent a stranger to me after my husband's brother and sister practically adopted her and she spent most of her time with them in London. I could not but feel estranged by the education that Charles Randall in particular provided for her... When I examined the pocket in this book and saw what my dear Richard had written, it came as a thunderbolt to me. I shall have to take some time to compose myself before I can face the family.

"Later. I have shed tears of regret over the discovery that in those last few weeks my husband was not as unable to comprehend what was happening as we all feared. It would have given me such pleasure to communicate with him even if only on paper. I always hoped that he did understand more than the doctor insisted he did, and here is the proof! But I think I can see why he hesitated to let us see that he could write – while no one but that boy was aware of it, he could not be pestered with trivialities. If he had not had that final stroke, he might in time have shown others what he could do, but sadly he seems to have foreseen how little time he had left.

"I ought to be angry with young Benjamin Wright for not telling anybody, and I suppose when my husband collapsed, the boy felt he should hide the document where he knew it had been kept. It must have been the day of that final stroke that Richard penned those last words. It means a great deal to me that the boy alerted me first of all, and I was able to be with my husband at the end. Yes, young Wright is a good lad and I am glad to know that he is now doing so well that there is talk of his employer taking him into partnership. And thank God I am the only person to know about this paper, it would have caused a great deal of trouble had it been seen at the time.

"Some of the things written here pierce my heart. It is some comfort to feel that however impatient I may have been at times, we grew closer over those last few years. Looking back, I now see that I was never as convinced as I pretended that it was the best thing for us to take Richard away from Sussex when that first stroke left him helpless for some months. I do not need his testimony to realise that he was not happy in that house they took for us. I never felt at home myself, and he must have missed all the interests of his estate even if he would not have been able to get about. He did not complain, possibly he felt that being so near our grandchildren was a great pleasure to me and was glad of it for my sake. I think he did derive some pleasure from Lucy's children, when he was well enough to do so. I am sure he would be glad to know that with young Hugh settling in at Old Manor, there is a real chance that some of our descendants will continue to live there.

"Perhaps the greatest shock I had in perusing these writings is to see Richard put into words feelings about our elder daughters that I had been trying to ignore. I now wish we had managed to discuss them, though I agree that we had an unspoken understanding. There is some truth in the suggestion that he did not assert himself enough, he was all too liable to slide away from having to take control of the

386

household. I know how it was, his formidable mother had ruled for years and discouraged him from taking control, and he had got in the habit of retreating from authority. By the time she took herself off to Cheltenham, I had begun to find that it was easier to order the household without consulting him. I did endeavour not to expose him to ridicule. Yet as a landlord and employer, he was excellent. I think old Mrs Randall was initially attempting to suppress the hot temper Richard had had as a child, but I think she undermined his confidence, almost disastrous when he should have stood firmer, most particularly where the older children were concerned.

"When I look back upon those early years it seems to me that things were simple enough at first. Baby Anna seemed a placid, pretty child, and was made much of by everyone, but when first a sister and then a brother joined her in the nursery, she perhaps resented the attention that they received, with their noticeable hair and lively ways. The original nurse did not complain, perhaps she managed them better, but when she left to get married, just after Lucy was born, the new woman was always telling me how the older girls fought each other. She favoured Anna, who certainly appeared to make the most fuss even though larger and older. Caroline with her father's temper and red hair was easily provoked, but I now have a feeling that she was responding to taunts. She, and her little brother were often in mischief, but Anna was good and obedient.

"Dear me, I have just recalled the time when Miss Yare came to us to be the children's governess, and Anna was no longer in the nursery. I never heard of Caroline quarrelling in that way with little Dick, all was peaceful until it was time for her to start lessons. She seemed unlikely to be any challenge to her older sister, a model pupil, I was told, and one would have assumed that Caroline would take badly to being confined to the schoolroom. But she surprised us all by proving eager to learn, soon reading and writing much better than Anna, and by the time we lost our little son, Miss Yare was beginning to say that that if Caroline progressed at this rate she would not merely outstrip her sister, she would advance beyond *her* capacities by the time she was twelve.

"I was too concerned with my boy's illness, and my forthcoming fifth child to notice those two girls, but I do not think Anna liked her sister surpassing her at lessons. Squabbles were breaking out again, and I must confess that I was somewhat relieved when my husband's younger brother Charles, offered to undertake his god-daughter's education, proposing that Caroline should live in Chelsea with him and the sister who was the oldest in the family.

"He had been struck by her intelligence when she and Anna stayed with him during that sad time. In many ways this seemed an ideal solution to the problem, Anna would not be mortified by the contrast with her sister and Caroline would have tuition from which she could benefit. It was not as if we were asked to give our daughter up to strangers and there was no question of adoption, she would still visit Sussex, and it did not occur to me that this would make Caroline unfit for life at home. My sister-in-law Lucy may have been a bit of a bluestocking, but she was an excellent needlewoman who would train her in the domestic arts quite as well as I would have done.

"Charles had made money as a solicitor beyond what he had inherited from his father, so it was an advantage from a worldly point. I have not admitted it until now, but I know I had some sympathy with her desire to study subjects not usually taught to girls, such as Latin. My husband and family never knew that when I was young, I longed to share the education my brothers were given, and for a short time it was permitted, but I do not think they cared for a female doing better than they did. I was no rebel, but the disappointment did perhaps influence me when I agreed to my daughter having a more classical education.

"Now I wonder, if Caroline had not gone to London, whether her father might not have exerted himself to train her mind. He was a scholar, even if he was not as brilliant as his brother, and until she left home for most of the year, he was perhaps closest to his second daughter. I would not accuse

Charles of teaching her to despise her father, but he may unconsciously have undermined her respect for Richard's learning.

"It seemed to be easier for Anna to have Caroline away so much – she was happier with her younger sisters, neither of whom were particularly bookish. I naturally expected her to marry, and she seemed to esteem that young curate, but she was so young when he sought her hand nor did she appear to care for him. Also neither my husband nor I thought him a suitable match. She seemed happy enough helping Miss Carter, our vicar's sister with work in the parish, at one point I almost thought their nephew might be taking an interest in her during one of his frequent visits, he was much the same age – but of course it was little Lucy who attracted him, he was kind to my younger daughters when they were small, and it wasn't till Lucy was sixteen that I think he started to fall in love with her. Anna did not appear to be distressed, or even mind that no other suitors came forward.

"If only my sister-in-law had not died when she did, the situation over Caroline remaining in London would not have arisen, I certainly expected her to return to us when she reached eighteen, in fact by that time I had almost forgotten that she and Anna had disagreed so much. I was not at all happy when it was proposed that Caroline should take her aunt's place as Charles Randall's housekeeper, at eighteen she seemed far too young, in my opinion, to be left in the company of the many Radical friends her uncle entertained. But he seemed certain to make her his heiress, even if she did not marry, and had he lived longer, till she was perhaps thirty, it might have been possible for her to remain in the house which he left her along with his money.

"Alas, Charles Randall only lived another four years, it was quite unsuitable for her to stay on in London – I was already aware that a few people had begun to look askance at her being there at all, and even if as she proposed, an older chaperone had kept her company, I felt that her reputation would have suffered. My husband writes that he wished he had taken a firmer stand over that, but at the time I was determined to prevail, sure that she would soon settle down and forget any nonsense she had learned from her uncle and his friends. She was sincerely grieving for Charles, and for the first few months was more subdued than I had ever known her. I had no idea how different her ideas had become.

"I had imagined that once the immediate period of mourning was over, she would marry, apart from good looks she was now a considerable heiress, but when we received applications for her hand she announced her intention of remaining single – this I did not take seriously, I was not then aware what she had read concerning the rights of women, particularly that notorious Mary Wolstoncroft Godwin who had had a daughter by another man before she married. Unfortunately the men who proposed themselves had her fortune in mind, one of them so blatantly that I think Richard and I would not have encouraged the match even had it not revolted her.

"I pick up my pen after a week, my daughter Anna has gone on a short visit to my second granddaughter who is named for her, and I feel urgently that it would be as well to complete this before she returns. I have today had a long conversation with Lucy about Caroline, as a mother herself she can enter my feelings more than any one else with whom I am in contact, but even there I cannot say all that is in my heart, and her younger children and her husband naturally demand a great deal of her attention. I have looked over Richard's remarks about Caroline returning home. I do not think he ever shared my conviction that she would abandon all radical ideas, I wish he had mentioned this to me at the time – though would I have believed him?

"It is unlikely that she would ever have met Thomas Martin then. By the time that happened, I was much more aware that those years in London had affected my daughter's thinking, also that to her mind, agreeing to return was on condition she might retain ideas that I had hoped she would abandon. She did not speak of her interests and it was chiefly in matters concerning marriage that she showed how she was thinking. Not merely in rejecting it for herself, but in the matter of Selina Coleman, her earliest friend. In assisting this young woman to make a match that her parents disapproved of instead of the one they proposed, she risked scandal even if they could not prove her involvement. My husband pointed out that there was some excuse, the match arranged would have been obnoxious to any decent family, nor was there any real objection to the Welshman she had already met. What is more, in later years the Colemans became reconciled to Selina's marriage.

"Undoubtedly it was when fate brought Thomas Martin to dine with us that Caroline made it apparent that for two years she had missed the sort of conversation she had become accustomed to. My husband's old friend Daniel Sturgis had been bringing his nephew to join a party that included the Carters, just before Sir Charles proposed to Lucy, the young John had an accident and the man he sent with a message was a friend from a respectable family in Lincolnshire but he had developed such Radical views at university that they has caused a rift with his father, views that he did not hesitate to air at our table, to which Caroline responded all too enthusiastically. I did my best to discourage her interest in this man, she insisted that it was purely intellectual, but I think she was more attracted to him than she realised. He was not as handsome as Sir Charles, but he was not unprepossessing either. However I had not believed that she would put into practice all the theories and consent to live with him and supply from her own pocket the support his father had withdrawn.

"My dear husband's remarks about our eldest daughter would be unbelievable to most people who imagine they know her – although I suspect that she does not endear herself to many of the servants – but as I approach the end of my life I cannot deny the truth of much of what he says. There seems to be very little affection in her manner of caring, it does not take his words to make me aware of how she would have treated him after his strokes, if I had permitted it. He says that he pitied Harriet, when Anna took over her care so completely, I was not happy about it myself, and tried to

391

distract her, but she appeared to consider that no one else could tender to the child.

"I know she did not approve of our continuing the preparations with Lucy's wedding, but we could scarcely postpone that until my youngest daughter died – Harriet herself would have been distressed, apart from anything else. Anna tended to become almost frantic if she was prevented from spending more time than anybody else with the invalid. I fear she was displeased not to do the same for her father, but I am so thankful that I would not allow that, now that I have seen how much he would have hated it.

"The will that left Old Manor to Anna for her lifetime and then specified Lucy's second son would have enabled her to take up residence there, but she did not seem to care for her old home, it was her idea that the lease there should be extended till young Hugh came of age, something she suggested after her visit to settle matters when her father died. Anna appeared content to remain in Hertfordshire. I was left comfortably off – I would not have minded a return to Sussex, in fact.

"Lucy, I think suspects that her sister is not the comfort to me that other people imagine, but even she cannot be aware how much my distress over Caroline is increased by the presence of Anna. Over the years I have become convinced that whether it was passion or kindness of heart that drove the former to go to Thomas Martin, she might not have taken that step if her sister had not made life unbearable for her. Much as Richard and I deplored the fact that she continued to pursue theories learnt at her uncle's, and to correspond with that wretched Mr Martin, she did not openly defy us and we had not to acknowledge the fact that we could do nothing. This state of affairs appeared to infuriate Anna, and she insisted on confronting us and demanding that we discipline her sister. This put us in a very difficult situation, since Charles Randall had left Caroline in complete control of her money, she was over twenty one, and we had no authority over her beyond what she consented to.

"We had not told anyone of this, least of all Anna in case she resented it, and I realise now that she did bitterly resent her sister's return. Considering her hot temper, I feel that Caroline did try hard not to quarrel with Anna, whose response to Thomas Martin was almost unbalanced, particularly when after a summer spent in Lewes with a wealthy friend he called to say farewell. I would certainly have prevented his being in contact with Harriet had I known, but he did her no harm, in fact it was Anna's behaviour that upset the child most.

"From that time on, Anna regarded Caroline as unfit to be near her little sister, which was a great pity since it would have done the child good to have more company, and dear Lucy was absorbed in preparations for her wedding, but any suggestion that she should help caused Anna such agitation I was fearful for the effect on Harriet. When I looked back on that proposal that we turned down, I began to wish that we had not objected to that curate. If we had urged her to marry, even though not very eager, at seventeen I think she would have been dutiful enough to comply. Heaven knows what sort of wife and mother she would have made, but she would not have been still at home when Caroline returned from London.

"And Caroline would I am sure have made an excellent wife and mother – if only she had not got all those ideas on the role of women into her head! I do feel that Thomas Martin took advantage of her sympathy. No doubt he was sincere enough in his ideals, but I do not think Charles Randall would have approved of his character. He seemed to rely on friends to supply his wants, so he did not really suffer from his father withholding his income. None of us ever heard of him, or our daughter again, my husband was forced to rule out any question of her inheriting any part of his estate, but I cannot think of her as a hardened sinner, may God forgive me if I am being too lenient, but I still pray that her life has not been utterly wasted. Oh, I must ensure that Anna does not read this – but when I think of the barely hidden triumph with which she heard of Caroline's departure, I find it hard not to sympathise more with the younger daughter.

"My descendants may condemn me, or not, but I hope they will understand, and I wish to state, Caroline Randall may have erred, but she was not a wicked person."

11th August, Thursday (Evening)

As I feared, typing all this took longer than I expected, and I did not finish till this morning. I was hoping to go straight to a description of our reaction to the second letter, but just as I picked up my pen, I was interrupted. Ginny and Bel turned up out of the blue, and insisted on taking me out to lunch, Ginny has passed her driving test and had borrowed her mother's car. It would have been difficult to refuse without seeming churlish, but I'm afraid I did not enjoy it much.

Those two were among my closest friends while we were at school, but I now feel as if I had left them behind. I couldn't take much interest in what went on during the Summer term, and it was a surprise to find that they pitied me for missing it. I was quite sure what we have been doing would not interest either of them, so I kept quiet. Now, Laura would have been interested – I must write and tell her about it. Ginny seemed to be hoping that Bel and I would be jealous of her driving, but after all, we knew that she had had the chance to practise on her uncle's land for a year or so, no wonder she did not need many lessons. I said I am hoping to learn as soon as possible, and Bel seems to have become rather silly and feminine about the whole thing. Her mother is a bit inclined to think that girls ought to rely on men for everything. I do hope those two had no idea how bored I was getting!

Luckily Mrs Harcourt wanted the car by five o'clock, we got back here by three forty-five, but Mummy offered them tea, so it was an hour before they left, and I'd already offered to get supper for Rick and me, as our parents were going out, which is why it's so late now. I'd better not embark on an account of our talk on Monday till tomorrow.

Oh, before I close this entry, I do want to record what Mum said to me while we were washing up after tea. She remarked that I looked a bit downcast, so I told her what I had felt during the day, how I didn't feel I had much in common with the girls, yet it was only a few months since I'd seen them regularly. She nodded. "You have moved on, love, and neither of them are going to University, are they? Away from school, you don't share many interests; it's not like Laura. I know how much you miss her, it is a shame that her family had to move to Aberdeen, but perhaps you can see her at Christmas, when we go and stay with Grandfather."

She emptied the washing-up bowl and said thoughtfully, "As to Ginny and Bel, I don't think you have been apart for the right sort of time. In a few years time when you meet school friends, you will see them as fellow adults. I know that when I did that, some of those I'd liked had become complete strangers to me, whereas others, like Josie, and Eleanor, have become closer friends since we grew up."

12th August, Friday

Patrick will be home this afternoon, and Mrs Sharpe is on holiday so I've been helping Mummy this morning but I now have time to write a little about what happened when we had heard Mrs Randall's letter. As Grannie and Granddad and Aunt Katie are coming to tea tomorrow, I expect I'll be covering much of the same ground then, but it has been quite long enough and I do want to record it while it is still fresh in my memory.

I think we all felt dazed when Richard stopped reading, both the older men seemed almost tearful, and reading it over as I stuck the typing in here, I found it hard not to cry. It certainly seemed to make the relationship undeniable, and Mr Carter looked round us all and shook hands to welcome us into the family, and touched me by giving me a kiss.

Rick looked over at me, "Do you know, if you had not got that new map and noticed the name of Randall on it, we would never have thought to look in Old Manor at all!" he said thoughtfully.

"But you took my findings seriously," I reminded him, "If you had laughed at me, we might never have found out all this."

"And I would have found those papers and been fascinated, but have had no means of discovering what had become of Caroline Randall," said Mr Carter, smiling at me. "I suppose that there is little doubt that this Thomas Martin – ?"

"Did become our ancestor?" Granddad finished for him. "It is tantalizing not to know more about him. Rick, do you think he left her when she became pregnant? Her mother does not seem to have a very high opinion of him as a man, quite apart from his radical leaning. This does explain how it was that she would have the money to support herself as a widow."

"Perhaps she saw through him in some way," I suggested. "If her money was all he wanted, he might not have got his hands on it very easily."

"He sounds weak to me, rather than bad, if he let all his friends support him," said Granddad. "Perhaps she felt she would rather pretend to be a widow than to marry him!"

"You may have something there," Richard observed. "It was long before the Married Women's Property Act was passed. If her uncle had left the money in trust, she'd have been protected from fortune hunters, but her mother says that she had full control of it. I wouldn't have thought that he would have abandoned her, but she might have left him."

We discussed all Mrs Randall had said about her daughters, especially the older one; it seemed pretty harsh for a mother to say such things. Mr Carter remarked that it was surely lucky that this parcel had not been opened before, and it suddenly occurred to me that this must be the Anna Randall whose epitaph had so intrigued the Rector near Corwood Hall, and Richard and I told Mr Carter about that.

"That strikes a chord," he said. "I told you I had some idea that there had been a rift with that branch of the family, there was some kind of family legend that it had to do with Great Aunt Anna, and the letters I came across recently threw some light on the matter. I only glanced at them, but I think Lucy's oldest son was upset about his mother not considering Anna's feelings – something about her inviting her widowed youngest daughter and child to come and live at the Dower House. He looked at my brother, "You will come and help me sort out all these papers, won't you?"

"Oh, definitely," said Richard. "I would have been interested even if there had not been the family connection."

So we will be keeping in touch with these Carters. He asked about the rest of our family, and expressed a wish to meet more of us, especially Pat, when we told him about the new interest in Architecture and said that we thought he'd enjoy hearing about Old Manor.

13th August, Saturday

(Evening) I was so glad I had got that typing done, so that the rest of the family could read it. Mummy, and Grannie, and Aunt Katie were really moved by the writings of Mr and Mrs Randall over a hundred years ago, and even Patrick seemed fascinated by what we had found out on our visit to Hove. In fact I think it cheered him up; he didn't seem to have enjoyed his camping trip as much as he did last year. I asked him about that and he said it all seemed rather childish. I decided to tell him a bit about my encounter with Ginny and Bel, it's not as if he will be leaving school yet, but he was older than most of the others this time, and he has grown out of most of their interests. It seems to me that our little brother is all of a sudden more of a companion to Richard and me.

Grannie had heard an account of what we had discovered from Granddad, but Aunt Katie had only had time to learn that Richard's theory had been proved. She was struck by the situation Caroline seemed to have found herself in at the end of 1794. "Life with a sister like that sounds like Hell," she commented. "Marion and I didn't always see eye to eye, and I do not have much patience with Helen sometimes, but there was and is no enmity. This Anna sounds like the classic case of the eldest child in a family feeling supplanted and bearing a grudge. It seems terrible that she should have turned her piety into a weapon."

"But it looks as if she endeared herself to her oldest nephew," I remarked. "Judging by the way she is remembered on her tombstone."

"Not to all the family, by the sound of it," said Aunt Katie. "I look forward to seeing those letters about her." She turned to Granddad. "Philip, you have certainly started something when you promised the family in Australia to look into the background of the Randalls! I wonder what they will think?"

Granddad said he was sure that they would take it in their stride, but turning to Richard, he asked how he thought the Carpenters would react.

"They seemed quite open-minded, and after all, Caroline Randall seems to have had a blameless existence as Mrs Carpenter so they need not bother about what came before. I should think they would feel that if we don't mind, why should they?"

Dear Grannie seemed delighted to think that Caroline appeared to have had the sort of family life that her mother would have wished for her, but they were all curious about Thomas Martin and what had become of him – could he in fact have died before he could marry her? That was one of the suggestions made.

"I will see if I can trace him," said Rick. "There isn't a lot to go on, but he was presumably in his early twenties at that point, and born in Lincolnshire. I doubt if we would get any benefit from contacting them, though, even if we could be sure. I shall certainly try to get in touch with the descendants of the Philip Randall who edited that magazine."

"You have been rather silent, Charlotte," said Aunt Katie as she helped me to get tea. "Is something bothering you?"

"I feel a bit disturbed," I said, "I can't help thinking that Caroline went to great lengths to conceal the truth about her past – I wonder how much she would mind us bringing it all out into the open like this."

"I doubt if she would mind, my dear, she protected those for whom it would matter at the time, and she did found a new Randall dynasty. No, from all we have learned about her, I think she might even be amused!"

THE END

Lightning Source UK Ltd.
Milton Keynes UK
UKOW06f2057180817
307484UK00012B/88/P

9 781780 038377